Elizabeth Waite was born in T_____ there until she was thirty-four years old. During the war she worked as a bus conductress at Merton Garage. In 1956 she and her husband moved to Dev___ and bought their first guesthouse.

Now retired, they live in East Sussex.

Also by Elizabeth Waite:

SKINNY LIZZIE
COCKNEY WAIF
COCKNEY FAMILY
THIRD TIME LUCKY
TROUBLE AND STRIFE
NIPPY
KINGSTON KATE
COCKNEY COURAGE
TIME WILL TELL
A LONDON LASS
COCKNEY DIAMOND
LIFE'S FOR LIVING
WHEELING AND DEALING

Second Chance

ELIZABETH WAITE

SPHERE

First published in Great Britain in 1995 by Warner Books
This paperback edition published in 2010 by Sphere

A CIP catalogue record for this book
is available from the British Library.

ISBN 978-0-7515-4489-3

Printed in Great Britain by
Clays Ltd, St Ives plc

Papers used by Sphere are natural, renewable and
recyclable products sourced from well-managed forests and certified
in accordance with the rules of the Forest Stewardship Council.

Sphere
An imprint of
Little, Brown Book Group
100 Victoria Embankment
London EC4Y 0DY

An Hachette UK Company
www.hachette.co.uk

www.littlebrown.co.uk

Chapter One

'COR, STONE THE CROWS!' the railway guard groaned to himself as he stared in disbelief at the young lady in the corner seat of the carriage. Still he hesitated, his fingers hooked into the brass handle of the carriage door.

This young lady was something else! And no mistake!

He was used to his female passengers, in the main, being dressed in heavy serge uniforms, dark in colour, sombre in style and worn with thick lisle stockings and brogue shoes to complete the outfit.

The War was over. After nearly six years of austerity, if this young lady was a promise of things to come, then all he could say was that it was a damn pity that he wasn't thirty years younger.

Taking a deep breath, the guard flexed his wrist and slid the carriage door open. 'All right now, Miss? Room to spread yourself out, eh?'

The young lady smiled her thanks as he clipped her ticket and returned it to her. With another appreciative glance at those long legs encased in the sheerest of silk stockings, the guard went on his way, certain of one thing now. And that was that a man's youth were the best years of his life and that he was a fool if he didn't make the most of them.

The London train bound for Plymouth had been packed until it reached Exeter, St David's. Now at Newton Abbot even more passengers had got out and Barbara Hamlin was left as the sole occupant of the carriage.

The engine suddenly let off steam with a roar, the wheels began to turn and the train was on its way once more.

Barbara relaxed in her corner seat, eased off her shoes and stretched her legs out to rest on the opposite seat. She knew from her reflection in the carriage mirror that she looked smart, stylish. For the journey she had chosen to wear a tailored suit, a classic for its simplicity in the ever popular shade of navy-blue, with a white silk blouse. The lacy jabot at her throat gave just the right touch of femininity. It was so hard to obtain new clothes, coupons still being needed, she was glad she had hung on to the basic items in her wardrobe that never seemed to date. Her legs were covered in a pair of the sheerest stockings, not the thick lisle type she had had to endure when on duty with the Red Cross. Her luxuriant dark hair had a sheen on it like a freshly-fallen chestnut and was coiled sleekly upwards, held in place by tortoiseshell combs.

Throughout the whole of this journey she had had misgivings. Was she doing right going off to Plymouth to marry Michael?

Well, it's a bit late now, she mused, still feeling sick at heart as to what the outcome might be.

'For goodness sake, stop being so foolish!' she said aloud.

She would have felt so much easier, she thought wistfully, if only she had told her parents that she was setting off for Plymouth to be married to Michael. Michael loved her, she was sure of that. Sometimes though, for no particular reason, doubts would creep in. The emptiness of Michael's background, the need to belong, to be loved, would overwhelm him, breaking down the easy-going, jaunty barriers which he had painfully built as a front to the world.

Their future together was an obsession with Michael: he wanted her and he wasn't secure enough to allow anyone else to be aware of the fact until they were safely married and she could be known as his wife.

Three weeks ago it had all sounded so marvellous. Barbara found herself smiling. She could not stop the memories from flooding back.

Thanks to a seven day leave Michael had been in London. Nobody, least of all herself, could resist Michael's charm.

'You have only one question to ask yourself,' he had said. 'Do you love me?'

Barbara didn't have to think about this. She answered immediately. 'With all my heart, Michael, but . . .'

He quickly cut her off, 'No buts! Trust me. If you really love me you'll trust me.'

'My parents?' she had hazarded.

Michael had shown anger, just for a moment. 'We've already been over that a dozen times. We'll send them a telegram. Stop being so anxious.' She had given in, but she had never quite got rid of the apprehension.

The anger had gone, the charm was back. 'Please, my darling, everything will be fine. I will make all the necessary arrangements.' His words were spoken with conviction.

In a show of determination that had impressed her and convinced her it was right for them to get married, he had repeated again and again, 'I love you Barbara, I want you for my wife. It has to be like this, there is no other way,' he had told her. Held close in his arms, his lips caressing her, she had done her best to put all her doubts to the back of her mind.

All the same, the thought of her parents' disapproval bothered her still. If only she could have gone to them and asked her father's permission, but on this thought she sighed, knowing full well there would have been little chance.

Her father was an unusual man, a barrister practising in the highest courts of England. His profession had allowed him to provide a protected life for her mother, herself and her two brothers. In the September of 1939 when Neville Chamberlain had spoken on the wireless, telling the nation that a state of war now existed between England and Germany, she had been fifteen-years-old, still at a private school for young ladies, in Brighton. Her brother William, aged twenty-one, had joined the army. Patrick, the eldest at twenty-three, had opted for the Royal Air Force.

The death of William in the early stages of the War, during the evacuation of Dunkirk in 1940, and later the news that Patrick had been shot down whilst on a raid over the Rhineland in June of 1941, had not made her parents bitter, just sad. Always loyal and devoted to each other, the pain and anguish of losing both their sons had made them supportive of each other and as time passed they became even more inseparable.

Their attitude towards Barbara, now their only child, did however become little short of possessive. It was in 1942, having reached the age of eighteen, that Barbara announced her intention of joining the forces. Her father had argued that there really no necessity for his only daughter to participate in the War effort. Her mother had cried.

Penny Rayford and Elizabeth Warren were both friends

of long standing, having been at school with Barbara. They had grown up with each other in the small village of Alfriston in East Sussex, had spent most of their school holidays together and together they had decided to volunteer to work for ambulances throughout the city of London. They shared a rented flat in Parsons Green, which was the north side of Putney Bridge. Most nights, or rather in the early hours of the morning, dog-tired the three girls would be only too glad to drop into bed. Then late in 1943 air raids by the Germans over Britain began to diminish and they were granted leave for ten days. That was when she and Michael had first met.

Barbara twisted restlessly in her corner seat of the train and gazed out of the window. Even the countryside seemed to sense that the War was over: it was a beautiful June day as the train rattled through the West Country. The sky was high and beneath it lay peaceful fields of green with gentle farm buildings intermittently flashing by. All the wild summer flowers were beginning to bloom along the banks. She thought, with amazement, how vastly different this part of the country was to what she had left behind, it was as if it had been isolated by not having participated in the atrocities of the War years. The length and breadth of London had been blasted by bombs, and flowers were a luxury, for long since the Government had decreed that folk should grow vegetables instead of flowers. Seven weeks ago Field Marshal Montgomery had reported to his Supreme Head Quarters that all enemy forces in Holland, Germany and Denmark had surrendered unconditionally and V.E. day, May 8th 1945, would be a day that British people would remember for the rest of their lives. Who could blame them for celebrating?

There was of course the awful knowledge that War was still being raged in the Pacific but the general feeling was the Japanese would capitulate very soon now. The young men would start to be demobbed, come home to their families, the memory of so many dead comrades would never be forgotten but life would have to start afresh. How would they cope? What about herself? Six years ago life had been so different. All youngsters then had been forced, by events over which they had no control, to grow up quickly. Certainly all the youthful innocence had been stripped from her whilst working on the ambulances. Families had been devastated, torn apart, her own included. Was she being fair to her mother and father rushing off to marry Michael, a man they almost certainly wouldn't approve of?

Barbara felt a moment of panic, things had happened so swiftly she had, like most other young folk, been borne along on this feeling of euphoria since V.E. day, and more so the last three weeks since Michael's leave. 'Michael,' she said his name aloud in the empty carriage and that strange, giddy feeling flooded through her veins. When he cupped her chin in his hand and gently put his lips to hers, it was as though he was hypnotising her. Even if she had wanted to she couldn't have pulled away, but then she had never wanted to. No matter where they were, or who they were with, it was as if they were the only two people in the whole world and all that mattered was that Michael should go on kissing her and holding her.

It had been one year and eight months that they had been parted: now he was back in England to stay, as handsome as she remembered with dark brown wavy hair and the clearest blue eyes, and pleading with her to be his wife.

Barbara took her feet down from the opposite seat, stood up, stretched her arms above her head and began to pace the narrow space between the two bench seats. Her thoughts now had flown back to the night she had met Michael for the first time.

The very first evening of their leave, Penny, Elizabeth and herself had done themselves up to the nines determined to have a good night out. To hell with the air raids, they were going to let off steam. Rainbow Corner in Piccadilly was an obvious choice.

The dance hall was full of servicemen and women, Canadians, Australians, Americans and many British. From the other side of the room her eyes had met and been held by this good-looking, able-bodied seaman. It was enough.

Right from that moment love had struck them so suddenly that as he rose and covered the distance between them she had stood up, stepped apart from her friends and stood waiting. No one professes to believe in the possibility of love at first sight, most would say it was a myth, yet it happened to both of them. They were convinced it did.

The tunes the big band played had been fantastic, they had danced the quickstep to *In The Mood*, dreamily moved through slow foxtrots while the big mirrored glass sphere, suspended high above the floor, caught the light as it revolved, showering everyone with multi-coloured prisms of light. Come midnight as the band played the romantic waltz *Who's Taking You Home Tonight*, Michael had become as committed to her as she was to him.

Later Barbara told herself the secret lay in Michael's beautiful blue eyes: they twinkled, sparkled with fire as they gazed at her and spoke volumes. The effect on her had been electrifying.

For the next seven days they had been inseparable. There was no uncertainty. They were madly in love with each other. She was nineteen and he was twenty-six and for that week it was as if the world had been made for them.

Her friends told her she was mad and so she was. 'Mad about Michael,' Penny had grudgingly remarked, adding regretfully, 'In a rough kind of way I suppose one has to admit he's a handsome son-of-a-bitch.'

Much more that that! Barbara had convinced herself.

To her Michael had the masculinity that both men and women respected. He was one inch short of being six foot tall, broad shouldered, clear complexion and those wonderful eyes that continually twinkled with good humour. She had learnt that his pre-War job had been manual labouring and this she felt had given him a wiry toughness. His naval uniform suited him admirably, nipped in at the waist, bell bottoms swishing as he rolled along, he looked robust – as if he had never known a day's illness in his life.

The whole of that week he had treated her as if she was special and she had experienced feelings that were entirely new to her.

Their last night together. Those seven days had been the shortest that Barbara had ever known, they'd seemed to fly by.

'Oh Barbara! You're so beautiful! Say you love me, say you'll wait for me, please darling.'

Her head was still high in the clouds as she clung to him and whispered 'I love you Michael. I'll count every day until you come back.'

Then he was gone. Back to service in submarines. Each and every night she had prayed, 'Please God keep him safe.'

During that long separation of twenty months their love had not diminished, kept alive only by letters, irregular ones at that. Whilst she had continued to write lengthy weekly letters to Michael, his to her would arrive in batches, sometimes with lengthy intervals, not through any fault on Michael's part.

'You're going to drive yourself really mad,' Penny had told her one morning when Barbara came back from standing on the doorstep and watching the postman walk by.

'But it's been weeks.'

'I know, love. It must be just as bad for all sailors' wives and sweethearts. I expect you'll get a whole bundle of letters soon now, he's been writing, you can be sure of that, but how the hell is he supposed to post them?'

She had smiled wryly to herself at this thought. Penny was right, of course! He could hardly have been expected to post letters from the bottom of the sea-bed.

Barbara glanced at her watch. The train was due to arrive in Plymouth in twenty-five minutes at three thirty. Michael would be there to meet her. She felt a warm glow flood over her body as she contemplated their reunion. She still wasn't sure that she was doing the right thing but Michael had become her whole life, he had the ability to have her feeling as if she were walking in air. Taking up her handbag from where it lay on the seat, she slid open the carriage door and went along the corridor to the toilet at the end. Having washed her hands she smeared a little rouge on her cheeks, powdered her nose, then applied the bright red lipstick to her mouth, which Elizabeth had so generously given her, at the same time reflecting how much her mother would disapprove of her use of make-up. Only Michael mattered today, for him she wanted to appear beautiful. She wanted him to exclaim out loud when he caught the first glimpse of her, and he would.

She made her way back to the carriage, reached her suitcase down from the luggage rack and was ready waiting as the train came to a halt in the station. It was a big station, bigger than she had expected, yet still it had a countryfied air, not in the least like the grimy smoky London terminals. There were many more people milling about than she had assumed there would be. Everyone was talking loudly, laughing and hugging each other, everyone seemed to be having a reunion with someone.

Barbara walked down the platform carrying her suitcase, reached the barrier, gave up her ticket to the collector, went through to the entrance hall beyond but there was no sign of Michael.

She stood for several moments straining her eyes for a glimpse of him, but all she saw were unknown sailors and ordinary men and women. A young woman went flying past her, running straight into the wide outstretched arms of a naval man. Barbara watched with envy as they kissed and clung to each other. She waited feeling lost and alone.

Five, ten, fifteen minutes dragged by, the platform had cleared. Slowly she walked the length of the waiting area and sat down on a wooden bench, placing her case at her feet. She was thoroughly upset that Michael wasn't there to meet her and as the time passed she became anxious and then restless.

Perhaps I've come on the wrong day, or even to the wrong station, she thought, panic rising up inside her, then immediately chided herself. Don't be so daft, it's Wednesday.

It was only the night before last, Monday, that she had spoken to Michael on the telephone. From a call box he had rung the flat, his spirits had been as high as a kite as he told her he had obtained the special licence.

Filled with self-pity she felt her eyes smart with tears. Now you're being utterly foolish, she told herself as she angrily brushed them away. Yet was she being foolish? This was a strange part of the world to her, she knew no one, had no idea as to where she could go. The last thing she wanted to do was return to London. To admit she had been fooled would provide a heyday of gossip among her friends, some she could name in particular who wouldn't hesitate to have a laugh at her expense. Both Penny and Elizabeth would be well within their rights to say, 'We told you so!'

Three-quarters of an hour now she had been waiting and she was fast becoming alarmed. As her mind turned over all the possibilities that could have happened to Michael she realised, if she were honest, she knew very little of his family or background. His mother had died when he'd been sixteen, his father had married again when Michael was twenty. As so often happens, his stepmother, who already had three children of her own, hadn't wanted Michael around. He'd walked out of the Blackburn council house in which he had been born and had never to this day gone back. She had had to press Michael to tell her even that much.

The joy of seeing Michael again after twenty months had been marvellous. To *know* that he had come home safely. When there had been long gaps between his letters

11

her nerves had been stretched to breaking point as her mind conjured up pictures of him entombed in that submarine. Even whilst driving through an air raid she had prayed silently, 'Please God keep Michael safe!' From the very first day of his return, nothing had changed. Michael had looked at her with as much love in his eyes as was in her own. He had spent his entire leave pressing her to marry him. He had been so persuasive about his reasons for doing it on the quiet. He wanted her for his wife now, with no delay and no objections from her family.

'I think we should be married just as soon as possible,' he had declared in a voice gruff with passion. 'We've wasted too much of our lives as it is.' In the end she had gone along with his decision: she was convinced it was the right one, at least she prayed that it was.

She had been hoping to get down to Sussex to see her parents before leaving London but there had not been time. Although V.E. day had come and gone and the peace treaty with Germany had been signed it would be a long time yet before things would be back to normal and, like all service personnel and war workers, she was still held to her duties. There would be Red Cross trains arriving regularly, hopefully bringing home the wounded service men and, please God, prisoners of war would also be coming back to these shores. Four days' leave was all that she had been able to wrangle and even that had been a privilege. She had toyed with the idea of asking Michael to wait, to postpone the idea of getting married for a while, but she had recognised immediately that hesitating wasn't part of Michael's nature. Marry him or lose him. She knew there had been no other choice, yet still a small voice in her head had warned her that each of them would need every ounce of courage and all of their love if they were to face the future together.

What a dilemma! Every instinct had told her that her parents would oppose this marriage. She might have been able to tell her mother and father face to face of her feelings for Michael and that they intended to get married, but it wasn't a matter for discussion over the telephone. She had decided to gamble. Once she was Michael's wife she hoped against hope that things would automatically come right. Surely her parents would take to Michael and he to them. Perhaps, in some slight way, Michael might be able to fill the gap that losing her two brothers had left in her parents' lives. Dear God, she hoped so!

'Oh, for Christ's sake,' she said angrily half-aloud, 'sitting here dwelling on all these disturbing thoughts isn't helping one bit. All you're doing is meeting trouble halfway.'

One hour and ten minutes since she had got off the train. Now and again little groups of people stopped to stare at her. Workmen on their way home glanced at her with what she took to be pity in their eyes. The ticket collector was turning the key in the lock of his offices, he too glanced in her direction and she thought she saw a hint of a smile hover on his lips, before he dropped the barrier. She sat rooted to the bench as she watched him turn and walk away. What should she do? Find a hotel for the night? She had just decided when she heard footsteps, her heart leapt with joy, she *knew* Michael would come, he wouldn't leave her sitting here on her own, not on purpose he wouldn't. She was in her feet in an instant, searching for Michael to come into view. It was a sailor, only it wasn't Michael and she had to bite her lip hard to stop herself from crying out loud. She held her breath as the man approached, her vision was blurred by tears of disappointment.

'Are you Miss Barbara Hamlin?' he asked as he drew near.

Barbara swallowed the lump which was stuck in her throat and nodded her head.

The sight of Barbara's tears and her obvious unhappiness embarrassed the young man. 'I'm sorry you've had such a long wait,' he murmured, 'I've brought you a note from Mike, he asked me to wait while you read it and then to see you safely to the hostel where he's booked a room for you.'

Barbara read the short note, gulped and licked her dry lips before saying, 'I see.'

'I don't blame you for being upset,' he said quietly, trying his best to smile.

Barbara just stared at him. The smile vanished. 'It really isn't Mike's fault. By the way, I'm David Patterson.'

He didn't offer his hand to Barbara, as he made the introduction: he gave her no chance to refuse his offer to accompany her, merely picked up her suitcase, turned on his heel and strode off ahead.

Barbara wasn't sure she liked this young man, he acted as if he didn't approve of her. Shaking her head she told herself not to be so unkind, at least he'd come to her rescue, so to speak. Doing Michael's dirty work, she thought, which couldn't be very pleasant for him. He looked quite smart and handsome, the insignia on his naval uniform showed that he also, like Michael, served in submarines and for such service surely they had to be brave men. There must be a host of things he'd rather be doing right now than escorting her to a hostel.

They walked side by side along the road and then not more than five hundred yards from the station David Patterson stopped, placed her suitcase at the bottom of a flight of stone steps, nodded his head upwards and said, 'You'll be fine in there, your room is booked and hopefully Mike will be down to see you in the morning . . .' His words tailed off.

'Wait! Just a minute, please,' Barbara put a hand out to prevent him walking off.

Two things had not only surprised her, they had knocked her for six. One, the sign above the entrance doors stated; YOUNG WOMEN'S CHRISTIAN ASSOCIATION; which meant Michael would not be allowed to join her there, and the second she voiced out loud.

'You said hopefully Michael will see me tomorrow, won't he be able to get out this evening?'

'No, sorry,' was all the answer he gave as he turned to go.

'Why *hopefully*?' Barbara quickly asked. 'Is there some doubt even about tomorrow?'

'Shouldn't think so, can't always tell.' He paused and shrugged, 'Try not to worry, get yourself a good night's sleep.'

Barbara laid her hand on his arm. 'Please, I must know. Why hasn't Michael come to meet me?'

A very embarrassed David Patterson sighed deeply before saying, 'Mike got involved in an argument – he swore at a superior rating. Landed himself five days' stoppage of shore leave and privileges.' With that he turned around and walked smartly away.

There was nothing else she could do. Picking up her suitcase, she walked up the steps and rang the bell.

Within seconds the door was opened and Barbara was looking at a grey-haired lady in her early sixties who immediately put out her hands and grabbed the suitcase from Barbara's hand and with a laugh in her voice said, 'You must be Miss Hamlin, we'd almost given you up, come on, come in.'

'Thank you,' Barbara smiled at the woman and knew straight away that she was going to like her. She was the sort of person who had devoted her life to good work and in the process had acquired the particular qualities needed to set folk at their ease. Thankfully Barbara heaved a sigh of relief, she had no time to take in more than a fleeting impression of her surroundings when the woman gave a loud laugh which startled her and she became aware that she was being given the once over.

'My, anyone can see you're from London! Your outfit will be the envy of all the girls – but I'm forgetting my manners, I'm Jean Bailey.' With that she took hold of Barbara's right hand shaking it hard, so hard that Barbara almost squirmed at the firmness of the grip.

'What's your Christian name? We don't stand on ceremony here.'

'Barbara.'

'Well come along Barbara. What's it to be, your bedroom or a cup of tea first in the kitchen?'

'Oh, oh tea please, if it's not too much trouble. I really am gasping.' Barbara followed the short woman down the hall into a room which no one could mistake for other than a kitchen. Beside an enormous gas stove, hanging on the wall were frying pans, saucepans and numerous kitchen utensils. The opposite wall was flanked by a huge dresser displaying row upon row of hanging cups, the shelves holding matching saucers and plates. Four young women were in the kitchen and as Barbara crossed the floor they all turned to gape at her.

Jean Bailey clapped her hands, 'Now, now, she is not a mirage, she's real enough.' Nodding her head at each in turn she named the girls. 'Peggy, Vera, Hilda and Kitty, this is Barbara and she is dying of thirst.'

After only a moment's hesitation they crossed the room and her hand was shaken by each of them.

So thirsty had Barbara been that she had downed her tea in only five gulps. As she put her cup and saucer down onto the wooden table a chorus of voices asked, 'Like another cup?'

Amid all the laughter that followed Jean Bailey pushed Barbara hard against her shoulder, an action that almost overbalanced her onto the floor. Her eyes full of merriment and her face wreathed in smiles, Jean put out a hand to steady her, saying at the same time, 'See, you've made friends already!'

The hostel itself was a surprise. When the bell had rang she had done as she was told and come downstairs for the evening meal. A door on the right from the hallway led into the dining room. Barbara was so surprised at the size of this room she hesitated in the doorway, it was more like a meeting hall, she guessed it to be almost fifty feet long and at least thirty foot wide. At the very far end a table was set out for a meal, as far as she could tell the settings were for approximately thirty people. The outside of the building hadn't been at all pretentious, certainly not suggesting it could house so many people nor boast such large rooms. To the forefront of this dining room stood rows of wooden chairs as if set out in readiness for a meeting. Barbara soon found her assumption to be right.

An evening service was held before the meal was served. Prayers were said but it was during the lusty singing of the hymns that Barbara came to realise that this hostel was affiliated to the Salvation Army.

The dinner turned out to be a simple one, yet very good indeed. Tomato soup, steak and kidney pie, mashed potatoes, carrots and peas, followed by bread and butter pudding. Barbara ate hungrily, enjoying every mouthful. All she had managed to obtain at lunchtime had been two cold sausage rolls from the snack bar on the train.

As she ate, Barbara observed her companions. About twenty girls and young women of different ages and six older types mainly like Jean Bailey, who appeared to be in charge. The conversation was mostly of their Christian work and Barbara reflected how isolated their existence must be within this hostel, but soon realised they wanted nothing different, they were uninterested in the world in general for as far as they were concerned this was their calling. The official seated next to Barbara thanked God continually in her conversation and soon Barbara saw the funny side of the situation and began to wonder idly what would happen if the woman were to be transferred to a larger establishment in London where certainly the pace of life would be quicker and the changeover of guests more rapid and varied.

Dinner over, Barbara excused herself and went to her room. The bedroom was comfortable enough: it held a three foot bed covered by a bright pink candlewick bed-spread, one upholstered armchair, a tall wardrobe with a full-length mirror set on the outside and a marble-topped stand holding a white china jug and basin, beside which two pink towels hung from a free standing wooden rack. She removed the jacket of her suit, refreshed herself with a cold wash, took her clothes out of the suitcase and hung them in the wardrobe.

The next few minutes she spent studying herself in the mirror through a blur of tears. Never in the whole of her life had she felt so lonely. What a trip this was turning out to be! She must try to stay calm. At least until she did get to see Michael. She began to wipe away the tears from her cheeks with the back of her hand, sighing heavily as she did so. The silence in the room was deafening. She didn't fancy going downstairs again. 'I'll go for a walk,' she said out loud to her reflection. 'At least that will help to pass the time.'

Barbara couldn't believe it! What was it she had said to herself coming along in the train? The War had bypassed the West Country, leaving it green and tranquil. Well, that certainly did not apply to Plymouth. The whole area was one vast bomb site. The amount of bombing the city must have suffered had to be on par with that of London. Working with the Red Cross she had seen enough sights to last her a lifetime, even helped to drag the injured and dead from beneath piles of rubble, but God help the voluntary services, the police and air raid wardens who had attended this lot. She was standing where the Metropole Hotel had once proudly faced the sea, now reduced to a pile of broken masonry and rubble. The town's older streets, where rows of working class houses had stood, were all eradicated. Even the main thoroughfare and high street shops hadn't escaped entirely. What was amazing was the amount of wild flowers which pierced through the debris, their colours bright, their heads held high, the roots of which were certainly not nurtured in earth or compost – only masses of solid rubble. One thing was for sure, she said to herself, nature is resilient.

On reaching the famous Plymouth Hoe, she found it good to breathe the salty, fresh sea air. She stood a long time leaning over the railings of the esplanade, watching the lights of the small crafts twinkling on the darkening green waters.

There was the statue of Sir Francis Drake, overlooking the Sound and she thought, what an awful lot of history has been made since I was at school learning of The Pilgrim Fathers and how they had sailed from this very city in *The Mayflower*, back in the seventeenth century.

In the far distance, as she retraced her footsteps, she could see the outline of the great naval station, its dockyards and barracks and she whispered aloud, 'Where are you, Michael?'

His note had told her nothing. She didn't know anything of his plans. In her head she could hear his voice as it had come over the telephone. 'I have the special licence, darling. We can be married within three days; come to Plymouth, it will be easier here. You will come, won't you, Barbara? Please. You will be my wife, say again that you will.'

It was rarely that depression ever settled on Barbara, but her feet dragged tonight as she turned back towards the Christian Hostel. She had come to Plymouth, just as Michael had begged her too, but where the hell was Michael?

Breakfast and the morning hymn and prayers were over.

Barbara was just about to leave the dining room when she felt a restraining hand on her arm. With a nod of her head Jean Bailey indicated that Barbara should follow her. Once inside the office, with the door closed, Jean's features assumed a look of pity as she took hold of Barbara's hand.

'I had a telephone call before breakfast, from your young man, Michael Henderson, he asked that I pass a message on to you.'

Barbara looked up quickly. 'Didn't he ask to speak to me personally?'

'Well no, but he did sound as if he were pushed for time,' this kindly woman said soothingly. 'I wrote the message down, wait a minute, I'll find it and read it to you and that way there won't be any mistake.'

Barbara frowned, as she watched Jean shift through an assortment of papers that littered her desk. She felt so humiliated. First Michael didn't turn up to meet her, then he telephoned the hostel leaving a message for her, apparently not even having asked to speak with her.

'Ah! Here it is,' Jean said thankfully, 'I'd written it on the bottom of today's menu. "Am unable to see Barbara today. Everything is all right. Will meet her at the Town Hall registry office tomorrow, Friday, at a quarter to eleven. The ceremony is booked for eleven o'clock. Have found two mates to act as witnesses." '

Jean Bailey came round from behind her desk and patted Barbara's shoulder. 'There now, luv. I expect there's a very good reason why he couldn't get away.'

Barbara was incapable of answering. She just gasped, struck dumb at the starkness of the words.

Once again Jean Bailey's eyes were full of compassion as she looked at Barbara. 'I know you are upset, even lonely, but think about tomorrow, you'll be getting married to your young man.'

Think about it! She had thought of little else.

Barbara was by now consumed by anger, so much so that she had difficulty in stopping herself from pushing this homely woman away from her side. It was so unfair of Michael to treat her like this!

Now as well as the anger there was a sense of shock and loss, a feeling of betrayal was washing over her. Was she a fool? Had Penny and Elizabeth been right all along?

Jean Bailey stooped and brushed a strand of dark hair from Barbara's hot forehead. 'You're not to get yourself upset. Come along, go for a nice walk, it's a lovely day and this time tomorrow you'll be wondering why you got so upset.' Her sympathy was stretched to the limit as she watched Barbara get up and make ready to leave her office. She prayed to God that this nice young lady hadn't come all the way from London on a fool's errand! She couldn't let her go. Not in the state she was in.

'Stay and talk to me if it will help,' she said softly.

Tears welled up in Barbara's eyes. This annoyed her, she wouldn't cry, not in front of this good woman who had been so kind to her. She couldn't help it. 'Two days I've been in Plymouth and I haven't set eyes on Michael,' she sobbed. 'He calmly leaves a message for me to be at the registrar's office. I don't even know how to get there. I can't believe this is happening, not like this.'

Jean held her hand until she was calm again and her sobbing only little hiccups.

'You do want to go ahead with this marriage – that is why you came all this way, isn't it?' Jean Bailey waited for Barbara to answer without taking her eyes from her face.

'You wouldn't rather go back to London today, would you?'

When finally Barbara tried to answer her words were jumbled. 'No! Oh I don't know, I suppose not. Somehow I think I have to go through with it now.'

'Dear me, that's no way to look at marriage.' Jean sounded shocked. 'Marriage has to be a commitment – for life.'

'Yes, yes – I know that.'

Barbara raised her eyes to those of the older woman and the uncertainty in them made Jean stretch out her arms to what she now thought was a very bewildered young lady. Feeling very anxious now, she asked, 'Will your parents be coming?'

Barbara shook her head.

'Do you love this young man?'

Barbara again nodded her head. 'Yes, of course I do.'

'Well wartime has robbed most of us of something, but it's nearly all over now my dear, and when you're settled with your husband I am sure God's love will shine on you both and life will be good to you.'

Barbara couldn't help wishing as she wiped her eyes and blew her nose that she herself felt as sure.

During the rest of the morning Barbara asked herself the same question a hundred times. How come she had let Michael talk her into coming to Plymouth? She had walked about for over an hour, turning matters over in her mind. Had Michael lied to her? Did he really love her? Do *I* really love him? That last question she could answer. Yes, God help me, I do!' Finding herself at the gates of an enclosed park she went in. Her feet were burning, she wasn't wearing the right type of shoes for walking about in, she made towards a bench-seat situated beneath a leafy tree; slowly and thankfully she settled herself down.

Tomorrow she was to be a bride! She had had no engagement, no ring and this wedding, if she turned up, would be nothing like she had always imagined her own would be. She wondered if Michael would have a best man, probably not. He'd got two witnesses, or so he'd told Jean Bailey over the phone. There would be no honeymoon, she only had leave for four days which meant she would have to return to London on Saturday. Naturally no wedding invitations had been sent out. There had been no time. She would write later to her close friends but Christ Almighty alone knew what she would find to say to her parents. Traditionally she should be walking down the aisle holding onto her father's arm, and Penny and Elizabeth should be her bridesmaids. Although clothing coupons were still in use a way would have been found around that and she had to stifle a sob as she thought of the gay old time the three of them would have had touring the shops of London, choosing their dresses and her trousseau.

Feeling utterly forlorn she got to her feet: where could she go now? The rest of the day stretched endlessly ahead.

At one o'clock she was in a side street gazing through the window of a working class café. She could perhaps go in, have a drink and a bite to eat; amongst the occupants seated at the white-topped tables were several young girls and women so she wouldn't be out of place. Inside she pulled a chair from the table and sat down.

'There's no service, luv, you've got to go to the counter ter get served.'

The voice from behind her made her jump. Turning her

head Barbara saw a plump dark haired girl smiling at her and in spite of the abruptness of her statement she felt the girl was trying to be friendly.

'Thank you,' Barbara murmured as she got to her feet again.

As she returned with a cup of coffee, made from Camp Liquid, and a buttered bun, the same girl pointed to a vacant chair and asked, 'D'yer wanna sit with us?'

Barbara swallowed deeply, then again said, 'Thank you.'

The girl and her two companions shifted their seats and made room for her. 'I'm Alice, she's Billy and she's Maggie.' The introductions were made with a prodding thumb and much laughter.

'I'm Barbara, how do you do.'

Great chuckles came from the three girls as Barbara's educated voice came across.

'You're from London aren't yer, midear? Talk about looking lost, from the expression on yer face we'd 'ave to think yer had lost a shilling and found a penny.'

'Or some sailor ain't turned up to meet yer.'

The flush that came to Barbara's cheeks told the oldest girl of the group that she had probably hit the nail on the head.

'Don't take it ter heart love, how did I know? It was only a guess. This is a naval town, what d'yer expect? There ain't one of us it ain't happened to, all of us love a sailor. Some more than others!' she said giving her plump friend such a nudge that she almost fell off her chair. Everyone including Barbara burst out laughing. The awkwardness left her. How could she be anything else than at ease with these friendly souls? It was good to have someone to talk to, to be with.

The café filled up and Barbara felt it was a liberty to sit there taking up space with empty mugs in front of them.

'May I buy you all another coffee?' she presently asked.

'No,' they answered in chorus. 'We don't like that muck but the tea's not bad.'

Barbara smiled broadly at all of them, 'Well, shall I make it four large teas?'

'Yeah, thanks very much, for a Londoner you ain't so bad.'

Forty-five minutes later when the three young women said they had to get back to work Barbara felt a sense of loss: they had been good company, telling her about their boyfriends who all worked in Devonport Dockyards and what they got up to at weekends, all with spontaneous good humour. There were smiles on their faces as they wished her good luck and said goodbye. Slowly now Barbara rose from her seat, she couldn't remain in the cafe any longer yet she still had at least three hours to while away on her own before returning to the hostel.

How was it possible to feel so lonely? She sighed heavily.

The eve of her wedding day! There should be so many things she should have to attend to, she should be surrounded by family, relatives and guests. Tomorrow should be the most special day of her life if she were going to marry Michael.

A sudden thought struck her and she bent her head as she walked so that passers-by wouldn't see the tears that were flowing down her cheeks. She hadn't been consulted nor had she had any involvement in any of the arrangements for her own wedding.

At last it was five o'clock, she could return to the hostel.

Barbara had taken off her skirt and blouse, had a good wash and was sitting on the edge of the bed when a tap came on the door.

'Come in,' Barbara called.

'The whole place is thrilled at the thought of your wedding.' The cheery words were spoken by Jean Bailey before she had hardly set foot in the room. 'The staff and the girls have decided to give you a little hen party this evening,' she hesitated, 'and – if you would like us to, myself and Mrs Brackhurst thought we would come with you to the Town Hall in the morning – sort of act as temporary relatives like, seeing as your own parents aren't able to get here. Only if you want us to that is.'

The reply from Barbara came quickly, 'Oh, how kind, I really would appreciate that, it would mean so much, I would not be on my own, well, you do understand what I mean. Thank you. Thank you very much.'

Jean Bailey beamed at her. 'That's settled then. Put your dress on, come along downstairs and after dinner the party will begin.'

Barbara wasn't able to answer for a moment and when she did there was a catch in her voice and tears glistened in her eyes. 'Oh, Jean, all of you here are strangers to me and yet you have all been so kind.'

Jean Bailey dismissed this sentiment with a wave of her hand. Outside of the room she stood at the top of the stairs and asked herself why was this well-bred young lady so far from home and getting married to a sailor with no kith nor kin of her own to be present at the ceremony. Having met the young man when he had called at the hostel to book a room for his fiancée she had thought him pleasant enough, but there was no getting away from the fact that he was only an ordinary A.B. Not an officer. Surely a naval man of some rank would be far more suitable for this young lady, who was obviously very well-educated. Don't be such a snob, she chided herself. The war had broken down many class barriers and the youngsters must grab their chances. Still she was asking herself as she made her way downstairs, do oil and water ever mix!

It wanted only five minutes to eleven o'clock. They were all standing on the pavement outside the Town Hall. Michael had been there when she arrived and the joy of feeling his arms around her and his lips on hers had gone a long way to dispelling her misgivings. Now, as for minutes Michael had kept up a jocular conversation with his two mates, it was as if he was afraid that a silence might settle between them.

'Time to go.' Jean Bailey pressed them forward towards the steps. Shown into an oak-panelled waiting room, Barbara was at last near to Michael. Sitting close to him now, his hand sought hers and their fingers linked tightly. So much she wanted to ask him. So many explanations she needed but this was not the time nor the place.

'You look lovely, Barbara.' His voice was soft and tender. 'I love you.'

She wanted to put her arms around his neck, to be held tightly, she needed reassurances such as this. Their names were being called, there was no time.

Barbara still couldn't take it in: this was her wedding day. A balding man in a dark double-breasted suit was standing behind a long table, reading from an open book held flat on the palm of his hand.

To the right of her stood two motherly-type ladies who

28

up until three days ago she had never before set eyes on, but dear God, she was grateful that they were there, yet if she had been asked to explain what she felt she would have been unable to give a reason. It was they who had insisted that they visit a florist shop where the young lady assistant had with great skill fashioned two pink carnations into buttonholes and swiftly made the sweetest of posies for herself to carry. With small tea roses and lily of the valley interwoven with maidenhair fern now held in front of her cream silk two piece suit, she at least outwardly looked like a bride.

'Forsaking all others, do you Barbara Catherine Hamlin, take Michael James Henderson for your wedded husband until death do you part?'

Forsaking all others!

The silence hung heavy in the room as Barbara swallowed the huge lump that was in her throat before she was able to answer.

Not until they were again outside in the street did the full realisation hit her. It was all over. Just like that. There was no going back. She had got herself married to Michael.

'It's the privilege of the best man to kiss the bride first.' Barbara heard Michael laugh as David Patterson, looking very slim and smart in his uniform, bent and kissed her gently on the cheek, whispering as he did so, 'Good luck!'

The other shipmate of Michael's, who had been introduced to her merely as Pete, now stepped forward placing his lips also to her cheek and with a broad smile said very loudly, 'Got yerself a good bloke, but you know what they say, change yer name an' not the letter, change fer worse an' not for better.'

Oh for Christ's sake! He's just what I don't need. Barbara

was angry now but was stopped from making a retort by Jean Bailey.

'Ignore him, don't let him get you down. You'll laugh about today in years to come,' she said softly to Barbara, as she held her close for a moment. Then it was Mrs Brackhurst's turn; she put her arms about her saying, All the very best Barbara, dear. Be happy.'

It was too much! She couldn't answer them, her throat was too full. She merely nodded and did her best to smile.

At one moment there had been six of them on the pavement and now suddenly she and Michael were alone.

He took hold of her hands and pulled her close. 'Well Mrs Henderson, how do you like being my wife?'

She nestled closer to him, the lump was back in her throat and tears stung her eyes, she made no answer.

'Oh, Barbara, I know everything didn't go as planned, but I *do* love you. Really I do. I'll spend my whole life making you happy. Say you've no regrets, no doubts, please.'

She looked up at him and smiled. 'No regrets, just a few doubts and a helluva lot of nerves.'

He smiled now and touched her cheek gently. 'I've a few of those myself, but we've got each other now, and our love,' he murmured as he lowered his head and, regardless of people passing by, began to kiss her passionately.

Chapter Two

BARBARA FELT THE anger surge through her veins. She could cheerfully strangle Michael, husband or no husband, with her own bare hands!

She was sitting in the Lord Nelson, a rowdy public house situated just yards from the Town Hall. Michael was leaning on the bar, surrounded by what she supposed were a host of his mates.

As well as the sense of shock that Michael should have brought her straight to such a place, she felt betrayed: How could he do this to me? He must be telling everyone that he's just got married, the way they're all carrying on, laughing and jeering, while I'm sitting here on my own.

'All right, my darling?' is what he had asked as he placed a gin and tonic on the table in front of her. Then without giving her time to reply he had laughed and gone back to prop up the bar. I feel such a fool! she thought. My wedding day! How can he treat me like this?

What would she tell Penny and Elizabeth when she got back? Certainly not the truth.

'What are you fretting about?'

Barbara looked up slowly. Michael set his pint glass down on the table and bent over her. 'What say we go through to the saloon bar, they do meals in there. Get ourselves a bite to eat, eh?'

Barbara brushed a strand of her hair away from her hot forehead. There were too many people around for her to

31

have a showdown with Michael. Maybe he didn't realise that today should be kind of special like, but surely he could have taken her to a restaurant for a meal? Not the fore ale bar of this noisy pub. Stop it. Right now. She chided herself. You've got to make the best of it. Give Michael the benefit of the doubt, don't work yourself into a rage.

'You'll have me all to yourself tonight,' Michael said in an emphatic whisper, suddenly sensing just how upset she was.

In the saloon bar they sat at a table in the corner and, to be fair, Michael was doing his best to make up for his previous lack of attention.

'That's rabbit food,' he teased her as a pretty young girl set a platter of cheese salad down in front of Barbara. 'Ah now, that's a damn sight better!' he said as he ravenously tucked into sausages, baked beans and a huge pile of chips.

There were three empty pint glasses on the table: evidence that they had been sitting there for more than an hour.

'Come on, Michael, please let's get out into the fresh air,' Barbara pleaded as she got to her feet.

The afternoon was warm, the sky cloudless and high and as they walked she slipped her hand into Michael's. A bad start, but she felt happier now. Their slow stroll through the streets inevitably led them to the Hoe, where they sunk down thankfully onto the grass. Michael promptly stretched out on his back but Barbara propped herself up on one elbow and quietly looked lovingly into his face.

She felt like laughing and crying at the same time and her heart felt as if it were ready to burst. This man she was gazing at was her husband. Here in a strange city, far away from her family and friends she had become his wife. She couldn't help herself, she still had this terrible feeling of guilt. She should have told her parents. They deserved that much. Michael just hadn't given her time because, as he said, they loved each other so much that no one else mattered. Now for better or worse her life was linked to his. She still wanted to talk to Michael about so many things but she laughed out loud now, his nose was twitching, his breathing was heavy and suddenly he began to snore. He was fast asleep.

She tried to doze but it was impossible, she couldn't get comfortable, it was too hot. She wished she was dressed differently, more casually.

She sat up, brought her legs up so that she could rest her chin on her knees and gazed at the view. It was fantastic. Wide expanses of grassland and, ahead, the sea stretched for miles before it merged with the line where the sea and sky seemed to meet. Way out, across the shimmering water, she was able to see the outline of several ships and small crafts and in her mind she dwelt on the fact that all must have been engaged in action over the past years. Yet now, with the sun shining and the sea so calm, the whole place seemed so peaceful.

As the sun set lower in the sky her throat was parched and she found herself longing for a cup of tea.

At last Michael woke up, stretched his arms above his head, glanced quickly at his watch, swiftly stood up and gave her his hand and pulled her to her feet saying, 'What ever came over me? Fancy falling asleep on me wedding day, you should have woke me.'

Then tenderly he reached for her, pulling her slender body close to his muscular frame. His arms about her felt strong and virile; all her doubts were swept away as she clung to him, trembling with anticipation at the thought of the night that lay ahead.

It wasn't how Barbara would have chosen to spend the first evening of her married life but she hadn't been given any option. When they had first entered the servicemen's club she had felt apprehensive, especially when Michael left her alone to join other servicemen of all ranks at the licensed bar. The music was nice, albeit only gramophone records. She felt much happier when Michael came and led her onto the dance floor and she thought how festive the organisers had managed to make the place look. They were dancing a dreamy waltz and Michael was holding her in an embrace on the packed floor. 'There's hardly any room to move,' he smiled down at her. 'We'll have another couple of drinks an' then we'll get going.'

She spent the next twenty minutes alone, watching and listening to Michael. He stood surrounded by a group of naval men, the centre of attention; every now and then the men would laugh loudly at something that had been said and all eyes would turn in her direction.

She had had enough!

She got to her feet, gathered up her bag and strode off to the ladies' room. Having been to the toilet she washed her hands then, glancing into the mirror above the wash-hand basin, she got a shock. Her hair was a mess and the two roses she had taken from her bouquet and pinned to her jacket had wilted. What an odd sort of day it had been! If and when she could drag Michael away from the bar they were to spend the night together. A night that would be the only honeymoon she was likely to get!

God, what a mess! She felt awful, lonely; this was supposed to be the happiest day of her life and all she wanted to do was bury her face in her hands and cry her eyes out.

She was prevented from doing so by the opening of the door. The washroom was filled with the echo of the music coming from the hall. The girl that had entered gave Barbara a smile and a nod, went into a cubicle and closed the door. Barbara turned the cold tap on again and cupping the water into her hands she held her face down towards it. That felt better.

She dabbed her eyes and cheeks dry on the roller-towel, then picking up her handbag she walked out to confront Michael.

She pushed her way through the group of men, ignoring the ribald remarks, until she was face to face with her husband.

'Michael, may we go now. I'm awfully tired.'

Of course it was the wrong thing to say.

'Oh, she's tired!'

'Hard luck Mike, all she wants ter do is sleep.'

'You'll get nought ternight Mike, might as well stay and get yerself a skin full.'

This exchange of crude jokes about the wedding night brought the colour flaming up into Barbara's cheeks but she wasn't about to be put down by this bunch of half-drunk mates of Michael's.

'If I were to say goodnight, *gentlemen*, I'd be labouring under a misapprehension wouldn't I?' came the terse reply from Barbara.

'Whoa! Got yerself an uppity one there, Mike!'

'Come on Barbara, we're going,' Michael said firmly, seeing the anger in her eyes. He knew he was in for a right old tirade for having left her on her own but there was no way he was going to allow her to slang him off, not in front of his mates.

Not for the first time today Barbara felt hurt but she shrugged it off. Now was not the time to air her grievances.

'Yes, you go ahead, Michael,' one of the group of men said quickly before Barbara could make further criticisms.

Saying his goodnights Michael began to walk away. With a lot more bravado than she was feeling Barbara held her head high and followed him.

The taxi came to a stop. The district was a poorer residential part of Plymouth well outside of the town. There were rows and rows of three storey terraced houses. The house which they were now standing in front of was numbered eighteen; there was no front garden, only a four foot pavement onto which the front door of the dwellings opened directly. Michael lifted the black knocker and gave it a sharp rat-a-tat-tat. After a moment while they stood together on the pavement without saying a word, the door opened. The woman in the doorway was thin, aged about forty, of medium height with fair hair drawn tightly back from her brow.

'Hallo Mike, me lad, you've made it then,' she said, letting out a great peal of coarse laughter.

The familiarity of the greeting puzzled Barbara but she had no time to ponder on it.

'Come in, come in. Don't just stand there wavering.' She shook her head, still laughing and made a wide sweeping gesture with her hand. Michael went forward first and, carrying her one and only suitcase, Barbara slowly followed him. They walked down a passage, it was far too narrow to be described as a hall, where at the end was a flight of stairs.

Nodding upwards the woman gave a smothered giggle as she said, 'You know which room it is, Mike, you don't need me ter come up with you.'

For answer Michael stretched out his arm and with the flat of his hand patted her buttocks. 'You're all right Daisy, stay where you are.' Then a little selfconsciously he turned to Barbara and said, 'We'll away up then, shall we?'

With no introductions having been made, Barbara felt there was nothing for her to say.

Reaching the first landing Michael stopped, pointed a finger and told her, 'The bathroom and toilet are down there, our room is up here, top of the house.'

With that he preceded her up a further flight of stairs at the top of which there was one door only. Flinging it open wide he waited until Barbara had passed him and now as she stood in the centre of the room he kicked the door shut behind himself and with a wide smile on his face came towards her.

Involuntarily she took a step backwards, evading his outstretched arms. Slowly she lifted her eyes and looked into his and what she uttered could have been a cry from a wounded animal.

'What the bloody 'ell's the matter?' he yelled at her.

She couldn't form an answer. The day had taken its toll, everything had become beyond her control, she was shaking with fear.

Michael, watching her, was annoyed and the amount of beer which he had drunk probably made him more insensitive than normal.

'You should be happy, over the moon, it wasn't easy to

wangle it so that we could be together tonight. It's our wedding night for Christ's sake.'

'I know. I know.' Her voice was barely audible.

'What then?'

She did her best to smile at him now as she glanced towards the double iron bedstead that seemed to dominate the entire floor space of this attic room.

'It's just – well, this place, not seeing you before the wedding, the actual wedding, oh *everything*, nothing feels right, nothing is as I always imagined it would be.'

'Oh yeah,' he sneered. 'What did you expect? Westminster Abbey? Organ music, flowers, choirboys?' His voice grew louder, tinted with rage.

Of course she hadn't expected anything like that, but the words he'd flung at her brought home the reality of just how sparse today's proceedings had really been.

Oh wouldn't it have been nice, all of that and a reception, hugs, kisses, congratulations, gifts. That thought brought her up sharply. Not a single wedding present had she received this day!

'Well you'd better get things straight from the beginning.' Michael's tone brought her back to reality as he continued to storm at her, 'I'm an A.B. in the navy, what I'll be when I get demobbed God only knows. I'm not part of the legal profession like your father and his cronies. I've been fighting the bloody War, not like some of the toffee-nosed sods you mix with. Conscientious objectors most of them, I dare say – did anything and everything to get out of being conscripted did they? Well I've got news fer you, my darling, I didn't wait ter get me calling-up papers, I bloody well volunteered I did.'

Barbara couldn't believe it. She couldn't take it in. This

wasn't Michael, she'd had no idea that he felt like this. The acrimony of his words and the temper he was displaying appalled her. She had to grab at the brass knob on the end of the bed to stop herself from falling as she staggered backwards.

Suddenly Michael's arms, which had been flaying the air, came down to dangle loosely at his sides, the anger on his face lessened, he took a step, faltered, then slumped heavily against the wall.

Barbara's heart was thumping away inside her chest. Her hands were clenched into fists and her breath was coming in short gasps. Her throat was dry and she knew that if she tried to speak to him she would begin to cry. The tears were already there, burning and stinging behind her eyes. She bit down so hard on her lip that she tasted blood.

This was a side to Michael she had never seen, never even imagined.

Slowly he crossed the room, wrapped his arms around her and held her gently. She wanted to resist, to tear herself away and run, but where to? Where would she go?

Michael made no apology for his outburst. Releasing her a little he stared into her misty eyes and very quietly asked, 'Do you love me Barbara?' Without giving her a chance to reply he spoke in an emotional whisper, 'Sometimes I'm sure you do. Your letters convinced me you did. Other times, like now, you make me feel I'm not good enough for you – that I won't be able to give you the things that you are used to having.'

Barbara felt a flush come up over her face and neck. 'Michael, of course I love you,' she protested.

'No! There's no of course about it. Either you do or

you don't and if you don't it's not too late, I'll clear out right now.'

But it was too late!

It was she who now made the move. Putting her hands out she cupped his face and said, 'I do love you, Michael, it began the first moment I saw you, it's just that – ' there was a break in her voice and she wasn't able to go on.

He guided her towards the bed and they sat side by side on the very edge. 'Come on, Barbara, finish what you were going to say.' His voice was now soft and caressing.

'Well, today it's as if I didn't know you at all. You're like a stranger. I've been so lonely here in Plymouth, you haven't explained why it was you couldn't meet me before today. Oh – I just don't know.'

Michael's face was very white. His dark, curly hair was damp and his hands were shaking so much it frightened her and suddenly he was the dear, sweet Michael that she had been writing to for so long.

'In plain words, you're having doubts?' He tried to smile at her but it did not quite work.

She leant towards him and gripped his hand. 'Michael, I'm not. Really I'm not, it's just that – '

He didn't let her finish.

'Good. Since you've felt I'm a stranger today we'd better start beginning to know each other. Do you agree?'

'Yes.'

When their long kisses was over, their lips now parted, the magic of this man was back. She knew she wanted him, he was her very own Michael, compelling, strong, irresistible.

Michael stood up and removed his dicky collar, making a great show of folding it properly.

'Oh, Barbara,' he said helplessly. 'I've known a number of girls in my time but, Babs, you are the only one I ever wanted to be my wife.'

It was the first time he had shortened her Christian name, she didn't like it, but let it go.

Having started talking it was as if he couldn't stop. The words came pouring out.

'Socially and in a great many other ways I know you're streets above me, I couldn't believe my luck when we first met and you felt towards me as you did. We didn't have long together, did we? I never expected you to write so often, so regularly, but you did, me mates mocked me about it, every port we put into there was a bundle of letters, never a "Dear John" as so many blokes got. Even me best mate, a married man, got a letter from his wife saying, "Sorry, but!" Separations aren't good, I know that and ours was a long one. Actually just how long have we had together? Add it all up and I don't suppose it amounts to much more than a month.'

Stripped to the waist now, his tunic folded and lying on the one and only chair, he began to pace the floor, still talking almost as if to himself.

'The effect you had on me right from the start hasn't altered, maybe it has for you. I'm not a good catch, not for you I'm not. When I get out of the navy I've no job, nowhere to live, no family to speak of, but I'm sure of one thing, Barbara, I love you.'

He paused in his pacing, turned his head to where she still sat perched on the edge of the bed, the look in his eyes implored her to believe him.

'I will try and be good to you, I promise. I don't blame you if you are having misgivings, I've rushed you along a

41

bit haven't I?' He came to stand in front of her and once more his arms were about her. Now her fear of him was gone and in its place was a loving sensation, a yearning for everything to be all right between them.

'Oh Michael, I *do* love you!' And at that moment she truly meant it.

What followed was inevitable.

To begin with it was wonderful. His lips were covering hers, his hands moving gently backwards and forwards across her body. She was wafted to heaven, Michael did love her. All the pent up frustration of wartime, when the occasional letter had been all she had to remind her of her good-looking, strapping sailor, the uncertainty of the last few days, hesitations over decisions, all were wiped away.

Even this dingy, top back-bedroom of a terraced lodging house, it no longer mattered. Michael was showing his love for her.

Abruptly things changed, it was no longer love. Passion wasn't even the right word. Brutality was. Her body was on fire as he lay on top of her and the fierceness of his movements went on and on. It was more than just physical hurt that he was inflicting on her, he was giving vent to his anger, using violence to show her the urgency of his needs.

His body became still at last, all his resentment had drained away. He rolled off her and within minutes he was fast asleep.

The tears that showed her bewilderment and pain fell silently and she tasted the salty bitterness of them in her mouth, as she lay beside him.

Oh, Michael, she thought, despairingly. Why didn't we

give ourselves more time? We've married in haste and I only hope to God that I shan't live to regret it.

Up on the rooftop a cat screeched and somewhere in the distance a dog barked, there was plenty of living things moving about in the night air. Yet as Barbara moved to the edge of the bed and curled herself up into a ball, she was feeling hurt and very much alone.

Tomorrow, she would be catching the train to London. Within six to seven hours she would be back in Parsons Green; would Penny and Elizabeth see a noticeable change in her? They had to, the hurt must show in her eyes if not on her face.

A wave of longing swept over her. If only she could turn the clock back. There had been no time and very little time to feel. Feeling would come later, when the reality of what she had done sank in. If only she hadn't agreed to marry Michael, but she had. It was done. There was no turning back.

Chapter Three

THE PIPS ON the wireless signified the time was just nine o'clock on this mid-January morning in 1947 and Barbara was at her wits' end not knowing what to do or which way to turn.

What the hell can I do? she asked herself.

As the weeks had turned into months and the months now into over a year she wondered whether they would ever get out of this South London area and if they did, would the hell of a life that she and Michael were leading really alter? She was afraid of his violent temper. She hated the jealousy that exploded into vile insults and accusations and, most of all, she hated his foul-mouth and filthy habits. His drinking sessions were having a terrible effect on Michael.

The first four months following her marriage had been fine. She had remained on, sharing the flat with Penny and Elizabeth, whilst Michael was shore-based at Plymouth awaiting his demob. Frequently he had obtained forty-eight hour weekend passes and it was she that booked them into small hotels in and around Chelsea. Only once had she done otherwise, choosing the charming Manor House Hotel set in gentle countryside by the river in Richmond, Surrey. It hadn't suited Michael and for the second time she was given a display of his bad temper. For a start, the hotel held no drinks licence and secondly he objected that the quietness of the countryside was driving him bloody mad.

Finally Michael was discharged from the Royal Navy and they were supposed to settle down and begin to lead a normal life. Like a good many more youngsters who had lived through the War, it wasn't as easy nor as straight forward as they had imagined.

It was Michael himself who had found these rooms to rent, situated above a corner shop in Latchmere Road, Battersea. The first sight of the building had dismayed her, yet even that had not prepared her for the interior. She had shuddered and murmured, 'It's horrible.'

That exclamation had been like a red rag to a bull. 'Why don't you climb down from your bleeding high horse for once,' he had spat at her, and went on at great length about how lucky they were to have found these rooms to rent.

When she had got over the initial shock it was a point she had had to agree was true. Many ex-servicemen, their wives and even their children were being housed in Nissen-huts on open common-land. With whole streets of houses having been demolished during the air raids over London rented accommodation was hard to find. True, the local councils had acted quickly: families wanted and needed to be together after long war years of separation. On wasteland and what space had been cleared of debris, workmen were set to erecting the huts to be used as temporary homes. Being just corrugated-iron sections bolted together to form semi-circular constructions they were ugly, but people still fought to be allocated one. With the rent set at only ten shillings a week they were regarded as a godsend by those fortunate to be assigned such a dwelling and many more would have jumped at the chance.

Whenever Barbara passed such a site something of the same feeling went through her mind, regardless of the fact that they were fast becoming slum dumps. Already the lines of washing, overflowing dustbins and litter were making the locations unsightly. Yet at least these tenants had privacy and each family had their own toilet. Which was a darn sight more than she and Michael had.

Faced with these two box-like rooms and the small kitchenette, finding out that the lavatory on the landing outside her living room had to be shared with the tenants on the top floor, a Mr and Mrs Singleton and their two adult sons, had been the last straw.

Her protests had been cut short by a string of obscenities from Michael. With no other option she had decided to make every effort and had set to with enthusiasm, determined that if that was where they were going to have to live, at least for the time being, she would do what she could to make the place into a decent home for both of them. First off she had cleaned the walls and ceilings, scraping away the grease and grime from the paint work. Michael had been no help at all.

Long since she had come to the conclusion that the two of them were totally incompatible. To be honest, she was like a fish out of water in his world and if the tables were ever turned he would probably be a damn sight worse off in hers. She also decided she had little in common with her neighbours and was now convinced that old Mrs Winters, who owned the shop below, was the only person of her new acquaintances she could consider to be a friend.

Out of sheer habit Barbara began to move about the room straightening things, plumping up the cushions in the two armchairs, emptying the ashtray that Michael had left in the grate. She paused in her moving about to look out of the window down into the street. As early as it was women were lolling in doorways, arms folded across their ample bosoms; each wore a wraparound flowered overall. She often wondered whether these women wore shapeless pinafores as a kind of uniform or more than likely as an announcement of their poverty.

When she'd first come to live in the district several wives had invited her to join them for a cup of tea. She had accepted once. A whole bunch of women crowded into another's stuffy living room to drink endless cups of strong sweet tea was not her idea of a pleasant outing. After the first time her refusal was not due entirely to snobbishness, the longing for company, any company some days, often had her wavering but she clung to her belief, there must be, there had to be, more to life than whiling away time by listening to gossip.

Down on the corner a group of small children were playing hopscotch; the pavement was permanently marked out with chalk into the appropriate squares and only renewed after a downpour of rain. As she watched, a small boy, a great tear in the seat of his trousers, tossed a stone. Instead of landing into a square it rolled away off the pavement into the gutter and as he dashed into the road to retrieve it a van drew to a shuddering stop. Unable to hear from where she stood, Barbara was in no doubt that a stream of foul language was screamed at the child by the driver from his cab. Although many of the children down there were old enough to be at school, their attendance was at best irregular and nobody, least of all their parents, seemed a bit bothered.

Barbara turned away from the window. Was this what she wanted for her children? She heaved a great sigh.

This was the main bone of contention between Michael and herself. He was adamant. He didn't want to start a family. 'I don't care if we never have any kids,' he had roared at her when she had first told him she was pregnant. For the next two days life had been unbearable. He had gone as far as using his fists on her to emphasise that he meant what he said and that he was determined to be master in his own house.

Within six months of living here in Battersea she had had two abortions. Acting on the knowledge she had gained from Mrs Winters the first had been self-induced, having missed only one period the result had not been too drastic. The second time she had delayed telling Michael, clinging to the hope that he might just relent and be as pleased as she was. He wasn't daft! When he had finally challenged her she had no alternative but to admit the truth. Her pleading to be allowed to have the baby had earned her a severe clout round the ear. Michael had been beside himself with rage, even throwing the accusation at her that the baby couldn't possibly be his.

'I can't say I 'old with it,' Mrs Winters had answered sadly, when Barbara had sought her help yet again.

Barbara had flushed with guilt.

'Oh, I know it ain't your fault, bless yer heart. How yer ever come ter get yerself tied up with that sodding lazy bleeder I'll never know. Perhaps it's as well. What kid would want a father what spends two-thirds of his life in the pub an' the other bloody third in the damn betting shop. All right, my luv, leave it with me, though Lord knows I won't sleep till I know it's over an' done with.'

Barbara smiled bleakly at her and once more felt a surge of gratitude towards this cockney woman who had become her friend.

A tall, thin yet big-breasted woman, with a face as wrinkled as a prune, Mrs Winters would have her customers and tenants believe that she was as hard as iron and just as tough. In most circumstances she was. Beneath that craggy exterior, though, there was kindness and compassion for those that she thought warranted her help. Barbara most certainly came top of that list.

For a fat fee a doctor had terminated her pregnancy. The following days of pain and suffering, not to mention the heartbreak, had caused Barbara to vow never again. Besides which, she was tormented by the thought that having numerous abortions might in time cause her to become sterile and a future, despite what Michael said and did, without children didn't bear thinking about, at least for her.

Christ! I've got to snap out of this fit of the blues. Even if by some miracle, and God knows it would take one, Michael did come round to my way of thinking, what future would there be for our children in such surroundings as these? she asked herself, but came up with no answer. If only she could go out to work. How many times had this thought come to her? Perhaps with a job in the city her mind would once more become active, give her a reason to make an effort, dress nicely, wear some make-up – and the money she'd earn wouldn't come amiss.

Taking a duster from the dresser drawer, with a lack of enthusiasm she began to wipe the furniture; coming now to the mirror which hung on the wall she sadly shook her head at her reflection. She looked awful. Tired and dishevelled. The endless nightly arguments between Michael and herself had taken their toll. Why did he always get the better of her? Why had he developed such a degree of possessiveness? The hardest thing to endure was his jealousy, it seemed now that he would do anything and everything within his power to humiliate her.

'You're a spoilt rich bitch,' was his favourite accusation.

Rich! That was a laugh, there was never a week when she had more than a few shillings in her purse.

Most probably she could obtain employment locally, in a shop or a small office, but Michael's threats were no idle matter. 'Men around here support their wives, they don't stand for them dolling themselves up and pissing off each day, so yer needn't delude yerself that you'll ever get to claim that you're the breadwinner. Not while I'm around you won't.' Having made that statement for all the street to hear, he'd been really irritable.

That was another laugh! He'd support his wife! What he really meant was that he'd lose face amongst his drinking mates if they found out that his wife was working.

Well, the way things were heading he'd lose the roof over their heads soon. Even so, he still threatened. 'Get yerself a job, work in a bloody office and I'll make sure they'll be damn sorry you ever set foot in the place. I'll be there to meet you, you needn't worry on that score, an' I'll not only raise hell, I'll rearrange the face of any bloody ponce that thinks for a few bob a week he can have my wife running around after him.' He left her in no doubt. He meant every word.

Nothing she said, none of her reasoning or imploring had been able to shift his bigoted beliefs. Michael was sticking to his guns. A woman's place was in the home, but what was there for her to do all day long in these two poky rooms? And he couldn't bear the thought of their starting a family. Why had they never got around to discussing these matters before they got married? She knew well enough why they hadn't! He hadn't given her the time. Would it have made any difference? She doubted it. Love is blind, so the saying goes, well time had certainly opened her eyes.

She suddenly became impatient with herself. Going over and over all this time and time again is only going to drive you round the bed. So stop it, it's not getting you anywhere, she told herself as she began the task of washing up the breakfast things. Taking the whistling, tin kettle from the gas stove she poured most of the boiling water into the enamel bowl, the single tap above the shallow, brown, stone sink gave only cold water. When drying the dishes and putting them away she left out one cup and saucer in order to make herself a cup of coffee. Michael always preferred to drink tea, on her own she could please herself. First she must go to the toilet, on the way she fervently hoped it would be vacant. It wasn't.

She had to wait ages, with her front door ajar, before she heard the chain being pulled and stout Mrs Singleton's laboured footsteps mount the stairs. Once inside the air made her feel sick, the smell was awful. She climbed up onto the wooden seat and wrestled with the small window, as usual she wasn't able to budge it an inch.

'It's nailed up,' was Michael's retort whenever she complained, but still every now and then she tried to shift it open.

She really did resent having to share this toilet with the tenants upstairs. How many times a week did she thoroughly clean this closet and the pan, only to find it filthy shortly afterwards? As to toilet rolls – they must eat them. No one other than herself seemed to provide them. More often than not the lavatory pan was choked with newspaper. Now she no longer left the roll in there, taking it with her each time and bringing it out when she left. Michael laughed at her, saying she had a fad about toilet rolls, but no, that wasn't it, she wouldn't have minded so much supplying them if others, at least sometimes, would do likewise. On many of the occasions she had been caught out, not only was there no paper left but no evidence that she had ever hung a roll through the string on the back of the door – even the cardboard centre cone was never there, albeit empty of tissue.

Another thing that got up Barbara's nose was the flight of stairs that led down to the street. The carpet (or was it linoleum?) that once had been laid on the stairs was now so well-worn and rotten in places as to be dangerous. When going down or coming up she could never stop herself from wrinkling her nose at the smell that prevailed throughout the building. Inside their own two rooms she had worked wonders, even Michael agreed on that, yet when once she had timidly suggested to Mrs Singleton that they cleaned together the walls, staircase and landing she had been glad when she had at last been able to get away from her. Even now the memory of that clash with Mrs Singleton made her shudder. Petrified she'd been as the bulk of the woman had barred her way.

With a mocking laugh Mrs Singleton had mimicked Barbara's voice, 'So, this place ain't quite good enough for you milady?'

Seeing Barbara cringe only edged Mrs Singleton on and

she reverted to her own guttural tone. 'A bit of sodding dirt never 'urt no one. We've all got ter eat a bushel 'fore we kick the bucket. My old man and me two sons all work on the building and if I did git down on me 'ands an' knees an' scrub them stairs they'd only be just as bad again by termorra what wiv their filfy boots an' all. No, you bloody upstart, you want the stairs scrubbed, get yer lazy sodding old man ter do 'em for yer, I've never seen 'im do a day's work since yer came 'ere. And while we're on the bleedin' subject if yer don't like it 'ere why the bloody 'ell d'yer stay? There's plenty as would be only too glad ter take over your rooms an' I sure as 'ell would be glad ter see the back of yer. You've got yer nose stuck so far up in the air that yer think your own shit don't stink, well let me tell you luv, you smell just as rotten as the rest of us around 'ere.'

Having finished her tirade, she'd waddled off, her breath coming in short ragged gaspings, and over and over again she was muttering, 'I'll kill the stuck-up bitch! I'll kill her! I will! I'll flatten her stone dead!'

The trouble was Barbara knew the old woman spoke the truth; there would be heaps of young couples more than glad to be given the chance to rent these rooms.

For days after that Barbara had gone to great lengths to avoid coming into contact with any member of the Single-ton family, and she had had to quickly cover her mouth with her hand to suppress a giggle when a week later she heard that Michael had got himself a job on the building sites.

He had joined a gang of demolition men. London, and most major cities the length and breadth of the country, needed these gangs to bulldoze the remains of buildings damaged by the bombing and to clear the sites ready for rebuilding.

As Barbara folded her duster and placed it back in the dresser drawer she cursed herself for having listened to Michael's glib tongue. Why, oh why had she allowed herself to be rushed into a marriage that at the moment didn't seem as if it would have a hope in hell of ever working out? But what was done was done. For better or worse, she had saddled herself with Michael Henderson as a husband and she just had to make the best of it .

At that moment she wondered what had happened to the gentle, loving, courteous Michael that she had fallen in love with. Seldom did she ever get a glimpse of him now.

'Michael,' she said aloud. 'Oh, Michael – what's to become of us?' She felt tears of self-pity prickle the backs of her eyes, and she angrily brushed them away.

Oh well, she sighed, better decide what to cook for his dinner tonight. With today being pay-day God knows what time he'll come home. A visit to the pub with his workmates would be of primary importance, none the more for that, whatever the time, Michael would expect his dinner to be ready and waiting for him. And God help her if it wasn't.

Searching through the larder didn't take long. She found two desiccated soup cubes, both oxtail flavoured, some lentils and pearl barley. In the vegetable box, thank God, she had plenty of carrots, onions and potatoes. She'd never have believed that one person could eat as many potatoes as Michael did. Right from the start he had soon made it clear that a dinner was not a dinner unless the plate was piled high with spuds, as he referred to them. One thing, he wasn't fussy about how they were cooked. Roasted, boiled, mashed or in their jackets he always asked for more – as for chips! – she could never get used to watching him eat great mounds of chips liberally smothered in vinegar and that revolting bottled tomato sauce he liked so much.

She laid the pot-herbs out on the wooden draining board and set the potatoes in the enamel bowl filled with cold water, looked around the living room and made certain that Michael could find nothing to complain about.

Going now into the bedroom, she put on her winter coat and wound a long cashmere scarf around her shoulders – it would be bitter-cold outside and the wind seem to bite right through to one's very bones. Not that she would be outdoors for very long, the market was only at the other end of the street.

She had decided to make a casserole and as she slipped her gloves on she gave a wry smile; better not say 'casserole' to Michael, he'd only repeat what he'd told her before. 'Posh name for a stew, that's all it is, so why not come straight out and call it a stew.'

Not that Michael minded having a stew for his dinner. The thicker the better, stand a fork up in it and if it held it must be good. Even cheap scrag of mutton, Michael wouldn't complain, he'd happily suck the meat from the bones while she attempted to use a knife and fork. An apple pie for sweet would be filling. Oh, there she went again, she must try and remember to think of it as a pudding or afters, though how a fruit pie could be known as pudding! Still, anything to keep the peace.

There was many a time now when Barbara had reason to be grateful for the cookery classes her school had insisted upon. She prided herself on her soups. They were excellent and nutritious. There again Michael annoyed her, with one bowl of soup as a start to their evening meal he would polish off half a loaf of bread, dunking great hunks of crust into the hot, rich soup – drawing the dripping bread upwards to his mouth, ignoring the fact that drops were being spilt onto the tablecloth.

She admitted to herself that this was more than likely half of their troubles: to Michael she was much too fastidious, whilst he to her at times was coarse, even uncouth.

Opening the door at the foot of the stairs which led out into the street, Barbara paused a moment and looked into the shop.

'Morning luv, 'ow are yer?' Mrs Winters called cheerfully to her and without waiting for a reply rushed on, 'Talk of the devil, I was just about to call up ter yer, kettle's boiling an' I've only got ter put tea in the pot. Come on – don't just stand there, put wood in the 'ole an' come and sit yerself down.'

'I've just had a coffee,' Barbara protested.

She might just as well have saved her breath. Ma Winters was pulling a heavy armchair nearer to the oil-stove. She plumped up an enormous cushion and placed it against the threadbare, upholstered arm of the chair.

'Plonk yer arse down in there,' she said, with a nod of her head. 'You ain't so busy that yer can't spare a few minutes to gossip with an old woman that'll be right glad of yer company.'

She poured tea into two enamel mugs and came and sat down facing Barbara. When they'd each taken a sip of the scalding tea, she leant forward and said in a low voice, "Ow are yer managing?'

Barbara was reluctant to answer. This blunt, straightforward type of woman who was her landlady had proved to be a friend – indeed, Barbara was not at all sure that she would have survived these past months without Mrs Winters to talk too. Honest as the day was long, was how Barbara regarded Mrs Winters. Never afraid to speak her mind, offend or please. Affluent compared with most folk around these parts, in as much as she owned a second-hand furniture shop plus the two flats above, which she rented to tenants. Barbara had no idea where Mrs Winters lived; ever ready to listen to Barbara's troubles, she was not one to discuss her own personal life. Life hadn't dealt kindly in other ways with this woman, in spite of the fact that she had prospered. Everyone took her to be elderly, at least in her sixties – her thin frame, pinched wrinkled features and greying light-brown hair made the assumption easy. If the truth were known she was in her late forties.

'Oi! You're miles away.' Mrs Winters' work-worn hand on her knee brought Barbara back from her daydreaming. 'You ain't answered my question yet. You would tell me if there was anything wrong, wouldn't you?'

'Of course I would', Barbara assured her, touched as always by the concern shown to her. 'I'm fine. Really I am, with Michael working now we'll manage a whole lot better.'

It wasn't often that Mrs Winters had a feeling of helplessness, life had taught her to be hard and she could hold her own with any man. When it came to Barbara she was utterly bewildered. Her every instinct told her that Michael Henderson was a right bastard! An arrogant sod! Then again, what on earth had possessed a lovely, gentle girl like Barbara to marry him in the first place? It must have broken her parents' hearts. One could tell just by looking at

Barbara her early life had been good, giving her breeding, education and money. She was totally unfitted for the life she was leading. But Mrs Winters wasn't in a position to interfere. Damn that bloody Michael, she cried to herself, just let him go too far and she'd see he got his just deserts. By hell she would!

'I'd better get going,' Barbara said, setting her empty mug down. 'Is there anything you want me to bring you back from the market?'

'No thanks, luv, an' don't you get 'anging about too long, it's cold enough out there to freeze the brass balls off a monkey.'

Barbara was still laughing to herself as she wound her scarf tightly round her shoulders and set out to do her shopping.

Turning the corner, Barbara was met by a chorus of wolf whistles, she smiled broadly and waved her hand in greeting towards the gang of men who were clearing the site where once had stood the Crown and Anchor Public House. A direct hit from a German bomb had erased it, leaving nothing but a pile of rubble. To the side of the crater a huge bonfire was burning – the acrid smell of rotting timber filled her nostrils, bringing back scenes she had witnessed during the air raids, scenes she would like to have obliterated from her mind. Thick dust covered the men and straight away she thought of Michael, doing exactly the same type of work on a larger scale in the West End of London. Every evening he came home thickly grimed with red brick-dust. It would be in his hair, his eyes, even under his fingernails. It was awful for him. She knew that, but he just wouldn't help himself. Having no bathroom was a disadvantage yet he could so easily have a

58

good wash down. On the ready each evening, she'd have two pans of water boiling, the tin bath placed in front of the gas stove and towels laid out on a chair. Michael could hardly ever be bothered, a quick sluice under the cold tap and he would be demanding his dinner.

Try as she would she couldn't begin to understand Michael.

With the weekend approaching it was a full market day, no empty spaces between the numerous stalls and already the pavement was thronged with many people. Strangely, Barbara loved the hustle and the bustle that greeted her from all sides. Those women, mostly with big families to feed, were bargaining ferociously with the men who owned the stalls, answering their cheeky comments with good humour, giving back as good as they got.

The scrag-end of mutton bought and stowed away in her shopping bag, Barbara now made for the largest of the fruit and vegetable stalls. For a moment she was tempted to ask for two extra-large apples, filled with golden syrup and sultanas they were delicious when baked. Better not. Michael hated stuffed baked apples.

'What can I do yer for, me luverly?' The trader yelled the question at her.

'Two pounds of Bramleys please.'

'They ain't Bramleys darling', he told her with open honesty. 'Wrong time of year, but they're luverly cookers – make a luverly pie and if yer old man don't appreciate it chuck 'im out an' invite me round for a bit.'

The women in the crowd roared with laughter and Barbara joined them. It was impossible to take offence at such cockney wisecracks, even though they were vulgar and loaded with a double meaning.

'There yer go, those five come to a tanner, want me ter take one off?'

'No,' she smiled her thanks at the man, 'they will do nicely.'

'Any fing else?' he asked as he tipped the apples into her shopping basket. She was about to say no when her eyes rested on the high display of grapefruits. It was such a long time since any such-like fruit had been available, quickly she said, 'Yes please, two grapefruits.'

Then the thought came to her if she bought potatoes today it would save her having to carry such a heavy load tomorrow when shopping for the weekend, so now she added, 'And may I have five pounds of potatoes please?'

'King Edwards at fourpence fer five pounds or Whites at threepence?'

'King Edwards please.'

'That the lot then?'

'Yes thank you.'

Barbara handed over a two shilling piece and the young barrow boy gave her sixpence in change, holding on to her hand for a lot longer than was necessary. 'Tat-Ah then luv, take care.' He was grinning at her, his eyes full of admiration.

In response she gave him an open smile. She was fully aware that the hawkers were skilled in the art of bantering with their customers; none the less for that, a little appreciation shown to her by a good-looking young man did an awful lot for her ego.

Snow was in the air: everyone was saying so, the clouds

were low, dark and foreboding as she walked home. The wind had dropped but then so had the temperature. The cold was raw now and the daylight seemed strange, even spookish, which certainly heralded a storm of some sort.

'Christ, I hope we aren't going to get a repeat of last year!'

Last winter had been terrible. Snow had lain in the streets for weeks and most of the country had experienced sub-zero temperatures. If that happened now Michael would be laid off, together with many other building workers and there would be no pay for any of them. Besides, she'd have him home all day cooped up in those two rooms! It didn't bear thinking about. The prospect wouldn't be any better for Michael, he seemed much happier since he had been working and had a few shillings in his pocket to spend.

Tonight I'll make an extra effort, she silently vowed. Have a real good hot dinner ready. I'll be loving to him, put my arms round him before either of us have time to get off on the wrong foot. I'll have the fire banked halfway up the chimney so that the place is really warm for when he comes home. But what time would he come home? Never mind, I won't even comment.

Saturday morning was typical. At nine o'clock she'd gone shopping, leaving Michael in bed. Eleven o'clock she was back and by twelve Michael had gone out. Shortly after three, when the pubs closed, he had come home, eaten an enormous dinner – on Saturdays and Sundays he preferred to have his main meal at this time – then slept the afternoon away slunk down in an armchair drawn close up to the fire.

'Cup of tea, Michael. It's gone six.' Barbara would just as soon let him sleep on but for him to miss a trip to the pub on a Saturday night just wasn't on.

He wriggled himself upwards in the chair, stretched his arms above his head and yawned loudly.

'Thanks Babs,' he said, leaning forward and taking his cup and saucer off of the edge of the table. Three or four gulps and the cup was empty. 'Fill it up, luv.'

He watched as she tipped the slops into the slop-bowl she insisted on using, then removed the quilted cosy from the pot before pouring him out a refill using a tea-strainer. What a bloody rigmarole! Still, with parents like hers and the way she'd been brought up it was a wonder she didn't use a clean cup and saucer every time.

'Gonna doll yerself up an' come with me tonight?' The question had been asked kindly and it surprised Barbara.

'I don't think so,' she answered quietly. 'You'll have your mates at the bar to talk to and I don't know any of the customers. I'd just as soon stay here and read my book.'

He didn't rant and rave or tell her she'd always got her head buried in a book. 'You never will get to know anyone if you stay cooped up in here every night of the week. Besides, I'd really like yer to come with me, it's about time I showed yer off to some of the blokes, I want to see their faces, their wives are proper old has-beens compared to you.' He got to his feet, came to where she sat and put his arm around her shoulders. 'Please Barbara, come with me.'

In the face of such gentle persuasion how could she refuse?

She took pains over her make-up, brushed her long hair

until the glints in it shone, then pinned it into a sophisticated French pleat at the back and piled neat curls on the
top and at the sides. A plain black dress with a wide red
belt and her high-heeled red court shoes and she was ready.

The look of approval in Michael's eyes as he held her coat
for her told her that her efforts had been well worthwhile.

If only he would wear a collar and tie, was what she was
thinking as she watched him wind a white silk muffler
around his neck. This habit favoured by all the local men
seemed as much a badge of poverty to her as did the
wrapround overalls the women constantly wore. She had
the sense not to comment.

Everything was normal for a Saturday evening. The
noise, commotion and smoky atmosphere were all as Barbara had feared. The bench seats set along the wall were
occupied by the older women, grey-haired, with an
unhealthy pallor and dressed in clothes that looked as
though they had been bought at a jumble sale. Pints of
draught Guinness with thick creamy heads were set in front
of each of them. In groups, nearer to the bar, were the
younger females. Peroxide blondes, redheads and brunettes,
all had had the curling-tongs at work on their hair. Rows
and rows of sausage curls enriched by ornaments neatly at
the nape of their necks. Perched on high stools, legs swinging, stocking seams running straight to where their short
skirts barely covered their behinds, now and again showing
bare thigh and a glimpse of a ribboned suspender, they
were – as they intended to be – an eyeful for the men at
the bar.

Having seated Barbara at a small table tucked away in
the corner and bought her a double gin and orange,
Michael had joined his mates at the counter. Centre of this

group of men was Pete Davis. A tall young man with the build of a rugby player, loud-mouthed and flashily dressed, Pete Davis was no stranger to Barbara. Michael had brought him back to their flat quite a few times. Never short of money, very generous – according to Michael – and popular with all the ladies. That was not how Barbara felt about him. She was uneasy whenever he was around. She always felt that she should tread warily where Pete Davis was concerned.

Barbara sighed heavily as she watched Michael pass another ten shilling note over the bar to pay for his round of drinks. He was a big man in every way when among his mates and very popular, yet she found herself wishing that he would get his priorities right. For some reason she suddenly felt very guilty. It was such a pity that they never seemed to want the same things. She did love him and she tried so hard to understand him yet she never seemed able to. At times like this, when he was showing his happy-go-lucky nature and his lovely smile, he was easy to love, just as he had been when they had first met. But the days when he was in a filthy mood and nothing she did was right were becoming far too frequent and it wasn't in her nature to give in to him all the time.

'Funny yer old man leaving yer so much on yer own,' observed the old woman seated nearest to Barbara.

'Not really,' said Barbara faintly. 'He likes to be with his mates.' The woman made a grim face. 'Wouldn't do me. Should 'ave thought the pair of yer would 'ave been canoodling up tergether like a pair of doves.'

Well yer thought wrong! was what Barbara wished she had the courage to snap at the old hag. She felt her cheeks flame but was saved from answering by the appearance of Michael.

He bent down until his face was level with hers. His eyes looked at her hungrily as he asked. 'Ready for another drink?'

Before Barbara had time to reply the woman who had been pestering her tugged at Michael's sleeve, ''Ow about buying me an' me friend just one little drink, Michael,' she wheedled.

'My pleasure, me darlin'. What's it ter be? Another Guinness or a drop of mother's ruin?'

'Oh, we'll 'ave a little drop of Gordons wiv you, won't we Mabel?'

As Michael made his way back to the bar, the woman who had been referred to as Mabel leant across her friend and poked Barbara in the ribs.

'Got any fags?' she asked.

'No, I don't smoke. Won't your friend give you one?'

'She ain't got no more. That was her last one she's just lit – see – the empty packet is in the ashtray.'

'Mike will buy us some,' said the woman who had asked for the drinks, and without more ado she yelled loudly, 'Mike, be a luv an' get us some fags.'

'Weights or Woodbines?' he called back.

This was carrying things too far. Barbara felt herself stiffen with the sheer audacity of the pair of them. She longed to tell the woman that they hadn't money to spare to be buying casual acquaintances drinks, never mind cigarettes as well, but Michael was enjoying playing the Big I Am and he wouldn't take kindly to her interfering and what would she do if he turned on her here in the pub. Still, it would be nice once in a while if he was as generous as this when it came to handing over the house-keeping money.

When at last the Landlord called 'Time, Gentlemen please', Barbara pulled herself together, squared her shoulders and with some effort pushed through the crowd to where Michael stood. She was determined that they should go straight home. She didn't want Michael sloping off to some late nightclub with Pete Davis, by the sound of his slurred speech he had had more than enough to drink for one night.

As Barbara opened the front door Michael began to sing at the top of his voice. 'Show me the way ter go 'ome, I'm tired an' I wanna go ter bed . . .'

Oh, he was driving her mad, being so contrary. Getting him upstairs was proving very difficult. With her arm around his waist to guide him, it was still case of up two stairs and back down one. Halfway up Michael began to laugh and pushed her flat against the wall. Laughing, tearing at the buttons on her coat, grabbing at her red belt, Barbara was instantly embarrassed. Suppose Mrs Singleton, or even one of her sons should come down to the landing?

'Come on, Michael,' she pleaded. 'Let's get indoors.'

He wouldn't budge and she felt she had to assert herself. With a hefty shove she broke free. 'I'm going on, I'll open up and put the lights on,' she said, doing her best to pacify him.

The heels of her shoes made a tapping sound on the threadbare linoleum as she quickened her pace. She heard him behind her, coming upwards on his hands and knees, whining away in a peevish voice. 'Wait. Oh, Babs please wait. I just wanna show yer 'ow much I luv yer.'

At last. She had him safely inside their living room and she thankfully closed the door.

'I'll boil the kettle, make us some tea. What would you like for your supper?'

'Who the bloody 'ell wants tea?' he roared at her. He made a grab for her, slipped and half fell, just saving himself by tugging at the hem of her dress and almost bringing her down to the floor with him.

She sighed heavily, best get him into the bedroom before he woke up the whole household. Michael tore at his clothing, smiling at her all the while. Much better to give in quietly, she decided, hoping against hope that perhaps, just this once he might treat her gently. Act as if he really did love her and not just want to use her.

She tried. Encouraging him to kiss her softly, showing him affection, hoping for some in return. To begin with he did treat her kindly, fondling her body, caressing slowly, then suddenly it wasn't at all like that. He was biting her. Hard and spitefully. Then he was on top of her, a short sharp blow of lust with no regard for her feelings and he was finished. Heaving a great satisfied sigh he flopped spread-eagled across her and it needed a huge effort on her part to push him off and roll him over to the other side of the bed.

Pulling the bedclothes up over him she felt her throat suddenly tighten. She closed her eyes rather than look at him. He stunk of beer and he was sweating like a pig.

Tears forced themselves from beneath her eyelids and slid down her cheeks. The whole act had been repugnant to her.

Chapter Four

IT HADN'T SNOWED, in fact the weather had improved. This Monday morning Michael had set off for work in a good mood for, according to him, the weekend had been great. Barbara was in a hurry now for she wanted to catch the eight twenty-five train to Eastbourne. She was going to visit her mother. Glancing around the living room she felt everything was neat and tidy, she had banked the fire down with wet slack and placed the guard in front of it. She'd have to hurry for she still had to walk to Clapham Junction railway station. She was excited and there was a spring to her step as she set out, filled with anticipation at the thought of the enjoyable day that lay ahead. She so seldom saw her parents these days.

She looked at her watch in desperation as she queued to buy her day return. She ran half the length of the platform and had just reached a carriage when the guard's whistle pierced the air. Doors banged, voices were raised, a man came running, catching the train by a hair's breadth. A kindly porter bundled her aboard, and slammed the door behind her.

The journey seemed to take forever. The train was icy cold, she couldn't be bothered to go in search of hot coffee. The carriage windows were none too clean and they rattled like mad; Barbara tugged hard on the leather strap in order to tighten it and hopefully stop the draught.

East Croydon was left behind and the view began to

change. Smoke-ridden walls of tenements, litter-filled yards of warehouses and busy suburban streets gave way to green fields and high barns and finally the train drew into Eastbourne.

Good grief! The rain was pouring down and it was still bitterly cold. Barbara's heart sank. She'd have to find a taxi. Then she spied her mother.

'Oh, you poor darling, I thought you must have missed the train. You look frozen.'

Everything was all right now, there were hugs and kisses, and being held close, and both of them talking at the same time, until finally as they reached the car and got into the two front seats there was laughter, because it was such a relief to be out of the cold and going home.

Home was Meads Lodge. A charming house situated just outside the village of Alfriston, surrounded by rolling downs and shaded by numerous huge old trees. No one knew the exact date it was built but her father said it dated back to the Elizabethan period. Tall chimneys and many leaded windows looked out over velvet lawns and flower beds. Two modern bathrooms had been installed while Barbara was only a toddler. The whole family loved the house and despite having one full-time and two part-time gardeners her mother devoted much of her time and energy to the grounds: they were her pride and joy. The stables were her father's dominion.

Her mother swept the car around the circular drive and brought it to a halt outside the main door. Stepping from the car, Barbara let her gaze take in the whole of the house, her bedroom with the pretty chintz curtains, the two rooms that had belonged to William and Patrick and the large room with the big bay windows that was her parents' bedroom, into which she had gone running many a morning to crawl into the warmth and loving arms of her mother for a cuddle. So many memories. Her home now was two rooms above a shop in Battersea. The comparison made her shudder.

'Leave your coat there. Come on straight through to the kitchen.'

The big, familiar room was bright and, oh, so lovely and warm. The fire in the range burnt bright red, a saucepan simmered at the back of the hob, the big kettle sang and a gorgeous smell was coming from the oven. Barbara took off her boots and warmed her hands, while her mother made a pot of tea and set home-made biscuits out on a plate which held a lace doyley. Before long they were sitting at the table, just as they had when she'd been small, drinking their tea and nibbling their biscuits and again both of them talking at once.

'I'm so glad you're here.'

'So am I.'

'You don't come home often enough.'

Barbara made no reply and her mother didn't push her, but she sighed as she looked at this lovely daughter of hers.

She looked the same, much as she had before she'd left home to volunteer for war work. She still had a beautiful figure, bit too thin really, her dark hair still had a sheen to it, still coiled sleekly upwards and held in place by side combs. Beautiful skin, still a few freckles, only her eyes seemed to have changed. Those lovely, deep-brown eyes, shielded by long, thick, dark eyelashes, were sad. There was no getting away from it. Her Barbara wasn't happy.

'It's so lovely to have you home. Are you sure you can't stay for a few days?'

How I wish I could, was what Barbara nearly said, instead she sniffed.

'Something smells good.'

'Beef casserole with mushrooms, tomatoes and baby onions.'

'Mmm, wonderful.'

'Go upstairs, freshen up in your room, and then we'll have a drink before lunch. I'm sure you could use one. I'll set the glasses out ready.'

Barbara picked up her handbag, crossed the kitchen and went up the thickly carpeted stairs, across the wide landing and into what had been her own bedroom for so many years of her life. It still looked exactly the same. The beige, closely fitted carpet, the high wide bed, with its brass-railed head-stand, the pretty bedspread that matched the curtains. The kidney-shaped dressing table and the white Lloyd Loom chairs. Her mother had given it the final touch, a deep-pink potted cyclamen set into a flowered plant pot, stood on the bedside table and Barbara, standing in the doorway, marvelled as she always did, at her mother's ability to create not only her own personality and warmth in a room but real visual pleasure.

Downstairs, Patricia Hamlin was torn with worry, it wasn't just a nasty suspicion that all was not well with Barbara and her marriage – it was stronger than that.

First and foremost Mrs Hamlin was the sort of mother everyone would have loved. She had given her life to the role of motherhood and being a good wife. Sadly that had all changed now, with both her sons having been killed in the War she was left with only Barbara to mother. The turn that events had taken by altering her only daughter's life to such an extent that she was only able to see her on rare occasions, not only saddened her but sickened her. The conditions under which Barbara was living just didn't bear thinking about. Why had she had to be so headstrong? Why had the marriage arrangements been carried out with so much stealth? Not even to have informed her own parents, let alone invite them to be present at the ceremony. That had hurt them badly.

Barbara had had the decency to send a telegram. She knew it off by heart: 'Married Michael this morning. Be happy for me. All my love, Barbara.'

Nothing in this world had ever hurt her husband as much as those words on that flimsy piece of paper.

'She might have given us some warning,' he had stormed angrily. 'To go off like that – and that Michael! – Dear God, what has she done?'

He had sat there, his fingers twisting and fumbling with the telegram. The silence that had followed was so awful she just had to break it.

'Phillip.'

He put out a hand, pulled her close.

'Phillip.'

She looked up him, and he shook his head. She knew that he did not want to discuss the matter, not now. Suddenly he seemed old. He had never seemed so to her before, but now she knew that he felt he had lost Barbara, the last of his children, and it was more than he could bear.

She got to her feet and went out of the room, closing the doors behind her. Upstairs in Barbara's room she had given way to her own tears.

Had Barbara found happiness? She could bear it if she had, but her only daughter! She should have been in church today, the bride's mother, watching her walk the length of the aisle, on her father's arm, a vision in white with a long train trailing behind. Instead nothing but a telegram.

All her children had gone. She had lain down on Barbara's single bed, burying her face in her pillow and cried for the sons that she would never see again and for the little girl who was now a married woman.

'Mother?'

'I'm here.'

Barbara found her in the dining room, not doing anything, just standing staring out of the long windows, deep in thought.

'What are you doing?' Barbara asked her.

'Just waiting for you. I'll dish up lunch now, and then I thought, as it's stopped raining, why don't we wrap up warm and take a tour round the grounds; might even get as far as the village, must be ages since you've been down into Alfriston. What do you think? Shall we eat first and then decide? Plenty of coats, wellies and stout sticks still in the vestibule if you feel that energetic.'

The dishes set out on the table said a lot for Patricia Hamlin's culinary skills, but more than that was the presentation. The fine china, cutlery and table linen were all perfect but the little touches made all the difference. Duchesse potatoes, their piped pyramid shapes coloured beautifully because of the egg yolks she had mixed into the creamed potato, spiced with nutmeg, browned under the grill and garnished with watercress. For added colour she had baked whole tomatoes and arranged these around a dish of asparagus spears. What a difference! Barbara couldn't help her thoughts. Michael would have only wanted a pile of mash and tinned peas with what he would term as stew.

Having done justice to the meal they went through to the back of the house and dressed themselves warmly in the lobby, then let themselves out through the conservatory and into the garden. Side by side they crossed the lawn. The early rain had soaked the turf and they left a trail of footprints on the damp grass. Past the flower borders and through to the rose garden and on into the orchard. Still more memories came flooding back to Barbara. The great chestnut tree way over in the corner which her brothers had been able to shin up like a couple of monkeys. The round patch of grey cinders, the remains of endless bonfires, and she could almost hear the shrieks of delight from long-gone firework nights. Beyond, they came upon the Cuckmere River, flowing deep and narrow between green covered banks. Was their old rowing boat still in the boathouse?

There were sheep on the Downs and away in the distance was Friston Forest. Walking at a steady pace they soon entered the village; the church, raised and built on a circular mound, looked out over the river valley and was, in its seclusion, a symbol of peace and tranquility. A watery sun came out as they crossed the field, making for the cobbled high street with its high pavements and causing steam to rise from the wet grass and give off a sweet smell. It was a lovely smell.

East Sussex, Barbara decided, was all quite beautiful, and she must have been out of her mind when she had rushed into marriage with Michael, thus forgoing the right to live in this lovely village with her parents. Just being with her mother made her view life so differently, here without the hustle and bustle of never-ending traffic she felt calm, safe and secure.

The church clock chimed the half hour, two thirty, oh dear the day was going far too quickly.

By the time they came to The Smugglers Inn set off from Market Square with its huge chestnut tree and market cross, they were both out of breath and warm with exertion.

'Do you remember when Eastbourne Foxhounds, horses and riders, your father amongst them, used to assemble here prior to leading off over the Downs?' Patricia asked her daughter.

'Yes I do,' she smiled, 'and when there were many racing stables in the area and jockeys, trainers and stable lads all lived locally.'

'Times have certainly changed,' her mother sighed sadly.

Seated now in the lounge, in front of a roaring fire, the tea-tray set out on a long low mahogany table in front of where her mother sat, it was Barbara who broke the strained silence which had fallen between them since they had got back from their walk.

'You and Daddy knew my marriage wouldn't work from the start didn't you?'

'Oh, Barbara.'

She met her mother's eyes, and saw that she was right.

'How could we not know, you had been used to so much, though I prayed love would be sufficient for you both to survive the odds.'

Barbara lowered her eyes, unable to meet the grief in those of her mother's.

'The only time you brought Michael here to meet us, he

was coarse, rude to your father and openly contemptuous of our way of life.'

'Oh, Mother, it didn't matter to me then, I loved him so much. Looking back it was more than likely envy which prompted Michael's bad behaviour. He never tires of telling me how spoilt I am.' Tears overcame Barbara for a moment, she hastily brushed them away. 'It didn't matter that Michael had no money, it wouldn't now, if only he would settle down, accept some responsibility. All I wanted was for us to be happy, the two of us together, loving each other, wanting the same things.'

Her mother sat perfectly still, silent for an instant, and then she said his name, 'Michael', as though it summed up every thing that was wrong.

'Yes, Michael. I know now. It was a ghastly mistake. Michael doesn't love me and he won't let me love him. I never dreamed it would be like this.'

'Perhaps things might change for the better if you were to start a family?'

This statement did nothing to comfort Barbara. How could she tell her mother that Michael was adamant about not wanting any children? How could she tell her of the two abortions she had had?

She sat there, in the comfortable lounge of the beautiful house that had been her childhood home, recalling how she had been so willing to give up everything convinced she and Michael were made for each other and would be happy together for the rest of their lives. But of course she had been wrong. Terribly wrong. Now it was too late, she realised to be fair to Michael that she was possibly the worst type of woman that he could have chosen to marry. She felt hot tears prick at the back of her eyes.

'Here,' ever practical, her mother produced a clean handkerchief scented with lavender. 'Wipe your eyes, crying won't help.'

Barbara took the handkerchief and did as she was told.

'Now. Tell me, what is wrong? I don't need to be clairvoyant to know that all is not right between you and Michael.'

'Oh, Mumma,' Barbara reverted to the name she had used for her mother when a child. Indeed she sounded now like a very small child. 'I know now I should never have married Michael.'

It was out. She had admitted it out loud. The relief was great. She looked up and again, met her mother's eyes, and saw them troubled.

'I should have realised that weekend I brought him home. He didn't fit in, did he?'

'I hope your father and I didn't show our disapproval.'

'Oh, of course you didn't,' Barbara hastened to assure her. 'You were very kind to him, both of you. I thought Daddy especially went out of his way to make him feel welcome. It was *him*. He was so insulting, sneering at every suggestion Daddy made. Look how he behaved when we had our meals. He ate like a pig. I think that was what upset you most, Mumma, and there was no need for it. Michael was doing it deliberately.'

'In fairness, darling, I don't think you can blame him too much for that weekend. He was out of his depth. He had obviously been brought up differently. You told me he did apologise afterwards.'

'Yes he did and I made allowances and forgave him.'

'That's hardly surprising, you were sure you truly loved him at the time.'

'And you're telling me you know that I'm not in love with Michael now?'

'No, my darling, I'm telling you no such thing. You have just admitted it yourself.'

Barbara sighed. 'What am I to do?'

'Only you can decide that. One thing is for sure, it's no good looking back. Give yourself time, do your best to improve the situation. Perhaps you may even be able to persuade Michael to visit us again, give your father and me another chance, things might turn out different. Michael might feel differently about us now that the War is over. What do you think?

Pigs might fly! is what Barbara was thinking, but what she said was, 'I'll try.'

'Good. Now, please, for my sake, cheer up and let me see you smile.'

Glancing at her watch, Barbara spoke her thoughts aloud, 'I would have loved to have seen Daddy.'

Eagerly her mother leant forward, placing her hand over Barbara's. 'Why don't you stay the night, or better still for a few days, your own bedroom is quite ready.'

Oh mother! Yes, *yes please* was what she wanted to cry out, instead what she said was, 'I must go home Mumma, it wouldn't be fair to Michael if I just stayed away without telling him.'

Patricia watched her daughter's hands twisting restlessly in her lap and she felt dreadful. 'Darling I'm sorry, that was selfish of me, perhaps another time, soon eh? Tell Michael in advance, I'm sure he won't object to you spending a few days with us, oh, I shall so look forward to having you home – and wait till I tell your father.'

Her mother's words sent a shiver through Barbara, she

didn't want to upset her father more than she had already. Such a kind and loving man. He was fifty-eight years old, but the death of his two sons had aged him. Since Barbara could remember, he had been a tall distinguished man, dark suited with bowler hat and rolled umbrella as befitted the legal profession, but only on weekdays. Saturdays, Sundays and holidays his clothes would be sporty and youthful when he took her and the boys walking up over the Downs, out on the river or scrambling over rocks, searching for seaweed when they went to the coast. She vowed to see if she couldn't change Michael's animosity towards her parents.

'Barbara, do you need money?'

The question brought Barbara up with a jerk.

'Your father would be only too pleased to help. You do know that, don't you? If only you could bring Michael round to thinking kindly of us, come and spend some time with your father. He misses you so. He loves you very much.'

'I know, Mother. I'll do my best.'

She knew well enough that her powers of persuasion were not that great. Even if she did screw up enough courage to broach the subject of them having a short holiday with her parents, Michael would cut her short with one solitary word: No. She had taken in what her mother had said about money, and she wondered again, as she frequently did, would money be a solution to all their problems? In her heart she knew it wouldn't really help. A stop gap, that's all it would be until Michael lost it all to the bookmakers or drank it away with his mates in the pub. Money wasn't the only difficulty, if only it were; they needed shared interests, a common ground on which to talk and that they didn't have.

Barbara sighed heavily. 'I shall have to be making a move now.'

Patricia put on a brave smile. 'All right, my darling, I'll go and start the car.'

At the station her mother handed her a brown paper parcel. 'A few books I know you will enjoy reading, some tobacco for Michael and some chocolates for you.'

'Oh, mother. Thank you.'

'Goodbye. Ring me when you can.' They kissed and held each other tight.

'Goodbye mother.'

By Wednesday of that week it did snow. Continuous squalls of heavy flakes accompanied by bitterly cold blustery winds. It lay in deep drifts and then it froze. The roads were treacherous. Michael was laid off, outside building work was impossible. With Michael home all day and money scarce the next two weeks were not pleasant but Barbara drew the rest of her savings out from the bank and survived as best she could.

Nevertheless the rot set in and things came to a head one Saturday morning. Michael's chin came out aggressively as he faced Barbara across the kitchen table. 'Are you gonna give me a few bob or shall I start taking this place apart until I find where you keep yer private hoard?'

His features were distorted with rage and Barbara was afraid of him but she didn't have the energy for yet another row. Turning she picked up her handbag from the dresser, opened her purse and checked the coins that were in it.

'Well, it ain't much is it? Hand it over,' he demanded, thrusting out his hand. He looked awful. Two days' stubble on his chin, the inevitable scarf tied in a knot around his

neck and now he had taken to wearing a huge checked
cap pulled well down over his forehead.

Barbara obeyed. Seventeen shillings and fourpence she
tipped into his open palm.

'And the notes.'

Dismay showed in her eyes, He couldn't leave her with
nothing, there was hardly any food in the house let alone
coal for the fire.

Michael's arm shot out. A hefty push sent her sprawling
backwards. He wrenched open the metal stud at the front
of her purse and took out the three notes from the wallet
section.

'A measly two quid!' He spat the words at her as he
folded the one pound note and the two ten shilling notes
before pushing them into his back pocket. He sneered at
her in triumph. 'I promise it will do me more good than
it would you. Honest love, I've got a great tip for the gee
gees, I'll be back later on with me winnings and you can
go down the market and get the weekend grub then.'

He strode off, banging the door, she heard him clomping
down the stairs, whistling as he went and Barbara burst
into tears.

Wrapped up warmly, clutching her shopping basket, Barbara nervously pushed open the door to Mrs Winters' shop.
Overloaded with second-hand furniture and more knick-
knacks than a person would collect in a lifetime, the smoky
smelly atmosphere was nevertheless warm and inviting.

'Allo, luv. Bloody cold terday ain't it? Fer Christ's sake
put the wood in the 'ole and come over 'ere by me stove.
It's great ter see yer.'

Knowing what she had come to ask, Barbara was

embarrassed by the affection. When Barbara remained silent Mrs Winters' smile turned into a suspicious glare.

'That bugger ain't bin knocking you about agin, 'as he?'

'No, nothing like that. Of course he's very moody lately, not being able to work gets him down.'

'Hram,' Mrs Winters sniffed. 'If anyone's got good reason ter be moody, it's you my luv. Tied up ter that no good 'usband. Missing work my arse! All he's missing is his sessions in the boozer with his bloody mates. Wouldn't know a good day's work if it was staring 'im in the face.'

She put her arms across her chest, heaved her bosoms higher and shot a puzzled glance in Barbara's direction. 'You're not sickening fer something are yer?'

'No, no really I'm very well.'

'Then what is it, Barbara? If you can't tell me what's troubling yer after all this time then it's a bloody bad do. I thought we were friends. Good friends, that you could come ter me no matter what the trouble was. Seems I was mistaken.'

'Oh, Mrs Winters, please don't be cross with me. We *are* friends. Without you I never could have survived this winter.'

'Here, sit your bottom down there,' she urged as she pulled forward a well-worn winged-back chair, 'and get to the point of what is the matter, cos I ain't no fool an' if you expect me to believe that all is right wiv your world you must think I was born yesterday.'

'I can't pay the rent,' Barbara murmured, her eyes lowered to the floor.

'So, what's new? No, it ain't the first time you've had to come ter tell me that an' yer know well enough by now that from you it don't bovver me. No, my girl it's more than that and yer better spit it out before I lose me temper.'

'I need some money,' Barbara stammered. Once started she couldn't stop, 'I haven't a penny-piece in cash. I pawned my gold watch two days ago. All the food I bought has gone. I will go and see my parents just as soon as I get the chance and then I could pay you back with interest. I hate to ask but Michael will go berserk if there's no coal for the fire and no dinner ready for him.'

'Bugger Michael. I don't give a sodding toss for him, but you just say how much you need my love and it's yours, and don't you ever let me 'ear no more talk about paying me interest.'

Barbara's eyes were brimming over with unshed tears as she gazed at this skinny scruffy woman who had a heart of gold.

Suddenly Mrs Winters bent down and grabbed hold of Barbara's shoulders. 'Christ orlmighty! You're pregnant again! Oh you silly little cow! Does Michael know?'

Barbara had gone pale and she looked scared as she shook her head. 'Well, one thing's fer certain, you ain't gettin' no more abortions, yer nearly killed yerself last time. I'll take meself off and find out where yer parents live and tell them a few things before I'll stand by and see yer do that ter yerself again. Yer got me? I mean every word I've said.'

Mrs Winters came and squatted beside her. Their eyes came level and she saw that Mrs Winters was quite serious in her threat to visit her parents – not to be in any way unkind, she was merely looking out for her welfare, afraid of what the consequences might be should she plunge into yet another abortion. What a good friend this woman had turned out to be. Her face was deeply lined and very weather-beaten, her clothes were an odd assortment, the top layer being a number of brightly coloured shawls, and on her head she wore the most elegant hat. Purple velour, adorned with artificial flowers of all shapes and sizes, and little wisps of her light-brown hair had escaped and were hanging down over her ears. Crumbs, the colours of some of those flowers! Suddenly Barbara lost all her self-control. Shaking with mirth, she tried in vain to struggle into an upright position in the deep armchair.

After a moment of shocked surprise, Mrs Winters' lips broke into a smile and soon she too was laughing fit to bust.

'Oh stoppit, stoppit!' puffed Mrs Winters. 'You're making me bleeding side ache. Barbara, if you don't take the bloody cake I'm damned if I know who does.'

Clutching her side with one hand and rubbing at her eyes with the other, Mrs Winters got to her feet.

'By Christ, this ain't the life you were meant ter be leading. Yer ain't got a penny piece in yer purse, you've got yerself in the bloody family way yet again, a fact that no-good 'usband of yours ain't gonna be exactly over the moon about an' you're sitting there laughing yer bleedin' head off. Gawd knows what's gonna become of yer!'

The jangle of the shop-door bell saved Barbara from having to answer.

'Here Ma, 'ow much d'yer want fer this brass fender yer got out 'ere?' The question came from a youngish man, well muffled up against the bitter weather; still, his face was pinched with the cold and his nose was bright red.

'Got a load of kids 'ave yer?' The question was flung at him.

'Got me fair share, I suppose, two boys and the new

baby's a girl. Bin looking fer a fender. Keep the kids from
playing wiv the fire and 'andy to air the napkins on.'

'Ten bob ter you then son. Fifteen ter any other bugger.'

'Yeah I know. I've 'eard your spiel before. How about
seven and a tanner?'

'Cheeky sod! Give us eight bob an' don't argue or I may
change me mind.'

'Yer a darling, Missus,' he said holding out the silver
coins. 'No need to come out, I'll carry it fine underneath
me arm. Ta-tah then.'

'Tat-ah lad, Gawd bless yer.

'Now,' she said, turning back to Barbara. 'I'll make us a
brew up and then we'll get you sorted. At least ter see yer
over the weekend.'

Barbara watched as she bustled about putting the tin
kettle onto the spirit stove, sorting out two enamel mugs
and wiping them out on a cloth that was as clean as
the driven snow. A mixture of contrasts was this cockney
woman.

Barbara was not sure which was worse, Michael when he
ranted and raved or this stony silence he had kept up since
they had had that awful row.

Michael hadn't got his way, not this time. To begin with
he had pleaded, then threatened and would have used
violence had not Mrs Winters waylaid him, giving what
she chose to call a friendly word of advice. Barbara had
turned a deaf ear: not another abortion! Besides she was
happy, she longed for a baby, it might just make a difference
between Michael and herself; he had to feel love for it
when it was born, especially if they were to have a son.

Half of her mind knew that to be a delusion, the other half insisted there was always that possibility.

Meanwhile you could cut the atmosphere with a knife. To look at Michael you would think something terrible had happened and his black mood was making her restless and nervy. He was back at work and still had his bet and spent time in the pub, more so at weekends, though he no longer asked her to accompany him. In fact she hardly ever went out, except to the market, meeting only a few neighbours and dear old Mrs Winters when she went downstairs for a chat.

What she wouldn't have given to be able to go home and stay with her parents for a few days. Their reaction to her news would be so different. The joy on their faces, to be clasped in their arms and told how wonderful it would be to have a baby in the family again. She thought about writing to some of her old friends, meeting up with them again. How could she invite them here? Never mind the state of the place, Michael's reaction would be more than enough to drive them away. She let her imagination run riot when her thoughts dwelt on Penny Rayford and Elizabeth Warren, but the outcome was too depressing. She missed those two girls. The three of them had been such close friends and had shared so many happy memories whilst growing up; together they had also experienced many sad events during the years of the War.

With Michael now treating her with contempt because of her determination to have this baby, she actually began to think that this was the loneliest phase of her life. What Michael was doing now was a deliberate, systematic campaign to break her spirit. His indifference alone was driving her mad. She could be invisible for all the notice he took of her and he could have been struck dumb when you considered the silence he maintained.

As March gave way to April, bringing with it the promise of spring, Michael's attitude softened a bit. He was not so aggressive when making love to her. In other ways there was no improvement. He steadfastly refused to even talk about her parents, let alone visit them. He still remained workshy. He could have found a regular secure job. But no, he preferred the odd few days' casual labouring on various sites, receiving his payment daily in cash. Also, she had found out that in addition to this cash in hand he signed on each week at the Labour Exchange, drawing benefit for her as well as himself she supposed, but what the amount of money was that he was entitled to she had no idea and she daren't ask. He was still convinced that, one day, he was going to make a pile of money by backing three winning horses in a row.

Whenever she attempted to open a discussion on the state of their finances he became hostile. He knew only too well by now that his aggressive temper frightened her and that knowledge gave him even more power to be abusive to her. The trouble was, right from the beginning she had given in to aggression and now had no defence against it.

For the past two weeks Barbara had known there was something wrong; Michael had given her no money and she had been supplementing their income from her own bank account which her father had topped up some months ago. Now there was little left for her to draw on and she would feel both guilty and embarrassed if she had to ask her father for more.

'Can yer let me 'ave fifty quid?'

Michael's blue eyes looked up at Barbara and there was deep malice in them; his voice sounded really strange as he made this request. When Barbara made no answer he dropped his eyes and continued to stare at the pages of the Sunday paper.

'I'm in dead trouble if I don't come up with that amount within the next coupla days. An' I mean *dead* trouble.'

'We're already up to our eyes in debt, you know that – don't you Michael? Where the hell do you think I'm going to be able to find fifty pounds. What do you need it so badly for?' she asked bluntly.

Michael pushed his empty breakfast plate away, tucked the newspaper under his arm and got up from the table.

'Hey, where are you going?' Barbara stood up and caught at his arm. 'We have to talk about this, Michael.'

He tried to pass her but she stood her ground and refused to move.

'I'm not joking. I have to have that fifty quid or I'll end up with a broken arm and maybe a broken leg as well.'

She shook her head blindly in desperation.

'You could get it for me if you wanted to, you callous bitch.' He rounded on her, 'It's a mere flea bite ter you, you've plenty, yer bloody daddy sees to that.' He reached out and grabbed her by the arm and squeezed hard.

'Well?' he hissed at her.

'I did have money in the bank but it's all gone once again. What do you think we've been living on?'

'You could get more if you wanted to, but I've yet ter see the damn day when you'd offer to put yerself out to 'elp me.' He gave her arm a final savage squeeze and then pushed her from him.

Barbara deliberately changed the tone of her voice to

one of pleading, 'Look Michael, let's get out of here, I'm so tired of being cooped up, let's go for a walk, watch the boats on the river; we can talk then, it is such a nice day it seems a pity to waste it indoors.'

He gave her a look of disgust and then to her surprise muttered, 'Okay. Why not?'

They strolled through the streets, across Battersea Bridge and into the park. Finally when she sat down on a seat Michael dropped down onto the grass at her feet. He lay on his back, his hands behind his head.

Presently she asked fearfully. 'What are we going to do, Michael?'

'About what?' The sarcasm was evident in his voice.

'You know very well, we haven't paid Mrs Winters the rent for three weeks, we have only the bare necessities of food indoors, the rental for the wireless is more than a month overdue, we still need coal, it's not yet warm enough to do without a fire but the coalman won't deliver unless he gets paid in cash there and then.'

He made no answer. Just lay looking up at the sky, displaying a pointed lack of interest.

Barbara was suddenly so angry that she became brave. She wasn't going to shoulder all these worries on her own any longer. She levered herself forward into a position where she could stare down at him, before she had got any words out Michael looked up and gruffly said, 'Ask your bloody parents, they're wealthy enough.'

Still angry, she did something she would not normally have done: her arm stretched out, her hand opened flat, she was about to slap his face.

All he did was laugh as he caught at her wrist before her

hand could make contact. Barbara snatched her arm away from his grasp and gave a bitter smile.

'I thought you wanted nothing from my family, you took such painstaking care to tell me it was only me you wanted when you pleaded with me to marry you. Been a very different story since, hasn't it?'

Michael's face went scarlet with rage, he sat up, pushed his face within inches of hers and hissed. 'You were different then.'

If they had been indoors she would have been intimidated by his voice alone, but out here in the open park with people around she wasn't about to let that remark pass without comment. Dropping her usual way of speaking she let her temper rip. 'So were you! By God you were! Now all you want is your working class mates. So long as you have money to go boozing with them and to squander playing the Big I Am with the bookies and at the dog-track you don't give a damn where the money comes from or who has to suffer just so long as you are all right. You accept no responsibility whatsoever. All you think about is yourself, you wouldn't do a day's work if you could get out of it.'

She paused to take a deep breath before sneering at him. 'You get a lot of pleasure out of scorning me for my upbringing; according to you I'm a rich spoilt bitch, but that never seems to stop you when you want something. This fifty quid, as you call it, who's pestering you for that? The bookmaker or the governor at the Falcon Arms? Seems you wouldn't have any objection to being financed by my folks' money in order to pay off this particular debt.'

Michael was astounded. Such hostility. She had retaliated before but never as fiercely as this.

He was up on his feet in seconds. Turning angrily towards her, his head jutting close to her face again, he snarled, 'The pubs are open – I'm going for a drink.'

'Well I'm sure you'll find enough money for that.' Her words were directed at his disappearing back.

Barbara remained sitting where she was for a long time. From her very first meeting with Michael she had been infatuated with him, willing to do almost anything he asked, afraid of losing him. She hadn't minded one bit using her own money to tide them over, but now it had almost run out. She couldn't go to her father yet again. In her heart she knew she would. That fifty pounds had to be paid and quickly, she was well aware of the code of honour that existed between these Londoners when it came to paying their debts. Treatment for welshers was always severe. Oh Michael! All they were doing was leading a day to day existence, forever at each other's throats. Where exactly were they heading? Sadly she knew she had no answer to her own question.

Michael had changed so much, he didn't give one jot now whether she was happy or not. She herself had changed somewhat, there was no disputing that. Would things change for the better if she were to give up fighting? She could so easily fall into slipshod ways. Become as some women were in the district. Would Michael notice if she didn't change the bed sheets so often, or dust the furniture, take pains over her appearance, spend less money on fresh food and use more tinned stuff – as to fresh flowers his opinion had always been voiced loud and harshly, 'Bloody waste of good money!'

Her lips twisted into a bitter smile as she got to her feet and began to walk across the grass. It wasn't only Michael's temperament that had altered since he had been demobbed from the navy; he didn't look anything like the happy strapping sailor she had fallen in love with. No longer was there a jaunty spring in his step or a swagger to his walk, his hair was now long and lank; yet it was his eyes that had taken on the most noticeable change, no more did they twinkle with laughter, more often than not they were veiled with stubborn antagonism. Sometimes, quite unintentionally, she would let slip a slight reference to her childhood or her parents and then God help her!

Why should he be like this? He had known of her background before he asked her to marry him. All the feelings he had for her mother and father and indeed for her most of the time, were bound up with bitterness. Then again, Michael felt bitter about a whole lot of things. The navy had been good for him and the discipline that went with it. He had felt himself a somebody, which indeed he had been, loyal and brave enough to have served in submarines. Now he was a labourer. The years stretching ahead held out no hope to him for betterment. Her father, who would have been able to help, was the one person that Michael would have nothing to do with. Sighing heavily, Barbara decided that she felt very sorry for Michael. Like so many men now out of the forces he was finding civvy street was not so easy. Good jobs not requiring qualifications were elusive. The War might be over but indirectly the repercussions were still being felt.

Glancing to her right, Barbara spied a crowd gathered around a speaker perched high on a box; his voice was loud and carried across to where she stood. The theme of the young man's speech was political. She laughed to herself.

Even Winston Churchill hadn't got the job he wanted or deserved.

People were fickle. In 1940 the Chamberlain Government had come under heavy criticism, had been dissolved and replaced by a coalition led by Churchill. During the succeeding War years Churchill had rallied the nation and led England to victory over Germany and Japan. The whole country owed Winston Churchill a great deal yet the outcome of the first general election since the end of World War Two had seen him become Leader of the Opposition, not Prime Minister. As Barbara walked on she told herself that circumstances did change people, of that she was in no doubt. Yet did all their hopes and dreams have to become stagnant? She stopped dead in her tracks and pondered on what the long term effect this marriage would have on both herself and Michael.

She shivered as if somebody had walked over her grave and she was suddenly afraid.

The weeks dragged by, the weather was fine, but matters between Michael and herself were not: open hostility was how Barbara described it to herself. Now apart from his daily antagonism there were the nights. Nights that were nightmarish. There was no way she could prevent Michael from taking his rights, as he put it. When it came to satisfying his needs he made no pretence of tenderness and his taking of her had become repulsive. It was hellish to have to lie there and allow her body to be used in such a brutal way. It was all too much at times. Her body was heavy with this pregnancy, even her brain was becoming weary; this was not what she had imagined being married to Michael would be like. She had got used to the idea that he was not a good provider, but oh, how she wished that he would show just a little consideration, some kindness once in a while.

He was still his own worst enemy, he wanted to rise above the rut he had got himself into, well there were times when he said he did, yet he made no bones of the fact that he despised the upper classes and in particular her parents.

She turned now and looked around her, it was ten minutes past ten in the morning and still she was sitting on a straight-backed chair at one end of the wooden table. The breakfast things spread out before her were still unwashed, the bed in the only other room remained unmade. What had she come to? How much lower could she sink? For another ten minutes or so she stayed still, when she finally forced herself to stand up her legs felt leaden and she realised she had almost reached the end of her tether.

From the wireless came the sweet sounds of the Inkspots as they sang: '*Into each life some rain must fall, but too much is falling in mine!*' True, how true. Tears slowly trickled down her cheeks.

As Barbara washed herself at the kitchen sink she moaned out loud as she lifted first one leg and then the other up to rest on the seat of a wooden chair, in order to be able to wash her legs and feet. She would readily admit that she still missed the privilege of being waited on, the space to walk about the house that had been her childhood home, her mother's lovely gardens, her father's horses, but if she were to be asked to pinpoint what she missed most there would be no hesitation, the bathrooms would be her answer. The very thought of stepping into a hot bath, perfumed bath salts, unlimited hot water gushing from the taps, large fluffy towels on the heated towel rail. Compared to a tin bath in the middle of the kitchen floor, filled only with water from kettles boiled on the gas rings of the old black enamelled stove, and then the backbreaking job of having to empty the water after she had washed herself down, the contrast didn't bear thinking about.

It had taken her ages but at least she was washed and dressed and felt much more able to cope with the day that stretched ahead.

'Barbara, Bar-bara,' Mrs Winters was yelling at her from the bottom of the stairs.

Opening the living room door, Barbara put her head out and called in answer, 'Yes, Mrs Winters?'

'There's a posh young woman down 'ere in me shop, says she's a friend of yours an' she wants ter see yer. Are yer coming down or shall I send 'er up?'

Barbara panicked. A friend, come here to Battersea?

'I'll be down, give me a couple of minutes. Thank you Mrs Winters.' She ran a comb through her thick hair, straightened her grey maternity skirt, wondered what friend had found out where she was living and slowly went downstairs. At the foot of the stairs stood Penny.

A shrill cry of pleasure, chuckles and then giggles from the pair of them. 'What on earth are you doing here?'

Then they were in each other's arms, hugging tight, touching each other with the familiarity that only comes with long natural friendship.

Upstairs as they entered the living room Barbara felt envious, just for a moment, Penny, she thought proudly, was still a good friend, and so beautiful, with her bright blonde hair and those amazing big blue eyes. No wonder she had always been so popular with the men. Today she looked marvellous. She wore a grey tailored suit, a red silk blouse, her shoes and handbag were red and tied to the handle of the bag was a navy-blue silk scarf. Everything about her was fresh, clean, and shiny, right down to her fingernails which were manicured and varnished.

Barbara swallowed hard to rid herself of the lump in her throat. Maybe I haven't let myself go, well not entirely, but beside Penny I must look decidedly dowdy!

Penny sprawled into one of the two armchairs, her long silk clad legs thrust out, her hands folded in her lap. Barbara sat down opposite with a thump.

'Why didn't you let me know you were coming?'

Penny gave a grin which spread from ear to ear. 'How? You haven't got a telephone, besides, since when did good friends have to make an appointment? By the way, don't get yourself too comfortable – you and I are going to celebrate.'

'Celebrate what?'

'My birthday, it's not actually until tomorrow but I decided to visit you today.'

Barbara raised her deep brown eyes to the ceiling, 'I don't get it, why come here?'

'Why not? To see you, of course, you daft old thing. Your mother told me you were a bit down so I'm taking you out to lunch and maybe on a shopping spree.'

So that was it! Her mother had asked Penny to come and spy out the land. No, maybe that was a little unfair. Her mother did worry about her wellbeing and her concern would have been genuine, her father cared too for that matter, and it was weeks now since she had been able to visit them and to be honest the letters that she dutifully posted each week never told her parents very much. If they had asked Penny to visit her their motives would have been of the best.

'Come on, move yourself Barbara, get changed, let's go.'

Barbara had to laugh. There was no arguing with Penny.

Kensington: it brought back a whole load of memories as together they walked down the busy High Street and Barbara paused for a moment, staring at the passers-by. There was a purpose in their steps, their bodies held straight, no fear in their actions as they strode along showing determination. Most were smartly dressed and self-consciously she looked down at her own suit; it was clean and well-pressed but old, that very fact had her pondering on just how long it had been since she had made up her face, dressed with care and gone out, out that is beyond the limits of Battersea.

Hardly were they through the main doors of John Barker's department store than Penny was exclaiming, 'Oh, I do like these, choose one, Barbara, I'll treat us both.'

Floor walkers paused to give Penny a second glance, she was bubbling with vitality. Through her hands she was trailing Italian pure silk scarves. John Barker's were known for the quality of their merchandise and these scarves were no exception.

Barbara felt her cheeks colour up, it was she that ought to be urging Penny to select a gift as a birthday present from her.

'Certainly not,' said Barbara fondly. 'There is no reason you should be buying anything for me.'

'I don't need a reason, Barbara, love, I just want to.'

Draping a long mauve scarf against the fawn of Barbara's jacket she asked, 'How about this one?' then suddenly changing her mind she selected from the stand a multi-coloured one, the main overtones being copper. 'Now that is you, yes, it picks up the glints in your hair, do you like it?'

Barbara hadn't the heart to dampen her dear friend's enthusiasm. Penny's jovial mood was contagious, Barbara laughed out loud, a laugh such as had not come from her for a very long time.

'Okay, that one for you and this one for me. These two please,' Penny was now saying to the sales assistant. Her own choice was an emerald green, brilliant in colour, exactly right with her fair hair and complexion. By one thirty the pair of them were sitting in the Platter Restaurant, Barbara was by now very much more at ease and thoroughly enjoying herself.

'Pleased I came and dragged you out?' Penny wanted to know as they waited for the waitress to bring their lunch.

'Oh, Penny, you know I am.'

'Good. You know I love doing things on the spur of the moment, they always work out so much better. I phoned Elizabeth and told her I was coming and she was mad at me for not giving her enough notice to arrange to come with me.'

'Really? How is Elizabeth? Do you two see each other often?'

'Elizabeth is fine, sends you buckets of love, and yes, we meet at least once a month.'

'What is Elizabeth doing with herself these days? And come to that, you haven't given me very much gen about yourself.'

'Me? I'm footloose and fancy-free. Well, I am at the moment. Elizabeth is deeply in love, has thrown up the job she had on one of the glossy magazines and gone to live in Windsor in a dear little house that has jasmine growing along the wall, a huge conservatory at the back that is filled with white cane furniture, a fish pond in the garden and she's talking about planting a magnolia tree.'

'Penny, you're making it all up.'

'I swear it's the truth.'

'Has she got married?'

'Don't even suggest such a thing. Elizabeth and Tim Holsworthy are having a trial period to find out if they are capable of living together harmoniously.'

Barbara began to giggle and soon the pair of them were laughing fit to bust.

While they were eating they went back over their memories, recalling the years of the War through which they had lived and worked together, sharing not only the horrors and the fears and the long nights with German planes droning overhead but, as well, the good times such as when the local off-licence had let them have a quart bottle of cider and the effect that it had had on them all, especially Elizabeth. Arms linked, making their way home through the black-out, Elizabeth had stumbled and falling over had dragged the pair of them down with her. At the time it had seemed hysterically funny, that was until an air raid warden had threatened to arrest them if they didn't stop waving their torches about.

'Do you remember what the old boy said as he tried to untangle us?' Before Barbara could make a reply, Penny assumed a stern expression and in a gruff voice stated, 'Aw my Gawd, I've a funny feeling you gals ain't all yer seem to be. Now, Miss, turn off that bleedin' torch or I shall be forced, 'erewith, to take yer all into custody fer signalling to the enemy.'

'How we ever got back to Putney that night, the Lord only knows,' Barbara said, wiping tears of laughter from her cheeks.

Most of the diners had left the restaurant and Penny and Barbara were lingering over their coffee. But now, for some reason, the laughter had gone. A silence fell between them, as though having talked so much, they had all at once run out of things to say. Barbara's felt Penny's eyes on her, and lifted her head to meet that steady gaze.

'You're very pensive all of a sudden, Barbara, is something wrong?' Penny asked the question cautiously and immediately felt a chump. A blind man could tell that Barbara wasn't happy.

'No, no of course not.' Barbara forced a smile and said to herself, How can I tell her, it would take hours to pinpoint everything that is wrong between me and Michael.

Penny's eyes were brimming as she looked at Barbara and said sadly, 'Your marriage isn't working out, is it?'

Barbara's hand shook as she set down her coffee cup and bowed her head.

'Anything you'd like to talk to me about, Barbara? You know it won't go any further and sometimes it helps to get a problem out into the open.' Then stretching out she clasped one of Barbara's hands between her own, adding, 'That's what friends are for.'

Neither of them spoke for a time then without warning Barbara began to cry, silently, the tears running unchecked down her cheeks. She blinked quickly but was unable to control the flow.

Penny had to turn her head away, the lump in her own throat was choking her. It wasn't fair! She couldn't bear to see her dearest friend so upset and as to the way she was living, it was appalling. She motioned for the waitress to bring them a fresh pot of coffee.

The clink of fresh cups and saucers being set out and the aromatic smell of the hot coffee which Penny was pouring from the silver plated pot gave Barbara time to regain her composure.

Penny handed a cup across the table and she deliberately made her voice brisk-sounding as she urged, 'Talk to me. Get it off your chest. You might even feel better if you do, you know a problem shared an' all that.'

'Oh Penny, don't be so kind to me. If the truth be told it's just as much my fault as Michael's, I do try, honestly I do Penny, but nothing ever seems to turn out right.'

After a further moment of silence Barbara began to really talk, the need was there to unburden herself and it was as if the floodgates were now open. Penny listened, her face turned towards Barbara, watching her intently.

'I've had two abortions, only because Michael insists he doesn't want children.'

'But you're having a baby now?'

'Yes, and Michael is making my life hell because of it. Penny, I want this baby, it could make such a difference, surely every baby that comes into the world brings love with it.'

Penny ignored this. She became practical. 'Have you tried to find better living accommodation, maybe in a better class area?'

'And what would we use for money?'

Penny shifted in her seat and sat up straight. Barbara lifted her head and met her friend's eyes, and saw on that beautiful face an expression of disbelief.

'We're in debt, way over our heads.'

'Is this why you haven't been to see your parents?'

'You think they know?'

'Well, not for certain. Your mother has been so worried. She felt you were unhappy and maybe regretted having married Michael, she knows full well you are in some sort of trouble.'

Barbara sighed deeply. 'Aren't I just!'

'Why didn't you tell your father before? He still makes you an allowance doesn't he?'

'Yes, but it is never enough. I did tell Daddy once, some months ago, and he put an extra two hundred pounds into my account, I can't keep asking him to bail us out.'

'Michael's working, isn't he? Is your rent very high?'

Barbara gave a bitter laugh. 'Oh yes, Michael's working but it's seldom that I get to see his wages. He used to have a bet on the horses now and again and that was bad enough, but suddenly it has become his way of life. He is a compulsive gambler, and what money the bookies don't have off of him goes to the local publicans.'

'Oh, Barbara dear, I had no idea things were as bad as this.'

Barbara stopped talking, closed her eyes and clenched her hands into tight fists. Not even to this dear, well-meaning friend could she bring herself to divulge all the sordid details of her life with Michael. The punches she suffered, the barbaric way he used her sexually. All she could bring herself to tell had been told, it had taken great effort on her part and now her whole body felt listless.

Penny watched Barbara's lips tremble and her heart ached for her. She sensed that she had only been told a fraction of the whole story.

'Will you answer me one question truthfully? Do you still love Michael?'

Barbara kept her eyes closed tight. It seemed a very long time since she had been able to answer yes to that question when put to herself. Now she made no attempt to answer. Penny moaned, she was holding Barbara's hand, gently stroking her fingers.

'You've got to do something, come to some decision, you know that don't you? Especially with the baby coming.'

Silently Barbara looked up at Penny, withdrew her hand, brushed at her eyes and began to shake her head from side to side.

In a voice as firm as she could make it, Penny told her, 'You just can't sacrifice the whole of your life because of one disastrous mistake.'

'I know. But just what can I do? There are times when I don't think I can go on much longer, with life I mean.' Barbara's voice had dropped to a mere whisper.

Quickly Penny scolded her, 'Now you are not to to talk like that!'

'I mean it Penny, I've made such a mess of my life, I can't see any future for Michael and me. It's no more his fault than it is mine if you look at it from his point of view; he just doesn't want from life the same things that I do, I mean I did, it doesn't seem to matter one way or the other now.'

Penny sighed deeply. 'You ought to go home to your parents, or at least go and see them, talk to them, tell them the whole story.'

A visible shudder ran through Barbara's body. 'Oh, no, I couldn't, they probably do suspect many things but to confirm their suspicions wouldn't be fair, not to them it wouldn't, they've taken enough knocks losing William and Patrick.'

'But they care about you, you shouldn't shut them out, wouldn't Michael go with you to visit them?'

'I've tried to persuade him. God knows I've tried. My father is probably the one man that could help Michael find a decent job and come to terms with himself. No, there's no budging him, come to that he seldom goes anywhere with me now.'

Penny realised how difficult all this was for Barbara, but the fear that things were far worse than Barbara was telling made her press on. With compassion obvious in her voice she spoke quietly, 'Barbara, you should think seriously about leaving Michael, go home, there would be no recriminations from your mother or your father.'

'No, I can't.' Then under her breath she added, 'If only Michael could bring himself to be pleased about this baby we might still make a go of it, but to be honest I don't think his attitude towards me will ever change.'

'Well then, if you feel you have done your best and I'm sure you have, why not give up, admit defeat, it's not a crime for couples to separate, get out before matters become even worse.'

Barbara's eyes were sad as she raised them to Penny's face. 'There was a time when I thought Michael was a wonderful person.'

Penny half smiled. 'We were all aware of how you felt about him, then Barbara, you left us in no doubt. But it was wartime when you two met, it was a matter of live for the day; now the War is over, we are all having to face reality. Everything about you and Michael is so different. With your background it was an impossibility from the start, only you couldn't see it then and you wouldn't have thanked any of your friends for pointing it out. For you, at that time, Michael was your knight in shining armour, or naval uniform if you like.'

With head bent low Barbara murmured, 'What's going to happen to me, Penny?'

Penny wished she knew, what she said was, 'Well for a start you have to face the situation squarely, neither of you are happy, so stop feeling sorry for yourself and make up your mind to do something about it. It's up to the both of you; can you not try to talk to Michael once more?'

'I've tried. Every day for months. He only sees his side of it, I feel so guilty, that is until his temper flares up – you can't imagine the hostility he feels towards me. He blames me for the whole state of our affairs, I know he does and I suppose I shouldn't blame him for that.'

Penny's eyebrows shot up in disbelief. 'Oh come on Barbara, I'm not going to have that! Most of the responsibility for this disastrous marriage must lie with Michael. Whichever way you look at it, it was Michael who rushed you along, it was him urged you down to Plymouth and what happened? You came back married to him. Not a word to your friends, let alone your parents, not a soul that knew you there to witness the ceremony. Talk about still waters running deep, we all wondered at the time, why all the secrecy? And since now we are down to the nitty gritties, has it never crossed your mind that for him you were an extremely good catch?' A bitter note had come into Penny's voice now as she urged, 'Go on, think about it now if you haven't ever before.'

'I don't think that's true.' Barbara was flustered, her voice faltered, 'I know he loved me, at first if not now. Besides, he hasn't benefited in any way.'

'*No*?' Penny stared long and hard at her friend whom she loved very much – but the time for sympathy was over.

'Have you any of your savings left? Do you still draw your allowance from your father? Doesn't Michael ever plead for you to tap your parents for more money?'

Barbara was shocked. How did Penny know these facts? Her mother must have discussed them. Now she knew for sure that was part of the reason Penny was with her today. She felt *so* humiliated, she didn't want her friends feeling sorry for her. Her mind was in a whirl, she had to remain calm and she did her best to convince herself that she should be grateful. Yes, that was it, she consoled herself, her parents not only worried about her, they loved her deeply and would Penny be sitting here with her now if she didn't care?

'Your resentment is showing, I'm sorry if I upset you.'

'No, really, it's all right. Perhaps we ought to get off the subject. What time does your train go?'

But Penny was not to be hurried. She hadn't finished having her say yet.

'When you talk about feeling guilty, Barbara, you make me mad, I don't feel any sympathy for Michael. What's done is done. As to him feeling hostile towards you – the boot should be on the other foot, it is you who has been deprived. Think about it and remember whatever you decide there is still a lot of living ahead of you.'

There had been moments this day when Penny had wanted to take hold of Barbara and shake her. What had this damned Michael done to her? It was almost as if he had her hypnotised. She shouldn't lie down and accept the kind

106

of treatment Michael was dishing out, she should stand up to him, show some guts. By God she hadn't been gutless during the War. Side by side she had worked with the wardens and police, seeing to the injured, digging with her bare hands to get to someone buried beneath a pile of rubble, ignoring the fact that incendiary bombs were dropping all around her. It wasn't fair. Barbara didn't deserve the way her life had turned out.

Now Penny leant slowly towards Barbara and the look she gave her was one of loving concern. 'We all make mistakes, darling, but that doesn't mean we have to go on paying for them for the rest of our lives, neither does it take away one's right to be happy.'

Barbara leant across the table and kissed Penny on the cheek. 'Thank you.' They both laughed in relief.

'All right, I know when I've made my point.' She began to gather up her purchases, bag and gloves.

Outside in the balmy sunshine their goodbyes were tearful.

'Thank you for today Penny, I hadn't realised just how much I miss you.'

'There are an awful lot of people, including me, who miss you Barbara.'

Their arms about each other they lingered for a moment, then as a taxi drew up to the kerb and as Penny was about to get into it she hesitated, turned her head to look back and speaking very softly she offered a last piece of advice. 'Cut loose now, Barbara.'

Within the next month Barbara was to wish many times that she had acted on it.

Chapter Five

BARBARA STOOD LOOKING out of the window, outside the rain was coming down in sheets, this was no April shower. Being Saturday, she had to go out to shop for the weekend, hesitating as to whether to wait any longer she made her decision; this rain wasn't about to let up, it was set in for the day. As she struggled into her macintosh she realised it was too tight, with this pregnancy she had put on a great deal of weight: it was impossible to do up the centre buttons. Drawing the belt around she knotted it to one side, that would have to do. Giving a final tug to her hat she took up the two shopping bags, closed the living room door before going down the stairs, out into the street.

'Lord, luv us, are you mad?' Mrs Winters had her head stuck around the shop doorway and was yelling after her. 'Come back, come on, come in the shop for a minute.'

Barbara did as she was bid, but asked, 'What am I supposed to do? I need to get a joint from the butchers, vegetables from the market and we haven't a slice of bread left in the house.'

'But it's teeming cats and dogs, you'll get drenched.'

Barbara screwed up her face, 'Can't be helped, I'll be as quick as I can.'

Mrs Winters stared at her and sighed heavily, but her smile was very kind. 'Well take care. I'll have the kettle on an' you come straight in 'ere an' get yer wet things off the minute yer get back.'

'Gawd save us,' gasped Mrs Winters as she watched Barbara struggle up the road, the force of the wind causing her to lower her head into her chest. She moaned aloud. It wasn't right. This beautiful healthy girl from an obviously well-to-do family was fading away, being dragged down more with every day that passed. She couldn't stand by and ignore all the things that worried her about Barbara. Not for much longer she couldn't.

'I'll let things ride over the weekend,' she said, thinking aloud. 'And then, by God, I'm gonna do something!'

Ever since Barbara had moved here she had felt that things weren't right, but these past few months were more than flesh an' blood could stand. There was Barbara, tired out with the cleaning, shopping and waiting on that lazy bastard of an 'usband and what did she get in return? Bugger all. All he dished out was verbal abuse, and that wasn't all. Oh no. It went a lot further than that. Well, it was time to put a stop to it. Let that bleedin' Michael call her a nosy old cow, better that than stand by an' do nothing until the sod went too far an' really did Barbara some harm. If it weren't for the fact that she was pregnant it might well have happened by now. One of these days that sod would come home the worse for drink and then what? Any day it could happen. The very thought made her tremble.

I'll find out the address of Barbara's parents if it's the last thing I do, she thought. I'd bet me last 'alf dollar they ain't got a clue as ter what their daughter 'as ter put up with.

Interference, that's what it would be. 'But the Lord, knows I've got ter do something,' breathed Mrs Winters as she filled her tin kettle and placed it on top of her portable stove.

Despite the rain Northcote Road market was busy, old women as well as young mums with nippers in tow, like herself, had to get food in. Barbara felt sorry for a lot of the old dears. Most wore hats but they still had scarves over them, knotted beneath their chins, to prevent the hats from being blown off. Legs bulging with varicose veins, swollen feet with bunions breaking out of split shoes, they still laughed and bantered with the stall holders who in reply called them all Ma and returned the good-natured teasing back at them.

Normally Barbara would make a couple of journeys but today she wanted to be finished, to get home in the dry. The shelves in the baker's shop were almost empty as she asked for two large split tins.

'Only got one tin left my love, will a cottage do?'

As Barbara hesitated the middle-aged woman took down the cottage loaf from the shelf, 'The nobbies are great, they're me favourite, smothered in butter, a chunk of cheese and a pickled onion, what could be better fer the ol' man's supper?'

Smiling her thanks Barbara took the two wrapped loaves, still warm to the touch, and placed them into her shopping bag. Dodging from one stall to another Barbara hoped she hadn't forgotten anything. It was still raining heavily and she paused in the butcher's shop doorway, mentally going over her purchases. Both shopping bags were full and already her arms were aching like mad. The bag with seven pounds of potatoes and all the vegetables was the worse. 'Oh, to hell with it!' she muttered out loud, 'What we haven't got we must do without. I'm going home.'

It took more than ten minutes to walk the length of the market for now she was battling into the wind which was driving the rain directly into her face. Her chin had been tucked deep into her scarf but she lifted her head as she neared the Falcon Public House and stepped over the brass rim into the shelter of the porch-way. Thankfully she let go of her heavy bags, propping them up against the wall. A thin, wiry man removed his cap, beat it against the wall, sending a shower of rain droplets flying in all directions, before stepping in, arm outstretched to push open the door to the saloon bar. Seeing Barbara he stopped in his tracks.

'Ere, you look all done in, Missus, yer can't go out agin in all this rain, you're drenched to the skin. Is yer ol' man inside? D'yer want me ter go an' fetch 'im for yer?'

'No, no thank you,' Barbara said quickly, 'I'm waiting for him, he'll be along in a minute. Thank you very much, all the same.'

'Yer welcome, lady,' said the man, pushing at the swing doors which when opened let out smoky warm air. Barbara leaned forward but although she saw familiar faces her gaze could not penetrate deep enough into the interior to see if Michael was there. To tell the truth she was half hoping that just maybe he would see her, come home with her – perhaps even relieve her of these heavy shopping bags. Then she remembered, this was the saloon bar. To Michael this pub was his second home, but his favourite haunt would of course be the public bar. She knew just where to find him, propping up the bar with his cronies. Maybe it was as well that this was the wrong bar. If Michael had caught a glimpse of her peering through the door he would have probably flown into a rage, accusing her of spying on him. The very thought of his anger and the way he would have sworn at her, made her shudder as she dragged her shopping bags home.

She said nothing because there was nothing to say when Michael came in soon after three o'clock. Much the worse for drink, he slobbered through his dinner, drew an armchair up to the fire and promptly went to sleep. Only once did Barbara disturb him by lifting his legs gently from the fender in order to replenish the dying embers. Wouldn't do to let the fire go out. If he woke up and the room was cold there would be hell to pay. She usually got severely cursed for her pains.

True to habit, Michael was ready to go out at eight o'clock sharp. Reaching the doorway, he stopped to pull his cap on over his hair that was oily with brilliantine. He gazed back to where Barbara was spreading a dark blanket over the table in preparation for doing some ironing. Something within him must have relented. In a voice that was soft for a change, not at all surly, he said, 'Do yerself a favour, come down the pub an' 'ave a drink.'

For a moment she was tempted, but only for a moment. Gently she declined the invitation knowing no good would come of it.

With the ironing out of the way the evening seemed to drag. Opening the dresser drawer, she took out her needlework basket and settled in front of the fire to embroider a small pillowcase she was making for the baby's cot. At ten o'clock she put away her work, undressed, gave herself a good wash down before donning her nightdress and dressing-gown. Once again she was sitting before the fire, drinking hot milk and wishing she might go to bed.

Michael kicked up such a fuss if he came home and found she wasn't waiting up for him.

It was a quarter past twelve when the side street door banged open and heavy footsteps sounded on the uncarpeted stairs. Michael was not alone. Her first thought was that she must get herself into the bedroom, but having been half asleep in the chair she wasn't quick enough. The minute she saw flashily dressed Pete Davis step into their living room behind Michael, she felt afraid. Good mates these two were, according to Michael but Pete had never made any secret of the fact that he had no time for Barbara. Never had he made any friendly moves toward her, not even the simple courtesies one would expect a man to pay to a friend's wife.

She was under no illusion as to what he thought of her. Once within her hearing he had referred to her as high and mighty, hoity-toity bloody Barbara and since then, whenever possible, she had taken care to avoid him. Barbara felt her face redden. She was so embarrassed, sitting here in her night clothes. Her belly felt swollen and stretched. She spread her hands across her back to help herself to get out of the chair.

It was unbelievable. Michael stood cocky and arrogant beside his mate. Pete Davis stood facing her, tall, heavily built, his long mousy hair lank and greasy, his eyes red-rimmed, bleary with drink. Both of them swayed where they stood, a leering smirk set about their lips. The fear that had already settled in her grew when Michael kicked the door to close it behind them. It seemed a long time before either of them spoke. Michael removed his jacket with great deliberation and unwound his white silk muffler from around his neck, then very quietly he asked, 'You

113

Elizabeth Waite

gonna be nice to Pete? You betta be cos he's me mate.'
There was a hard-bitten expression on his face that she'd
never seen before.

Suddenly it was not fear that Barbara felt but stark terror.
'I'll put the kettle on, make some black coffee. You've
obviously had too much to drink.' Even to herself her voice
sounded strange.

They both roared with laughter. 'It's not bleedin' coffee
I've brought Pete 'ome for, yer daft bloody mare.'

'Too much ter drink,' Pete Davis flung the words at her.
'What would you know about it, yer toffee-nosed bitch.
We can never 'ave too much ter drink can we Mike?'

'Don't you dare speak to me like that,' Barbara spoke
resentfully without stopping to think, 'I'd like you to leave
now or I'll – '

'Or you'll what?' Michael cut her words off short. 'Let
me tell you something. Pete didn't wanna come back 'ere
with me tonight – but I made 'im. I told 'im what a
smashing cook you are – yeah an' I also told 'im you'd give
'im a tasty titbit fer his afters.' Michael was tottering on his
feet, his words smeared apart, his hands waving in the air.

By now Barbara was petrified, 'Shut up! Shut up! You're
drunk out of your mind, you don't know what you're
saying.' She cut off her own words abruptly, looked from
Michael's blood shot eyes to Pete's laughing gaping face
and the truth hit her. Michael meant what he said. In every
sense.

What could she do? What help could she summon? To
bang on the floor would be useless: Mrs Winters' shop was
only a lock-up premises. The Singletons upstairs might
hear if she screamed, but they'd do nothing. Probably be
delighted that a row was taking place; so often did that

family indulge in screaming matches, that more often than not led to fights, they certainly wouldn't come down and interfere.

Unexpectedly Pete lunged towards her, opened his mouth slurring his words. 'Come on luv, try being nice to me – Mike said he don't mind an' I promise I won't treat yer rough.'

He actually meant it! These awful words, tossed casually at her, made Barbara lose control. She had to get out of here. She had to. Heaven knows what will happen if we all stand around here much longer, she thought. She was terribly afraid. With courage she was far from feeling, Barbara pointed a finger in Pete's direction. 'I think you had better leave, go home and sleep it off.'

Suddenly Michael was shaking with rage, his face scarlet. All the anger that he had been feeling against Barbara ever since she had told him she was pregnant again, and that she intended to have the baby, suddenly came to boiling point. The sting of his hand as he slapped her face sent her reeling. 'So that's it, is it? I bring a friend 'ome an' you think you can tell 'im to bugger off Well, he'll not be leaving. Not till he's had what I invited 'im 'ere for. You're gonna find out what mates are for and get a taste of what mates can do fer each other, an' any more of yer lip an' you'll live ter regret it.'

Poor Barbara was doing her best not to cry but was frozen with fear, her hands and face were clammy, her stomach such a bulge that she knew she couldn't move quickly enough to escape these two drunken louts. The horror of it all was making her feel dizzy, waves of sickness rose into her throat. She had to get to the toilet; if she could get that far onto the landing, who knows but she might be able to get down the stairs and out into the street. *Dear God help me.*

She crossed the room sidestepping Michael, but Pete Davis barred her way. Mocking her, he was. Reaching out, touching her face, stroking her breast. If she had had a gun in her hand she would have shot him.

'Relax darling,' he told her, his face so near to hers she could smell his foul breath. 'Yer wanna know something? I think you're a tasty tart. Don't matter none that you're in the pudden club, all the better really, ain't it? True yer know, what Mike said, a slice orf a cut loaf don't make no difference.'

Barbara was speechless for a second, then anger took over and spurred her on. Reaching behind her she grabbed at a glass vase, swung her arm forwards and upwards and brought it smashing down onto Pete Davis's head. If she had her way it would have been thrust into his lecherous face. Barbara expected him to retaliate savagely and steeled herself against his blows as she flinched and backed away.

The glass of the vase had been thin; it had smashed into fragments doing little damage. A shake of his head sent the pieces of glass showering from Pete's mop of hair onto the floor.

Michael and Pete looked at each other and burst out laughing. They were both so drunk the sight of them made Barbara shudder. She felt the colour drain from her face as she backed away so quickly that she almost toppled over, and the more she trembled the more they laughed.

Michael crossed the room, stood in front of her, his eyes staring into hers, his breath hot on her face. Slowly he pinned her shoulders against the wall with one hand and with the other hand he ripped open the front of her nightdress. She struggled furiously. Tried in vain to bring her knee up into his groin, tore at his face with her nails, all the while yelling at the top of her voice, 'I *hate* you, Michael! I *hate* you.'

He didn't care that she was frightened or that she was on the verge of collapsing. All he heard were the angry cries and the note of revulsion, and so he really lost his temper.

His arm shot out, swiping her hard across the mouth: it was enough to stifle her screams. His hands were back on her shoulders, holding her in a vice-like grip. 'Now you listen to me.' The words came from between his lips with a spray of spittle. She was panic-stricken – Michael would stop at nothing. His look was not just full of hatred, it was pure loathing.

His voice changed, now it was menacing. 'That's no way ter treat me best mate. Smashing 'im over the head like that. Pete's a good bloke. One of the best. He's bin buying me beer all night. Yer wanna know why? I'll tell yer. Cos I ain't got no bloody money, not a bleedin' brass farthing. That's what you've reduced me to, sponging orf me mates.

'Well, now Barbara dear, you're gonna find out I like ter pay my debts, one way or another, and since you're all I've got, Gawd 'elp me, you're gonna 'ave ter 'elp me by being nice to Pete. Got it now 'ave yer?' We can do it all nice an' friendly or you can treat me an' Pete like we ain't fit ter lick yer boots, in which case it's gonna be you that's gonna come off the worse.'

Barbara's heart was thumping, her hands were wet, her mouth swollen and painful. 'Michael!' she begged. Their eyes met for a second before he gripped her arm tighter and although she wriggled and squirmed she could not jerk

117

it away. Forcing her head to one side he sucked savagely at the flesh of her neck; as he withdrew his lips and brought them together they made a loud plopping sound. His laughter could have been heard half a mile away. 'You, my dear wife, should feel honoured, I have just given you a lovebite.'

'How much bleedin' longer you gonna play around?' Pete Davis's face was flushed with anger as he glared at them both.

Michael put both his hands under Barbara's back and knees, sweeping her up against his chest. 'Open the door Pete, the bedroom's through there. You'll be all right mate – I don't break my promises.'

Barbara gritted her teeth when he threw her down onto the bed. By now she was terror-stricken.

'Michael!' she begged again. 'Think of the baby.'

'Damn the baby,' he yelled.

Then Pete Davis was the other side of the bed, fending Michael off with both hands and shouting.

Michael shouted too, 'Stay still yer silly bitch, that way yer won't get hurt so much.'

'No! Leave me alone! Don't you dare touch me. Go away! Please, both of you, just go away.'

Barbara's heart was beating so rapidly that she thought she might be having a heart attack.

Pete Davis heaved his body onto the bed beside her.

'No, no!' Barbara pleaded yet again. 'Michael, you're never going to stand by and let this happen? Please, please, say something to stop him. You'll regret this when you sober up. I'd rather be dead than let this animal touch me.' Getting no response she screamed. Really screamed.

A whack around the head from Pete's ham-like fist soon put paid to that. There were moments when she was fully conscious when the most dreadful pain and humiliation were such that she hoped death would come. She tried her best to convince herself this was a nightmare. Only it wasn't. It was frightening, horrific reality. It was torture, so much so that her head swam and the blood pounded in her ears.

She wanted to scream and scream and scream, but what was the use, it would most likely bring her another savage blow.

As children in a fit of temper might use a rag doll, they used her. She might have endured the humiliation of being raped by a stranger – just, but this wasn't rape. It had nothing to do with the sex act. This was beastly, savage persecution and even revenge on Michael's part. There were moments when the infliction of pain made her black out, only to be revived by the biting, twisting and pinching of her bare flesh. In their drunken state these two men were vulgar brutes. The soreness of her inner thighs became unbearable as one after the other they used her.

She woke with a start and for a moment she had no idea where she was. The room was quiet. She was alone. Then the nightmare situation that she had been forced to endure returned full force. Looking at the sticky mess of tangled bedclothes, she put her head in her hands and wept. How long had she been asleep? Minutes? Or hours? How could she have slept at all, with all that had happened? What the hell am I going to do? Barbara whimpered to herself. Movement of any kind brought spasms of fire searing through her bruised body. Her legs felt painful, like severe cramp, only worse. What shreds of clothing she still had on were stuck to her body which was running with sweat. Her head hurt like hell. Cautiously she lifted a corner of the bed-sheet and wiped the blood from the side of her forehead. The pain in her stomach was a constant throbbing, attempts at deep breathing only made it worse.

She tried to lie still. There was one thing she clung to: this night had swept away all doubts and uncertainties. She wouldn't spend another day under the same roof as Michael. She wasn't going to be around when he sobered up and made an attempt to express his regret. Forgive him? Never! He had not been a bystander, he had participated. Every blow, every humiliating action had been premeditated. Drink had made him brave and he had sought retaliation on her for everything that had gone wrong since he had been demobbed from the navy. Her social class was like a thorn in his side. Well he wouldn't have to bear with her ever again. Something, a voice, came back to her, much too terrible to remember, yet how would she ever blot it from her mind? Pete Davis growling, 'Some bleedin' wife you've got 'ere, she wouldn't even make a good whore.'

She cried quietly for a long time. She felt no better, only empty, bruised and sick.

When the room began to grow lighter, she got up. What she wouldn't give to be able to lie in a hot bath, but that wasn't possible. Warily she slipped out of the bedroom, then found she need not have bothered. Apart from herself the flat was empty. The air in the living room was foul, the whole place a mess: one chair lay on its side with the back broken away from the seat, and there were cigarette butts ground out on the linoleum everywhere.

Barbara held the tin kettle under the cold water tap until it was half full, then, setting it down on a gas jet, she struck a match, turned on the gas tap and ignited the flame. When the kettle came to the boil she made a pot of tea and immediately refilled the kettle to the brim, placing it once more over the naked flame.

She felt so cold, chilled to the bone, as she sank into the chair and clasped her hands around the cup of tea. Every limb of hers felt numbed and heavy, she ached from head to toe. She looked around the room, stared at the dead ashes in the grate. What did the mess matter? What did anything matter now? Painfully she rose and poured herself a second cup of tea from the brown china teapot.

The sound of the tin lid of the kettle wobbling up and down signified that once more the kettle was boiling. Having poured the water into an enamel bowl and added cold water from the tap, with the bar of soap between her hands she worked up a lather. She couldn't bear to use a flannel: her body was too sore. Gently she washed herself from head to toe, flinching as she cleansed between her thighs, dabbing herself dry on a clean towel. She had to come out of the scullery and go back into the living room in order to sit down.

She felt so ill. The effort of washing herself had been so great. I'm an absolute mess, she thought angrily. It would have been bad enough if Michael had come home drunk out of his mind and used her spitefully, it wouldn't have been the first time; but to have brought that bastard Pete Davis and not only allowed him to rape her but to have actually encouraged him! I hope to God I never set eyes on Michael again, because if I do, so help me I'll murder him, she thought.

It was some time before her anger was spent and she could bring herself to stand up again and get herself into clean clothes. Eventually she was ready. Without even bothering to close the door or with any inclination of where she was going, she went down the stairs and out into the street. Only one thing was she certain of – nothing nor no one would ever induce her to set foot in that place again.

Everywhere was strangely quiet. Despair overwhelmed her: which way should she go? Feeling so unwell, so confused, she didn't rightly know. Just one predominant thought was in her mind; she had to get away. Still being only a little after seven o'clock on this Sunday morning, no one was rushing off to work, no totters toured the streets, no children played in the gutters. Even the permanent chalked games of hopscotch on the pavement had disappeared, washed away by yesterday's torrential rain. She had to stop for a rest, get her breath back. Walking was agony. She leaned against the wall of the working man's café, usually so busy; now its shutters were down, its sign turned to 'closed'. Over the far side of the road scruffy mongrel dogs were rummaging amongst the litter dumped on the disused bomb-site, apparently Sunday made no difference to them. With its three huge brass balls, the pawn shop on the corner was also closed. Come tomorrow morning there would be a queue of women there pawning various articles in order to get a few shillings to see them through the week. There was a gaudy sign above these premises which announced, 'We pay thirty-three shillings and threepence for gold sovereigns.' Who the hell in this neighbourhood possessed a hoard of sovereigns?

It was no good, if she didn't make herself get on the move again she would most likely fall down. With dragging footsteps and interminable stops she finally saw Clapham Junction railway station ahead of her.

In a voice that was little more than a croak, she asked for a single ticket to Victoria.

'Forty minutes to wait, Missus,' the ticket operator told her as he passed over her change. Then pushing his head forward and peering closely at Barbara's swollen mouth and the bruise on the side of her temple, he added kindly, 'Buffet bar is open, pop along there, get yerself a nice hot cuppa an' 'ave a sit down.' Barbara quietly thanked him.

He watched her slowly walk away and, shaking his head, said to himself, 'Another Saturday night family feud. It's always the women what comes off the worse an' by Christ that one's taking a rare old bashing, an' no mistake.'

At the counter of the refreshment bar Barbara passed over a sixpence and took her cup of coffee to a table in the far corner where she thankfully sat down. She tried to take a sip of the coffee but she quickly set the cup back down; she would have to wait for it to cool. Her lips were so swollen the scalding liquid hurt. Time passed, she felt dreadfully ill.

Dear God what am I going to do? she thought. I can't possibly go home to my parents, not in the state that I'm in.

It wouldn't be fair on them and if Michael were to come looking for her that would be most likely the first place that he would try. What was the alternative? Her friends' homes? Both Penny and Elizabeth would be glad to help, they wouldn't turn her away. No, no, of course not, the idea was inconceivable. What could she say to them or they to her? The thing that mattered most to her was that no one should ever know the contemptible things that Michael and his mate had done to her.

Never, never, would she be able to relate those details to anyone. She began to panic, giving in to fear, her insides ached so much; what if she were to have a miscarriage? She had to face the fact that she was entirely on her own, and find somewhere to hide away from prying eyes, at least until she felt better. She had finished her coffee long since and got up now to go outside. She felt a wave of dizziness overtake her and would have fallen if an arm had not gone around her waist and a gentle voice seemingly from far away urged her to sit down again. Two hands lightly pressed her head down until it hung between her knees, soft fingers drew her long hair back and gently stroked her neck.

When her vision cleared Barbara saw that the lady who was befriending her looked a little like a nun, but not completely so. The robe she wore was not floor-length but reached only to her calves and the colour was navy-blue, not black as would be that of a nun from a Holy Order. Around her head and shoulders she wore a veil of the same blue material as that of her robe, held in place by a stiff white band which lay across her forehead encircling a sweet, kind, gentle face. Wisps of golden hair escaped from the sides. She touched Barbara twice on the arm before asking, 'Do you feel any better now?'

Barbara couldn't bring herself to answer, she felt so awful. Suddenly she coughed then made a choking sound as she dropped her head forward onto her chest. It seemed that all the muscles of her face were twitching now. She couldn't control her lips in order to speak. Presently she lifted her head and gazed at the face of the young woman who was obviously affiliated to the Church and in that moment Barbara envied her the quality of peace that shone from her clear blue eyes.

'You need help, my dear. Where were you going?'

For answer Barbara reached into her coat pocket and withdrew her train ticket, holding it out in front of her.

'Victoria. So was I, but we've missed the train now. Were friends meeting you?'

Barbara sadly shook her head.

'Did you have any destination in mind on arrival?'

Again Barbara could only shake her head, evading an answer. There was a long silence. The glass doors opened, two men entered, hoots from shunting trains sounded ominous. The Church lady stood thoughtfully watching Barbara who was having difficulty with her breathing.

Finally she said, 'I'm Sister Francis, I belong to the Church of England Nursing Order. Will you trust me? Will you come with me, if only to rest for a while?'

Then, not waiting for an answer, she softly patted Barbara's arm, 'Wait here, sit quietly. I'll be back in a few minutes.'

Barbara had no idea how long she sat there; no one bothered her and she never raised her glance from the floor until the gentle voice came to her again, saying practically, 'Can you manage to walk? I've a taxi waiting outside.'

They walked together, Sister Francis with her hand placed firmly on Barbara's elbow. They had scarcely covered half the distance when they were forced to stop. Barbara's chest was heaving, the pain in her was everywhere making her feel sick. The taxi driver came to meet them and with his help they finally reached the waiting cab. Barbara got into the back and sank gratefully against the upholstery.

The taxi drove up St John's Hill, turned left into Spencer Park and skirted the row of tall elegant terraced houses which formed a triangle around the lovely green of Spencer Park. They might just as well have been going to the North Pole. Barbara was oblivious as to what direction the driver had taken. Her eyelids had dropped but although she dozed dry sobs shook her even now and then. She did open her eyes as she felt the taxi come to a stop.

The driver was opening the door and got her out with the help of Sister Francis. Panic shot through Barbara, for a fleeting second she thought she had come to her parents' home. As she stood with her hand in the crook of Sister Francis's arm she looked hard at the house. The impression she got was that it was a mansion. Large, dark red bricked, ivy-clad walls and many many tall windows. Beautiful grounds and a long winding drive.

Even with the help of Sister Francis, walking was sheer agony. Barbara kept telling herself to stay calm, take small steps and go slowly, but still she was forced to stop every few yards. Her mouth was dry, her limbs were trembling – she didn't think she could make it, she would have to drop to the ground.

Ahead of them the main door opened and a woman, dressed similarly to Sister Francis, hurried down the stone steps and came towards them. An older woman, quite stout, her face was round and red as any apple. Taking hold of Barbara's other arm she smiled, the smile lit up her homely face and again Barbara saw the same quality of peace and tranquillity that she had first seen in the eyes of Sister Francis. Her voice was soothing as she said, 'Come along my dear, let's get you inside.'

Clustered together, the sisters one each side of Barbara, they moved slowly forward up the flight of steps through the open doorway and into a vast oak panelled entrance hall. The stout sister went ahead and they followed her into what appeared to be a sitting room.

Barbara stood still and breathed a sigh of relief, then

muttered a silent prayer: 'Thank God'. It was a lovely spacious room, but it was the overall feeling of peacefulness that descended upon her as she allowed Sister Francis to press her down onto a chintz-covered settee that she was grateful for. Everything spoke of serenity. In the centre of a round polished table stood a bowl of fresh flowers; at the end of the room French windows stood opened outwards, from which flimsy beige curtains fluttered in the breeze.

Both sisters drew an armchair close and seated themselves facing Barbara. The stout one spoke first and still her voice had such a calming effect that Barbara began to relax.

'I'm Sister Marion, this is Beechgrove House and you will be quite safe here. While we are waiting for some tea to be brought to us by Dorothy, she is one of our helpers, would you like to talk to us?'

Receiving no answer she asked, 'What is your name, my dear? That at least would be a good starting point.'

Barbara bowed her head; tears were trickling down her cheeks. It was their kindness to her. It was too much.

When her head fell lower and sobs began to shake her body Sister Francis rose and came to sit beside her. Slowly she slid her arms across Barbara's shoulders, drawing her head onto her own chest and sat there gently holding her close, her own chin resting on Barbara's bent head. Many minutes passed, the silence only broken by the sound of Barbara's grief, until Sister Marion suggested, 'Let's get her upstairs and into bed, and then I think it would be best if we ask the doctor to come along and have a look at her.'

Compassionate hands had removed her clothes as though she were a baby. A thin cotton nightdress had been slipped over her head and now she was in bed in a room that was small in size, yet she savoured the relief. Everything was so clean and bright. She lay back, propped up against a stack of pillows. The feeling of being between soft clean linen was heavenly but terrible pain still gripped her and the tension was still there. Every thought tormented her.

Where was she? What was going to happen to her? Where would she have gone if Sister Francis hadn't come along? When would these terrible pains go away and when would she stop feeling so sick?

When a knock came on the door Barbara jumped, for it startled her. The door opened, a loud cockney voice announced, 'I've brought yer some tea.' A thin young girl in a skimpy green dress came across the room, setting a tea-tray down on a small cupboard which was placed beside the bed.

She grinned at Barbara and held out her hand to her. 'Me name's Dorothy, Dolly ter me friends. Bin in the wars 'ave yer? Well yer've landed in the right place, like 'eaven on earth this place is. The sisters are bloody angels. Oh, sorry luv, keep forgetting I ain't supposed to swear, but that's wot they are – bloody angels.'

When Barbara made no move Dorothy leant across her and quietly now she said, 'Everyfink will seem better tomorra. After you've 'ad a nice cuppa tea you get yer 'ead down, sleep it orf, yer'll see, a good sleep can work wonders.' Her voice dropped almost to a whisper, 'I've got ter go now, there's twenty of us living 'ere – not counting the staff nor the babies – so there's always plenty ter do. But I'll tell yer one fing, we've all bin frew the mill, one way or another we 'ave, but we've come frew and so my luv will you, you'll see. Ta-tar fer now. Don't let yer tea go cold.'

Left alone, tears were again stinging at the back of Barbara's eyelids. She felt a sense of unreality, none of this was really happening. Last night and how she came to be in this place had to be a dreadful dream. It was so good to feel cleanliness about her, yet she screwed her eyes up tight at the thought of how she had been abused. Her body would never again feel totally clean. Not inside it wouldn't. She felt now that she would like to blot out everything and everyone, even the kind sisters who had suddenly come into her life, and pull the sheets over her head and hide away from the world.

It was all too much. The fragile thread of self-preservation to which she had clung, snapped. She felt a drumming in her ears and it was as though she was falling down into a bottomless pit. And she didn't care. She wanted to go and never come back.

Over the next few days the doctor was worried. Injections had brought about a form of sedation but not entirely so; indeed the sisters reported that Barbara couldn't speak properly or control her movements and she suffered from terrible nightmares. More than once he had wondered whether he should suggest to the sisters that the police be notified, for most surely this young woman had been cruelly used. He was used to being called to Beechgrove House and having battered wives as his patients, but this case was different. The severity of her injuries was appalling. One small wound on her forearm shocked him beyond belief. A small, deep, festering hole that refused to heal caused by, he was in no doubt, a lighted cigarette having been ground into her flesh.

The sisters asked themselves if Barbara had lost her reason. For two days she had tossed and turned, rambling all the time. At one point in the middle of the night she had pushed herself up on her elbow and, staring wide-eyed into space, had yelled, 'I'll kill you, I will, I'll kill you!'

The look in her eyes had been dreadful to see, then her voice had trailed away, her head flopped back down onto the pillow whilst her whole body trembled.

The fourth morning Barbara's breathing was easier. She no longer tossed from side to side but lay still, only occasionally she still moaned. The opinion of the sisters who had nursed her day and night was that she had lived through an horrendous experience.

At the end of the week Barbara got out of bed for the first time since her arrival. She now knew that Beechgrove House was mainly a home for unmarried mothers. Sitting in an armchair by the window, gazing out at the beautiful grounds, her mind pondered on how fate had sent Sister Francis to the railway station on that Sunday morning. Had God sent help to her?

If that were the case, where had God been during the hours she had called in vain for his help? What had she ever done that was so bad that God had deemed fit that she should suffer such perversion?

Chapter Six

DOWNSTAIRS THE GIRLS, almost all from the working classes, were at first cautious of Barbara and she was reserved towards them, even a little shy, but with the help of the friendly Dolly barriers were broken down on both sides as the days wore on. Much time was given by trained members of the staff to Barbara. She no longer had to see the physician daily, for her body was healing. Nothing was physically wrong with her and the kindly old doctor advised her that her pregnancy was safe.

That fact was not accepted by her with any relief. When she had first felt the baby move inside her she had been overwhelmed with an almost unbearable tenderness. Yet she thought, how can I feel like that now, knowing the father is a ruthless sadistic pig? Will I be able to cradle this baby in my arms? More important, will I be able to love this child? What if it should look like Michael, a constant reminder?

It didn't bear thinking about. Should she keep the child, try for an abortion, have it adopted? Despite herself she sighed, heavy-hearted. She had tried. But now, after what she had been put through, whatever she decided she knew full well that the memory of that night would return to haunt her, like some ghastly nightmare, for the rest of her life.

Was she frightened that Michael might come looking for her?

Of course she was frightened. The very thought terrified her. Cowardly, she made a resolution: to push all thoughts of the baby to the back of her mind, at least for the time being.

She had needed little persuasion to accept the offer of the sisters' hospitality to remain as a resident at Beechgrove House until after her baby was born. Where else could she go?

Inevitably there were still signs of what she had been through. She looked nothing like her former self, now she was washed out and pallid, there were still dark circles beneath her eyes. Her lips and the area around her mouth were still swollen and bruised. A bald patch at the side of her head, where the hair had been cut away to enable the wound to be stitched, was a constant reminder whenever she looked into a mirror, of the spiteful way Pete Davis had struck her.

For all the kindly counselling Barbara received no matter how many times the direct question was put to her as to whether she had any parents or relatives living, she never answered. Only the barest facts as to what had happened to her and her married name was all that the sisters could persuade her to tell them.

Soon she settled into a routine. Given the choice, she had opted to work alongside Dolly and four other young women in the kitchens – Sally, Mary, Vera and Peggy.

The girls accepted her and she them. Two were common, even bawdy in their humour, but who was she to criticise? Their friendly gestures to her were unstinting and as such she accepted them and was grateful. Mornings they mostly prepared vegetables which were grown in the grounds, while two of the younger sisters made bread, scones and potato-cakes.

'Are you rich?' Sally, the quietest of their group, asked Barbara as the two of them scraped away at freshly dug carrots, while the others peeled potatoes.

'Of course I'm not rich.'

'Then how is it you speak so posh?'

'Probably because of the school I went to.'

Sally made a face. 'Wish some one had taught me to talk like you do, maybe I wouldn't 'ave ended up in 'ere in the state I'm in.' She patted her own swollen belly.

The group glanced at each other and burst out laughing. Even the dark haired Vera, who was strangely secretive, joined in.

'Yer silly cow!' Mary, the oldest of the kitchen skivvies, as Dolly was wont to refer to them as, playfully pushed Sally's shoulder.

'Her talking different to us ain't stopped 'er from taking a bashing nor from getting 'erself in the pudden club 'as it? She ain't no better off than the rest of us.'

Turning to Barbara, Mary added, 'My old man brought a floosie 'ome with 'im one Saturday night. There was me, in bed, fast asleep, and the two of them climbs in and start their hanky-panky. I split 'is head open, used the brass lamp 'is muvver gave us fer a wedding present. Didn't do me no good. Chased me up the stairs he did, we lived in a basement flat just off the Fulham Road, knife in 'is 'and, blood streaming down 'is face and that's 'ow I come to 'ave this great scar on me neck.'

Dolly sent Barbara a long amused look, and Barbara grinned.

Now it was the turn of Peggy and Sally to explain in

detail as to how they had come to be living at Beechgrove House. It was as if Barbara had been accepted into their club and they had all decided to confide in her in a single burst.

'Booze, that was my Alf's ruination. Nice enough bloke when he was sober, but a bleedin' pig when he'd 'ad a session down the pub.'

Barbara glanced across at Peggy and felt a great deal of sympathy for her.

'Nothing like that about my Jim, good as gold ter me.' Sally came out with the words quickly. 'No. Only thing wrong with Jim, he took a liking to other folk's goods. Been inside a few times before he took up wiv me. Drove a laundry van fer a few months and then one Friday night came 'ome with the takings. Had a smashing weekend down in Brighton we did, 'ad our dinner in a cafe two nights, steak an' chips and we 'ad afters. They was waiting fer 'im on the Monday morning, silly sod went ter work, large as life. He's in Wandsworth jail now. Landlord didn't waste no time kicking me out of our upstairs flat, he knew me an' Jim weren't never properly married. I didn't 'ave a leg ter stand on.'

Vera wasn't about to disclose her life story to anyone. Dolly screwed up her child-like face and winked at Barbara. 'Ain't everyone this lot confides in. Mostly they tell anyone asking questions to eff orf!'

'I don't remember asking for any details,' Barbara murmured.

'All the more honoured then, ain't cher? One day maybe I might get around ter telling yer why I'm still 'ere after two years an' yer won't 'ear none of the sisters asking me ter go. Then agin I might not tell yer.'

How sad Dolly sounded, her circumstances must have been pretty grim.

Wisely Barbara kept her thoughts to herself as she sliced the carrots into a saucepan and went to strain the peelings at the sink and throw away the dirty water.

Now, two months later, Barbara had become accustomed to Beechgrove House. She was grateful for the quiet, for peace, for time to rest, read a book, even for the kitchen work of a morning and the jolly company of the girls. It was a gorgeous day, the afternoon sun hot, the sky blue and cloudless. She sat in a deck chair beneath a tall shady tree, her hands lying idle in her lap. Dolly sat near, hemming sides of sheets that had become worn in the middle and were now being made up into cot sheets. George, one of the gardeners, was way over to her right, quietly digging and making the flower beds look fresh with the newly-turned earth. Barbara watched his dry, gnarled old hands and wondered why on such a hot day he still wore a tweed coat and flat cap.

A blackbird came down to drink from the stone bird bath and faintly she could hear the hum of traffic, which at most times was deadened by the great tall leafy trees. She thought of home. Not Battersea and Michael, but her real home: Alfriston, where her mother and father were. Suddenly she wanted to be there, safe and sound, to be a young girl again growing up surrounded by love.

She had written to Mrs Winters, merely saying that she had left Michael and thanking her for all her kindness. The letter to her parents had been harder. Much the same explanation, assuring them that she was well and that she would be home to see them in the not too distant future.

Would she? Even now she was not sure that she would go home, face the love and hurt that she would see in their faces. Well, she had sent the letter, that had to be enough for now, she couldn't face any major decisions at the moment.

She felt mean. She could at least telephone. In the entrance hall there was a pay phone, there was no excuse for not ringing her father. It would be so simple. It wouldn't take a minute. 'Daddy it's me,' she would say, and tell him where she was, outline what had happened, only briefly, but it would be enough and he would be here to fetch her in no time.

One evening she had almost gone into the box. Holding onto the door she had hesitated, trying to pluck up courage. But the telling of the story was beyond her.

She imagined the conversation.

'Daddy?'

'Oh, Barbara! We've been *so* worried about you. Where are you?'

'In a home for battered wives and unmarried mothers.'

She couldn't go on. Not even in fantasy. Her courage failed her and she had crossed the hall with tears in her eyes and shut herself away in her bedroom.

Barbara felt Dolly was watching her and looked up to meet her eye to eye. Dolly was not an attractive person, certainly not pretty. But she had a scrubbed, immaculate look to her. Her hair was short and spiky, cut so that it framed her face, and – Barbara had come to know – discreetly covered a disfigurement that ran down the side of her left ear. Her eyes were brown, her face the sort that one would call an out-of-doors sort of face and she looked and acted much older than Barbara now knew her to be, which was only seventeen.

'Penny for them,' Dolly offered as she laid her needle-work down and gave her full attention to Barbara.

Barbara sighed, half sadly and half relieved to have some-one to talk to.

'I was thinking about my parents.'

'Do they know where you are?'

'No.'

'Will they be worried about you?'

'Very much so, I imagine.'

'Then you're very lucky. Wish I 'ad a family that worried about me. By the way, Barbara, yer never mention yer 'usband. Not that yer talk much at all but when yer do it's only ever about yer mum an' dad.'

Barbara saw no reason to comment on that, instead she asked a question. 'Don't you have any family at all, Dolly?'

'No, me mum died when I was eleven. An uncle I'd never even 'eard of before wrote and said me two bruvvers, who were both older than me, could go an' live wiv 'im and his missus in New Zealand. Ain't never 'eard of them from that day ter this.'

'What about your father? Did you live with him?'

'If you're just being nosy an' wanna know 'ow I come ter be living 'ere why don't yer come right out in the open an' damn well ask?'

'You started this conversation,' Barbara pointed out.

'Yeah, I know,' said Dolly shortly. 'All right, don't let me an' you argue. Ter tell yer the truth I get on better wiv you than I 'ave wiv anyone since I bin 'ere.'

Barbara smiled, kept her silence and watched the old gardener pack his tools in a canvas bag which he hung on the handlebars of a bicycle, then fling his leg over the crossbar and wobble off down the pathway.

Dolly straightened her lean frame and took a deep breath, as if to say she had come to a decision.

'Yeah, I lived wiv me father. Lived to regret it an' all. He made use of me most nights as if I was 'is wife.'

Barbara had to stifle her emotions, not let so much as a glimmer of sympathy show on her face.

'Why don't yer ask me why I didn't tell someone, go to the police, or me teacher at school? Yer wouldn't 'ave ter ask if you knew my father. Big an' brutal. He didn't bother to threaten, he just gave me an 'ammering now an' again – just a taste. of what I would get if I was ter open me mouth. I was fourteen when me monthlies started, that keep 'im at bay for a while. Then one night he wanted me ter do somefink different and I wasn't 'aving any. I 'ad stood fer all I was going to. Yelled an' screamed, I did. Said this time I was gonna tell the police. He set fire ter the bed. Locked the bedroom door an' buggered off an' left me.'

Barbara felt so inadequate, wanting to hug Dolly and to say something that would ease the memory. She was so angry that men should be able to abuse women, but a little girl of eleven! Her anger was short-lived. Thank God for the wonderful kind sisters and the sanctuary of Beechgrove House.

'Must be about tea-time,' Dolly said matter-of-factly as she folded her work away and got to her feet.

It was decision time. Barbara had an appointment with the gynaecologist and Sister Francis had promised to be there.

Taking out a cotton dress from the cupboard in her

room, she removed her working overall, washed her hands and face at the hand-basin which stood in the corner and pulled the dress over her head. It hung long and loosely over her swollen stomach. Unexpectedly a thought struck her. Every single article of clothing she wore – even her sandals – had been provided by the sisters. Did she have any money of her own? Was her father still paying her monthly allowance into her bank account? With this thought she sat down on the edge of the bed. Guilt filled her mind: she had been so selfish, taking everything that was offered by the sisters without giving a thought as to how Beechgrove House was funded.

There had been plenty of opportunities when she could have gone out, paid a visit to any branch of her bank and checked on her financial position, but she had shrunk from putting a foot outside of these walls. She had never even offered to make a contribution towards her keep, just taking everything for granted.

Well, once she had had this baby and was able to go back and live in the outside world fortunately she would be able to put matters to rights. She would have no qualms about requesting her father to make a donation to this Church nursing order and he would be more than generous, of that she was quite sure.

Down the stairs and into the hall she went. The door leading to the garden stood open, there was no wind, the sun shone, the grass was like an emerald carpet, the trees stood tall and abundant with leaves. What a beautiful place this was, what a haven it had been for her. Not for much longer though.

She turned right, went down the corridor that led to the hospital wing and sat herself down on one of the vacant chairs that were lined up outside of the room which served as a clinic.

'Hi yer Barbara, won't be long now an' you'll be doing this, eh?' Sally sat opposite, unaffected, breast exposed, her three-week-old daughter sucking contentedly at the nipple.

Barbara stood up, went across and smiled tenderly down at the wee mite whose head was covered in blonde hair that was so fine it shone like silk. 'She really is a lovely baby,' Barbara murmured.

'Yeah, ain't she just?' The look of tenderness on Sally's face was unbelievable. With everyone watching, Sally pulled Barbara's head down and, placing her lips near to Barbara's ear, she whispered, 'Her Dad's gonna think the world of 'er. I ain't told no one this, he's a married man, his wife can't 'ave no kids.'

'Then she'll be very precious to the both of you,' said Barbara, kindly but much embarrassed. How will she cope when she leaves here? Barbara wondered. Scarcely more than a child herself, Sally was obviously thrilled to be a mother.

Every patient had been seen in turn and now it only remained for Barbara to be called. The door opened and Sister Francis put her head round the corner. 'Come along in, Barbara, Doctor Osbourne is all ready for you.' The smile and friendliness were as usual a joy to behold and went a long way towards calming Barbara's attack of nerves.

Anita Osbourne was a beautiful woman, tall and slim. What set her apart for Barbara was her striking combination of lightly-tanned skin, dark brown eyes, and copper-coloured hair with more than a hint of red in it which she wore short and cut close to her head like a young lad.

Doctor Osbourne put down the pen with which she

had been writing, swivelled round in her chair to face Barbara and let her strong hands with their long fingers and unvarnished nails hang loose between her knees. 'Um, well, have you come to a decision?'

Soothed by the intimate tone of her voice, Barbara felt her spirits rise and told herself to speak up sensibly, not to give way to all of her half-acknowledged doubts but to be firm and stick to her guns. After all, the girls all agreed that Doctor Osbourne was as much a social worker as a doctor when it came to giving advice as to how to solve their problems.

Anita Osbourne would have agreed. She seemed to spend a great deal of her time either filling in forms on behalf of her patients or talking on the telephone to social workers. Barbara Hamlin was to her a case apart. She would have given a great deal to be in possession of the facts that had led to a well-bred young woman such as Barbara seeking shelter in Beechgrove House.

Sister Francis dipped her head in Barbara's direction and before Barbara had a chance to reply to the doctor's question she asked, 'Is anything wrong?'

'Why do you ask that?' Barbara retaliated quickly.

'You look so pale. Are you sure you have come to the right decision?'

'Yes.'

'You weren't so sure yesterday and you weren't very anxious to talk about it.'

'Only because it had to be my own decision. Made entirely off my own bat and with no one else involved.'

'Good girl,' the doctor said pleasantly. 'I'm sure she is absolutely right, don't you agree, Sister?'

'Yes. If she had wanted to ask my advice I am sure she

would have done so by now. Though it is not too late, perhaps I could still help.'

Nobody can help, Barbara said to herself. Nobody can do anything. Barbara thought for the umpteenth time of how much she had wanted this baby, longed for it, but not now. It wouldn't be fair to the child. She would never be able to look at its face without remembering what Michael, yes, and Pete Davis had done to her. It wasn't the child's fault but then neither was it hers. So, if she couldn't bring herself to love this unborn baby, far better that it should go to parents who would love and care for it and, please God, it would never learn the reason why she had signed it away even before it was born.

'I want this baby to be adopted. I don't even want to see it.'

A pin would have been heard had it dropped in the room at that moment. Sister Francis leaned across, took Barbara's hand between both of her own and softly said, 'Oh Barbara.' The sadness in her voice had turned to a sob.

Very briskly Anita Osbourne shuffled and tidied the papers that were scattered across her desk and in a voice free from emotion announced, 'I will set the wheels in motion.'

On the first day of October 1948, Barbara gave birth to a son. Quite naturally her labour had not been without pain, but she had endured it, biting her bottom lip and seldom crying out. She kept telling herself over and over again that childbirth was natural and women the world over went through it daily, besides which she kept reminding herself that this suffering was not being maliciously inflicted.

One final push and with a great whoosh the baby entered the world.

Barbara lay flat, her hair damp with sweat, her eyes shut tight, and she heaved a great sigh.

The last link with Michael was severed.

She never saw the child; indeed she would not have known the sex of it had she not heard a nurse murmur, 'Would you look at the amount of hair he has!'

Anita Osbourne spent the next six weeks fighting her own conscience. She had had Barbara's baby moved to another home, feeling that was in the best interest of everyone concerned.

This child would not be difficult to place. It was a perfect male child. There were very few normal, healthy British babies available for childless couples to adopt. Some authorities had so many potential parents waiting that they were closing their lists.

Anita stood in the doorway of the utility room and watched Barbara, whose back was to her, fold sheets. She would have one more go to try and prevent this young woman from making a decision that she would probably end up regretting for the rest of her life.

'Barbara, when you've finished in here, would you like to come and have a cup of coffee with me? I'll be in my office.' She turned and walked away without waiting for an answer.

Barbara knew what this would be about. More persuasion. She went just the same.

Anita made small talk for the first few minutes, while she poured out the coffee. Then she started to plead. 'Barbara, stop being so ashamed of your feelings. You've never once asked for help. Talking about what you've been through would maybe release all those pent up emotions. Wouldn't you just like to take a look at your baby?' Barbara never lifted her head. It was like talking to a brick wall. 'Is there no one among your friends and family who would be willing to take your baby?'

For one fleeting moment Barbara imagined herself looking over the side of the cot. Lifting the baby out. Taking it home to her parents.

The moment was gone, instantly suppressed by the memory of Michael and his cruelty.

Anita watched with a heavy heart as a single tear escaped and rolled down Barbara's cheek. Oh, dear God, how this girl must have suffered.

'Let me refill your cup,' she said, placing an arm across Barbara's shoulders and wishing like hell that there was more that she could do to help.

The six weeks were up. Barbara signed the adoption papers without giving a second thought as to the untruths she had stated: married, but separated. Father of child unknown.

For herself police action didn't worry her one jot, and should Michael ever surface and want to know about the child that would be a different matter all together. Threaten him she most certainly would.

Two days later, it was time for her to leave. Breakfast was over and everyone trooped out across the hall and through the front door to see her go. It was goodbye to the friendly, peaceful Beechgrove House, to the sanctuary it had given her, to the lovely gardens. Goodbye to the camaraderie that had become so natural between herself and the other girls. Goodbye to the sisters who were indeed angels.

'Thank you for everything.' Barbara held out her arms wide to include each and every person that had helped to save her life. Well, if not her life her reason, for without the care and protection of Beechgrove House what would have been the outcome?

She smiled at them all with sadness lingering in her eyes. They had been there when she needed them, given her a home for as long as she had wanted to stay.

Sister Francis stepped close, enfolding her lovingly within her arms. Gently she kissed Barbara on each cheek, then with her voice full of emotion for she had come to love what she considered this strange lost soul, she murmured, 'Take care, Barbara. Put the past behind you, and may God bless you always.'

Barbara turned blindly away, her eyes brimming with tears, so much of her life was being left here at Beechgrove House. As she walked the path to where a taxicab stood waiting it was the down-to-earth words of Dolly that reached her ears.

'Keep yer chin up luv, there must be some good blokes out there somewhere.'

Oh, Dolly! It was too much. Barbara turned.

Dolly opened her arms wide and Barbara ran back to her. They hugged so tightly they both nearly lost their balance.

'Who knows? We may meet again, one day,' Dolly said in a voice that was husky with emotion. Then she kissed Barbara, hard, and gave her a little push. 'Go on, on yer way, goodbye Barbara.'

Barbara was too choked to reply.

She almost ran to the taxi. The cabby started up the engine and moved off. There was scarcely time for Barbara to turn to the window and wave a last farewell. Just a final glimpse of fat, rosy-faced Sister Marion waving her handkerchief and a group of people, all of whom had become her friends, standing there on the gravel drive in front of that lovely old house.

Then they were gone.

Ahead lay only the busy road and traffic that seemed to be moving much too fast.

Chapter Seven

MRS HAMLIN WAS thrilled to have Barbara back home but at the same time both she and her husband were terribly worried. Although they were both Victorian in their outlook and adhered to a strict sense of moral values, they felt a great deal of compassion towards their daughter. It was so obvious that Barbara had suffered some terrible ordeal. But what?

The happy young girl that had been Barbara had changed so much it actually caused them pain to watch her. She was so secretive. Where had she been these last months? Something dreadful must have happened to cause her to cut herself so completely off from them and indeed from her friends.

Apparently she had left Michael, but under what circumstances and for what reason?

'Can't say I feel any regret about that man no longer being on the scene,' Phillip Hamlin admitted to his wife when they were alone in their bedroom. 'Actually, to be honest I feel relieved. I couldn't bring myself to trust that fellow, right from the start. Think about it.'

'As if I've done anything else but think about it from the very day I heard the name Michael Henderson,' Patricia Hamlin muttered beneath her breath.

'How could our only daughter have taken up with such a man in the first place? Then, without a word to us, take off, marry him and end up living in such appalling conditions. What a mess she has made of her life. It is astounding really!' He laid his silver-backed hairbrushes down on the glass-topped dressing-table, smoothed the sides of his hair flat with his hands, picked up his glasses and a book and walked to his side of the bed. He paused, as though deep in thought, 'Patricia, do you know if Barbara has given a thought to divorce?'

'Probably hasn't, but if you are thinking along those lines then I am entirely with you. I won't be a moment, I'll just wipe this cream off my face and then I will switch the main light off. Be a dear and switch my bedside light on as well as your own. Think I shall read for a while.'

Her husband couldn't settle to reading; like a dog with a bone he couldn't leave the subject alone.

'Best thing that could happen.' He spoke aloud but more than half to himself. 'Obtain a divorce. As speedily and as painlessly as possible.' Some things he couldn't discuss with his wife. His heart racked within him whenever Barbara, unaware that he was observing her, allowed the anguish to show through in her eyes. No doubt about it, his little girl had been to hell and back.

He put down his book, took off his reading glasses and turned to face Patricia. Firmly he said, 'We must at all costs tread warily. Sufficient for the moment that Barbara is safely back home with us.'

Patricia looked at her husband, his hair had turned iron-grey since the loss of their sons. She had loved him as a young law graduate, married him whilst he still served as a pupil to other barristers, sustained him through endless exams and burst with pride the day he had donned his wig and gown, proclaiming himself a barrister. She loved him still. He radiated strength and character. Barbara was with-

holding dark secrets, there was no doubt about that. She
had been made to suffer and if the truth should ever be
told, what then? She shuddered. How would her husband
react?

'Darling, don't you want to tell me where you have been
these last months?'

Barbara and her mother were together in the lounge
having afternoon tea.

'No mother, let's change the subject. That was the past,
let's talk about the future.'

Her mother laughed and Barbara had not heard her
laugh so spontaneously or so happily for a long time.

'I'm so glad to have you home but, Barbara, I do hope
you are not going to become a recluse. You haven't been
outside this house since you returned.'

Barbara smiled to herself. She was amused that her
mother thought she may become a recluse. Quite the
reverse were her intentions. When the time was right, she
had a lot of living to make up for: the War and the depri-
vations that had followed were for her at last truly over.

Her mother's voice sounded gentle as she rebuked her.
'You seem to have lost all your feminine ways. If you are
going to go around looking as you do now, you can hardly
expect to mix with your old friends – let alone attract new
ones.'

Barbara had the grace to look away as she felt her cheeks
flush up. Seated opposite to her, her mother was a picture
of softness, even regal; her grey hair was immaculate as
always, her small strong hands were clasped together in the
lap of her simple yet elegant blue dress, its severity softened
only by the gold cameo brooch on her shoulder. Barbara

couldn't help but feel a twinge of guilt. Her own hair was drawn back into an elastic band, her attire anything but neat: black slacks and an old grey jumper hardly suggested that she had dressed with care.

Defiantly Barbara shrugged her shoulders. 'I couldn't care less at the moment,' she declared, 'and if by attract new friends you mean men, don't bother, I never want a permanent relationship ever again.'

'Well my darling, unless you do something about your appearance it's highly unlikely you will ever get the chance. You are so thin, you only pick at your meals, why won't you eat properly? And your hair! It always used to look so attractive.'

'Mother, just give me time, please. I know you and Daddy are worried about me but there's no need, honestly. The important thing at the moment is that I am home, here with you, *safe*.' The last word had been little more than a whisper.

Her mother sighed heavily. If only Barbara would talk to her. Confide in her, it would be such a relief. Ugly thoughts had preyed on her mind for weeks since she had a visit from the kindly Mrs Winters, who herself had been worried sick since Barbara's sudden disappearance. She had learnt enough about Michael to know that anger and alcohol had turned him into a man that Barbara had found impossible to love.

'Why do you say "safe", Barbara? Why not get whatever terrible experiences you have suffered out into the open? If you don't know where to begin then just blurt it all out. It is often the best way to talk about something unpleasant and surely you know by now I really can be a good listener.'

Barbara nodded, choking back tears, her hands were

twitching nervously. What she wouldn't give to tell it all! Deliverance from the guilt of having signed away her baby. She was on the very point of speaking when she saw the look of concern in her mother's eyes. It was after all her grandchild she had given away. Then again she had had no choice. The birth of the baby and the subsequent adoption was the end of that part of her life. If she were to let go and divulge those facts she would have to give her reasons, begin at the beginning as it were, and for that to happen she would have to relive all the horrors and that much she could not bring herself to do. The necessary words wouldn't come from her lips. Not coherently they wouldn't. Her courage deserted her.

Sinking back further into the cushions of the chair, she put her head in her hands, holding back hot, painful tears Still, the bitterness was there but she dare not let it overflow. The tears came then, rolling salty into her mouth. She cried until she felt there were no more tears left in her, and then she felt her mother's arms encircle her, holding her close. Her bitterness had surprised even herself, and she knew she could not bear to go on constantly thinking of the past and whether or not she had made the right decision.

Minutes passed in silence. The tea in their cups now stone cold, the dainty cakes uneaten on the silver cake-stand. Innumerable questions ran through her mother's mind, but she reserved them for later.

'Sorry Mother,' Barbara raised her tear-stained face. 'Please just give me time, let's leave it for now shall we? I promise you quite soon I will be much better, more like my old self.'

'Yes, well, I think it is about time I made a fresh pot of

tea and we both cheered up and put a smile on our faces before your father gets home.'

Patricia looked fondly at her daughter as she poured fresh tea into their cups. 'Shall we have a day out shopping? Eastbourne maybe, or how about doing something really marvellous, like going off to London, stay the night, really scour the shops – after all you do badly need clothes, you've hardly anything here. Could be quite an adventure, what d'you say?'

In spite of herself Barbara sniffed away the remains of her tears and smiled. 'You sound really excited, Mother. All right, give me a few more days then have your cheque book ready and we will go up to town together.'

Her mother grinned. 'Yes, well, just so long as you mean what you say. I don't want you becoming spinsterish.'

Barbara smiled again, the lines of anxiety erased from her forehead. 'You'll have your chance, Mother. Just a little more time and then I'll go the whole hog, hairdo, facial, manicure, new clothes, shoes, the lot. How does that sound?'

Her mother looked at her shrewdly but was prevented from having to think of an answer. To her surprise the door had opened, her husband was home.

'Hallo darling, you're back early,' she said, looking across the room at him. He moved to stand behind her chair and putting his arms around her neck kissed the top of her head. Having done the same to Barbara, he said softly, 'This is a nice surprise, afternoon tea all ready, the pair of you looking so cosy. I thought perhaps you would be out.'

There was such a rush of love welling within Barbara as she gazed at her father. He was a real man, kind and considerate. How could she ever have turned her back on such wonderful parents?

'Come on then, Barbara,' he said. 'How about a cup of tea for a hard working man who has been stuck in the smoky city all day. I'm parched!'

'You!' she pushed him away playfully.

Suddenly the laughter from the pair of them was like manna from heaven to Patricia. 'We were talking about having a couple of days in town, Barbara and I. Your daughter is threatening to bankrupt you and have the whole works – will your bank balance stand it?'

Phillip lifted his eyebrows as he met his wife's gaze. Smiling broadly he shrugged indulgently. Money was not important. Only the return to normality and the future happiness of his daughter mattered. It was on the tip of his tongue to tell them they could have the earth so long as that ruffian Michael Henderson remained well and truly out of their lives, but he had the good sense to remain silent.

Barbara was alone in the room, her mother had taken the tea-tray to the kitchen and her father had gone upstairs to have a bath before dinner. She rose from her chair and went to the window and stood gazing out across the lawns. Though summer had long gone the garden still looked beautiful, the grass so green as to be like a velvet carpet, a few shrubs were still a blaze of colour and those that had ceased to flower were abundant with foliage. Away to the left were the stables. She hadn't realised until now how much she had missed the horses. Oh, to ride again. To feel a horse beneath her once again. Without warning her heart lifted, there was joy to be found in the future, she did not have to spend the rest of her life paying for her mistakes, she had to make a more determined effort to put the past behind her.

To make such an effort, it had taken several days. The nights were the worst because more often than not she would have a brief but vivid dream in which she relived every sordid detail of her night of terror, and she would wake saturated in sweat and with every limb trembling. But she had survived it.

It was shortly after seven o'clock in the morning when Barbara left the house and walked towards the stables. She was glad she had still been able to get into her close-fitting jodhpurs and her riding habit felt good across her shoulders. Amongst others her father had two magnificent thorough-bred horses which a couple of lads from the stables in the village of Jevington came up to exercise daily. She returned the lads' cheerful greetings with a friendly wave. In the stable yard she saw Colin Peterson leading the two bays. He doffed his cap and said, 'Good morning Miss Barbara. We've one of the hacks all ready for you. I'll be with you in a minute, just set the lads off.'

'There's no hurry Colin, take your time,' Barbara told him.

Colin Peterson was a new addition to her father's staff since the end of the War, and Barbara had only made his acquaintance during the few weeks she had been home. Apparently there had been no hesitation on her father's part when engaging this man; indeed he counted himself lucky, for Colin Peterson had served in one of the regiments of the Royal Household Cavalry.

Barbara liked the clean-cut tall man if only for the way

he handled the horses. Minutes later Colin led a grey horse forward, bringing it to a standstill when he came up to her. The horse flung its head up and down and snorted loudly as if in greeting and they both laughed as he handed her up into the saddle.

Barbara soon left the main road, taking the side roads through the Sussex villages that led to the open Downs and gazed about her as she rode.

I never appreciated how beautiful Sussex is, she softly told herself, and clean, oh yes so clean. The trees were dressed in full autumn glory of reds and golds, the rolling Downs appeared as green as ever – while in some fields the earth was newly turned, ready for the winter frosts. Then there was the silence. Not a silence that one longed to be broken, but nature's silence, interrupted only with songs from the birds, or a low moo occasionally from the lazy cattle as they sought shelter beneath the hedges. So utterly peaceful. A fair exchange for the hustle and bustle of street traders, motor vehicles and noisy children with nowhere to play except in the confines of narrow, dusty backstreets.

It was difficult to believe that all this splendour lay less than two hours' travelling from London, or that the small children with whom she had become so familiar had never set eyes on living cattle or frolicking young lambs – let alone climbed trees while playing in the woods. Here one could breathe great lungfuls of fresh air, not air tainted by fumes from the gas works. The tranquillity of it all was as a balm to her soul. Autumn would soon give way to winter, then the ground would become hard and slippery in parts under the horses' feet, while in some parts of countryside the animals would more than likely have to plough through quagmires. This, however, Barbara promised herself would not deter her. From now on she was determined she wouldn't miss a single day, come rain or snow she would ride every morning – for it had been quite a while since she had known such serenity.

After four days spent in London with her mother, Barbara's lifestyle took on a new routine. Her main ambition now was to enjoy life. Her days were spent riding, swimming, playing golf, even indoor-tennis and excessive eating and drinking. The nights were a ceaseless round of parties, society gatherings and visits to West End theatres. Her objective, it seemed now, was to pay back the whole world for the pain she had suffered.

Barbara still found it hard and embarrassing to admit exactly why her marriage had broken up. In time her friends and relatives stopped referring to the fact that she had ever been anyone than Barbara Hamlin and Penny Rayford never once asked what had happened to her baby.

To be fair to her, initially, when Barbara had settled back home with her parents, she had toyed with the idea of registering as a medical student at one of the London hospitals. Unable to do so because of insufficient qualifications, she had rebuked herself severely. What a God-awful mess she'd made of her life. Why, oh why had she spurned education when the chance had been given her? She wasn't unintelligent, she had worked just hard enough to satisfy her teachers. The War and London had called her to what, at the time, she thought of as an exciting life. Even so, when the armistice had been declared she could have gone back to studying, even gone on to university, but no, she had wanted Michael, to be married, and to have a home of her own. Well, she had got all three, plus a great many regrets. All of that was behind her now, so why did she constantly feel this terrible guilt, the feeling that she had abandoned her baby before it was ever born? Why the hell are we all so wise after the event? she angrily asked herself.

Even though Barbara was leading a very different lifestyle, regret still played a large part in her thinking. She had mental scars that wouldn't heal. She had married a working class man and he had rejected her. More than that – he had abused her. She had thought loving him would have been enough, she had used charm to bring forth his talents, to stir him to have a purpose, to be ambitious. To no avail. Since being demobbed from the navy Michael had had a chip on his shoulder, the world owed him a living and he was content to lead a shallow life.

Now suddenly, her own behaviour was very different. Outwardly at least. All restraint had gone by the board, at times it would seem that she had no regard for anyone. Her innermost thoughts she kept secret, sometimes telling herself quietly, one day I might even succeed in wiping out the memory of life with Michael Henderson. Even that last ghastly night I might be able to suppress.

But that wasn't enough. She was tired of trying to push it to the back of her mind. If only she were able to erase it completely, for there were still lonesome moments when she felt paralysed with fear, when she couldn't move and she would tremble, her whole body racked with great silent sobs, her cheeks crimson at the recollection of what had been done to her. At such times she would withdraw into herself, giving no one the chance to show sympathy. That was the last thing she wanted. All was now right in her world was the impression she strove to create.

Christmas was only seven days away. In London today, shopping with Penny, Christmas had suddenly lost its appeal for Barbara. She must put on a cheerful face for the sake of her friend, yet her thoughts were filled with regrets. Elizabeth Warren, now happily Mrs Elizabeth Holsworthy, had given birth to twin boys and while she was thrilled for Elizabeth, Barbara could not help comparing her own circumstances. Barbara had been enjoying her day in London – the crowds of Christmas shoppers jostling and pushing, carol-singers at the kerbside and brightly lit shop-windows – but it wasn't over yet, Penny seemed hell-bent on spending more money. They had already pushed their way down Oxford Street, loaded themselves with purchases from Selfridges, bought fabulous gifts from the expensive shops of Bond Street and finally hailed a taxi to take them to Regent Street. As she and Penny alighted from the taxi Penny exclaimed in delight, 'Oh Hamleys, we must go in and see the toys. Besides, we can buy presents for Elizabeth's new twins.'

No sooner had Penny made this declaration than Barbara felt herself being edged towards the revolving doors. Hamleys, always a paradise for children, was filled with nice bright youngsters eagerly pointing out to their parents the gifts they hoped to receive for Christmas. The cold December wind outside was forgotten. Some adults walked the department store briskly, making their purchases without hesitation, whilst others – mainly those accompanied by children – lingered. The queue to visit the plump red-faced Father Christmas caught Penny's eye and she and Barbara stood a while watching the kiddies, their faces wreathed in smiles as each was given a colourful wrapped gift.

Each department looked beautiful with special displays created for the festive season. Little girls' eyes sparkled as they viewed the miniature golden coach complete with occupants in period costume. Small boys tore around the bicycles, the motor cars real in every detail in scaled-down sizes, the aeroplanes that were guaranteed to fly. It was odds on that almost every item would be sold by the time the store closed on Christmas Eve. Grandparents happily clutched their purchases of which each one was tied with a gay red ribbon. Oh yes, Barbara thought to herself, Christmas is a time for children.

But sorrowfully her mind went back to the kiddies in Battersea. Would they fare as well as the children from well-off parents? Probably not, but there again, what they had never had they wouldn't miss and most would feel loved and wanted even without the trappings of lavish presents.

The two of them now stood in the middle of the soft toy region. Barbara couldn't tear her eyes away from the massive arrangement of teddy bears; she picked up a conventional brown one which had a blue bow tied around its neck and hugged it close to her chest. There were innumerable shelves running around the walls and soaring up to the ceiling, holding hundreds of different bears in various colours alongside dogs, bunny-rabbits, tiny kittens and baby lambs – each with a coat of the softest fur. Oh, she liked them all.

Now Penny crossed the floor and called to Barbara, 'Come and see the dolls.'

Barbara's face broke into a surprised but delighted smile. 'Aren't they gorgeous!' she exclaimed. Her eyes caught the display of real china dolls: their wax-like faces appearing so delicate, the finery in which these dolls were clothed was exquisite. She couldn't remember seeing dolls of this quality for sale ever before. Probably because of the War. Dolls such as these were heirlooms, so she had thought, only handed down to children from grandparents and never regarded as toys to be played with.

'Choose one, come on – make your choice,' Penny urged.

Barbara was a little more cautious in her enthusiasm, 'Aren't Elizabeth's twins both boys?'

'Of course you're right. Damn! Can't very well buy them a doll then can we? But there is nothing to stop us having one each for ourselves. Look marvellous laid out on your bed.'

Barbara laughed aloud, 'All right, I am going to have this one, its label says it is one of seven from the story *Little Women*.'

'Then I'm going to have this crinoline lady, her dress will spread wide if I sit her up.'

They had to wait while the lady assistant carefully boxed their choices and neatly wrapped them in decorative paper. 'They're so beautiful, seems a shame to give them to young children,' she remarked as she handed them over the counter.

They looked at each other and burst out laughing. 'They are for us. A Christmas present to ourselves.'

'Nice to be able to afford to indulge one's every whim,' the assistant muttered to herself as she turned towards her next customer.

'Now for these presents,' Penny said.

Barbara laughed, 'I've already decided, one honey-col-oured teddy bear and one pale blue one.'

'So what does that leave me?'

'Oh don't be so daft, there's hundreds to choose from.'

Penny made a show of thinking hard and examining several of the cuddly toys before settling on two snow-white baby lambs, each bore a different coloured silk ribbon holding a tinkling silver bell around its neck.

The bedroom in the private nursing home was hung with Christmas decorations. A crystal vase on a side table held long-stemmed red roses. Elizabeth, impeccably attired in a peach silk nightgown and matching bed-jacket, rested back against a mound of pillows, her silky brown hair immaculate above her pale face.

'Hallo darlings,' she eagerly greeted her friends.

Penny and Barbara, in turn, bent low and gave Elizabeth a kiss on each cheek that was the recognised salutation amongst their circle of friends. Penny perched herself on the end of the bed while Barbara settled in a winged armchair beside Elizabeth. Barbara looked around, even knowing it was a private hospital she had not been prepared for the room to be so luxurious. Elizabeth was smiling at them both now.

'It really is good to see you and I don't feel so envious now that you both have such slim figures.'

They all laughed as Elizabeth patted her now flattened stomach.

'You must see the twins. Do you know, Tim told me last night that now we have two sons our life will change radically because of our responsibilities, and I told him it had better be for the better.'

Penny was the one to reply, 'Of course it will be, Elizabeth. Children give shape and meaning to everything.'

What happened to the young light-hearted girls we used to be? Barbara thought wistfully. That profound comment was out of character for Penny but they were both saved from answering by a nurse entering the room. 'You rang, Mrs Holsworthy. Is there something I can get you?'

'Yes please nurse. May we have a tray of tea for three and while we're waiting, would it be possible for my friends to see my babies?'

'Certainly, Mrs Holsworthy.' With a nod in the direction of Penny and Barbara, the slim young nurse asked, 'Would you like to follow me?'

Penny squealed with enchantment as she gazed at the two wee babies. Barbara's hand trembled as she held onto the side of the cots and her eyes misted over. The two little boys were delightful, perfect, their fingers moved nonstop, their eyes were screwed up tight so there was no chance to note the colour, but each tiny head was covered with hair so fine and blond it shone like silk.

Grief welled up in Barbara's chest and her arms ached for the son she had never held; she thought, if only I could put the clock back. Tears were stinging the back of her eyelids but she forced them back. This was Elizabeth's day. She wouldn't spoil it.

Sleety rain was falling when Penny and Barbara left the nursing home. They turned up the collars of their coats and made a dash for the taxi rank.

Their goodbyes were lingering, each wishing the other a Merry Christmas, promising to keep in touch by phone and to meet for New Year's Eve. As Penny's cab set off in the opposite direction she looked back through the rear window, unable to see anything for the rain was now coming down in torrents. Barbara was the centre of her thoughts. While they had been admiring the babies she had studied her, thinking how sad she looked, but what had upset her? Surely she was pleased that Elizabeth had come through her confinement so well and produced two fine healthy sons?

Barbara didn't have a jealous bone in her body, she was too nice a person for that, she had been thrilled when told that Elizabeth and Tim had finally decided to marry. Besides, those babies would bring such a lot of pleasure.

Seeing as how the three of them had been life-long friends it was more than probable Elizabeth would ask Barbara and herself to be godmothers. That would be nice. The christening would be a big social event and, as the babies grew into toddlers and then young lads, she and Barbara would be viewed as aunts with a stake in their future.

Then again, she thought, when I get married and Barbara puts her wretched past behind her and finds a more suitable husband at the second attempt, why, the both of us will have babies of our own and all the children will regard each other as cousins. Penny realised she was laughing to herself. I'm becoming quite broody, she thought, but wouldn't it be nice if things did work out that way for all of us?

Quite abruptly, the vision of Barbara's face as she had gazed down upon those twins burst into Penny's mind, and she remembered, the only emotion revealed in Barbara's eyes had been sadness.

Oh, my God! It came to her in a flash. The day they had spent together, shopping in Kensington, Barbara had been pregnant!

There had been Barbara's disappearance, surfacing only months afterwards, looking nothing like the bright young girl she had been before she had made that disastrous marriage. No mention had been made of her having given birth, not then, nor since. What a dope! What a heartless friend she was! Had Barbara suffered a miscarriage? Barbara's mother and her father had been almost out of their minds with worry, it had been painfully obvious that Barbara had suffered hell and yet they had never talked about it.

She hadn't asked Barbara any questions, just assumed that Michael had been giving her a hard time and that at long last she had had the sense to leave him. Penny chided herself, you haven't pried so far and you mustn't start now, Barbara will tell me if and when she is good and ready.

She was aware from her talks with Mrs Hamlin that Barbara had told her parents very little. 'Oh Christ! Poor Barbara!' she muttered aloud. Fancy, dragging her off to see Elizabeth. She must think me an insensitive bitch. She leant hard into the corner of the seat now and, her face between her hands, she rocked herself and groaned, 'Why the hell didn't I think?' Making such a fuss of Elizabeth and slobbering over the babies and Barbara had never said a word. Oh, God Almighty!

Barbara was drenched by the time she got into the railway carriage and she shrugged out of her wet coat, tossing it careless onto the opposite seat. Taking a handkerchief out of her handbag, she wiped her streaming face before lighting a cigarette. She drew the smoke deep down into her lungs. It wasn't very often that she smoked and never in her mother's presence but, by God, she needed to now. Her hand shook as she replaced her lighter in her bag. It was not surprising she was trembling – she had thought she was going to pass out back there in the nursing home. She had been almost abrupt with Penny, making all that fuss about getting home, refusing to stay in town for a meal. She shouldn't have allowed her emotions to get the better of her. She should be stronger by now.

What had set her off? Well, first off there had been that gleeful celebratory atmosphere in Hamleys, the immaturity of adults as they played with their toddlers, the choosing of cuddly toys for Elizabeth's two boys. Thoughts were in her mind now that never should have been there, thoughts that she had sworn she would never dwell on, thoughts of the past that was over and done with and had no part in her life now whatsoever.

Still she found herself wondering who was having the joy of buying Christmas presents for her son? Someone kind and loving? She prayed then as she had never prayed before. For a moment she wished she knew to whom her child had been given.

No. No I don't, she angrily muttered to herself. That knowledge would be intolerable. I would want to race away to see him, trying to kid myself that all I wanted would be a glimpse of him when all the time I would know that I was lying to myself.

Dear God, help me remember that my decision was the right one and that it is irrevocable.

The house looked wonderful, in the bow-window of the lounge stood a grand fir-tree, rich dark green in colour and its branches were thick and bushy.

'Hallo Barbara. You're back early.'

Barbara turned around as her mother entered the room

and walked towards the open fireplace, holding out her hands to the blaze.

'Hallo Mother. Yes, I decided not to stay in town with Penny. I had finished all my shopping so I thought I would come home and dress the tree.'

'Oh that is nice, your father will be pleased. Would you like a drink before dinner?'

'That's an excellent idea, I'll have a glass of sherry please.'

Despite the fact that her mother knew Barbara was withholding many things from her, a great companionship had developed between the two of them since Barbara had returned home. Essentially different as they were in experience and age, they were now very much at ease with each other, and although this understanding was not spoken of, it was none the less there and both of them were grateful. Barbara was quite aware that her mother knew something of the terrible anguish she had suffered and one day, please God, she might be able to bring herself to confide in her mother, but not all the gory details. No, never that.

Count your blessings, she daily insisted to herself and indeed that was what she was striving to do. She had wonderful parents and friends, a lovely house in which to live and no shortage of money. Painstakingly she decorated the tree, taking her time as to where each glittering bauble should hang, but her own face was a mask.

Patricia Hamlin was not deceived. She handed Barbara a glass of sherry and her thoughts were very much the same as Penny's had been. No matter how or when Barbara smiled, the smile never reached her eyes. Such sadness! What she wouldn't give to be able to ease her daughter's heartache? Now it was her turn to pray and all she asked was that Barbara might be granted peace of mind.

Chapter Eight

ON THE MORNING of the first day of the year 1949, Barbara woke up reluctantly. She had a hangover, her whole body ached – it was too heavy to drag out of bed. The previous night's party with its boisterous activity, too much food and far too much wine had taken its toll on her. She could faintly hear sounds of liveliness coming from downstairs. She squinted towards her bedside clock. It was a quarter past ten, she had promised to go riding with Penny and others of her parents' house guests at half past eight. Still she made no move to get up. She lay staring into space, willing herself to get a move on, draw a bath and get dressed.

New Year's Eve had been great. Off with the old and on with the new, was what her friends had urged. Right after a marvellous dinner the fun had begun, the library floor had been cleared for dancing and games, and the younger members of the party had availed themselves of this with enthusiasm.

Penny's brother Tony, a tall lean handsome young man, had partnered Barbara in a quickstep to the lively beat of a Squadronaires gramophone record. He had swung her around the room and out into the hall, swift and sure footed. She had thoroughly enjoyed the whole dance. Her parents and their friends had withdrawn to the lounge with their preference for bridge, yet even the oldest member had smiled tolerantly at the young ones' antics.

A little before midnight everyone had assembled in the dining room with glasses charged with champagne. Flushed and excited they had waited for the twelve strokes of Big Ben to boom forth from the cabinet wireless set. 'Happy New Year!' voices echoed from all corners of the room. Streamers were unfurled, balloons were popped, everyone was laughing. Patricia Hamlin separated and began to circulate, embracing everyone in the room. Amid all the hugging and kissing going on all around her, Barbara sought out her father. 'Happy New Year, Daddy.'

'And to you, my dearest. The past is well and truly behind you now, eh? Make an effort and you have a new beginning.' He pulled her close to his chest and held her gently, his cheek resting against the top of her head. Minutes passed before he released her and Barbara was able to reach up and kiss him. Softly, in a voice filled with emotion, she whispered, 'You and Mother are two of a rare species.'

The sadness in her voice had wrenched at her father's heart and he was unable to speak and could only cup her face in his hands and kiss her tenderly. He looked past Barbara to Patricia, and, as their eyes met, he saw traces of tears and knew that they had been shed for their lovely wilful daughter, so dearly loved and yet so headstrong. But she was home now, in their care and starting a new life. God grant her this second chance, he prayed silently.

'I'll come with you if you want,' Penny offered. 'But to be honest I'm bushed, I was out on the Downs this morning while you were still in bed.' Lunch was over and Barbara, having drunk several cups of coffee, felt very much better.

'No, you stay and have a yarn with the others.'

'Oh yeah,' Penny answered with a grin. 'If I can find a quiet corner I'm getting my head down, it's me for a snooze.'

Barbara grinned back at her friend, remembering the capers she had got up to last night and wondered how on earth she had managed to rise so early this morning and go riding.

'I'll see you later then. Sleep well.'

Barbara walked into the stable yard just as the hands of the wall clock showed two o'clock. Despite the fact that a weak sun had broken through the clouds, it was a sharp, bitter cold day. Black ice, formed during the night, still persisted in sheltered spots. Colin Peterson led her horse out of the stall; its hooves clattered and it slithered awkwardly on the uneven cobblestones of the yard, its breath condensing in clouds of steam in the cold air.

'I'll be gone when you get back, Miss Barbara. Will you mind rubbing him down yourself?'

'Of course not Colin,' Barbara bent over and patted the horse's neck. 'We're not going far, are we boy? Just a a few lungfuls of fresh air to clear away the effect of last night and we'll be back.'

'That's all right then. It gets dark so quickly now, don't want you out on your own once the light goes, do we?'

'I'll be fine, thanks Colin.'

Barbara gave her horse the signal to trot and in a very short time they were down the lane and out of sight of the house. A rabbit scurried across their path, making for the thick undergrowth. Her horse shied and Barbara tightened the reins and laughed softly. 'Steady boy, he's as entitled to come out for an airing as we are.'

For a long while she trotted him slowly, passing no one.

It was as if she had the whole of the countryside to herself. Reaching high ground she realised the top of the cliffs were invisible, a mist was coming down and far below the sea was grey. She thought to herself it was a long time since she had seen the waves so high and rolling in with such force. A shudder went through her. Fancy being at sea on such a rough night as this was likely to be.

'Time to turn for home, eh boy?' she said, bending forward and giving her horse a soft pat on the side of its neck. 'This damp cold sinks right into one's bones.'

As she dismounted and led her horse into the stable a shadow fell suddenly across her. Since the time when she was raped she had not been able to control her fears. Any unexpected or strange situation caused her heart to start thumping and the blood to rise in her cheeks.

Startled, she peered into the dim interior. Michael was standing a few yards ahead, barring her way. He stood not with the upright bearing and the cheeky grin of the young sailor she had fallen in love with, but with a careless slouch – his face showing nothing but meanness.

'*Oh my God,*' she muttered out loud, the slow words were both an exclamation of sheer terror and an anguished prayer for help.

She felt the icy clutch of dread take over, she stood stock-still shivering with fright.

For that first few seconds he appeared as tongue-tied as she was.

Her eyes, now accustomed to the dimness, saw that his eyes were fixed upon her face and there was no mistaking the hatred he was directing at her.

She made to run. Michael moved quickly, his movements crab-like until he was behind her. She jerked herself around,

glancing to the left and to the right. There was no escape.
Without warning her horse whinnied as if conscious of
danger, the sound echoed loudly, other horses in their stalls
raised their heads, stamped their hooves and they too began
to neigh. If only the noise had been heard up at the house,
would the men come running? It was a vain hope. The
horses, having expressed their annoyance, snorted once or
twice and turned their attention back to their feed-bags.

'Well, ain't you going to wish me Happy New Year?'

Barbara found she couldn't speak, her voice had deserted
her entirely. All she could feel was this dreadful thumping
of her heart against her ribs and a breathless feeling of
suffocation. She had never, in the whole of her life, felt so
frightened. Finally, without looking at him she managed to
say, 'Oh, Michael,' and despite all her efforts her voice
trembled with fear.

'Sorry I didn't let you know I was coming,' he said with
a sneer. 'Got to thinking about you and about the baby,
thought it was about time I accepted my responsibilities.'
There was no mistaking the sarcasm. 'On the spur of the
moment I borrowed a car from one of me mates – see,
darling, I've still got some mates – came down on the off
chance, like. Don't tell me you ain't thrilled to see me?'

Barbara's agitation was now visible and Michael looked
at her with contempt as she let go of the reins of her horse
and stepped further back.

'Oh no, you bloody well don't!' He came at her with a
rush. 'I wanna talk to you, we've plenty to discuss. Besides,
I want you to come back ter me.' He expected her to
return to Battersea! To live with him as his wife!

The horse, now free from restraint, stamped on the
concrete floor, backed up a little, turned and bolted out

into the open. His clattering hooves, resounding at first, gradually lessened until an ominous silence settled once more around them. Michael moved right up close to her and his nearness was like a physical shock. Her knees began to shake and she had to clench her hands into fists to stop them from trembling.

She decided to try and play for time. 'Have you got a job now?'

'I'm surprised you care enough to even ask.'

'Of course I care.'

'Balls! Don't be such a bloody hypocrite. You walked off, back to yer mummy and daddy without so much as a word.'

Some of the fear of him vanished and her voice became much stronger. 'After what you did! What did you expect me to do?'

He reached out and touched her arm, 'I'm sorry, really I am. You never gave me a chance to explain.'

Explain! For Christ's sake! She hated his wheedling almost as much as his anger.

'It wasn't that bad Barbara, things got out of hand, you wouldn't go along with me, I needed help. It all went too far, it was the drink. Honest I'm sorry.'

It wasn't that bad! Barbara was thunderstruck, barely able to believe what she was hearing.

'Wasn't it always too much drink with you?'

'There you go again – always criticising.'

Deliberately she didn't answer: to provoke him was the last thing she wanted. Desperately she racked her brains for a way to pacify him.

'Michael, you really can't be serious – suggesting we start all over again in that awful flat.'

'I don't give a damn where we live just so long as you come back to me. You seem to forget you're still my wife. I only came cos I miss you so much and I wanted to find out 'ow you got on when you had the baby.'

'Oh wonderful, suddenly you care.'

In the eerie quiet she knew she had blown it. Terrified now, her heart was thumping like a sledge hammer. Why hadn't she kept quiet? Her every instinct told her that taunt had been like waving a red rag at a bull.

He lunged at her. She turned her head in disgust at the beery smell of his breath and this seemed to infuriate him further. She flinched even before his hand struck the stinging smack to the side of her face.

He brought his arms up on each side of her and pushed her backwards until he had her pinned against the wall. He lowered his head and brutishly pressed his lips against her mouth. He tore furiously at the buttons of her riding habit and then his fingers were on the silk of her shirt and he was spitefully squeezing her left breast, grunting and dribbling as he assaulted her. 'Jesus, I'd forgotten how good you always smell. I want you Barbara, now, after all I'm only asking for me rights.'

Fortified by alcohol, he had come looking for her and incredibly found her on her own – he wasn't about to pass up a chance such as this. Her struggles only encouraged him, and her tears and entreaties were ignored. She tried to scream but felt she was choking as she had to swallow the bile that had risen in her throat. Despairingly she pushed at his hands and eventually she got the words out from between clenched teeth, 'Michael, let's go somewhere else, I must—' he cut the words off by covering her lips with his open mouth, thrusting his tongue deeply towards the back of her throat.

She couldn't help it – she choked. Michael jerked his head away from her face and with two hands banged her head against the wall. 'That's it – I've stood enough, get those trousers undone. Come on be quick, rip them open down the front.' He gestured with one hand what it was he wanted her to do. She watched his face whilst she attempted to open the thick corded material of her jodhpurs.

'That won't do. Take them off, I'll 'ave a fag while you do a striptease for me, I've waited long enough – a few more minutes won't matter.' He took a packet of Players and a box of matches from his jacket pocket. His eyes never left her as he placed a cigarette between his lips, struck a match and lit it.

Still desperately playing for time, Barbara pleaded, 'Michael, wouldn't you rather we went somewhere more comfortable?'

He blew smoke directly into her face, then raised his fist menacingly, 'Suppose we discuss that later, right now all I want is for you to get those bloody daft trousers off.'

Something snapped in Barbara. Not this time! There was going to be no repetition of that night that still haunted her. She would rather die here and now than endure yet more horrors. She might go down fighting but this hateful beast was not going to use her as a whore.

Michael flicked his cigarette stub out into the open and with a leer on his lips he stepped forward and pressed himself hard against her. She turned her face away but as she did so she brought her knee high and fiercely up between his legs.

Although he instinctively doubled over, his anger erupted. 'You cow!' Pain spurred him on as he retaliated. The blow he struck caught her sharply on her cheekbone, the smarting agony served to make her more determined.

With a rapid movement her hand felt along the wall until her fingers came into contact with what she was seeking. Hatred swamped her, her eyes were burning, her heavy breathing choking her. If she didn't defend herself now she would drown in her own shame, but it wasn't going to be as Michael wanted it – she would fight him off or die in the attempt.

Her trembling hand now held a brush used for grooming the horses, its bristles really sharp. In the second before she struck him Barbara knew that he had guessed what she was about to do, but quick as he was her movement was more speedy. She held her arm high, tightened her hold on the wooden handle of the brush and with vengeance uppermost in her mind, she smashed at Michael's face, raking the pine-like needles deeply from his forehead down to his chin.

'You are a pig, a detestable pig!' she screamed at him, then her voice rising with every word, she added, 'I hate you! Do you hear me – I hate you! Did Pete Davis buy you more beer for what you allowed him to do to me? You're not a man – ' She didn't get to say another word. The next moment his hands were round her throat and he was shaking her violently.

'And you are a stuck-up bloody bitch!' he yelled. His hands tightened viciously around her throat and she could feel herself choking and the blood pounding in her head. She tried to pull feebly at his hands but the pressure seemed to increase. Suddenly he let go of her and she fell to the

Chapter Nine

LOOKING AT HER daughter, who was unable to move her head and barely able to speak, Patricia Hamlin wanted to cry. Sometimes in these past three days she had ranted at God. She supposed that was wicked of her, but hadn't Barbara been through enough? 'Oh, my darling!' she muttered aloud, her sad eyes never leaving the face of this beloved daughter, now her only child.

At the beginning of the War Barbara had been all youth and freshness, as innocent of life as a baby, with her silky chestnut bright hair, her unblemished skin and a mouth that always seemed to be smiling. With Penny and Elizabeth they had set off for London, so keen to make their own effort to help win the War.

Why, oh why had Barbara been fated to meet Michael? No actual details of the previous ill-treatment Michael had administered to Barbara had ever been brought out into the open. Nevertheless one would have to be blind not to see that the awful effects had become long-term and now just as she was showing signs of becoming more settled, he had reappeared. How could she and her husband have been so careless as to have let his second attack on Barbara take place? Normally she didn't use blasphemous words but now she found herself clenching her fists and saying, 'Damn and blast that man!'

Thank God the men had found the horse still saddled and without a rider. Running to the stables to mount their own horses and begin the search for Barbara, they had found her crumpled body. When at first Barbara had been gently carried into the house Patricia had been convinced that her daughter was going to die. Deep anxiety for Barbara made the next twenty-four hours an absolute nightmare for her parents. She was only twenty-four-years-old and her life lay in ruins.

Her father was so angry, the anger levelled largely at himself. He was overwhelmed with guilt. That this could happen twice to his beloved Barbara and this second time within the bounds of their own home. A damn good whipping was what he would like dealt out to that fellow, and with the mood he was in right now he would have no hesitation in offering to wield the lash himself.

Police enquiries as to Michael's whereabouts had proved fruitless but their investigation had turned up one certainty: Michael Henderson had spent a considerable time in The Smugglers Inn that same lunch-time, consuming pints of bitter with whisky chasers until the landlord had refused to serve him any more. The landlord's statement was that Henderson had been very much the worse for drink and on being asked to leave the premises had hurled curses and threats at all members of the staff.

Phillip Hamlin came quietly into the bedroom where his wife sat at the bedside of their daughter. Looking from one to the other, he asked, 'How is she?'

'She is sleeping but very fitfully.'

'Well now dear, you go and make us a nice pot of tea. I'll stay here for a while.'

Almost reluctantly his wife rose and left the room. Phillip

seated himself in the chair Patricia had vacated and gazed down at Barbara, horrified by what he saw. It was not only her neck covered in bandages which did not entirely conceal the thick ugly weal or the dark bruises that upset him, but also the traces of suffering on Barbara's face.

How could this have happened in a few short years? he thought. It seemed only yesterday that Barbara had volunteered to work for the Red Cross and now she looked so much older than the beautiful girl that had left this house. To think he and his wife had been condemning her for not visiting them more often, and all the time she had been suffering at the hands of that brute!

Suddenly Barbara struggled to sit up, she tried to speak but could only make strange croaking noises as she tried to form the words.

'Barbara, Barbara,' her father kept repeating in a distraught voice. She stared up at him, her eyes wide with fear. 'It's all right,' he soothed her. 'You'll feel better soon, my darling.' Fortunately her mother returned at that moment carrying a laden tea-tray. Placing the tray on top of the chest of drawers, she took from it a feeding cup which she had filled with home-made lemonade and ice-cubes.

She raised Barbara's head and dribbled some of the cold liquid through the spout of the feeding cup into her mouth. 'Try to swallow some, my dear,' her mother urged. The effort brought tears to Barbara's eyes but at last she managed to swallow the liquid and her mother patiently fed the rest of the drink into her mouth, and then gently laid her back down onto her pillows. Barbara touched her mother's hand in gratitude.

While Patricia poured cups of tea for herself and Phillip,

he moved back to sit beside the bed. All the while he was making consoling murmurs, assuring Barbara she was safe now and that they would not leave her alone. Gently he stroked her hair back from her forehead until she finally drifted off into sleep.

Phillip spent the rest of the day in Barbara's bedroom and towards evening he had closed his eyes but opened them again to find Patricia standing beside him. This time she had brought thin creamy soup in the feeding cup, and now Barbara found it a little easier to swallow as her father supported her with his arm. His face wrinkled in fury as he felt the weal that Michael's hands had left around Barbara's neck. The doctor had told them it would fade with time but he knew he would see it to his dying day. His thoughts were tormenting him. He had always felt that the young man Barbara had chosen to marry was most unsuitable but now his strong dislike of him had increased to the point of utter hatred. If Henderson's stance had been more steady that riding crop could have decapitated Barbara! That man should be behind bars – locked away for good.

Phillip had not needed to be told the horrific details of why his daughter had left her husband. In the early days of her home-coming he had spent many sleepless nights listening to Barbara thrash about in agony as she lived through her nightmares, praying to God to ease her suffering and grant her peace of mind. Now he was obsessed by the need to ensure his daughter's mental as much as physical survival. Overruling his wife's protests, he had moved a single bed into Barbara's room and for the past two nights had lain alongside her, soothing her with words, exerting every ounce of his own strong will to give her the wish to pull through. 'Fight back, Barbara! Come on my darling, don't let him win,' he implored her over and over again. There was no responsiveness and that fact only served to make him hate Henderson all the more. He wished him in hell!

Barbara had been depressed when first she had returned home and just when her outlook on life seemed to be so very much brighter this had to happen. Was there to be no end to the unhappiness that man could cause her?

'I'll get Henderson into court if it's the last thing I ever do,' he vowed to himself. On his own ground Phillip knew full well he would be verbally more than a match for the likes of him.

Barbara opened her eyes and saw the look of anger that had spread across her father's face. 'Daddy.' The word came from her lips as a croak forced up from her damaged throat. Her tongue felt enormous and she still fought for breath, but she managed to smile. Her father wept with relief. She put out her hand which he took in between both of his and they stayed like that until Barbara muzzily drifted off to sleep again.

It was ten days later before Barbara came downstairs for the first time. She was having lunch in the dining room with her parents. The doctor had visited her daily, asked numerous questions and suggested she tried to put the whole incident from her mind. Diversion was what she needed now, he had told her father.

Barbara felt she had spent the past days in a long twilight, sick to her soul. Without encouragement from her mother and father she could have so easily have let go. During her conscious spells one or the other of them had always been there. She still shrank away in revulsion whenever her mind slipped back to what Michael had once again tried to do to her.

She loved this house, always had, only now she appreciated it, especially so her own room. It had given her sanctuary. She had lain for hours staring at the walls. The softly shaded lamp beside her bed, in the stillness of the night, had shone on the pastel wallpaper, and on the old polished woodwork of the furniture. The love of her parents and the peacefulness and privacy of that room had saved her reason.

Patricia was worried because Barbara was still eating hardly anything. When the soup plates had been cleared away by Mrs Clarkson, the daily treasure who had been with the family for nearly twenty years, and the main course set on the table, Barbara asked to be excused.

'Barbara, please stay and try to eat a little,' her mother implored.

'Just a few vegetables, mashed with gravy?' her father coaxed, for all the world as if she were a young child.

'I couldn't. Really.'

Her mother gave in. 'All right darling. It's really warm in the lounge, I lit the fire hours ago. Draw an armchair up and perhaps you could do a little of my jigsaw puzzle — it's a very difficult one.'

Barbara smiled in an offhand way at both of them and left the room. She sunk thankfully into the depths of the armchair and stared into the flames of the fire. Outwardly she knew she appeared calm and uncomplicated, but the thoughts within her head were anything but. What was she going to do? Where could she go to be safe? If Michael's visits were going to continue, with him popping up any time the fancy took him, she would never be able to cope.

It wasn't fair! It just wasn't fair. The uncertainty of the situation appalled her. She couldn't take any more of his violence. Michael had become a twisted, perverted bastard. One thing she was quite definite about: never again would he get the chance to practise his abnormalities on her. 'I'll kill him first. I swear I will,' she solemnly promised herself.

She had thought, fleetingly, of filing for divorce but she knew she was not yet emotionally ready to cope with this step. Her father in his wisdom had told her to leave such matters in his hands. 'The future will take care of itself,' he had assured her. But it was the future that worried her.

One week later and still Phillip could not look at his daughter without an ache in his heart. The ticking of the clock on the mantelshelf, the only sound in the room, was hypnotic. The flames in the fire turned blue, showing frost was in the air outside. A log crackled and disintegrated, sending a shower of sparks up the open chimney. Phillip quickly glanced to where Barbara lay on the settee, thankfully she was still fast asleep.

It was early dusk when Patricia kicked gently at the lounge door, pushing it open with her foot. Her husband rose from his chair, crossed the room and held the door open wide. She carried a tea-tray on which she had also placed a plate of thinly cut sandwiches which she had decorated with watercress and wedges of tomatoes. She did everything she could think of to tempt Barbara to eat. As Patricia placed the tray on a small mahogany table Barbara opened her eyes, yawned and stretched very much like a contented cat. Her parents smiled at each other: it was a good sign. Spreading a napkin across Barbara's knees and handing her a plate, Patricia said, 'Take one of each, ham and cheese, and I've made a few cakes which – if I do say so myself – look very tempting.'

Barbara laughed as she pulled herself up into a sitting position. 'All right Mother, if it will make you happy I promise to try your fancy cakes.' The three of them ate in companionable silence, though when Barbara sipped from her cup the hot tea was still difficult for her to swallow.

The doorbell rang. Phillip looked questioningly at his wife, 'Not expecting anybody, are we dear?'

She raised her eyebrows and shrugged her shoulders as he rose and crossed the room. Barbara and her mother heard the opening of the front door, then the voices of more than one man. Minutes later her father re-entered the room. There were two men with him, one dressed in police uniform and the other in a long fawn raincoat.

The look of dread on her husband's face and the sight of the policeman caused Patricia's heart to race and the colour to drain from Barbara's cheeks.

'This gentleman is Inspector Watkins,' Phillip stated. The policeman stood back against the wall and was not introduced.

The inspector looked to where Barbara lay propped up against the cushions. 'Mrs Henderson?'

She looked up at him, startled, and the cup which she held rattled as she placed it back down on its saucer. 'Yes.' Her answer was barely audible.

The inspector placed his hand over his mouth, coughed loudly to clear his throat and, in a quiet voice that sounded apologetic, said, 'Ma'am, there is no easy way to tell you this – ' again he hesitated and the pause was ominous. The words now came out rapidly. 'The coastguards have recovered a body from the bottom of the cliffs at Beachy

Head. We have reason to believe it may be that of your husband.'

Barbara said nothing, just held her face between her two hands which were visibly trembling.

Her father walked towards the blazing fire whose flames were illuminating the room on this dark afternoon and with his hands resting on the high mantelshelf he stared into it.

'Are you sure?' Patricia shuddered as she asked the question.

The inspector nodded. The silence was frightening.

Some time passed before the inspector spoke and then it was an utterance filled with compassion. 'We shall need you, Mrs Henderson, to make formal identification.'

Barbara felt her stomach churn. She struggled desperately to stay calm.

'No!' The one word shot at the inspector made Barbara jump. She was not used to hearing her father's voice raised in anger.

'There will be no need for that, my daughter is not well enough. I will identify the body if it is that of my son-in-law.' The words were snapped out by Phillip Hamlin in a manner that surprised even his wife.

Barbara's eyes quickly flashed to the inspector's face. Would he allow that? She didn't think she would be capable of doing it.

'As you wish, Sir. I'm sure that will be quite all right.'

The sigh of relief which came from Barbara was very loud.

The inspector took a pair of gloves from the pocket of his raincoat and drew them onto his hands and with a nod to his constable turned towards the door, pausing only to say, 'We won't disturb you further just now, but we shall have to return again tomorrow morning. We need to take statements.'

While her husband went to show the officers out, Patricia moved across to sit on the end of the settee and sat holding both of Barbara's hands tightly – as if she could pump reassurance through them to her daughter.

Barbara never moved but a deep groan came from her throat. 'Dear God,' she moaned.

Inspector Watkins returned alone next morning.

The raincoat had been replaced by a navy-blue melton overcoat. This thin, sallow-looking man seemed embarrassed as he stood twirling his trilby hat between his hands. Endeavouring to put the man at his ease, Patricia smiled, 'Let me take your hat and coat, Inspector. Shall we go into the dining room?' She led the way, opening the door and standing back to allow him to enter first.

Seeing Mr Hamlin and Barbara, the inspector's first words were, 'I'm glad to find you all here.'

When they were all seated around the dining room table he began to go over the events of the night of Michael's last visit.

'Who found him?'

The inspector and both of her parents were surprised when Barbara put the question.

'It was the coastguard who discovered the body, if you remember,' the inspector said gently.

'Yes.' She must have been told that yesterday. Vaguely she remembered, but no doubt she had been too shocked to register anything other than the fact that Michael was dead.

'You said you struck your husband with a grooming brush, Mrs Henderson. How badly was he hurt?' The inspector's tone was now neutral, neither accusatory nor protective.

'His face was deeply scratched, he was bleeding badly.'

'Did he fall to the ground?'

'Oh no.' How she wished that he had. 'It was then that . . . he . . . became more vicious,' Barbara's chest was heaving and her face was as white as a sheet. 'I'm sorry . . . I don't remember much else.'

'May I be excused for a few moments?' When the inspector nodded, Patricia got up from her seat and left the room.

Some ten minutes passed before she came back with Mrs Clarkson. The two women began offering coffee and small cakes and biscuits which they had set out on doyley-covered plates. Inspector Watkins ate and drank, said 'Thank you,' and went back to writing in his notebook. Now it was the turn of her parents. Mrs Hamlin was confused and her answers were not clearly expressed. Mr Hamlin, however, was in complete control. His version of himself and the three other men finding his daughter, battered and bloody in the stables, was given in precise clipped terms – very much in the same manner as he was accustomed to use in legal battles when in court.

Looking up from his notes the inspector paused, his eyes taking in all three of them.

'The coroner has been notified of the death, he will arrange for a post-mortem to be held; as the death was sudden, probably an accident, your consent is not needed. The coroner will almost certainly decide to hold an inquest, in which case you will be required to attend.'

Patricia felt she couldn't sit still any longer, so she rose from her chair and collected the cups and saucers, stacking them in an orderly manner on the tray.

The inspector began all over again. Endless questions directed at each of them in turn. Phillip, his voice steady as a rock, repeated his version of the events.

Patricia, her voice trembling, told how her daughter had been carried into the house.

The inspector twisted round in his chair to look directly at Barbara, 'Are your husband's parents living?'

Barbara hesitated. It seemed absurd that she knew so little about Michael's background. 'His mother died some years ago, but I think his father is still alive.'

'Can you not give me more details than that?'

'Not really.' This truly was an embarrassment for her. 'His father married again, a lady who already had several children, and Michael being the only one I think felt out of things, perhaps even neglected. He joined the navy as soon as he was old enough and, as far as I know, has not been in contact with his father since.'

Kindly now, the inspector said, 'Don't worry, Mrs Henderson, we'll trace his father through his naval records. He will be notified. One last question – in your opinion was your husband very much the worse for drink when he came to the house?'

Barbara kept her eyes downcast. 'Yes,' she murmured.

'Do you know if he had any bottles about his person?'

She shook her head, 'I'm sorry, I haven't any idea.'

'Nothing else you can remember about that afternoon, no little detail that you have left out?'

Again she shook her head, 'Just what I have told you.'

At last he closed his writing-pad, said, 'Thank you all for bearing with me,' and stood up.

Phillip came forward, 'I'll get your hat and coat and see you to the door.'

Barbara and her mother were both close to tears when the inspector finally left.

Within a week of Michael's death the coroner held a preliminary hearing. It had been decided that Phillip Hamlin's presence would be enough. With dragging footsteps he walked along the cold corridor and thankfully sat down on a bench. This past week had been exhausting. He wasn't sure if he was relieved or surprised that neither he nor Barbara had heard from Michael's father. He couldn't fathom how a man could lose touch with his only son. It seemed cruel and hard for no one to express sorrow at Michael's death, but hypocrisy was not in his own nature.

He couldn't erase from his mind the picture of his lovely daughter, with her gentle voice and gentle ways, lying on that cold stone floor of the stable. Abused, bloody and beaten. Barely alive. He had detested the man and the urge to kill him had been strong – at least to have him locked away for a very long time, anything so long as it prevented him from ever again having the opportunity to come near Barbara. Only now Michael was dead, leaving behind him deep shadows and scars.

'This hearing is for purposes of identification only and formal evidence of the identity of the body.' It was all over in minutes. The coroner gave the order for the body to be released and so allow the cremation to take place. 'The inquest proper will take place three weeks from today and will be an inquiry into the cause of death,' the coroner declared, looking somewhat sympathetically at Phillip Hamlin.

Barbara insisted, against all advice, on attending the service at the crematorium. There were a few male mourners in the chapel when Barbara arrived with her parents, but she never raised her eyes to notice who they were. She looked wan and sad, as indeed she felt, in her black suit and hat. It was the way that Michael had died that had hit her hard and she did her best during the short service to think back to the way they had felt about each other when they had first met. Her first mistake had been to go to Plymouth without even telling her parents and her second, and by far the biggest, mistake had been to marry Michael in such haste. From that day things had only gone from bad to worse.

It was midday when they arrived back at the house. Mrs Clarkson had hot refreshments set out ready in the lounge. Three armchairs were grouped close to the fireplace in which a roaring fire burnt halfway up the chimney, looking so cheerful and giving out such comforting warmth.

Her father broke the silence by touching on the subject they had all been avoiding during the past days.

'You must remember, Barbara, Michael had been drinking heavily, he didn't know what he was doing and it is almost certain that they will bring in a verdict of accidental death.'

Barbara made no reply but she thought about it. She wasn't sure if that made it better or worse.

With concern in his voice, her father asked, 'Would you like for your mother and me to take you abroad for a while?'

Barbara sipped at her hot coffee before answering, 'No, Daddy, I don't feel the urge to run away.'

'Are you sure? A holiday might do us all good.' His deep-set kindly eyes looked into hers. Had there been a little tinge of longing in the smile with which she had softened her refusal? 'There is nothing you have to prove to anyone, you know that by now, don't you Barbara?'

'I think so.' She replaced her cup and saucer on the table, reached out and covered his large bony hand with her own – it felt warm and reassuring.

'You are intending to stay here, live with your mother and me, at least for the time being? We both want you to stay so much.'

'Hmm! Just what the doctor ordered,' she smiled. 'Who else would love me as you do? And spoil me.' Reaching up, she touched his cheek. 'Oh Daddy!'

Her father breathed out and relaxed. 'Poor Barbara. It's been a hell of a time for you, but you must put it all behind you now. There is a future ahead and I hope it leads you to a happy road.'

'Thank you Daddy.' Barbara's voice was little more than a whisper and he could tell that tears were not far away.

He took her by the shoulders and pulled her close. Watched by her mother he put his arms around her, giving her the protective love that only parents can offer. Phillip looked sadly at his wife.

After a while, Patricia sighed, hauled herself out of her chair, knelt down on the floor and placed her hand on Barbara's head. Very gently, very slowly, she began to stroke her daughter's hair.

'It's all over now, my love. Please, Barbara, please dear,

don't cry. Let's have no more tears. Your father and I will take care of you. Don't be afraid any more.'

Barbara raised her head and brushed her hand over her eyes. 'I'll try not to be,' she whispered, knowing how lucky she was to have parents that not only loved her but were free with their sympathy and understanding. She reached out and took her mother's hand.

Patricia smiled. 'Good girl.' Then clambering to her feet she added, 'I'll see about refilling the coffee pot.'

Barbara felt compelled to attend the inquest.

Her mother and father sat either side of her in the cold corridor. The sound of the heavy rain lashing against the window panes did nothing to lift her spirits.

'Time to go in.' The tall official had a military bearing and an odd expression. He swallowed as if he had a lump in his throat.

'Shouldn't take long. Fairly straight forward.' He made the statement kindly.

The inquiry opened with the doctor who had performed the autopsy stating that Michael's body had contained an excessive amount of alcohol. This was confirmed by the evidence given by the landlord of The Smugglers Inn.

The coroner presiding at the inquest was an elderly but efficient gentleman. He gave his judgement in precise terms. 'Michael James Henderson had been intoxicated at the time of his death and the verdict of this court is accidental death.'

Chapter Ten

BARBARA LIVED THE next few weeks day by day, grateful for the refuge her old home provided, frightened to look back yet refusing to look ahead.

Mornings she walked the grounds a lot, wearing stout shoes and a sheepskin coat, with no other company than her own, and the afternoons she spent in the solitude of her bedroom. There were days when rain turned to sleet at times and pelted against the windows. Then, later, the sleet turned to snow, and her parents gave up trying to encourage her to venture further afield. The wind howled and yet the white snow presented a pretty picture, covering the lawns, mantling the hedgerows, and lying white on the dark boughs of the bare trees.

Friends and relatives visited, asked questions and showed concern for Barbara's health. Their talk flowed over her and she scarcely heard it. She found the time now spent at home alone with her parents strangely soothing. It was like going back into times past, except that her brothers were missing and her mirror told her she was no longer a little girl.

Her mother did her best to get her to talk. The two of them lunching alone one day seemed the ideal opportunity.

'Have you thought what you'll do with the rest of your life?' her mother fearfully asked.

Barbara had. Often. As yet she hadn't come to any decision.

Receiving no reply Patricia pressed on, 'Darling, I know you're not fit enough to do anything too strenuous at the moment, but wouldn't you like to go out a little? See some of your old friends?'

As if speaking to herself, Barbara said in an undertone, 'I hadn't realised how bitter Michael had become.' The comment was uttered in little more than a whisper and her mother had to lean forward to catch the words.

'Stop it! – do you hear me? You cannot go on blaming yourself for what has happened, Barbara, it is about time that you tried facing the truth.' The exasperated tone of her mother's voice caused Barbara to look up sharply. It was totally out of character for her mother to lose her temper.

'The thing is,' her mother insisted, 'if things hadn't happened as they did, God alone knows what the outcome would have been. Your life would never have been free of his threats. Michael was a menace to himself.' She took a deep breath, regretting her outburst, but that damned man had been the ruination of Barbara and it was time she put all thoughts of him from her head and got on with her own life. She forced her voice down to quieter tones.

'Please Barbara, try to look at things in realistic terms. You didn't do anything harmful to Michael. He did it to himself.'

Taking Barbara's hand between her own she sat stroking it. When she spoke again there were tears in her voice. 'Your father and I care about you, Barbara, we just can't stand by and see you fading away. You made a disastrous mistake, fair enough – we all do at some point in our lives – but no one expects you to go on paying for it for the rest of your life. Make an effort. Please. Promise me you will try. How about beginning right now by giving your old mother a smile?'

Penny had said almost the selfsame words to her months ago. What a pity she hadn't heeded them then, left Michael and come home, Barbara was thinking to herself.

'You're not old, Mother, and yes I will try and buck myself up.' There was sorrow still in her voice but she had forced a smile to her lips.

Spring came. Daffodils bloomed in their hundreds, not in neat flower beds, but higgledy-piggledy in clumps around the base of great tree-trunks and tucked away beneath the hedges. Lambs were born in the fields, their plaintive bleating sounding wonderful as they skipped around their mothers. It was all new life. Did it bring new life to Barbara? One evening late in April, dinner over, she asked her mother if she might use her car. 'Of course you may, dear,' her mother readily agreed, smiling happily that at last her daughter was going off somewhere.

In the garage her father's gleaming car looked enormous against the modest black Morris thousand which her mother used. Barbara settled herself in the driver's seat of the small car and was pleased when the engine fired first time. She drove slowly with the window wound down. The air was sweet as wine, fresh and fragrant with the scent from the hedgerows, and as always the smell reminded her of her childhood. Now she was appreciative of all the countryside that surrounded her. In her mind's eye she could see again those two rooms in which she and Michael had lived. The time spent there had been an endless struggle against the dirt and grime. But all that was over. There were times now when she felt cleansed, even renewed, yet other times when the nightmare would still return. Then the filth and sweat of Michael and Pete Davis's actions was so real and horrible that she would panic and feel dirty again.

She drove for twenty minutes, by which time she had left the villages behind and was now approaching the main Brighton road. At the top of the incline she turned the car to the left, taking the winding road which had open fields on each side. Climbing now to higher grounds, Birling Gap with its long low hotel and coastguard cottages was left behind.

When she brought the car to a stop on the cliffs above Beachy Head, she asked herself if it had been her intention from the start to make for this place, and the answer was yes, only she hadn't thought she would have the courage to go through with it. Ever since the thought had come into her mind it had stayed with her, eating away a little more each day. It had to be done or she could not go on living with herself.

'So,' she said aloud, 'I'm here now but why? Exactly why?'

Face the truth, she sternly told herself. This is the place where Michael had died and what she wanted, if she was ever to find peace and start to rebuild her life, was to exonerate herself from Michael's death.

It was ages before she could bring herself to get out of the car, and when she finally did it was dark. She walked up the grass bank, staying well away from the edge of the high precipice. It was a fine starry night. The sea sounded so gentle as it lapped softly against the foot of the cliffs, and the beam from the lighthouse spread out over the water. She felt isolated. Swamped in a cold sweat as she stood there feeling fear and trepidation. For a few seconds she almost lost consciousness. When she recovered she gave a gasp of dismay. This whole area was scary. What the hell was she doing there? Michael was gone, he should be at peace and he should now leave her in peace.

She took a great breath of salt air into her lungs and called out loudly, 'Michael!' The sound reverberated above the quiet night and the small waves which broke and splashed against the shingle far below.

She listened. No human voice answered her. Only the seagulls, disturbed by the sudden burst of sound, wheeled up overhead calling and screeching. Then all at once they ceased, settling again quietly into the crevices of the cliffs. Her eyes stared out into the distance and her innermost thoughts questioned as to whether Michael could hear her wherever he was.

Words. They were so important and she had come here to say so much. With a great effort she thought of all the happy times she and Michael had shared. With the end of the War things had changed. Perhaps, like a good many more, they had been drunk with sudden freedom. With the madness of war behind them came the beginning of reality. A new lifestyle. Poor living accommodation, not enough money, so many responsibilities. Life had become so different.

Shock of having to fend for themselves, in the forces all decisions had been made for them. Quarrels, laying the blame on each other. More sad days than happy days. She thought again of the love there had been between them in the beginning and all the sweet letters they had written to each other. She thought of their son and the thought brought a lump to her throat and the sting of tears to her eyes. Michael had expected her to abort the baby as she had twice previously. She had stuck to her guns and given him birth only to reject him without ever holding him in her arms. Had that gesture been made as a retaliation against Michael? If so, her own action had been wicked. She shuddered – as if someone has just walked over my grave, she thought, as the saying goes. She put both her hands to her head, tugging her fingers through her hair.

She wished they had never rushed into marriage, it had been as unfair to Michael as to herself. With hindsight it had been a crazy thing to do, but then she had been cooped up in London, hedged in by the air raids, seeing sights that were gruesome while Michael had spent endless days and nights submerged in the depth of foreign seas. On first meeting they had been dazzled by each other. Given a different time and different circumstances – who knows? – they might have made it.

She moved, cramped and cold, and started back to the car. This place was thick with shadows but it wasn't haunted. 'There aren't any ghosts,' she softly said, and knew that she was right. Only sky, stars, grassy hills and the sea below. No ghosts.

As she drove her mother's car back along the country roads, Barbara vowed to close her mind to the past. It was over. A strange feeling came over her: she no longer hated Michael.

Chapter Eleven

BARBARA NOW SET about leading her life with a swiftness that surprised all who knew her. Plunging into a kind of desperate routine. Barbara was suddenly no longer the frightened, subdued young lady who had returned to the safe-haven of Alfriston. She filled her time. Life went on. An endless round of parties and social occasions.

That was the Barbara on public view. The other one was known only to herself and only glimpsed briefly by her parents. She saw a lot of Elizabeth and Tim Holsworthy; how quickly the twins were growing. Barbara often looked at them through tears that stung. How different everything might have been! There were days when she thought she had forgotten – well, almost forgotten – how it might have been.

Goodness only knew, she had tried to forget.

Then there were the days when she tormented herself. What did her little boy look like? Did he have kind and loving parents? Did he have wonderful grandparents? Oh, how her mother and father would have loved and spoilt him. She would feel her heart ache inside her. Don't think of such things. Don't think of what can't be helped, she would fiercely scold herself. If only she could bring herself to tell her mother, yes, and her father too. Lose the whole load of guilt and maybe free her conscience.

Never. No, never. She had made the decision and she had to live with it forever. How could she tell the two people she loved most in the world that she had been callous enough to sign away their grandson without even looking at him?

Patricia Hamlin repeatedly asked herself if Barbara was now happy or was it all a sham. Once she had found her sitting looking out of the window, hands idle in her lap. There was such an expression on her face! Something so set, ferocious and sad! When she had softly spoken to her she started, she had to repeat her words and she saw her blink, shaking her head to bring herself back to the room from wherever she had been.

Both she and her husband still worried about Barbara. They recognised the occasional signs of strain in their daughter, perhaps by an unusual sharpness in her normally composed and gentle voice, or a morbid opinion which Barbara would express openly. They made no comment but it worried them.

We've a lot to be grateful for, she often thought to herself. Barbara does love us both very much. We have no great problems, she and I, we can talk to each other about most things. But she's more attached to her father. He adores her, she's the light of his life. But then, that's the way it often is between fathers and daughters. If only Barbara could put Michael and that episode of her life away at the back of her mind. Blot it out. What sense is there in thinking of what might have been? Or in wondering who should take the blame? No sense, and yet I wonder. I'm still not sure that I have been told the full facts, in fact I'm certain it is what has never been brought out in the open that's playing on Barbara's mind.

Patricia sighed, a long quivering sigh, more like a sob. I

mustn't let myself dwell on what has happened either, she thought. All we can hope is that Barbara will confide in us eventually. Given time, everything would work out all right. Time was a great healer, she assured herself – but without much conviction.

Were they happy times in this post-war era? Barbara did her best to convince herself they were. Carefree and fun, bringing new-found opportunities, but she missed Penny Rayford who was away on a cruise. The new look came in. Hemlines were not now acceptable just below the knee – they had to be lengthened, reaching now well below the calf. Some items in one's wardrobe could be extended, but for Barbara and her friends it was justification to indulge in a shopping spree. Chic elegant suits, with skirts that became known as hobble skirts, jackets with velvet collars. The whole bunch of them spent a great deal of money and never turned a hair. Delicate dainty camiknickers and lace-trimmed, long slips to complement new dresses. Outstanding colourful accessories. The price didn't come into it, but all the same money didn't buy happiness.

Barbara arrived home after midnight from a party. Her mother had gone to bed but her father was reading in the lounge. Barbara came in and curled up on the floor beside his chair. 'Good party?' her father asked, not giving her his full attention. Barbara sighed deeply. Her father looked up and quickly put down his book. 'That sounded ominous,' he said lightly. 'What's the matter, Barbara?'

She laid her hand on his knee. 'Oh, I don't know, Daddy. Well, yes I do. I've made such a mess of my life and now I just can't seem to get things together. There doesn't seem to be any purpose. I don't even enjoy these parties I get invited to. Does that sound silly?'

'No, of course not, my dear. This much I know, Michael disappointed you cruelly and because of that you have become very vulnerable. Given time you will work your own destiny out, but you must try and keep things in perspective. There is no way you can alter the past, but you could make the future a whole lot different if you really tried.'

Barbara smiled at him, 'Daddy, how did you ever become such a wise old bird?'

'Takes a lot of living and a whole lot of practice,' he joked. 'But then I have been blessed with two beautiful women who are fully qualified to keep my life running smoothly.'

'No one could say you've lost your persuasive charm, that's for sure. One thing I will tell you though, you don't have to sit up to all hours waiting for your baby girl to come home.' She said the words softly, letting him know that she appreciated and loved him. 'I'm a big girl now, Father,' she added sternly, 'and you should be in your bed.'

His face creased up with laughter. 'Yes, and so should you, my girl.' He held out his hands to help pull her up and they rose to their feet together.

'Good night, Daddy.'

'Good night, my darling.'

Later, when she was in bed, Barbara lay awake for a long time, musing on her father's good advice.

Barbara stood alone in the lounge, trying to decide how to fill her day. Her mother had gone up to town with her father.

This room never failed to delight her. Beautiful furniture, huge wide open-hearth to the fireplace with its marble surround, but best of all the high, wide windows that reached from floor to ceiling – giving views over the green lawns and flowering shrubs. She thought again of the shabby rooms she and Michael had shared. The smell! She had never got used to that. Should she have tried harder? Many folk had to live in similar places for the whole of their lives.

Maybe she could have coped better if she had been born into different circumstances. God forbid.

'Hallo! Hallo! Anybody home?'

Surprised, Barbara looked up quickly.

The door had opened and there stood Penny Rayford.

'Good Heavens! I didn't expect to see you, when did you get back? Who let you in?'

'Whoa, hold it, one question at a time,' she laughed. 'I came through the grounds, Mrs Clarkson saw me and let me in through the kitchen.' Penny had a happy-go-lucky air about her and, to Barbara, she seemed considerably pleased with herself. She looked so well. Dressed in a beige linen safari-style suit and a brown, cotton, tailored shirt which contrasted so well. Her make-up was perfect, her mouth outlined in bronze coloured lipstick, her soft brown leather shoes had low heels. I shouldn't be so surprised, Barbara thought to herself as she watched Penny cross the floor, Penny is always elegantly attired no matter what the occasion.

'Barbara – oh, Barbara!' The arms of Penny wrapped Barbara in a tight embrace. She rocked her life-long friend for a moment whilst the two of them shed happy tears at their reunion. It had been more than four months since they'd met and though for the life of her Penny would not mention it, she found the change in Barbara, once again, to be shocking.

Penny broke the embrace. 'Enough of this melancholy. I've missed you but now I'm back to remind you life is for the living and life can be wonderful.'

'Yeah, so you say.'

'Yes, I *do* say, so wipe those tears and give me a smile to show you're glad to see me.'

'Penny, you know I am. You are always such an optimist, aren't you? You find the cup half full, you always did.'

'And you find it half empty?'

'Well, often I do.'

Penny gave her a lovely smile, 'Then we must rush to fill it for you, mustn't we?'

The love and vitality of Penny came across strongly to Barbara. She with her air of sophistication, beautiful blue eyes and the bright blonde hair. Undoubtedly she was well-travelled, well-educated, kind and intelligent – despite her devil-may-care attitude – and so loyal to those she loved. When it came down to making an appraisal of Penny, well, she was certainly very different from most people.

'You can't possibly know how glad I am to see you,' Barbara said softly. A tear slid down her cheek, she brushed at it with her hand impatiently. 'Oh, I must stop feeling sorry for myself.'

'Yes you must. Snap out of it. You need company; just as well I decided to invite myself for a few days. I seem to be needed. Now, go upstairs, dress yourself up, meanwhile I'll mix us both a drink. Then, we'll decide where to go for lunch.'

'All right, give me about twenty minutes.' The tone of her voice still sounded strangely subdued.

Penny was thoughtful as she watched Barbara leave the room. It was tragic really. That awful marriage, a sheer disaster. Barbara had certainly had a rough time of it. More so because of the terrible way it had ended.

Anyway, it was over. She would see to it that Barbara now started to live a little. There was still a lot that had happened that Barbara hadn't felt able to talk about, she felt positive about that. All in good time, she rebuked herself, and told herself not to pry.

From that day on both Penny and Barbara had a strange hunger for living. Penny steered Barbara to dinner-parties made up of the eminent and the rich. The wealth had been inherited. That was not an assumption on Barbara's part, just a well known fact. Barbara, having experienced poverty at first hand while living in Battersea, was sometimes embarrassed by the show of riches. In this stream of social waters Barbara was given several opportunities to choose a suitable man to be her second husband. Yes, she cast her eyes over the man allocated to her as an escort, but the bitter truth was she was afraid. She wouldn't allow herself to be interested.

At the insistence of Penny, Barbara was now completely fashion-conscious. Always looking the height of elegance with her expensive dresses and tailored suits. Now her lips and nails were fashionably coloured and her facial make-up included eyeshadow. Her chestnut hair, which had begun to show signs of grey after the last meeting with Michael, was now regularly tinted. The changes in her, however, were only external. Under the veneer of sophistication Barbara was very sensitive. She backed off from forming any lasting new friendships, especially with men.

It was taking far too long for Barbara to come out of the protective shell she had drawn round herself – those were Penny's thoughts on the matter.

Over coffee one morning Penny felt herself become exasperated. The silence between them held faint sadness and she sought for a way to break it. Offend or please – she was going to have to say what was on her mind.

'Honestly Barbara, you're becoming unreal. Half the time beneath all that veneer you look like a ghost. Oh I know you're the life and soul of the party when there's a crowd around you, but let a man come within five yards of you and you run scared. You've got a long time to live yet – a whole life in front of you – you're not being fair to yourself.'

Barbara accepted the telling-off with good grace. Penny only had her well-being at heart. She knew full well that what Penny said was right. She couldn't help it, she preferred not to be left alone with a man, however nice he seemed. She wasn't ready to cope with a compromising situation. Frequently she had been asked out by bachelors and when attending dinner-parties was well aware that her hostess made sure she was seated next to someone supposedly eligible. But always the past came back to taunt her and she reacted against the situation.

Barbara lifted her eyes to the level of her dear friend and in a voice that held a plea asked, 'Why is it so important for me to take up with another man, why can't I just enjoy life?'

'That's just the point,' Penny came quickly back at her. 'You are *not* enjoying life. You're afraid all the time.' More gently now, Penny insisted, 'Barbara, it's easy to see that you're not happy and that makes me unhappy for you.'

'So you think if I took up with one of these chinless wonders you keep producing for me, all my problems would be solved?'

Penny's colour flared up and she made an impatient gesture, 'That's very unfair, Barbara, and you know it.'

'I'm sorry, oh Penny, I wouldn't upset you for the world. I didn't mean to be spiteful, I'm sorry.'

She's still very frightened, Penny thought with a swift burst of sympathy, she's still afraid . . . and yet she tries so hard not to show it.

Barbara's voice cut into her thoughts, 'I've a good mind to give up going to these social functions.'

'You *won't*, you know. You won't do anything of the kind. I won't let you!'

'Well, what do you suggest that I do?'

'You know very well what I think. You should find some suitable man, good family, that sort of thing. Most important though, give yourself a chance, get rid of that deep-seated sense of suspicion. You know, Barbara, there are still some good people left in this world, try trusting your friends.'

Now, in the manner of a woman to whom the past had brought heartache and suffering, Barbara knew the wisdom of Penny's words. It was true. She was distrustful of everyone.

Penny decided to be candid. 'It's still Michael, isn't it? You can't lay him to rest can you?'

Barbara turned her head away.

'To this day I've never been able to fathom out why you

stayed with him, let things go so far. Neither of you were happy.'

'Well Penny, there's no easy answer to that.' She drew a deep breath, sighing to herself, trying to find the right words without disclosing awful details that she had vowed she would tell to no one. 'I won't pretend that I'm proud of that period of my life, you know well enough I'm not. You have also made a good guess that when it comes to the truth I have ever only told my parents and you half of what really did take place. Now I'm not sure I could make you understand if I wanted to.'

'Try me,' Penny quietly suggested.

If only she dare! Unleash all her guilt into Penny's sympathetic ear. It would be better than telling her parents. *No!* Even now she couldn't bring herself to tell a living soul that she had not only been raped by her husband but that he had encouraged his mate to take a turn at her as payment for beer which they had drunk together and for which her husband couldn't pay his share. The baby? That was another matter altogether. She couldn't, she wouldn't even think about that. Not in broad daylight. Those thoughts were her own, that only came out of the deep recess of her mind in the darkest hours of the night.

Barbara waved her hands angrily, 'It all went so wrong.'

Again a silence settled between them, Penny had no answer to that. Their half-drunk cups of coffee stood on the table, cold and curdled, unwanted.

It was some time before Penny could bring herself to move. Barbara's face was so sad. She leaned forward, peering at Barbara intently. It was curious the way Barbara's thoughts always reflected in her face. It made one's heart ache just to look at her. Penny leant across the table and grasped Barbara's hand in a gesture of warm affection. 'We both seem to be suffering a fit of the blues. Come on now, buck up. Just promise me one thing, not to shy away from life anymore.'

Barbara nodded. The sad look on Barbara's face made Penny want to put out her arms to her, she wanted to hold her, she wanted her to open up and talk to her, tell her exactly what had happened in those last days before she had finally found the courage to leave Michael. Most of all she wanted Barbara to stop bottling up her secrets – to tell her about the baby. Had she given birth? Had she been driven to having an abortion? So many questions that she knew she'd get no answers to, so what she said was, 'Promise me you will try, please?'

'I'll try, Penny. You shouldn't worry about me so much.'

And the glance they exchanged now was full of understanding and simultaneously they reached for each other.

This friendship between them was very valuable.

Chapter Twelve

THE WHOLE COUNTRY was intoxicated. Everywhere there was a sense of anticipation and excitement, for this was 1953, Coronation Year. The War was long over, men had died in their hundreds and thousands, yet life had continued. The wealthy kept their place in society while the working classes fought for jobs, higher pay and better conditions. For the moment there was no resentment. People had found a common cause in which they were united. Queen Elizabeth II was to be crowned in a ceremony that for the first time millions would be able to see on a television screen.

For the past three years Barbara and Penny had been inseparable. They had taken river boat rides from Tower Bridge, toured museums and Madame Tussaud's – the famous waxwork show in Baker Street. Obtained tickets for every first night West End theatre showing. Been twice to see *Gone with the Wind*; each had come away from the film with the longing to find a real life Rhett Butler for themselves. Afternoon tea was taken either at the Ritz or the Savoy. They were constantly seen wherever it was socially important to be.

The company of these two young ladies provided a challenge to many of the best hostesses in the land. Their time was fully engaged and on the surface Barbara appeared to be enjoying life to the full, though her mother still often thought her frivolous attitude was feigned.

The pursuits of the two of them were the talk of Sussex. Not everyone was charitable when voicing their opinions. Awful rumours reached Phillip and Patricia Hamlin about the way Barbara and her friend Penny carried on, drinking to excess, noisy late parties, gambling heavily at race meetings, driving at speeds well above the law. Moving in circles neither set of parents approved of. Many a time Patricia shivered with apprehension. Her own daughter, did she really get up to bad things? She wished often that Barbara would abandon this whirl of self-indulgence.

Phillip Hamlin, still a wealthy man, ignored the rumours. Whatever had happened between Barbara and Michael, he knew the damage inflicted on his daughter was considerable. Her periodically horrific nightmares alone were proof and for that very reason he made great allowances for her behaviour. He denied her nothing.

Now June 2nd would provide the most brilliant social event of their lives. Princess Elizabeth, eldest daughter of King George VI and Queen Elizabeth, was to be crowned Queen of England. Despite the weather being cold and wet, thousands had camped overnight in The Mall. Stands had been erected along most of the route. Tickets for these seats had changed hands on the black market for vast sums of money, while more than a million people stood shoulder to shoulder, most of whom had waited up all night to catch a glimpse of their young Queen.

Thanks to Phillip's influence the Hamlins were asked to join a party in offices which boasted a balcony to the front of the building. A choice site overlooking the route. Inside the premises a television set had been installed in the main office, giving these privileged people the best of both worlds. Included in the party were Penny and her parents. Penny and Barbara were among the young folk who leaned low over the balcony to cheer the royal party on its way to Westminster Abbey. Then, thanks to the television, they were able to see Queen Elizabeth II crowned. The television cameras showed the crowned heads of all Europe looking seemingly impressed as the roar of the crowds outside announced the arrival of the young Queen.

It was a ritual going back centuries but with all the pomp and splendour of the greatest royal occasions. Everyone agreed the television set was marvellous. It enabled them to see in detail the Archbishop of Canterbury place the crown on Elizabeth's head, then watch as she was invested with the robes and emblems of high office.

'Rather her than me,' Barbara sighed as she watched men kneel to pay homage to the new Queen. 'She looks so young and kind of lost.'

'Oh, I don't know,' Penny chirped up, 'I wouldn't mind having a go at it for a while. Imagine the power one would have.'

'That's just it,' Elizabeth Holsworthy laughed. 'It's like getting married, isn't it Tim? You can't have a go at it just for a while, especially not if you find yourself with twin boys. Being Queen is like becoming a mother, it's a job for life. More so in the Queen's case. She has the whole British Empire as her family.'

This statement caught Barbara on the raw, even more so as she watched Tim Holsworthy look tenderly at his wife and say, 'Well, if Prince Philip is blessed with as much good fortune as we have been, he won't have gone far wrong, will he?'

'Whoa! Serious, serious!' This exclamation came from

one of the young lawyers who had helped swell their numbers today, and all the young folk laughed.

Back outside, crushed together on the balcony, the older men opened bottles of champagne. 'Long live the Queen!' was the toast they drank to and this was echoed around the street parties in the suburbs and towns of all England, while the crowds who had poured into London roared their approval as their newly invested Queen rode in the golden coach back to the Palace.

Afterwards the Hamlins and several mutual friends had been invited to a party given by Jane and Stephen Mortimer in their lovely old house in Hampstead. Stephen was a judge and most of the male guests were members of the legal profession. Champagne flowed, food was plentiful and delicious. Talk was mainly of the glittering pageantry that they had witnessed in London today. Every man present was of the opinion that no other country in the world could accomplish such a magnificent show as well as the British.

Barbara was surrounded by women, all talking loudly. She looked away to where her father stood and wondered – with so many brilliant young men in the company today, was he thinking of her two brothers? He never deliberately avoided talking about them, yet on the other hand he never entered into a conversation should her brothers be the topic under discussion. Surely he must have so many regrets, she thought now, this room is filled with men who have pursued their education to such lengths in order to be qualified to plead cases in the high courts and Daddy has no one to follow in his footsteps – no one he can encourage and pass on his knowledge to. What she saw was a vigorous man in a well-cut grey suit, a kind and loving man where she was concerned. He was in good shape. Didn't look his age. He hadn't run to fat like a good many of his older colleagues had.

He must have felt Barbara's eyes on him for he turned his head, caught her glance and immediately smiled and beckoned her to come over, 'Barbara, dear, I would like to introduce you to James Ferguson, an up-and-coming young man – unless I am very much mistaken. James, this is my daughter Barbara.'

The colour flooded into Barbara's cheeks and what she wanted to cry out was, Oh no, not you Daddy! With everyone else having a go at match making, doing their best to see that I'm always paired off with a suitable young man, I don't need you to start.

Instead she held out her hand and raised her eyes to meet the clearest blue eyes she had ever seen. James Ferguson was not handsome, more the rugged type, with fair hair and a fair complexion. He was in his early thirties, with the assurance of wealthy parents and position charmingly concealed by an attractive good nature and perfect manners.

'I really am very pleased to meet you, Barbara,' he said and taking her hand between the both of his, he raised it to his lips and kissed her fingers. There was to be no standing on ceremony with this man! Her pulse in her wrist was beating hard, hastily she withdrew her hand hoping James hadn't had a chance to notice this.

Placing an arm around Barbara's shoulders, her father bent his head and, speaking softly, he said to her, 'I'm going to mingle a bit. Should really go and have a chat with Stephen, it was awfully good of him to lay all of this on.'

'Your father is a great man,' James stated as he bent towards her. 'Feared by many when he has them at his mercy in a court room. Can't say I've ever felt the wrong side of his tongue, quite the reverse — he has been very valuable to me as I've slogged to climb the slippery slope. Unstinting in both help and advice.'

Barbara felt he was only talking so fast to put her at ease and she appreciated his efforts.

'If you want to go and join the men, please don't feel you have to stay.' Her words sounded stilted even to her own ears, 'I should go and find my mother.'

He threw back his head and laughed. 'Oh dear, have we got off on the wrong foot or are you usually this hostile — or perhaps it is only us legal beadles that ruffle your feathers?'

Barbara had the good grace to murmur, 'I'm sorry.'

'Not at all. I was rather foisted on you, but it is a day for celebrations so what say I fetch us both something to drink and we'll see how we go from there. Yes?'

Despite her attempt to be aloof Barbara found herself smiling. And her answer to this was simply, 'Thank you.'

'There! See! It isn't so difficult to be friendly with the natives, is it?' Without waiting for her reply he moved away and Barbara was left to ponder on this lively young man, who seemed so determined to be friendly.

From across the room Penny had been watching. She found the situation easy to read. James was smitten and Barbara now seemed sufficiently at ease to allow her to hope that something good might come from their meeting.

They talked as they sipped their drinks and Barbara was surprised to find that she really was enjoying his company. How could she put it to herself? Well, James was easy to be with and, yes, if she was honest, she didn't want him to go away.

They became aware of talk and movement in the room. People began saying their goodbyes, hugs and kisses, promises to phone one another, meet again soon. The day was coming to an end.

'My folks live at Eastbourne, quite near you isn't it?'

'Yes it is,' Barbara agreed.

'I shall be coming down at the weekend. Do you ride?'

'Yes I do,' she was studying his face as she answered.

'Then we'll meet on the bridle path, foot of the Downs, Sunday morning, eight a.m. sharp.'

There was no sign of nervousness in Barbara now as she smiled with pleasure.

Walking to their car her father grinned to himself, her mother kissed her warmly, hugging her with affection, and Barbara found herself looking forward to the weekend and wondering how a stranger could so quickly become a friend.

It was three weeks before Barbara really let herself think about how happy she was. Life as a whole had suddenly become good. People were good – especially James. There was a longing inside her for this relationship to be a lasting one. Whether it would turn out to be, well, that was another question. It was a quarter to eleven on this Tuesday morning and she was alone in the house. Seated on her low stool, knees tucked under her kidney-shaped dressing table, she had her elbows resting on the glass top and her chin cupped in her hands.

She stared at her reflection in the mirror and sighed. She was twenty-nine-years-old. Old enough to know her own mind. But did she? Her love for Michael had been instantaneous, or so she had thought at the time, and how quickly that love had turned to hate, even fear. Did she know the difference between love and infatuation?

Here in the safety and comfort of this lovely house, the serenity of not having to worry about money, the caring love of both her parents, and the sweet smelling air of Sussex, yes, she had to admit that there were times when she could completely blot out the episode of life lived in two rooms in Battersea. She didn't hate Michael any more. Hate was a useless emotion, more so when directed at a person who was no longer alive. But he had sent her to hell and back. Twice. That fact would be with her for as long as she lived. Reaching out she picked up her silver-backed hairbrush and began slowly to brush her hair. Nodding at her mirror image she felt the anger rise in her.

'You're too hard on yourself,' she said aloud. 'You put up with everything that Michael dared to dish out for so long because you hadn't the guts to admit you'd made a mistake and walk out. Michael treated you in a manner that no man should – many a man has been sent to prison for less. So let me remind you that you stood enough from that marriage to make you bitter, but by now you have found out that being bitter doesn't get you anywhere. Nor does putting on a brave front and letting the world think that you don't give a damn for anyone but yourself.

'You've been offered a second chance, well maybe not quite that yet, but at least a friendship with a decent man, a man from a good family, so what are you going to do about it?' She laid down her hairbrush, stood up and went to stand at the window, to stare out over the beautiful grounds. She thought for a moment with sadness, how different her life might have been if she had never met Michael. When the War was over she would have come home, lived a privileged life, mixed with all the right people, fallen in love with a suitable man, and perhaps had two or three children by now. Instead, what had happened to her?

'Oh, enough of this talking to yourself, what is the good of keeping harping on the past and what might have been. It isn't going to do you any good, surely you've learnt that by now?' She knew that, if she allowed it, love for James could easily grow. But would it turn sour with time, be as savagely painful as it had been with Michael?

Did anyone really have a say in their own lives? Or was it God that ordered and set the pattern? She didn't know, but whoever it was it seemed one had no choice but to go through with it. But that didn't alter the fact that sometimes you were given more than you could bear, and when good times cropped up why was it that one felt so frightened, fearful that this was not for real, that it wouldn't last? Should one grab an opportunity to be happy, to form a relationship – knowing full well that there were no guarantees to be had? Already, in James she half-believed she'd found the man who could bring her happiness. One who could wipe out the nightmares from her mind. To be honest, she admitted, she felt the physical pull whenever she was near to James. In these few short weeks she had only met him at weekends and yet she was fascinated with this sophisticated man who led an exciting busy life and promised her a wonderful future – if only she had the courage to reach out and take hold of it.

Chapter Thirteen

AT THE LAST minute her parents remembered that they had a previous engagement and Barbara would have to be hostess alone to James Ferguson. It was a thinly veiled excuse. They might have been more open about it, Barbara smiled to herself. As if it would make any difference! It was just one more try to throw them together. Her father was always praising his brilliance, indeed he had prayed that such a man might come into her life. She knew that. She only hoped that James wasn't offended: he was by no means stupid, he would surely know what they were doing.

She was afraid. They had been together, but never exactly alone, except when riding and that was slightly different. What would they talk about during the meal and then there would be the long evening . . .

Mrs Clarkson put her head around the door, 'I've seen to the melon; soup only needs heating; salad, ham and chicken already in the fridge.'

'Thanks, Mrs Clarkson, but I'm not looking forward to this dinner one bit.'

'Good heavens, why ever not? You should be over the moon. He's a real nice man, your Mr Ferguson. I took a liking to him the first time he came to this house. It were when you were so ill, he was a great comfort to your father. Apparently he took on a lot of your father's cases. I'm telling you, you've got a good one there.'

'I didn't know about that. I like him, too. I just feel

awkward, as if Daddy is thrusting me onto him. It was him that invited James here for tonight, wasn't it?'

'Never mind about who invited him, he's coming an' like I've told you he likes you, I could tell he did. I bet he'll be ever so glad to have you all to himself. You'll see.'

'I hope you're right.'

'Course I am. Well, I'm off now. Relax, enjoy yourself, I'll see you tomorrow,' and as she closed the door Mrs Clarkson muttered to herself, 'God above knows you deserve a bit of happiness, my love. If anybody does, you do.'

Barbara didn't know why she felt so nervous. It might be rather nice to have dinner alone with James. So why did such a simple thing seem so difficult?

'What's that scent I can smell?' James asked when she opened the front door in answer to his ring.

'It's pinks. My mother planted a whole heap of them under that hedge.' Barbara turned on the outside light though it was not yet quite dark: the pink, white and deep red of these heavily-scented flowers made a pretty show. 'They smell very much like cloves, I always think. My mother loves the old-fashioned cottage type of flowers.'

James said quietly, 'It seems so peaceful out here, even Eastbourne seems miles away. Do you really know how wonderful this home of yours is?'

'Oh, yes.' She answered too quickly. There was no way in which she could explain to him exactly how and why she appreciated her home and parents as much as she did. 'It is a lovely house, isn't it?'

'I didn't mean the house. I meant your wonderful parents. Warm, good people. Gentle, caring people. Losing

220

two sons would have turned many a soul bitter, but not them.'

'I think they comfort each other, kind of anticipating the needs of each other. It's not only that, of course. But that's part of it and the main thing is that they love each other.' Now she felt embarrassed as she looked into those clear blue eyes, but he wasn't talking for the sake of talking: he really did have a great admiration for her father and her mother, and she felt herself drawn to him.

'Will you pour us both a drink?' she asked as they walked into the lounge, 'I'll have a sherry but there is plenty of whisky there so, please, do help yourself.'

With his drink in his hand, James walked to the end of the room, picked up a book from a side-table, glanced at it and replaced it. 'Are you happy now Barbara?' The question was out of the blue and caught her entirely unawares. She was astonished, unable to form an answer.

'Forgive me. That was out of order. I feel a great deal of distress when I think how very ill you were only a short time ago and, since I have come to know you, your happiness and well being do mean a great deal to me. I wasn't meaning to pry, you do know that don't you?'

Barbara was suddenly aware that he knew a good deal more about her than she did about him.

'I don't mind answering your question,' she said shyly. 'Yes, I am very much happier now that I live at home.'

'So? What are you interested in? What do you aim to do with the rest of your life?'

'Well, one thing's for sure – I can't continue on this perpetual round of gaiety. Every day wasted, frittered away, there has to be more to life than an endless round of parties and race-meetings. I think I would like to work with children. Children that aren't very well cared for. Children that need help. I don't know exactly what I could do – offer my services to some organisation, perhaps one that deals with handicapped children . . .' She was talking too much, and she finished abruptly, 'I guess I really want to do something useful, only I don't know what.'

'You can be very solemn at times,' James said thoughtfully. 'I know a lot about your childhood, how you grew up here, in this house and where you went to school, but very little else. Tell me about your Red Cross work during the War.'

'I was a driver. At times it was dangerous and dirty, often very sad. But then again we had our moments and a good many laughs. Did you know there were the three of us? Elizabeth, Penny and myself. We thought we were so grown-up. We knew it all. Had our own flat in Putney.'

Why was she talking so much? This man drew the words from her.

'Since my father went to such lengths to contrive that we should be alone, I think we had better go and eat this meal.'

They looked at each other and burst out laughing, and then James's laughter broke off. He stared at her. 'You're the most extraordinary girl!'

'I'm not. I happen to be able to see through my Dad's schemes, that's all.'

He stood up and came to where she was sitting. He took her hands and pulled her lightly to her feet, 'Barbara, I'm going to say this right out while I have the courage. I want to see a great deal more of you. I want us to become close. Can you think of a good reason why we shouldn't be?'

She didn't answer. She hung her head.

'Because I think we get on so well together. I don't know about you, but I haven't felt so happy to be with someone, or so much at ease like this for a long time.'

Was it possible? Could it be she was to have a second chance? Would things work out between them or – like before – would it all go so terribly wrong? Still she didn't answer.

He put his hand beneath her chin, forcing her face up. She looked into his eyes, which were gentle and kind. She saw he meant every word he had said.

Her eyes filled with tears.

He pulled her closer and kissed her forehead. 'I don't know what that means,' he whispered. 'Does it mean yes or no?'

'I think . . . I think it means yes,' she murmured, doing her best to keep back the tears.

'Barbara, that's great. I hoped so much you felt the same way but I had to be so careful not to rush you.' He pulled out his handkerchief and dried her eyes, 'No need for tears, we'll have a terrific time, I promise we will.'

She nodded, laughed, and still a tear rolled down her cheek. She wanted to explain why she was crying, because she had half hoped this might happen and yet feared that it never would. Because she was almost thirty years old, because she had made such a mess of her life. Because she and Michael had been so wrong for each other. Because he had died so tragically. Because she had a son somewhere, a son she would never see, never hold in her arms. And now James was offering her a new start, maybe a happy future. With him.

The meal was a success. They were comfortable with

each other and their laughter rang all through the house as they talked away nineteen to the dozen.

'Black or white?' Barbara asked, as she came back from the kitchen carrying a tray on which she had set out the coffee things.

'Is it milk or cream?'

'Only milk I'm afraid, there didn't seem to be any cream in the fridge.'

'That's good. I like my coffee half an' half, made with boiling milk.'

'That's funny, that's the way I prefer it and I did boil the milk – it's in that separate jug.'

'We shall get to know all these little preferences. We have a lot to learn about each other, don't we Barbara? And, by the way, I think a very good time to start finding out such things would be at Henley.'

'Henley?' She raised her eyebrows in question.

'Yes, Henley Regatta, it's the principal rowing event in England. The best oarsmen from all over the world come to Henley-on-Thames for this event every July. You *must* have heard of it.'

'Of course I've heard of it – I was even there on one occasion – but when you said "Henley", just like that out of the blue, I didn't catch your meaning.'

'My meaning, Barbara dear, is to have you to myself for a whole weekend. Well, not exactly to myself, my whole family will be there but I'm sure we'll be able to give them the slip at some point or other. Say you'll come, please.'

Barbara was almost ashamed of the joy she felt as she listened to his enthusiasm. She hadn't been this happy for so long.

'The weekend will be very informal,' he was saying, with

224

laughter in his voice. 'It will be a great chance to get to know each other better. My mother arranges marvellous picnics. My sister Chloe told me a long time ago I should pay more attention to you. You want to know something? I think she was right.'

'Barbara, relax,' James scolded as he negotiated a roundabout on the outskirts of Henley. 'We're going to have a great weekend.'

'Do your parents know you're bringing me?' she asked for the third time.

'They know,' he said patiently. 'They're all looking forward to meeting you. They will love you.' He took one hand from the steering wheel and squeezed Barbara's hand in reassurance.

'James, I want them to like me. Do they know anything about me?'

'Only that you were married a long time ago, your husband died and for a while you were very ill. No more than that.'

He drove slowly now along the road that ran parallel with the Thames. It had been a lovely hot day. Too hot. The breeze coming from off the river felt marvellous and the sun, not yet set, still glimmered on the water.

'I'll have to park up at the back of the house,' James told her as he slowed the car down. 'You won't see the beauty of the house until we are inside. Its frontage runs right down to the river's edge. It belongs to my grandfather, much too big for him now, more so since my grandmother died, but he'll die before he thinks of parting with it and I can't say that I blame him. See what you think.'

The door stood wide open and as they crossed the

grass they heard the sound of laughter inside. 'Seems we've arrived in time for dinner,' James grinned as he sniffed the savoury aromas of roasting meat and fresh baking which filtered out into the hallway.

Waiting to greet them was a small, fair-haired lady. Barbara knew instantly it was James's mother.

'Mother, this is Barbara, Barbara Hamlin.'

'We're all so pleased that you accepted our invitation to spend the weekend with us and even the weather is set fine for you.'

In minutes Barbara was surrounded by James's father, his sister Ann, and her five-year-old twins Harry and Lucy. 'Are you Uncle James's girlfriend?' Harry asked, giving her a cheeky grin.

'It's rude to ask things like that, isn't it, Mummy?' And without waiting for an answer Lucy added, 'I think you're very pretty.'

Everyone laughed.

'Thank you, Lucy.' Impulsively Barbara bent down and hugged her.

'Where's Chloe and Roddy?' James looked around.

'I'm here, have you got a kiss for your baby sister?' James moved forward to kiss a taller, younger edition of his mother.

Chloe came towards Barbara when James released her, arms outstretched. 'I really am pleased you're here,' she said, giving Barbara a hug. 'I know your father. Well, perhaps I shouldn't say *know*, rather know *of*, but I do admire him. I made a point of going to the Old Bailey every day for two weeks when your father was acting for the defence. The whole trial fascinated me. Your father is an absolute wizard.'

'Are we going to stand in this entrance hall for the whole night? I'm starving.'

Lucy, a bundle of energy, darted to the side of a grey-haired, tall, broad-shouldered man, took hold of his large hand and announced, 'This is our Great-Grandfather Ferguson.'

'And this is Uncle James's girlfriend,' piped up Harry.

Lucy giggled as her grandfather scooped her up in his arms.

In a few minutes James's brother Rodney and his wife Elaine appeared. There was no mistaking that James and Rodney were brothers; alike as two peas in a pod, Barbara thought as she watched them slap each other on the back. His wife, Elaine, was taller than the Ferguson women and had very dark hair swept up at the back and fixed with a comb. The welcome they gave to Barbara was spontaneous and she liked them both, sensing that they would be fun to be with. After introductions had been made, Mrs Ferguson ordered everyone to the table.

To Barbara the sense of affection that surrounded the dining room was incredible. Under the table James reached for her hand. From that moment she had a feeling of belonging.

'So, Dad, tell us what you're doing with yourself these days?' James asked. 'Are you enjoying retirement?'

Mr Ferguson's eyes met his wife's. 'Forget about retiring,' he chuckled. 'That's like saying you've finished with life and are waiting to die. With a wife like I've got I will never be idle.' He spoke directly to Barbara. 'What with all the committee and charity work, the children, whom she still thinks aren't able to fend for themselves, and the grand-children, I'm never allowed a moment's peace – never mind a day on the golf course. No other man would put up with it, I'm telling you!'

Barbara looked to where Mrs Ferguson was sitting, a sweet smile hovering around her lips, and she decided that James's mother came into the same category as her own mother. They were two of life's real ladies.

'I'm one of Grandad's children, aren't I, Dad?' Young Harry shot the question to a thickset man who had just entered the room.

'Sorry I'm so late, bit hectic in Fleet Street today,' he said. Making towards Ann, he bent over her shoulder and kissed her cheek.

'My son-in-law, Jack Tully,' Mr Ferguson nodded towards Barbara. 'You'll have gathered he's my daughter's husband and, for his sins, a newspaper editor.'

'Pleased to meet you,' Jack put out a hand to Barbara. 'Have my nippers been driving you mad?'

'That lady is Uncle James's girlfriend!' Harry had no intention of being ignored.

'You are a precocious brat, Harry, an' I'll deal with you later,' Ann said loudly her cheeks turning red. 'I do apologise, Barbara.'

'No need,' Barbara quickly assured her and then she laughed. Her laughter was contagious and soon everyone was chuckling.

By the time dinner was over, Barbara felt exhilarated. She had been accepted by James's loving family.

'I want to take you to a party,' James said, as they left the dining room. 'You have just one hour in which to tog yourself up, then I'm going to show you off. The party is being held on board a boat that belongs to a colleague of mine, Peter Bradley. You'll like him.'

Fifty minutes later Barbara came down the stairs. She was wearing a loose shift dress of pale green, with two long strands of coral beads. As she moved, the necklace caught the lights and glittered in multicolour. The events of the day seemed to have released the tension within her. James couldn't take his eyes off her. How nice to see Barbara so happy, he thought, and then what he exclaimed was, 'Barbara, you look stunning!'

'Why, thank you,' she answered, flashing him a sudden, radiant smile that instantly transformed her normal sad-looking face.

They strolled along the tow-path, James's hand at her elbow. The boats looked marvellous, gleaming and sparkling against the grassy banks. Their woodwork glowed and the brass shone.

Barbara looked flushed and excited as she climbed aboard the long sleek craft whose name on the side showed it to be *Special Lady*.

James led her down a narrow corridor that was rich with the smell of polish. At the end was the saloon. The room was crowded and alive with a medley of raised voices. Almost everyone held a glass.

'Jamie!' A tall broad-shouldered man with the kind of astounding good looks one normally associated with sports-men, was striding towards them, shouldering aside groups of guests who were in his way.

'Jamie,' he repeated as he drew level, 'you made it, I was beginning to think you weren't going to.'

'Wouldn't miss a bout of your hospitality for the world, Peter, you know that. And in any case I wanted to introduce you to Barbara, Barbara Hamlin; this is my work-shy companion, Peter Bradley.'

His teeth flashed as he smiled at her and took her hand between both of his, holding onto it for far too long.

She heard James laugh once, a burst of amusement. As for herself, she took in his immaculate white trousers, shirtsleeves rolled high revealing strong suntanned arms, and she thought this friend of James was almost too good to be true. A steward offered a glass of champagne to each of them, then, out of the blue Peter asked, 'And are you two thinking of living happily ever after?'

'Ah!' James pondered. 'That remains to be seen, time will tell. This is damn fine champagne – drink up Barbara, Peter can well afford it!'

Barbara shot a glance towards James, he winked and she laughed.

'I get the message,' Peter said, flickering his eyes to take in the two of them. 'Taboo subject at the moment, is it? Well, my topper and morning suit are available when you decide to tie the knot. Meanwhile, enjoy yourselves, only just make sure you're both sober enough to watch me row to victory tomorrow.'

Enjoy themselves they did. Much more than Barbara would have thought possible. To dance with James was like moving in a dream. His arms about her, his footsteps light, she was happier tonight than she had ever thought she would be again.

James was unsure of himself. He stood very close to Barbara as they leaned against the rail and looked out over the water. To date he had never found anyone who met his criterion of an ideal wife: that was the only reason he had never married. He hadn't led a celibate life. He'd enjoyed several affairs, which had been accepted by both parties as temporary and without obligation. That was not what he wanted now. He wanted Barbara. Something in the past had frightened her, he would give a lot to know the details. She was like a young fawn, go too close and she would cringe away. He would have to tread very carefully.

An inky blackness had settled over the river, but on either bank small boats and large yachts bobbed at their moorings. Threads of light from the portholes wove a pattern of ribbons in the fast flowing water.

'Fascinating, isn't it?' James asked as he slid his arm around her waist.

'Yes,' she murmured. 'Absolutely beautiful.'

'Time we made tracks,' he whispered. 'Should be a good day tomorrow.'

Barbara felt sure that it would be.

James stowed the oars, letting the boat dance of its own will. There was something different about him today and it disturbed Barbara. The weekend had been glorious, brilliant sunshine, blue skies and wonderful company. The weather had been ideal for the Regatta. The chief races had drawn the crowds and the Ferguson family had had the advantage of being able to watch from their upstairs balcony which looked directly down onto the river.

The loudest cheers, in Barbara's opinion, had been for the Ladies Challenge Cup. The fashions displayed by the young women and men alike had amused her and at the same time fascinated her. Everywhere there had been bright colours. With the dreary War years not so far behind, it had made an unusual, and sometimes comical, spectacular show.

The boat bobbed. James leaned forward in his seat and took hold of Barbara's hand. A funny look came to James's face. Barbara thought he looked as if something had upset him. 'Barbara, have you been happy being here with my family?'

She knew that if she were to answer her voice would come out very strange. There was a pain in her throat and her eyes were stinging like mad. She didn't want to cry. She was too happy for that, but how could she convey that to James?

For a while James didn't say anything. Then he began to talk in that way he had which was so gentle, as if he were almost talking to himself and not expecting any answers. 'I realise I know very little of what happened to you. This much I do know, if I could erase those bad memories, which seem to haunt you, from your mind I would. For what seems to me a very long time I have loved you. You don't have to say anything, I've seen you on the edge of tears whenever anyone speaks kindly to you. If you should ever, at any time, feel you are able to talk to me I want you to know that I will always be there. You don't have to tell me that your first marriage was a nightmare, that much I've worked out for myself. You've had more trouble than most. More than your fair share. It's about time there was a little happiness in your life. I hope I can be the one to help you find it.'

It was too much. Suddenly she was crying like a child, sobbing, her breath coming in gasps. James was so kind. So good. She didn't deserve him, she could never bring herself to tell him that she had given up her own son for adoption. Could she?

In a little while she felt a handkerchief being thrust into her hand. She wiped her nose and eyes, and looked up. 'If I could talk to anyone it would be you.'

James didn't answer right away. Instead, he took the oars and the boat sprang ahead. They had to bow their heads under a low sweep of willows, and in this hidden cool dark place at the water's edge he put the oars down again. The boat gently rocked.

Suddenly Barbara began to speak and in seconds the words came rushing out, 'James, if there is to be any chance for us you should know the truth. I don't know any other way to tell you but like this. I was pregnant. Michael abused me and stood by watching while his mate raped me.

'It was the end. I couldn't take any more aggression. I left him. I was in a home for unmarried mothers and women with problems until the birth. I never saw the baby, I couldn't bring myself to look at him. I only know it was a boy because I heard a nurse say so.' Never once had she raised her eyes to look at him, and her words were spoken so softly James had to strain to hear them.

Minutes ticked by as James watched her struggle to speak further. Tears burnt at the back of his eyes but he knew he had to stay still, say nothing, until Barbara had finished.

With what seemed a great effort, Barbara took a deep breath and began to talk again. 'At the time I thought any life would be better than the one I could give him. I thought I would never be able to love him, every time I looked at him I would have been reminded of his father. I couldn't stand the thought of what that would do to a small child. I signed adoption papers.'

There! She had done what she had sworn she never would. She had told someone. But James wasn't just someone. Would he understand? Or would he now despise her? Loathe the sight of her?

She covered her face with her hands. Unable to look at

James. There were no tears now, she doubted that there were any left inside of her. She gave a long shudder and then sat perfectly still.

'Oh, Barbara!' His voice was so sad it tore at her heart-strings. 'You went through all of that on your own! You've never told a soul?'

She shook her head without looking up.

There was a long silence until he leant forward, putting his face on a level with hers. 'Barbara, you have to come to terms with the fact that you made the right decision. At the time no other choice was open to you. You are the one that was sinned against. If you don't believe that, you'll drive yourself crazy.'

'I suppose you think I should have told you before now?' Now Barbara was thinking out loud, 'I wouldn't blame you if you decided to have nothing more to do with me.'

Beyond the screen of foliage a motorboat shot by, rocking the quiet water. Still neither of them spoke. James was searching his mind for the right words to use to break the silence and to tell Barbara he loved her to such lengths that at that moment he would gladly kill for her. The bastard! What if her father had known this! It was better that he didn't!

'Barbara, I want to say just one thing and I want you to remember that it is the truth. Will you do that, no matter what?'

She nodded.

James still had tears in his eyes as he said, 'I love you, Barbara and I always will.'

Minutes passed, then James bent to the oars and began to row, parting the green-coloured curtain of leaves. They came out into the sunlight that still sparkled on the water.

The boat drew up at the dock with a soft bump and James stepped ashore and tied the rope. They walked hand-in-hand across the lawn towards the house.

'You will remember what I said, Barbara? I mean it. From now on I shall devote my life to making you happy and perhaps one day you will feel able to put the past behind you.'

They had reached the house. Barbara forced herself to smile. James straightened up, and with one hand resting on Barbara's shoulder, they walked towards where the family were sitting.

Chapter Fourteen

IT WAS FOUR o'clock on a Tuesday afternoon in the first week of August, hot and sticky, the pavements burning the bottom of their feet through the soles of their shoes.

'I think we must have been in and out of every shop in the West End,' Penny sighed. 'Please, girls, let's call it a day and find somewhere to park our behinds before I fall to the ground in a dead faint.'

Elizabeth looked at Barbara, and they both laughed. 'Aren't you the cheeky one?' Elizabeth complained. 'Barbara and I were for stopping for lunch hours ago, but no, you had to try on one more outfit and then one more pair of shoes and now you're the one that's moaning about being dead beat.'

'Okay, it's too damned hot to argue. Here – grab some of these bags, stay where you are and I'll try and flag down a taxi for us.'

Elizabeth and Barbara had no option but to stay put. Despite the hot weather the pavements around Regent Street were thronged with shoppers and now the pair of them were surrounded by parcels.

'I've told the driver we're going to The Wayfarers, is that all right?' Penny asked as she picked up some of their purchases and herded them to the waiting taxi.

'I wouldn't care if it was Joe's café, as long as they serve long cold drinks,' Barbara muttered as she sank back gratefully into the cushioned seat.

The coolness of the restaurant and the camaraderie of the ladies in their summer-suits and dresses was infinitely preferable to tramping through any more stores. A plump, amiable waitress in her forties led them to a long table set in the recess of a bay window. 'Salads?' queried Elizabeth.

'Yes,' they all agreed. 'And long, cold fruit juices with loads of ice, please.'

'Are you sure you're all right, Elizabeth?' Penny asked, suddenly showing concern.

'Of course I am. Being pregnant isn't an illness, though I will admit this hot weather does tend to sap my energy.'

'Well, I haven't noticed you dropping behind,' Barbara said kindly.

'No, and I think I've spent an absolute fortune, nearly as much as Penny has.'

'Why pick on me,' Penny laughed loudly. 'Neither of you needed any encouragement to spend. Anyway, how long since the three of us had such a binge?'

'Elizabeth certainly looks well, doesn't she, Penny?' Barbara asked as she smiled at her friend.

'She most certainly does. Be quite the little mother with a brood of three, bet you are hoping for a girl this time?'

'I am, but Tim wouldn't mind another boy, I just hope he hasn't any ideas of forming his own rugby club.'

They all three giggled. It was true: pregnancy did suit Elizabeth. She was blooming, her freckled face was faintly tanned by the recent good weather but pregnancy had also given her skin a fine glow of health.

'What about you two?' Elizabeth asked briskly. 'Leaving it a bit late to start a family, aren't you? No sound of wedding bells in either direction from what I can make out, lost all those feminine wiles in your old age?'

They were prevented from answering by their waitress, who, having cleared away their plates, was now setting glass bowls filled with fresh fruit salad and topped with thick clotted cream in front of each of them.

'Umm, lovely,' they chorused.

Some minutes passed before Barbara took up the conversation again, but not before she had heaved a great sigh, 'You're right, Elizabeth. I hear what you say and I'm scared.

'Be fair Penny,' she said, turning her gaze towards Penny, 'we lead a useless frivolous life. To be honest, when do we ever give a thought to anyone but ourselves? I don't know about you, but I feel I'm getting older and parties and dinners are becoming less important. The day will come when I'll be regarded as a maiden aunt. I'll be trailing around looking for a good time, a headache to any hostess who will be hard pushed to find an escort for me.'

Penny was staring at her in disbelief. Then she put down her dessertspoon, threw back her head, and burst out laughing, 'Oh, for God's sake, Barbara, don't paint such a depressing picture, you'll have yourself believing you're edging onto fifty instead of thirty. And what's all this nonsense about nobody wanting you? James is crazy about you – if only you'd open your eyes! So you've been married once and it didn't work out. Stop being such a coward and be grateful that you are being offered a second chance. James is a good man and anyone a mile off can see he's in love with you, willing to give up his freedom. He's told you he's not interested in having an affair – he wants marriage and it's you he wants as his wife. What more do you want, men don't come with a guarantee.'

Elizabeth put out a hand to console Barbara. 'Penny means well,' she assured her.

Barbara took a deep breath. 'I'll admit all you say is true. I think James *is* in love with me, but I wish he would be more cautious. How can I know that it would work out any better this time? I think maybe I do love James, but is that because of the security he can offer me? As a companion he's marvellous and, to be truthful, I'm afraid of loneliness.'

'There are worse reasons for getting married than being good comrades,' Elizabeth said gently, directing her words at both of her companions. 'A husband still has to be a good friend.'

'Right!' Penny exclaimed. 'Since we have to dispel all this gloom and doom that had settled on us, I may as well drop my bombshell and then we'll order a pot of tea. I've a feeling you two are going to need it,' she ended on a laugh.

Barbara and Elizabeth exchanged amused glances but stayed silent.

'I'm going to marry Neil Chapman!'

'What!' Both girls doubted they had heard right.

Elizabeth was the first to recover, 'Penny, is this some kind of a joke? You've always referred to Neil as a wet blanket.'

'You're so offhand with him,' Barbara murmured. 'Sometimes I've even felt sorry for the man.'

'I know, but that was then, now I've learnt to sort the wheat from the chaff. As you so rightly said, Barbara, age is creeping up and I suppose you could say I've gained experience and with it has come this terrible kind of wisdom. I want you both to know that Neil loves me. And God help me, I find I love him.'

'Heavens!' Barbara marvelled. 'This is not the Penny we

all love and fear.' While she silently rejoiced that at long last her friend was going to settle down, she also wondered why she had not seen the signs. Neil was a good man. He did not have the height and breadth she herself liked in a man, but he was handsome in a way, with his sandy hair, blue eyes and clear skin. And his speaking voice was so attractive. Thinking back Neil and Penny had been practically inseparable for months now. Unexpectedly Barbara began to chuckle, Elizabeth couldn't help herself either and soon they were both laughing fit to bust.

'Oh, blow the pair of you, I knew you wouldn't take my news seriously. Is it so hard to believe Neil knows all about me and still wants me for his wife? Warts an' all.'

Barbara wiped at her eyes, conscience-stricken, 'Of course not Penny. Oh please don't be mad, I'm happy for you, really I am, it's smashing news – it's just that you've hoodwinked everyone, most especially me.'

'By gosh, some bombshell!' Elizabeth exclaimed. 'There's me rattling on about you two becoming old maids and all the time each of you have charming eligible men tucked away. I can see it's true, Penny; you do love him and, thinking back, Neil has adored you for years. It's not just puppy love with you two is it?'

Penny looked at her with some surprise. 'For an old married woman you're a lot wiser than you ever let on, aren't you?' She drew herself upright in her chair, 'Come on let's order that tea, I don't know why I allow you two to be so much trouble to me.'

They linked arms, their faces wreathed in smiles. 'Here's to births, engagements, marriages, friendships and a happy future for us all,' Penny said quietly.

'We'll settle for that.'

'Yes, one hundred per cent.' Barbara and Elizabeth responded.

Chapter Fifteen

IN EARLY OCTOBER Barbara gave in to James's urging and agreed to join him at his father's holiday cottage in the Lake District for a few days. It was not high season, there would not be crowds of holiday-makers about, but even so the weather was delightful, promising an Indian summer.

The house was quite small, set into a hillside, approached only by a narrow track just wide enough for one car to negotiate.

As Barbara stepped from the car, she stretched her arms above her head and gazed at her surroundings. The garden gave a sweeping view of the countryside. Autumn, she decided, was lovely.

The interior of the cottage was divided into two. The front door opened into a large room that held two lounge chairs, two high-backed wooden chairs, a settee which folded down to serve as a double bed, a pine-wood topped table for eating at and a small desk set back against the wall. The main attraction was the open fireplace, flanked by a stone surround and wide hearth. To the rear, a section had been made into a kitchen. Upstairs there was one large bedroom with a double bed and its own washbasin. Next door a tiled bathroom with a shower unit fixed to the wall and a lavatory with a wooden seat.

They had stopped for lunch, breaking the journey, and it was still too early to start to think about dinner. With the cases brought in from the car, James said, 'You know what I'd like to do? Have a swim.'

Half an hour later she and James walked from the house across the lawn to the swimming pool. 'I much prefer the sea,' James told her, 'to walk beside it or to romp in the waves. Still, Father is rather proud of owning his own pool.'

In swimming trunks, James looked like a young lad. His shoulders were broad, his waist slim, his stomach firm and flat. She thought how fit he looked. 'Come on!' he yelled as he made ready to dive. 'Let's see how cold the water is.'

It was very cold but exhilarating. Barbara came up for air and with swift strong strokes made for the side, pulled herself up and out, grabbed for a towel which she quickly wrapped around herself and then pushed her arms into the sleeves of a white towelling robe, one of many that had been stored in the cupboard under the stairs. The air was different, she could smell the faint dampness from the trees and grass and hear horses neighing in a nearby field. Oh, she was going to like it here.

James stood up, laughed and waved to her. 'Had enough?' he called.

'Yes, I'm shivering.'

Within minutes they were racing across the grass. Wood sticks, rolled newspapers and logs were set ready in the iron fire-basket. One match set the flames crackling and soon the room was glowing and warm.

Barbara appreciated James's attention whilst they were having dinner, which she had cooked using the provisions her mother had thoughtfully packed and insisted that she bring with her. He praised every dish she set on the table, though Barbara suspected that he was playing the gentleman. A role he played to perfection.

After dinner, James suggested that they go for a walk. 'But pull a heavy jersey on,' he instructed. 'It can get very cold up here at night.'

They walked hand-in-hand in comfortable silence. She never felt out of place with James, nor forced to make conversation. Suddenly her mind went back and she wondered had she ever really relaxed with Michael? Stop it! she immediately scolded herself. That was all a long time ago.

The light began to fade, the sky darkened and soon the stars would be out.

'Barbara, I don't want you to give me an answer yet, I don't expect one,' James said softly, 'but you must know how I feel about you. I'm in love with you, have loved your dearly almost from the moment we met. Will you marry me? Please?'

She stopped dead, her heart pounding.

'James, I – I don't know . . .'

'Take your time, my love. I've told you I don't need an answer now, just your promise that you will think about it.'

Think about it! She had thought about nothing else for weeks. The prospect of life without James was fearful. And yet the prospect of living with him . . . could she? She floundered.

'James,' she uttered his name and it came out on a sob. 'I keep telling myself that life with you would be wonderful, it would be different. Yet there is this awful unreasonable conflict that goes on in my head. Yes, I want to be with you, all the time, but I can't seem to blot out the memory of how wrong it was with Michael, no matter how hard I try. I still have nightmares, all the abuse, the terror, it still looms up vividly sometimes. It wouldn't be fair to you.'

'Nonsense.'

'Is it?' she quietly asked.

'Barbara, the past has gone. I have to find some way of proving to you that there is no life for me without you. The one thing I long for is for you to say that you'll be my wife. For the moment there is no problem, I shan't rush you. It has to be your decision. The best thing I can promise you is that I shall go on loving you and each day I shall not only tell you so, but do my utmost to prove it to you. All right?'

She gazed at him, tears welling in her eyes. How kind and gentle James could be – despite his sophistication, his powerful position with the law firm of Bradley and Summerford. Tonight he seemed like a boy, a boy that was truly in love, earnest in every word he said.

When he lifted her face to kiss her, she prayed. Should she take this second chance? If only it were possible.

That night James slept downstairs on the bed-settee. He made no effort to come into the double room which she was occupying. Barbara told herself that she was relieved: James was a gentleman, he was giving her time to think. But she was more disappointed than she would have cared to admit.

But did she want to have sex with James? With any man? Wouldn't sleeping with James bring back all the terror and humiliation of the night when Michael and Pete Davis had forcibly raped her. Then again, maybe, just maybe, making love with someone as loving as James would wipe out forever that horrific memory. If only she could be sure.

Each day was more wonderful than the previous one. The weather continued to be kind to them. They hired bicycles and toured the pretty village of Coniston, with its white-washed cottages sheltering in the shadow of the mountains, had a cream tea in Grasmere, took a steamer cruise on Lake Windermere, had dinner at Bowness in a restaurant that looked out across the lake. The fact that the trees and shrubs grew right down to the edge of the lakes, their autumn colours rich and glowing, where the calm water gently lapped against the dark earth, held Barbara spell-bound. She caught her breath at the beauty of it all and felt so happy and contented. At peace with the world. These days had meant such a great deal to her.

Friday dawned bleak and chilly. 'Let's go walking before it rains,' James suggested as they cleared their breakfast things from the table. 'You'll need a scarf around your head because the wind seems pretty fierce.'

The view was obscured today by a curtain of mist, which swirled around the hilltops. Every now and then a listless sun did its best to shine before sliding back behind the clouds. The wind tore at Barbara's scarf. It drowned their voices so that they had to shout at one another to be heard and so they walked on without speaking. They passed no one and there was no one in sight. A few birds left the shelter of the trees and took flight as they approached. At the edge of the lake ducks quacked and squabbled for the bread that Barbara crumbled and threw to them. The water wasn't calm today.

'Let's go back,' James shouted. 'The house should have warmed up by now.'

Back at the cottage James threw more logs onto the fire and they rubbed their hands in the welcome warmth. In a few minutes the extra logs had caught, flames spread, fluttering, the bark crackling. Barbara watched while James, on his knees, fanned and used the poker.

'You're really quite domesticated,' she said slowly. 'I feel as if I never really knew you until we came here.'

James rose from his knees and straightened up. 'This place has done us both good. Do you feel better for the break?'

So much better than he would ever know, but she was too embarrassed to put her feelings into words. 'Yes, oh yes,' she said hurriedly. 'I'll see about making us some coffee.' She moved towards the kitchen.

He waved her back. 'No, you take that jersey off and stretch out in front of the fire.'

When James came back with the coffee things on the tray they both sat down on the rug in front of the fire. Barbara poured the coffee and as she handed a cup to James their fingers touched. She felt a stirring, a tenseness. They glanced at each other and then quickly looked away. It felt as if this was the first time they had ever been alone together. She was puzzled and thrilled at the same time. Her eyes filled with tears and she turned her head away. But he had seen.

James stroked her hair. 'You've suffered too much. You were too young.' Lifting her face, he kissed away a few tears on her eyelashes, kissed her cheeks, until finally his lips found her mouth.

It was tender, soft and gentle. He clasped her closer and her doubts were swept away. For a while they lay back in the firelight, she quite content to have his arms hold her, while he revelled in the fact that she no longer seemed afraid of him. What happened then seemed so natural. She was not aware of anything at all but that James was making love to her. Pure sweet unselfish love.

A long time later came a deep calm while his arms were still holding her close. Perhaps, Barbara thought as they lay quietly side by side, perhaps there is more hope for James and me to have a happy marriage than I'd ever have believed possible.

'We are going to be very happy together, you and I, Barbara. Do you believe that now?' James asked, anxiously scanning her face.

She swallowed deeply before answering. She wouldn't be able to lie to James, he was sharp, neither would she get away with trying to hide anything from him. 'I'm still trying to convince myself that I haven't imagined it. Can love between two people really be that good?'

He laughed. 'If they each have love, one for the other, then the answer is yes. Always!'

The sight of his triumphant pleasure brought a smile to Barbara's lips, and then a laugh. It was a laugh such as she had not brought forth for months. She would try her damnedest to put all the sorrow of the past behind her. Even when this holiday was over and gone she wouldn't allow thoughts of Michael to surge again; she would remember this cottage, this hour and the tender yet passionate way that James had showed her how fantastic lovemaking could really be, for the rest of her days.

As if he were able to read her mind, James said, 'I knew it would be like that between you and me. It is the most wondrous thing two people in love can do.'

Later, when they were dressed, they came back to the fire. The logs were burning down, and the afternoon outside was darkening.

'I'll start the car up and we'll go out for dinner,' he said. 'But first will you tell me something? If it can be like this when you and I are together for the first time, how can you still have doubts as to whether you would be happy with me?

Barbara considered and answered slowly. 'How do we know it would last? Maybe you would stop loving me.'

'Oh Barbara! What do I have to do to convince you? I know I said earlier in the week that there was no hurry and that I wouldn't press you for an answer but . . . please, Barbara, marry me.'

She shook her head. 'I still can't be sure, perhaps – '

He interrupted, 'You can't blame yourself forever for what happened in the past. As to your baby, you have to forgive yourself even for that. It was the right decision at the time. It's over. Gone. You can't live for a hope that is never going to come true.'

Barbara gave a cry. It was a sobbing sound from deep inside.

'You think I've been brutal, that I should never have mentioned the baby. Don't you see, my darling, he's not dead, he has other parents now – two, a mother and a father, you can be sure of that. And sure that they love him. People don't adopt babies unless they are longing to have a child, a child they can love and take care of. You did me the honour of confiding in me, therefore it is not a taboo subject between us, it never will be. We can be happy for him, talk openly about him, remember him with love. Between us it is not a secret and as to other folk, they just don't matter. You trusted me when you told me what had happened, it made no difference as to how I felt about you. Please, trust me now.'

Barbara sighed. It was still a sorrowful sound. 'You are a good man, James, just give me a little more time.'

James stood up, he gave her his hands to pull her to her feet. 'All right, my darling, sufficient unto the day, and today you have been mine, I can afford to be patient.'

Barbara began to weep. James pulled her close and stood there holding her, very gently and without saying a word. When Barbara made to break away James only held her closer against his strong body, her head tucked beneath his chin.

'I meant this to happen, though you never did,' he admitted.

'I dare say I'll survive.' She was doing her best to sound flippant.

'No, we'll survive *together*, Barbara. I had to prove to you that making love with the person you are in love with can and will be a marvellous thing. You no longer need to be frightened. No more doubts, eh?'

Foolishly all she could think of to say was, 'We'll see.'

James still held her tightly and she knew he was smiling. 'We shall indeed, my love.'

Chapter Sixteen

THE BANNS HAD been called for Penny and Neil and the wedding fixed for the first Saturday in December, to take place in Alfriston. Besides all the relatives, it seemed almost everyone in the village would attend. Penny's mother had made three cakes of different sizes and Barbara's mother had been roped in to ice and decorate each tier. After the ceremony there would be a sit-down dinner in The Smuggler's Inn for the main guests and in the evening a buffet set up with a dance band to play in the village hall, to which everyone would be invited.

It seemed to Barbara that everything in Alfriston revolved around plans for Penny's wedding. No one seemed to talk of anything else.

Boys had been selected to sing in the choir, the vicar had agreed to the request that the bells should be rung.

Elizabeth declined the offer to be matron of honour, merely because her pregnancy was showing, and Barbara shuddered at the thought of being a bridesmaid. Neil had no relatives other than two aunts and his elderly mother and father, so in the end Penny asked James's sister Chloe if she would be a bridesmaid and settled on having Elizabeth's twin boys, William and John, as pageboys.

After three days of torrential rain the wedding day dawned bright and clear, the sky deep-blue and cloudless. Barbara was woken early by her father. 'I've brought you a cup of tea,' he said and Barbara squinted as he pulled open the curtains.

'Thank God, it's stopped raining,' she muttered.

'Amen to that,' her father replied. 'But it is still very cold. Tim and the boys went out about an hour ago, I think Tim was afraid that they would have the whole house in a turmoil if he didn't keep them occupied. Your mother has just gone in to wake Elizabeth. You know, love, she is so pleased to have Elizabeth and Tim staying here.'

'I know she is, Daddy, and it's so much better for Elizabeth. Are you going to fetch her father here or take him straight to the church?'

'I'm off to pick him up now. He always seems happy enough to be in that residential home – suppose it was the best thing when his wife died – but he must look forward to having a break, see fresh faces.' He was about to add that it was a pity that Mr and Mrs Warren had only had the one child, Elizabeth, but he caught his breath and checked himself. He and Patricia had had three children, and now because of the War they only had Barbara. Thank God for her.

He himself was the third generation of Hamlins to practise law. There would not now be a fourth. Who knew what fate had in store for anyone? He sometimes thought when he looked at his wife, whom he loved even more with the passing of time, that if God were good he would take couples together, not leave one partner to flounder along on their own after a lifetime of loving companionship.

'Penny for them, Daddy,' Barbara said as she replaced her cup and saucer down on her bedside table.

Phillip shook his head. 'Just dreaming, pet. Weddings

have a way of making us look back. Anyway, time I was off and you got yourself moving.'

By eleven-thirty everyone in the Hamlin household was ready. Tim had gone some time ago, for he was to be one of the ushers and was also picking his parents up from the hotel where they were staying, having travelled down from Yorkshire. Elizabeth had confided to Barbara that the only reason Tim's parents had accepted the invitation was the fact that their grandsons had been chosen to be pageboys. And who could blame them?

'Are you sure being a pageboy is important?' William asked.

'Really and truly,' Elizabeth promised.

'Auntie Penny told us it was' John said solemnly.

Barbara felt a lump rise up in her throat at the sight of the twins. She had vowed she wouldn't get upset today but it was going to be hard. The boys looked a picture. Dark-blue velvet suits, white shirts with ruffles at the neck and cuffs. Elizabeth had brushed their fine golden hair, which fell over their foreheads, until it shone. It was coming up to their fifth birthday. They were ten weeks younger than the son who was lost to her because she had let him go on the day he had been born. Michael had wronged her and she had wronged her baby. Oh, but it had been right to agree to that, she assured herself, at the same time offering up the prayer that she did so often: 'Please let his adoptive parents love him.'

Was there ever a more beautiful setting for a wedding than that of the parish church of St Andrew, Alfriston? Set alone on a huge grassy circular mound at the far side of a green field, which boasted huge leafy trees, and numerous wooden seats mostly set in the shade. A typical peaceful village scene. The church was surrounded by a splendid, low, flint stone wall, behind which lay the carefully tended family graves of local residents, watched over by the single spire of the church which rose high towards the sky. Inside, the winter sun shone through the stained glass windows, the eight wooden pews each side of the aisle were full, the small Lady chapel to the right of the high altar also had every seat occupied.

Penny looked radiant in her wedding gown. How different, so handsome, Neil looked in his cut-away jacket, pearl-grey waistcoat and dark trousers.

James reached for Barbara's hand as they listened to their friends take their vows. The vicar was pronouncing them man and wife when Barbara glanced up at Penny and Neil there at the chancel steps. Neil's eyes were on Penny, his gaze held hers, and it was as if they were the only two people in the whole world. Then Penny took Neil's arm, and he and his bride began to move towards the vestry.

Barbara sunk to her knees. They had some time to wait until the bridal pair would reappear and everyone would surge out into the daylight. The truth was, she wanted to pray. She needed to pray. If in the near future she was to become a bride herself, wife to James, then she needed guidance and reassurance. How could she deserve the wonderful happiness that James was offering her when she had made such a mess of her previous marriage? Most of all she prayed that James would often look at her with as much love in his eyes as Neil had when he looked at Penny.

The taking of the photographs, the kisses and the hugs, the good wishes and congratulations, the wedding breakfast and the speeches were all over. The evening festivities could begin. The scene in the village hall was superb. Children, including William and John, were running around like it was a school playground. 'Leave them be,' Mrs Rayford beamed at Elizabeth. 'Childish high spirits – nothing more. Everything went well, don't you think?'

'Oh, yes,' Barbara and Elizabeth both agreed.

'Began to think our Penny was going to play fast and loose forever. Still, she's settled well with Neil. You'll remember this day when your children get married,' she smiled as she nodded towards Elizabeth's bulge. 'Well, I'd better circulate. I'll send the men over with drinks for you.'

'Hi, you two, why are you hiding away in the corner?' Chloe came up on them from behind. For the wedding Chloe had worn an Edwardian-styled cream-coloured dress with a shoulder cloak made from the same blue velvet as that of the pageboy suits. Now she had changed into a slinky pale-blue dress that looked as if she had been poured into it. She looked fantastic, her fair hair swept up into a pile of curls, her cheeks glowing with excitement. At that moment, James, and Tim appeared bringing a tray of beverages.

'Sis, Anthony has been looking for you; we told him the vicar had made off with you to have his wicked way,' her brother told her, a wide grin which spread from one ear to the other on his face.

'Don't be so irreverent,' Chloe scolded her brother. 'I'll go and find Anthony and bring him back and introduce you to him,' she told the girls, but as she turned away she did a half-turn backwards. 'He's gorgeous, you'll see.'

They all laughed. 'She's well an' truly smitten,' James stated. 'She could do a whole lot worse, though. Tony does happen to be a very nice chap – don't you agree, Tim?'

'Yes I do,' Tim answered without hesitation, 'and from what I hear he does a heck of a good job.'

No one would ever call Anthony Holt good looking, Barbara thought as introductions were made. He was far too serious for that. Three to four inches taller than Chloe, only twenty-nine-years-old and already his light-brown hair was receding, his high forehead shone as if it had been polished and his gold-rimmed glasses added to the dedicated look of the medical profession.

'How d'you do, Mrs Holdsworthy,' he said, smiling at Elizabeth. 'How d'you do, Miss Hamlin.'

'Surely we are not going to be formal?' murmured Barbara, as she took his hand, immediately thinking how soft it was and how long his fingers were. 'I'm going to call you Anthony, so that you may call me Barbara.'

'Anthony and I work in the same hospital,' Chloe added eagerly, by way of explanation.

'Chloe, you work in the dispensary, yes?' Elizabeth queried.

'That's right,' Chloe agreed. 'And Anthony is a paediatrician,' she added, while all the time she gazed lovingly up into his face.

The band struck up and everyone stopped talking and watched as Penny and Neil took to the floor for the first waltz.

Having circled the floor once, other couples joined them. 'May I?' James asked, holding out his arms to Barbara. The lights dimmed, the music was dreamy and Barbara felt she was floating on a cloud as James expertly twirled her across the floor.

All too soon the married couple were saying their good-byes. Penny, now dressed in a going-away, beige-coloured

costume with coffee-coloured accessories, the very simplicity of which belied the enormous sum she had paid for
it, bent low to embrace Elizabeth, 'Now, make sure you
take care, I'll see you in the New Year.' Having left Barbara
until last, Penny threw her arms around her and whispered
in her ear, 'When I get home I want to hear that you've
said yes to James.'

Barbara felt her cheeks flush and playfully she pushed at
Penny, 'Get on with you, have a good time, I'll miss you.'

Neil, having shaken hands with Anthony and James,
turned his attention to Tim, 'Keep your nose to the grind-
stone, buddy,' he said, punching at Tim's shoulder. 'I don't
want to come back and find my desk loaded with ledgers,
be kind to me, eh?'

Tim threw back his head and laughed loudly, 'That'll be
the day when you tackle more than one set of books at
any one time. Besides, you'll probably need a rest, having
been on your honeymoon.'

Tim and Neil both worked for the same firm of account-
ants, the only difference being that Neil's father owned the
firm – hence the four weeks off to go cruising with his
new wife.

A lull settled over the hall when the bride and groom
finally left and the caterers began to hand out refreshments.

James had steered Barbara into a corner and, with plates
balanced on their knees, he grinned, 'Got you to myself at
last. Keep next weekend free, Barbara, there's a house I
want to take you to see, I'd appreciate your opinion.'

Barbara lifted her head and looked directly at him, 'Are
you telling me you've bought a house?'

'No, no,' he stuttered, his mouth full of smoked salmon,
'I've owned it a long time.'

'You mean someone died and left it to you?'

'That's exactly it,' he grinned. 'I'm not joking. Two of my mother's maiden aunts lived in it for years. It was left to me by my mother's parents, I shouldn't think any other members of the family would have wanted it.'

Barbara was curious by now and it showed on her face. 'Where is this house – is one allowed to ask?'

'Of course.' He made a mocking bow. 'The other side of Jevington. Not a million miles from here, eh?'

'But I go through Jevington almost every time I go out riding. I don't know any empty properties in the village.'

'Who said it was empty? And I didn't say it was in the village.'

'Oh, now you're teasing me. Tell me about it.'

'It isn't all that grand, you know. Actually the large stables and the three acres of land are its best features. Say you'll come with me next weekend and give it the once over?'

Wild horses weren't going to keep her away, was what she was thinking but what she actually said was, 'I shall be looking forward to it, honestly I shall.'

Later as Barbara undressed and made herself ready for bed she decided it had been quite a day, one way and another.

Saturday was dull and cloudy but the weather did nothing to dampen Barbara's spirits. 'I thought we'd have lunch in the Eight-Bells,' James told her as he drove away from Alfriston. 'You look marvellous. You know that don't you? That silly hat becomes you.'

'I still like to hear you say that I do, and my hat is not in the least bit silly.'

It was true she had taken a heck of a long time to decide

what she would wear today, but she was pleased with the finished result. A dark-brown wool dress topped with a heavy camel coat; the cloche hat made gay by the small feather that was stuck in the band, covered her ears and would be warm; a stout pair of shoes in case they had to go tramping across fields, she looked quite the countryfied lady.

James was lucky to find a parking space in the small car park. The bar was inviting, warm and cosy with great logs burning in the open fireplace, giving off that wonderful smoky smell of winter. Having taken Barbara's coat and settled her at a round table just big enough for two, he asked, 'What'll it be?'

Without any hesitation she replied, 'A whisky-mac and a ploughman's, please.'

They chattered as they ate, James laughing to himself at the enthusiasm Barbara was showing for this outing and he only hoped she wouldn't be terribly disappointed.

It still was not one o'clock when they came out from the Eight-bells. James had meant for them to have an early lunch so as to give them the benefit of the daylight. It got dark so early these December days. About a mile after having left the car park, James took a turning to the left, driving now down a lane that was flanked with gigantic hedges to protect the fields from excessive winds. Further along he swung the car between high wrought-iron gates which were wide open, secured back against the stout flint walls. The drive was long and winding but suddenly Barbara caught a glimpse of a long, low, very old house with a deep-eaved roof and very small windows. She couldn't wait for the car to stop.

'It's absolutely charming!' she cried, breaking into a run and heading for the porchway that sheltered the front door.

With quick strides, James caught up with her. 'Hey, steady on,' he ordered as he pushed open the wicker gate and they walked up the weed-covered path. Clematis, which must have looked beautiful when in bloom, still struggled to cling to the porchway.

The oak door opened easily enough to the key James used. The smell of musty damp came to them at once. What a shame, was Barbara's first thought; everything looked so dusty and neglected. The huge inglenook fireplace still held dead ashes from long-forgotten log fires. Barbara ignored the doors that led off from the wide hall and made straight for the staircase.

'There'll be much more of a view from up here,' she called down.

Laughing happily, James took the stairs two at a time.

Barbara was right. From the upstairs bedroom windows, the garden view was breathtaking. A neglected garden, almost a wilderness, lay close to the house and an apple orchard behind, which had also been left to run wild. Beyond, she looked out over rolling fields, sheltered by the high hills of the South Downs. The ceilings in the bedrooms showed damp patches, window frames needed refitting but the deep window-seats were her favourites. The floor boards creaked as they walked and would need replacing, nevertheless by the time they came to the bathroom, Barbara was in love with this house. It was, she felt, like stepping back into a time warp.

'That Victorian bath is something else, don't you agree?' James could hardly contain his mirth as he watched Barbara gaze in wonderment at the size of it.

'Magnificent,' she muttered. 'The weight of it must be colossal, look at those great claw feet.' She turned her attention to the huge washbasin and the toilet with its rusty cistern and wooden seat.

Reading her thoughts, James said, 'There would be an awful lot of work to be done, if I even think of keeping this place.'

'James! You wouldn't part with it, would you?'

'I've given it some thought. My father's advice is to sell.'

Barbara's face fell.

'On the other hand, knowing from the start the work that would be entailed, it could be great fun. We could use local workmen. Replace that rickety staircase for a start, making sure it was fashioned authentically. The reward could be a very nice home.'

'Oh, you tease! You've no intention of parting with this lovely old house, have you?'

'Not if you like it, I haven't; but to be honest you have seen the worst part first. Come on, we'll do a tour of the stables and I'll introduce you to the man that keeps that part of the estate running efficiently and economically. Besides, I'm sure you want to come an' see the horses.'

'Horses? You have horses stabled here?' asked Barbara with the enthusiasm he had expected.

'No, unfortunately. The stables are leased out to owners and trainers, but we do have our own manager, my father was adamant about that. He does a damn fine job too.'

The stables were well away from the house, purpose-built and well maintained. Gallops, sprints and hurdles were set out on fine flat grassland which looked rich and well cared for to Barbara's keen eye.

A wonderful sight met them. Jockeys were bringing in

a stream of horses from a canter that had presumably gone well.

'Afternoon, Mr Ferguson. You're earlier than I expected.'

'Never mind us,' James replied. 'Let me introduce you to my fiancée, then we'll get out of your way. Miss Barbara Hamlin, meet Clement Tompson, known to his friends and acquaintances as Clem, an' to employees as Mr Clem.'

Barbara smiled as he shook her hand. She already liked this man for the way he had greeted each horse in turn before he was aware that either James or herself had arrived. She was also secretly smiling to herself: James had introduced her as his fiancée!

Clem Tompson was a small, compact man, with a ruddy complexion and rather unusual features. A different sort of face that was utterly transformed when he smiled. He wore tweeds, leggings and brogues, a yellow scarf around his neck and a brown corduroy flat cap. He looked what he was: a man that had been around horses for the whole of his life.

'Do you ride, Miss Hamlin?' Clem asked.

'Whenever I can,' she replied.

'We'll always find you a mount, be our pleasure.'

'Miss Hamlin might just take you up on that in the not-too-distant future, Clem, when she's out this way – or better still, she can ride over and let you give her own horse the once over.'

Clem regarded Barbara for a few seconds before he said, 'Miss Barbara, that rings a bell.' Then, slapping his forehead with the palm of his hand, he asked, 'Phillip Hamlin! He is your father, yes?'

Barbara smiled as she nodded.

'Sorry, Miss. Should have made the connection sooner.

Had a lot of dealings with Phillip, one way an' another. I went with him, after the War, to look some horses over. We've become great mates over the years.'

'Does your father have horses here?' Barbara asked James.

'No, this is really not our territory. We own the stables and the land, or I suppose *I* do, strictly speaking, but as I told you it is all leased out and we leave it all in the capable hands of Clem here.' He added, 'It's time we were going.'

'Goodbye, Miss, Remember me to your parents and I hope to see you here again soon.' Clem Tomson gave Barbara a smiling nod of farewell, then shook hands with James before he hustled away, his heavy shoes clacking on the flagstones of the yard.

Back in the car James was suddenly very calm, and his voice sounded very intense. 'Barbara, why do we have to wait any longer?'

With restless fingers she twisted at her handkerchief, she could hear cattle lowing in the distance. The silence between them lengthened.

'Well?' James asked a little sharply.

Barbara turned her head away. 'I suppose it's no good pretending, James. I do want to spend the rest of my life with you, but marriage, it still frightens me.'

This time the quiet was fraught with question.

'I thought . . .' she said at last, 'that you would realise what that commitment would mean to me.' She turned her head back, gave a brave smile and looked directly into his eyes.

'Couldn't we just live together . . . for a while . . . kind of see how it works out?'

He was staring sharply at her, Barbara felt her cheeks flush up.

Abruptly he shook his head. 'No! That's *not* what I want. I love you, I want you to be my wife. I want to go to sleep at night with you in my arms and I want to wake up in the morning knowing that I'll find you lying beside me. I want us to have children, a family of our own. Barbara, if you really love me, surely that is what you want too?'

'But what if –'

He stopped her words by reaching for her, hugging her close.

She leaned against him, her hat now lopsided, wisps of hair dangling across her forehead. 'If only we could see into the future,' she sighed.

'Oh Barbara, darling, why won't you trust me? Don't you know by now I would never hurt you?'

The misery of the past, the quarrelling, the awful things Michael had said and done to her, were still imprinted in her mind; yet she knew with sudden awful clearness that should James go out of her life, if she were to lose him now she stood no chance of ever finding real happiness ever again.

She shivered a little, though it wasn't cold in the car. Silently she prayed: This time, dear God, let it be right for both of us. Then she told James that she would marry him.

'Oh, my darling,' she heard him say. 'Oh Barbara!' Slowly he moved, his lips came gently down over hers, then he was whispering, 'I love you, Barbara. I love you *so* much.'

She stayed leaning against him, his arms holding her close, and now she felt blissfully warm. She thought, This is so right. How could she have ever thought that she didn't really want to marry James?

Now it was her turn to tell him how much she loved him, 'Oh James! I can't believe how happy I suddenly feel!

It's like my life has all at once become peaceful, no more fears or doubts, I really do love you.'

'For us life will only get better from now on, you'll see,' he promised her. 'Now, the question is, *when* will you marry me? Please, Barbara, make it soon. I can't wait.'

'Nor I,' she answered. 'I'll marry you as soon as you like.' In each other's arms the minutes ticked away in silence.

In the end it was Barbara who spoke. 'Are we going to go and tell your parents first, or mine?' she asked.

'Neither,' James said. 'We'll tell no one today. Today is just for you and me. Nobody else matters.'

Chapter Seventeen

'MOTHER, I'M GLAD you asked Tim and Elizabeth here for Christmas,' Barbara said. 'It means Mr Warren will be able to be with them on Christmas Day and Boxing Day, whereas I doubt very much that he would have wanted to travel to Windsor. It will be so nice to spend it all together here, in Alfriston, especially having the twins.'

She was trimming the Christmas tree which stood in the bay window of the lounge; it had become her task each year since she had returned home.

'You seem to have a great deal more enthusiasm for Christmas this year,' her mother remarked. 'Are you happier now?'

'Yes Mother, I am. Does it show?'

'Of course it does. It wouldn't have anything to do with James being around, would it?'

Barbara smiled, like a satisfied cat, 'You'll have to wait until tomorrow morning before I give you the answer to that question.'

'Well, I'll not try to guess then.' Her mother turned away in order to hide her knowing smile; she was hoping against hope that James and her daughter were going to announce that they were to be married. Oh, wouldn't that be the perfect gift that she and her husband could receive – to know that after everything that Barbara had suffered she had at last found happiness. James was such a kind man, it would be an ideal match.

Barbara stepped back to view her work. She was really pleased with it. 'And when all the presents are placed around the base this evening it will look even better!' she said. 'We've had all these baubles for years, haven't we, Mother?'

'Most of them. In any case I prefer familiar things, they bring back such happy memories. That one there, the sleigh, and the one of Father Christmas with his sack, your brothers chose them; I remember them taking so long to decide which ones they were going to buy. That was a long time ago now,' her mother said sadly, 'so they're rather precious.'

'I know they are. I'll move them, hang them near the top of the tree so they won't get knocked off by the twins.'

'Hallo, you two. Hard at it, I see.'

They both looked around in surprise. 'Daddy! How nice you are home early,' his daughter greeted him.

Patricia kissed her husband and said, 'I'd better pour you a drink, dinner will be some time yet.'

'Have Elizabeth and Tim arrived yet?' he asked.

'Yes, ages ago. They've taken William and John off to see their grandfather; apparently Gildredge Grange put on some kind of a tea party for the residents to invite their grandchildren to. All the boys wanted to know was whether Father Christmas was going to be there and would they be getting a present from him.'

Phillip threw back his head and laughed. 'What it is to be young! Must say, it will be nice to have the house full for a change and real nice to have the boys around.'

Patricia laid her hand lightly on her husband's shoulder. She knew what was behind his last remark, knew he too was thinking of when they had had two small sons of their own. Sons that they had loved deeply.

'Did James travel down from town with you, Daddy?' Barbara asked, aware of her parents' feelings and wanting to steer the conversation onto happier topics.

'No. James was still tied up with paperwork.'

'Any idea of what time he'll be home?'

'Who knows? The trains will be at sixes and sevens with it being Christmas Eve. But knowing James, he'll ring you before he leaves the office.'

Barbara's smile said it all: James was so thoughtful.

'He'll be tired,' her father said. 'Last week was a blinder for him. Acting for the defence in a fraud case at the Old Bailey is never an easy task.'

'Hmm,' Barbara murmured. 'Will you tell me something, Daddy, does James practise almost exclusively in the criminal courts?'

'No, I wouldn't say exclusively,' he grinned to himself before adding, 'but I would agree that James shows a certain amount of skill when it comes to crime.'

'Really, Phillip!' Patricia protested. 'You make it sound as if law was some kind of a game.'

'Well, put it this way, all the time London has industrious criminals there will always be work for men of James's calibre.'

Before either of them could take this discussion further there was a commotion at the front door.

'That means Elizabeth is back with the boys,' Patricia said. The twins never moved quietly, but wherever they went they brought sunshine with them; as they did now, coming into the lounge on this drab December day. Elizabeth's appearance was also lovely. Very much pregnant, her skin glowing from the cold, her light hair escaping from each side of her felt hat.

'It's freezing out there!' she exclaimed. 'Wouldn't it be wonderful if it snowed for Christmas! Tim won't be back for dinner, he's staying to have a meal with my father.'

'Oh, that is nice. Did you tell your father we are picking him up early in the morning?'

'Yes, I did. And he is very grateful and so am I, Auntie Pat, it really is good of you an' Uncle Phillip to allow us to descend on you like this.'

'Nonsense, we're thrilled to have you here. Will make our holiday,' Phillip assured her.

'We *did* get presents,' William said, including everyone in his statement, 'an' a jolly good tea!'

'True,' John stated. 'But tell Auntie Barbara what we decided.'

'Oh yes, there are too many old people living in that house where Grandad's staying; they ought to invite some younger people as well.'

'I don't suppose you two are offering to go and live there?' she teased.

'No, we've got Mummy and Daddy to look after us,' he protested.

'Yes, of course you have – silly old me,' Barbara said.

'Would you two like to stay up for dinner?' Patricia asked. 'I have asked your mother's permission and she said as it is Christmas Eve you may if you want to.'

'Yes please,' they chorused eagerly.

When they sat down at the long table in the dining room both Barbara's mother and father looked at the laden table and thought how lucky they were. Their daughter looked so different. She had come a long way, hopefully put the past behind her and with James, please God, she would have a happy future.

'Why aren't we having Christmas pudding?' John asked.

'Christmas pudding is for tomorrow,' his mother said.

'Will there be sixpences hidden in it?' William wanted to know.

'You'll have to wait and see,' Aunt Patricia told him patiently.

'Why?'

They were all saved from giving an answer by the ringing of the telephone in the hall.

'I'll answer it,' Barbara said. 'It'll be James.'

She rushed out of the room. Everyone at the table smiled at each other. It seemed ages before they heard the faint click as Barbara replaced the receiver and came back into the room.

'It was James,' she said. 'He's leaving the office now. He wont' be coming here tonight. He said he'll spend the evening with his family, help fill stockings for Harry and Lucy. They're his sister Ann's children,' Barbara explained to Elizabeth. 'Like you she was lucky, had twins. Two babies at one go must be very nice,' she added wistfully.

'He'll be here about eleven in the morning.' It was as if she was floating on a cloud, everything about her shone, she couldn't conceal her happiness.

'May I be excused, please? Time I saw my two sons into bed. It's very late for them,' Elizabeth said, rising from the table.

'Mother, would you mind if I went with Elizabeth?'

'Of course not, darling, you go up with the children,' her mother told her. 'Your father will help me to clear the table.'

When Elizabeth and Barbara came downstairs, Tim was back and everyone had moved into the lounge.

'The tree looks splendid!' Tim said. 'You did a good job there, Barbara.'

'Yes, you did,' her father agreed. 'And now we're all going to have a glass of hot toddy.' He handed the glasses around, wondering if he had guessed right and that tomorrow they would be toasting Barbara and James as a happy couple.

It was well after midnight when everyone went to bed.

Patricia was brushing her hair. Phillip came up behind her and looked at her reflection in the mirror.

'I love it when you let your hair down, it's like silk and it always smells so fresh.' He leant over, buried his face in her hair. She turned around and drew his head down to hers, her lips finding his.

'Come to bed,' Phillip said.

After all the years their lovemaking was still satisfying to both of them.

'We've got a lot to still be grateful for,' she murmured later, as he drew her head into the hollow of his shoulder, put his arms around her and they settled down to sleep.

In her bedroom across the hall, their daughter was thinking very much the same thoughts.

When Barbara went downstairs next morning Tim was up and dressed, making tea in the kitchen.

'Hope the boys didn't wake you,' he said. 'They were up before the birds this morning, came bursting into our room like a tornado. Forgot – I haven't wished you a Merry Christmas yet.' He leaned forward and planted a kiss on

271

her cheek. 'Merry Christmas, Barbara; Merry Christmas, Patricia,' he added as Mrs Hamlin came into the kitchen behind Barbara. 'I was about to bring tea in bed for everyone.'

'That was a nice thought, Tim. You take a tray up for your father and Elizabeth, Barbara. Tim and I will have ours down here.'

Upstairs, Barbara knocked then entered her father's room, 'Happy Christmas, Daddy. I've brought you some tea.'

'Happy Christmas, my darling. The boys sound excited.' He raised himself to a sitting position and Barbara planted a kiss on his forehead.

'Yes, I'm about to go in an' see them.'

Elizabeth put out a welcoming hand to Barbara as she entered the room, 'Come an' sit on the bed, love. Have they woken the whole household?'

The two boys had toys spread out all over the floor.

'There was a sugar mouse in the toe of my stocking,' John told Barbara.

'Really?'

'Yes, look,' he said, holding up the white mouse by a length of string that was supposedly its tail.

Not to be outdone, William cried, 'Look at this, Auntie Barbara! A fire engine and the bell does work.' His face was beaming as he pulled the short rope which set the bell clanging.

John wasn't going to lose his aunt's attention that quickly. 'I've got a racing car, its lights flash. They didn't till Daddy put the batteries in. Good job Father Christmas remembered to bring me some batteries, wasn't it?'

'Yes, it was very thoughtful of him,' Barbara said, doing her best to keep a straight face.

'Come on now, back to your own room and get washed and dressed,' their mother urged them. 'There'll be a whole lot more presents once breakfast is over.' It was all the encouragement they needed. Both Elizabeth and Barbara were grinning broadly as they watched the pair of them scarper.

Barbara was on edge all through breakfast.

Everyone was thrilled by the presents that were exchanged when the meal was over. Screams of delight turned into shouts as the twins tore the gaily-coloured paper from the frames of their new bicycles.

'Daddy!' Barbara exclaimed with glee as she unpacked new riding boots, but all the time she had one eye on the clock.

She heard the motor and was out in the hall before the wheels had stopped turning. She opened the door, stepped out and ran to meet James. He caught her in his arms.

'Happy Christmas, Barbara.'

'Oh, it will be. Happy Christmas, James.'

Barbara was dressed for the seasonal holiday. She wore a grey silk skirt which flared out at the knees, a soft bolero to match, beneath which she wore a red silk blouse. Two silver chains fastened around her neck added a festive touch.

James thought she had never looked more appealing. He took her face between his hands and kissed her lightly on the lips. When he broke away she was smiling, then her smile turned into a laugh, not a loud laugh but a soft laugh of true contentment.

He reached into his pocket and pulled out a small leather box.

'I've waited a long time for this,' he said.

She opened it. She gazed at the ring resting between dark-blue velvet and she gasped, tears welling up in her eyes.

'James, it's so beautiful.'

'Let me put it on.' He lifted the diamond cluster set on a band of platinum and slipped it onto the third finger of her left hand.

Then he tilted her face and really kissed her.

Her mother and father had stood well back from the bay window but they had missed nothing. Silently Phillip held his arms out to his wife, they stood close for several seconds before he whispered to her, 'See, prayers *are* answered.'

'Well, sometimes they are,' she whispered back.

Chapter Eighteen

JANUARY BEGAN MILD and everyone said it would shorten the winter. Come the last week, though, and it was a different story; it blew itself out with a gale which tore branches from the trees and dislodged roof-tiles all over the village. February came in bitterly cold, with dark skies and a warning that snow was on the way.

It was Thursday of the third week in February and only seven-forty-five in the morning when Barbara heard her mother calling her from the hall downstairs.

'Barbara, come down, James is on the telephone.'

Barbara didn't wait to put on her dressing-gown, just pushed her feet into her slippers and, clad only in her nightdress, ran down the stairs.

'James?'

'Yes, darling, sorry to get you up. How do you fancy a trip to Jersey?'

'Very much so, but why call about it now?'

'Because I have to leave for Jersey tonight. Long story! You know I've been in Kingston all week at the Surrey assizes; well the lawyers acting for the Crown have sprung a surprise on us. Offshore investments. I'll explain more fully later. Thing is, if I'm there ready first thing in the morning, I can deal with what I have to and we'll have the whole weekend to ourselves.'

'That's lovely, James. Where do you want me to meet

you? Shall I phone for an hotel reservation? What about flights?'

'No, calm down; I can get all that dealt with by one of the office secretaries, but it would help if you could be at my parents' home say about four? Depends on how the hearing goes today as to what time I get away, should be home by five. I've asked my mother to pack me a bag. There's a flight from Gatwick about eight-forty-five.'

Barbara was beaming. 'Sounds as if you've planned things well. I'll be in Eastbourne when you get there. Oh, there is one thing, the weather forecast last night was not so good; did you hear it?'

'Yes. Forecast snow. All the more reason we should escape to sunny Jersey. Must go. See you this evening. Love you.'

'I love you too.'

Very much, she added to herself as she replaced the receiver.

By the time Barbara had bathed and dressed, Mrs Ferguson was on the telephone. 'James rang me, Barbara. Don't wait till this evening, can you come for lunch? Lovely as this old house is, it seems very lonely when there is no one but me rattling around in it. Everyone is about their own business today. You'd be doing me a kindness.'

'Of course I'll come – love to. I'll be there by one.'

'That will be nice,' her mother exclaimed when Barbara had told her the gist of the conversation. 'Can I help with your packing?'

'Mother, don't start fussing! I'm only going to Eastbourne for lunch and to Jersey for the weekend. I'm not taking a trunk!'

'Don't be so cheeky,' her mother retaliated. But in spite

of herself she couldn't hide her smiles. Oh, it was good to
see Barbara so happy. She blessed the day that Phillip had
introduced their daughter to James Ferguson.

Home to the Fergusons was a five-storey house in the
Meads, one of the highest points in Eastbourne. Almost at
the foot of the South Downs, Meads Village was sheltered
and yet only a short walk from the seashore. It was also a
place unaltered by time. Only a few shops, but shops where
courtesy and service was given without question. The village boasted two pubs, The Ship and The Pilot; neither
were ordinary public houses but were places where folk
met to enjoy conversation, a nice drink in congenial surroundings.

When the houses in Darley Road were built no expense
had been spared. High, wide and grand was what sprang
to Barbara's mind each time she visited. From the flight of
steps leading to the heavy front door, the pillars which
supported the porch, the tall bay windows and the long
wide hall: everything was huge. Even the wainscoting
throughout was at least eighteen inches high and the cost
of the curtains in the main rooms didn't bear thinking
about.

It was a house built for a family. A family who in years
gone by would have employed many servants. It didn't
seem to bother the Fergusons, apparently they got by with
a couple of cleaning ladies. At get-togethers, when the
whole family, including in-laws and children, would turn
up, Barbara had been amazed at how smoothly things were
planned. Everyone mucked in, children and adults alike,
each had their allotted tasks and performed them without

any resentment. Above all it was a happy house, and Barbara always looked forward to going there.

It had started to snow as Barbara drove out of Alfriston and by the time she reached Eastbourne it was snowing heavily. She received a very warm welcome from Mrs Ferguson and the two of them enjoyed a most companionable lunch, eaten in the vast, but somehow cosy, basement kitchen.

It was dark by four o'clock, still snowing and Barbara was starting to worry. At a quarter past five Chloe and her father arrived home together.

'Damned hazardous weather, is this,' Mr Ferguson grumbled to his wife as he shook the snow from his overcoat. 'Look at it and I've only walked across the drive from the garage.' Turning, he saw Barbara, 'Hallo my dear, fancy you being out in this weather. Not that I'm not delighted to see you,' he hastened to add.

'Hallo Barbara!' Chloe came into the lounge, rubbing her hands to get some warmth back into them. 'Nice to see you; rotten weather though, bet you'll have to stay here tonight.'

Explanations were left to Mrs Ferguson. 'She's meant to be flying to Jersey with James this evening. They have to be at Gatwick by eight.'

'No sign of James, eh?' Mr Ferguson tut-tutted.

Chloe put a reassuring arm across Barbara's shoulders. 'He'll ring soon, I shouldn't wonder. The roads were very slippery in places. I was driving, it was awful trying to see, wipers couldn't cope. More like a blizzard than a snowfall and trouble is there are patches of ice forming where you least expect them.'

'Stop frightening the girl,' her father rebuked Chloe. He

took hold of Barbara by the elbow and led her to an armchair close to the fire. 'Sit you down my dear, stop worrying. How about some coffee? Know I could do with a cup. Come along, stretch your legs out, James will make it home. Relax.'

'Dinner's ready, move yourselves. I've set it downstairs in the kitchen, it's lovely an' warm down there.' Mrs Ferguson had opened the door to the lounge and popped her head in, disappearing again before they had time to answer.

The scene was certainly cosy. She had pulled the big square table close to the fire and set the four chairs to be facing the range.

Muriel Ferguson was doing her best to hide the fact that she was worried about her son, she had drawn her husband aside and in a low voice asked him, 'Robert, isn't there anyone we can telephone? It isn't like James not to call.'

'If James is on the road there is no way I have to contact him,' he quietly told her. 'Serve the dinner, my dear, and try not to let Barbara see that we are worried.'

Muriel put the food on the table and the four of them sat doing their best to do justice to the meal, hardly speaking, except that once Chloe said, 'I expect James has holed up somewhere, we would have heard – ' but at a look from her father she didn't finish the sentence. Barbara helped Chloe to wash-up while Mrs Ferguson made coffee, which they carried back up to the lounge. Robert Ferguson sat in his armchair with the evening paper, not really reading it. The wind coming from off the sea rattled the windows. This February night was turning out to be a very long one.

It was almost nine o'clock when the doorbell rang. Mr Ferguson rose to answer it. Hearing male voices, the three women were sure it was bad news. It was a few minutes before he returned to the lounge, walking slowly, followed by a policeman who must have removed his overcoat or macintosh in the hall because his uniform was dry.

'There's been . . . I have to tell you,' the young man began. He stopped – obviously he hadn't had much experience with this sort of thing.

Robert Ferguson took over. 'James has been involved in an accident,' he said softly.

Barbara was impatient to know the details: 'Hurry up, tell us if James is badly hurt. Where is he? In which hospital? was what she wanted to yell; instead she remained quiet.

The policeman took a deep breath, 'The roads are really treacherous with icy patches. Seems the car skidded on a curve.'

'You're not telling us he is *dead*?' Muriel, her voice rising to a high pitch, flung the question at the policeman.

'*No!* Sorry – no, nothing as bad as that. In fact, from what I've been told, the ambulance was called by another motorist and they got your son out and away to hospital pretty quickly.'

The sigh of relief hung in the air.

Mr Ferguson took down details and telephone numbers obligingly offered by the constable, and then went to the door with him to see him out.

The three women, now alone, held out a hand to each other. That brought the tears.

'I'm going into my study to make a few calls,' Mr Ferguson told them. 'I'll be as quick as I can an' then I'll come back and let you know exactly what I have been able to find out.' At the doorway he hesitated, half-turned and said to Barbara, 'My dear, I think you should call your parents, tell them what has happened and let them know you'll be stopping here tonight. Use the phone that's down in the kitchen.'

'We'll come with you,' Chloe said, speaking for her mother as well as herself. 'I'll make some tea. Be glad of something to do.'

The telephone lines were fine: You wouldn't know there was a blizzard raging outside, Barbara thought as she listened to her mother say how sorry she was. 'Please, darling, phone us again as soon as you have any news.'

'I will, Mother. For the moment at least James has been taken to Kingston General Hospital. Just pray that the roads are not going to be too bad; anyway, even if we have to come by train, Mr Ferguson has promised to get us there as soon as he can. Goodnight, Mummy. Say goodnight to Daddy for me. God bless you.'

'Don't hang up for a minute, Barbara.' Her mother's voice sounded tense. 'Tim rang soon after you left this morning: Elizabeth has had her baby, a little girl, six pounds six ounces, born in the early hours of this morning.'

'Is she all right?'

'Yes. Tim is over the moon. Said mother an' baby are both doing well.'

'Thank God for that.'

Barbara couldn't help herself: as she turned to tell Chloe and Mrs Ferguson about Elizabeth she was feeling downright envious.

Why did everything go so right for some in this life and so terribly wrong for others?

In the past three weeks everything that could be done for James had been done. He had been taken from Kingston

Hospital to the London Clinic and put into the care of Mr Brooks, a Harley Street specialist. James's family had shown Barbara nothing but kindness, but somehow she often felt shut out. All decisions and information came to her second-hand through his father. Only right, she would tell herself: she wasn't James's wife. James had undergone surgery for a broken pelvis, that much was certain, but there was so much more that she hadn't been told. For one thing – why was James unconscious for such long periods and why did he seem to be in constant pain?

Dry-eyed, Barbara had kept a watch by him through long lonely days, taking her turn with his family. Most times he drifted in the half-world of delirium. As she listened to his all but unintelligible mutterings, the one name she did hear over and over again was her own.

Today she had cause to be joyful: James was awake and clear-headed.

As she entered his room he tried in vain to raise his head from the pillow. His kind gentle eyes and her own tear-filled ones met, then his own brand of humour saved the moment, 'Tied me down good an' proper, have you darling?'

She took his hand between her own. 'Yes,' she said, simply. 'You, my love, will have great difficulty in ever getting away from me again.'

She kissed his forehead, his cheeks and then his lips and was thrilled to see the wide smile which came to his face before he once more drifted off to sleep.

She hoped against hope the worst was over. Those awful days she had lived through asking time and time again, dear Jesus, how bad is he? Is he going to die? Then quickly rebuking herself: Don't think of that. Don't even think it. Instead she would try her best to think of Henley, a boat on the river, James telling her to let go of the past and love him, of riding their horses across the Downs, of their stay in the Lake District and their wonderful lovemaking.

She would go and get some exercise while James slept.

It was still bitterly cold. The snow hadn't really cleared, it lay in dirty piles of slush along the kerbstones and gutters. A cold wetness touched her cheek, and then another. In the glow of the embankment lights, small white flakes drifted down. More snow? The tow-path was dry, but already the white flakes were drifting into layers along the wall. Flakes fastened onto her eyelashes as she walked. Others landed on her uncovered head, making her hair wet. She had walked a lot further than she had intended.

A taxi appeared and she hailed it, and soon she was back in the warmth of the hospital.

With some relief she found no medical staff in James's room, but Barbara had barely removed her coat, thinking how lovely and warm it was in here, before a nurse entered bringing coffee with her. 'I saw you come back, Miss Hamlin. You must be frozen, I knew you'd be ready for a hot drink.

'Mr Brooks left a message for you, would you go along to his office before you leave?'

Barbara smiled her thanks. The coffee was delicious, unexpectedly so.

The summons to the specialist's office had her worried. Her pulse began to race as she heard him bid her come in in answer to her knock.

'Ah, Miss Hamlin,' Mr Brooks rose from behind his desk

as she slowly walked across the carpet. He was a large, broad-shouldered man, immaculate in his dark suit and white shirt.

'Come and sit down. Mr Ferguson senior has asked me to have this little chat with you. Only fair in the circumstances. I understand you and James are engaged to be married?'

Barbara felt he was an instantly likeable man with a relaxed, comfortable manner, but who nevertheless looked and sounded like the serious doctor he was.

Mr Brooks got right down to business and Barbara was grateful for his forthrightness, and that he wasn't trying to raise false hopes in her. He watched her as she let out a long shuddering sigh and, used as he was to delivering sad news, he felt compassion for this elegant young woman who was so obviously in love with James Ferguson.

Barbara had heard right. James was paralysed, yet she had this weird idea that this strong capable doctor was talking to the wrong person. It couldn't be James he was speaking about. No, of course it couldn't be, James was so much better today, alert – even humorous.

'I am so sorry, Miss Hamlin. James will in all other aspects be healthy. Unfortunately his spinal cord was snapped, it is irrevocably damaged. With the best will in the world, there is nothing more anyone can do for him. Short of a miracle the nerve-ends will not mend.'

He stood up again and came around his desk to where Barbara sat. He took hold of her hand and very gently told her, 'There is no damage to his brain. That must be a lot to be thankful for. The top half of his body will quite soon be strong and healthy. He'll need a wheelchair to get about in, but you'll see, he'll cope. James will even be able to continue with his profession, if he so chooses. With time things will improve.'

'Yes, yes.' She managed to nod her head. 'Thank you,' she stammered. Her brown eyes were shining with unshed tears as she raised her head and looked at him.

She'll cope, Mr Brooks said to himself, she won't desert the man, she will remain steadfast and loyal – of that he felt certain.

The experience of the past weeks was over. James was coming home. They say that money smooths all paths. In James's case that was true. His father had had two rooms, on the ground floor of their Eastbourne home, turned into a suite for James. A special bed had been ordered and delivered. At a touch of a button the bed could be raised or lowered. A backrest worked in a similar way, allowing the patient to sit or lie in several positions. A pulley swung over head, a chain ran through a grooved rim attached to which was a wooden handle: by pulling on this, James would be able to raise himself to a sitting position.

'Thank God his arms are strong,' his mother had remarked as she watched it being fitted.

Paul Soames had been engaged to take care of James; he would sleep in the room adjacent to that occupied by James.

Barbara had finally come to terms with the fact that up until now she had never been willing to admit, even to herself: James would never walk again. Barbara felt she loved James even more since the accident, if that were possible, but she was only human and she did sometimes harbour a deep resentment. Why James? Why him? She had been given this second chance, they were so happy together. All their plans! It wasn't fair!

But then, as she had discovered to her cost, only a fool thought life was fair. Life was cruel, unjust.

James was aware of his dependence on Paul Soames, but rather this than on others. Paul not only acted as his male nurse but as a good companion; at thirty-two years of age he had performed his war service in the RAF as a ground engineer. James and his father had agreed to employ Paul not for his medical knowledge, but rather for his brawny physique. His powerful, strong arms and massive shoulders made simple work of preparing James to face the day. When it came to lifting him from his bed and into the specially installed bathroom there was no exertion. Paul would carry him as a baby, James's useless legs dangling over his forearms.

They talked together discussing many subjects, the biggest bonus being that Paul did not regard him as a helpless invalid.

Doubtless James had his bad days, when he longed for the clock to be turned back to when he had been a whole man − a man with a good life stretching before him. On a good day he counted his blessings. His mind had not been impaired, he could carry on his work with Bradley and Summerford. In that quarter he had been very lucky − every member of the firm had visited him, assured him they were expecting him to return to the practice and to pull his weight in full.

Even without working money would be no problem, for since his grandfather's death ten years ago he had been a wealthy young man. Besides the house near Jevington he owned several acres of land there about. But that wasn't the point: he could never lead an idle life. The profession he had chosen to follow was one that intrigued him, it was never dull, it stimulated his brain and kept his mind active. Yet he was only human. There were times when he wanted to bawl his eyes out, so overwhelmed was he by his love for Barbara. She had suffered so much in her life and he had promised her such a rosy future. What could he offer her now?

What girl in her right mind would want to saddle herself with a man who was paralysed from the waist down?

Heavy-hearted, for it had been one of James's bad days, Barbara returned early one evening from Eastbourne to find Penny keeping her mother company.

'God, am I glad to see you!' she told Penny, holding her at arm's-length after they had embraced. 'You look marvellous, Neil must be treating you right.'

'Oh he's doing that all right, but he's away to Scotland till the end of the week, some important account that had to be dealt with in person. Still, ill wind an' all that. I rang, and your mother said I was welcome to stay here, so here I am.'

'Thank you, Mummy. I can make a guess at what you thought.'

'And you'd be right too. Penny will be a tonic for you, and for me come to that.'

During dinner the two girls never stopped chatting for a moment. Penny prattled on about the cruise, 'Service was fantastic! Wish for something an' somehow it appeared.'

Mrs Hamlin was well aware that all the idle gossip between the pair of them was only to put off the awkward moment when the matter of James would have to come under discussion. She was relieved when, at the coffee stage, Phillip announced he had a lot of papers to go through and would take his coffee into his study.

'You are never going to go through with the wedding!' Penny cried in dismay when Barbara at last let it be known how she felt.

Even her mother let out a gasp, too upset to comment.

'Listen, both of you,' Barbara began, 'I'm not quite sure how to explain my feelings and I don't expect you to understand.'

'Understand!' Penny roughly interrupted. 'Darling, you can't have thought things through. As I understand it, James will need professional nursing.'

'Have you *really* thought about it, Barbara?' her mother gently asked.

'Yes, for hours on end, if you really want to know, Mother, and I am still going to go through with it. That's if James will have me.'

'You mean the two of you haven't discussed it?' Penny asked.

'No, not yet. But look at it like this, if James hadn't had the accident he would have taken care of me. I love him, very much,' she had to pause there and swallow the sob that rose in her throat. 'I hope he loves me, I'm sure he does, nothing between us has altered.'

'*Please*, Barbara,' Penny was pleading with her now. 'Don't commit yourself, not for the second time. You're fooling yourself. What kind of a marriage can it possibly be? You told me yourself James will never again be an able-bodied man.'

Barbara gave an impatient shrug to her shoulders. 'Don't

you think I've said all these things, and more, to myself over and over again?'

Emotions were running high and Patricia groped for words, 'Darling, it's early days yet. Your father was saying the same thing to me this morning, be patient, let things take their course. We both of us want your happiness more than anything on earth. But at the moment what you are contemplating would test the love of *any* two people.'

She paused and sighed heavily and, when neither of the girls uttered a word, she went on speaking in a very soft voice, 'I don't know a finer man than James, and your father has great admiration for him and for what he has accomplished. We do know how much you care for each other. But there are so many things I am sure you have not given a thought to. What about children? You're not getting any younger, won't it break your heart to know you can never have a family?'

Oh Mother! Barbara was on the point of screaming. Children! She had to bring that up, didn't she? I've thought of nothing else. Regrets, all her life seemed to be made up of regrets. Being sorry didn't alter the facts though, did it? She took a deep breath, she wouldn't cry – she couldn't anyway, she hadn't any tears left to shed.

'What else can I say to you, Barbara, dear?'

Barbara forced herself to answer very quietly, 'Nothing, Mother, that I haven't said to myself.'

Somehow, Barbara's quiet words touched Penny. She rose to her feet, went across to where Barbara sat and put her arms around her, gently kissing her on her cheek.

'You really are determined, aren't you? Well if that's the case, darling, you had better sort things out with the groom and we'd better get on with the preparations, don't you think, Auntie Pat?'

Patricia was sadly telling herself that, as parents, she and her husband couldn't protect Barbara from all the bad times, even those she didn't deserve. We just have to continue to love her, to be here when she needs us, she vowed as she held her hands out to her daughter.

'If you've made up your mind, if this is *truly* what you want, then, my darling, what can I say but God give you strength.'

Thank you, Mummy,' Barbara answered, throwing herself into her mother's arms. 'It won't be all doom an' gloom, you'll see. James will get stronger. I know he'll never be one hundred per cent but we shall be happy.'

Barbara looked from her mother to her friend; she managed a smile, yet for all that it was a solemn smile that still held a trace of sadness. Now, she thought to herself, all I have to do is bring James round to my way of thinking.

Patricia decided she could offer no more advice or make any further comment. She bent her head to receive a good-night kiss from the girls, put her head round the study door and said, 'I'm going up, darling, I'll read for a while.'

Phillip raised his head and smiled at his wife, 'All right, my love, I won't be too long myself, just winding up here and I'll follow you up.'

In her room, however, Patricia was unable to read let alone sleep, but lay there fretting for hours with worry that her dear daughter was about to be hurt again.

It had become a custom of Paul Soames to nip out of the house and go tramping across the fields towards the village when Barbara arrived to sit with James. Usually he was back within the hour. On this particular day, however, James was wide awake, had all his wits about him and when Barbara arrived seemingly full of the joys of spring, it was immediately obvious to Paul that something was afoot. He wasn't wrong.

'I'll walk to the door with you,' Barbara said cheerfully, as Paul took his leave from James.

She hesitated, then screwed up courage, 'Paul,' she began, 'Would you . . . do you think . . .'

'Walk a bit further today, give you and James a little more time on your own?' Paul quietly suggested.

'Yes, would you mind?' Barbara asked half-heartedly.

'Not at all, I'm sure James will be fine,' said Paul and a moment later was gone out of the hall, leaving it strangely empty and Barbara's mood dropped. Now she felt forlorn. How would James react to her proposal?

Only one thing for it, she vowed: jump in feet first.

Seated by the side of the bed, James's hand held between both of hers, she could contain herself no longer.

'How would you like to discuss our wedding plans, James? I can't see any reason why we should wait,' Barbara continued.

With a sober sincerity that almost broke her heart, James said 'Is it a matter worth discussing?'

After a moment's hesitation, Barbara answered. 'Yes, it is.'

James sighed. 'I can see so many problems – for both of us.'

Barbara paused and then, with a touch of sorrow in her voice, admitted, 'Frankly, James, so can I. But we shouldn't let anything stand in our way. You're going to advise me to wait, aren't you? I don't want to wait, James. I want us to be married as soon as possible.'

James managed a trace of a smile and didn't try to avoid Barbara's eyes.

'I don't deserve you,' he whispered.

And I don't deserve you, was what she said to herself; instead she said aloud, 'Shall we talk about wedding plans?'

'Hey! Not so fast,' he pleaded.

'Why? Are you going to tell me that you aren't in love with me any more?'

'Oh, Barbara! Nothing could be further from the truth.'

'Well then?'

The look on James's face softened. 'Barbara, let's talk sensibly about this. To have you for my wife is what I've dreamed about. I've told you over and over again, I love you. I wanted nothing more from life then to spend everyday with you. But now . . .'

'But *now*, what? You are still you, and I am still me. Let's be grateful you weren't killed.'

'That's all very well, Barbara, but life wouldn't be a bed of roses, for you or for me. We would both us feel utterly frustrated at times, remorseful for what might have been. No, my darling, I love you too much to let you sacrifice the rest of your life tied to a cripple.'

He turned his face to the wall and his body shook. Barbara's heart ached for him, but if she let the matter rest there she might just as well get up now and walk away. He deserved better than that.

'A cripple, you said! T'hell with that! Is *that* what you see yourself as?'

'The paralysis of my legs is permanent.' He rubbed at his eyes with the corner of the sheet. 'I can't be the same as I was. I never will be. How can I be your husband, Barbara?'

'There are thousands worse than you. Men who lost limbs, even their sight, during the War. Did their wives desert them? If you haven't got the courage to tell me to my face that you don't want to marry me, well, that would be a different story. But I need to know right now.'

'Don't be so bloody daft.'

She didn't touch him, didn't comfort him. She let him cry, watching the tears roll slowly down his cheeks.

After what seemed an eternity she got up from her chair, went into the bathroom and came back with a wet face-flannel and a dry towel. Without a word she handed them to James and stood by while he washed his face. From the bureau which stood against the wall she fetched a silver-backed hairbrush and again waited while he brushed his tousled fair hair.

'Now I'm going to tell you one more thing and then I shall go in search of some tea for us.'

'Is there any way I could stop you?' he asked with a touch of his old humour.

The laugh Barbara gave almost bordered on hysteria but she pressed on, 'When Mr Brooks spoke to me he didn't pull any punches. He told me everything that was negative about your condition but he also pointed out all that was positive. Mostly he emphasised there was no damage to your brain. I've clung to that, and James, you should too. You are not a vegetable, your mind is *not* crippled, it is still as brilliant and active as ever. You have been told by your firm that in time they expect you to go back, to continue to practise law, even Daddy says there is no reason why you shouldn't . . .' Her eyes were full, her throat choking; she couldn't go on pleading for much longer. 'You see . . . if only you would marry me you'd still be able to keep me in the type of luxury you promised.' She was making an attempt to be flippant now, before adding, 'I'm not trying to be a martyr, honestly, James, I'm not. I love you *so* much. I can't think of what my life would be like without you.'

It happened naturally. Their arms automatically went round each other, their faces touched and their tears mingled. Outside the cold dry day grew darker, but in that room nothing and no one mattered but the two of them.

'If you're quite sure?' James softly queried, much later. 'It won't be easy.'

With much more brightness than she was feeling, Barbara said, 'Nobody's suggesting it will be easy, we'll learn to cross each bridge as we come to it. Together. Now may we talk of wedding plans? Set a date!'

What was going through her mind was the fact that nothing worth having ever seemed to come easily. At least, not to her!

Chapter Nineteen

TIME NO LONGER hung heavy on Barbara's hands and she was never short of a topic of conversation or a funny incident to relay to James. Their decision to make the house in Jevington their home after they were married was a unanimous one. James's father entered into the spirit of the operation and proved himself invaluable when it came to finding the exact workman for each and every job that needed to be done. On all points he consulted Barbara, asking not only for her views but demanding that she voiced her preference wherever there was a choice to be had. They were in complete agreement that, by and large, the house should retain its character.

On one point only did she dig her heels in: the huge bath with its iron claw feet was to stay. Workmen argued, plumbers pleaded. James laughed his head off, Barbara didn't give a damn.

'Work around it,' she implored. 'Paint the feet, install mirrors on the wall, put up a new ceiling, new washbasins, a modern toilet – anything you like, but leave the bath in the centre of the room. It looks majestic.' The workmen smiled behind her back. Mr Ferguson aired his views, all to no avail. The bath stayed put.

Barbara would now burst into James's room, armed with wallpaper-pattern books, carpet samples, catalogues showing pictures of kitchen units and cooking stoves. His mother would put her head around the door to ask if they were ready for tea.

On more than one occasion, Paul, who would be involved in all the discussions, would say, 'You come and sit here, Mrs Ferguson. See what you think about this paper for the hall. I'll go an' make the tea.'

Muriel Ferguson's heart was a whole lot lighter these days. Since Barbara and James had decided that their wedding would go ahead, it was as if James had taken on a whole new lease of life. She thanked God each night that James had come to terms with his disability and she prayed that her son and Barbara would indeed find happiness. She did her best not to let her thoughts dwell on the limitations there would be to this marriage. Sufficient unto the day, please God.

Barbara and James had both been determined James wouldn't be confined upstairs and out of touch with what was going on. So plans had been drawn up, agreed on and passed by the local council for an extension to be built onto the end of the house. A door was cut through the main wall and James would be able to wheel himself through the hallway, from which led off the main lounge, dining room, and the kitchen. In the new building would be James's large bedroom, another bed-sitting-room for Paul Soames and a big bathroom with special fittings to help with James's disablement, also a smaller room which would in time serve as his office.

It had been James himself who had held meetings with the architect, and his influence and preference that had determined the outcome of the finished plans.

Most days would find Barbara down there, walking the grounds, thinking it was a marvellous old house of great character and charm. The thick natural stone walls that surrounded the garden gave it security and privacy. It had all the eccentricities and the beauty of an old village house. Long, low, leaded windows downstairs, small ones upstairs. Low doorways and arches that led to the fields beyond and, further afield, the stables.

It was a house that should happily ring with the sound of children's laughter.

When such thoughts came into Barbara's mind she would do her best to banish them. Nobody has everything in this life!

James wasn't bright and cheerful every day. Who could expect him to be?

On such days when she didn't know how to comfort him and his dark mood would peeve her, she would make the effort to drive to Jevington and trudge off to the stables. She'd liked Clem Tompson since the first day she'd set foot on the place and he always seemed so pleased to see her.

She would change her clothes and shoes in the locker-room and wait in the yard for one of the lads to bring her a mount. Clem usually made sure it was the same one, Lady, a grey filly with a sweet, passive temperament that suited her mood.

Barbara would mount up and let Lady amble down the track that led to the Downs, giving the horse her head only when they were beyond the bridle paths. Born and bred around horses, the weather held no fear for Barbara. Should it be raining she would accept the offer of an oilskin cape and ride out to find the smell of fresh horse manure, wet grass and dripping trees truly exhilarating. Later she would return to the yard to share a mug of steaming coffee with Clem. Always able to judge Barbara's moods, Clem would talk of what was happening in the racing game and, more often than not, had a message for her to relate to James from several trainers, most of whom had a considerable reputation in the world of racing.

The day came when Barbara was in a relaxed mood.

'James getting stronger?' Clem Tompson asked, handing Barbara a mug and warning her that the coffee was scalding.

'Improving every day,' she beamed in delight. 'Honestly, Clem, you should see him manipulate that electric wheelchair. He can turn it on a sixpence, wonder he doesn't give his poor mother a heart attack. She cringes when he comes flying across the room – fearful for her beautiful furniture – still, as yet he has managed to avoid bashing into it.'

'So, shall we be hearing wedding bells before too long? Or am I not allowed to ask?'

Barbara slid her arm across Clem's shoulder, and tilted her head in a saucy gesture. 'Clem, it won't be long now, you'll know in good time to tog yourself up!' Then her face became serious. 'Thanks isn't enough, Clem, for what you've done for me. Many a day you've saved my reason.'

'Get on with you, love, all I've done is see you've had a mount. Not much to that.'

He turned his head away. He didn't want her to see how much her words had meant to him. His heart had ached for the pair of them. All these months James had been laid up, knowing he'd never walk again – and them with everything in the world to live for. Didn't seem but yesterday that the two of them had stood in this yard, fit an' able the both of them; telling him of their plans to do the old house up and live in it. Man and wife. God this lass was plucky! She'd stood by James. But then James deserved no less. He'd known the lad since he was a nipper, never did a wrong turn to anyone, nice lad was James. Never seems to be those that deserve it that get the bottom knocked out of their world, he was thinking to himself as he watched Barbara walk back across the yard.

The year had gone by; Elizabeth had had her baby daughter christened Hannah. Barbara hadn't gone down to Windsor for the event, she wouldn't leave James for that length of time. Both her parents had attended, so had Penny and Neil and Penny's parents also. The reports brought back to Barbara was that the baby was gorgeous and had behaved very well, only crying when the vicar had sprinkled her forehead with the holy water.

The house was almost ready. Christmas had come and gone again and Barbara and James were all set to have an Easter wedding. The awareness that soon they would be man and wife lent a special intensity to their relationship. Each day Barbara would arrive in Eastbourne not knowing what to expect. If James was perky, full of good humour and so loving towards her, she thanked God. If he was withdrawn she would be choked with emotion, sad for him and even more so for herself, knowing that there was no way she could reach him. All she could do was talk to him and wait.

Some days seemed to drag on interminably until suddenly James suggested that he taught her how to play chess. For that she was eternally grateful. She learnt quickly and from then on she never had to coax him into a game, it was something they both enjoyed.

Poor James! Paul Soames knew more than anyone what he was going through. His bride-to-be was beautiful. Tall, slim, long dark hair that glistened with chestnut glints whenever the sun caught it, skin that was as fresh and clear as porcelain and a personality that would charm the birds out of the trees. Of course James felt frustrated! What man wouldn't!

Paul had become extremely fond of both Barbara and James; he knew by now that they had a special kind of love, a love for each other that seemed to him to be very rare, and there wasn't anything he wouldn't do to help either one of them. What he asked himself was, how were the two of them going to survive in a marriage that could never be fully fulfilled? Could they survive?

Easter Saturday, Patricia Hamlin watched as her husband donned his jacket, then carefully she placed the white carnation into his buttonhole. The expression on her face showed sadness.

'If only James hadn't had that accident,' she spoke half to herself. 'It hurts that Barbara will not really have a normal married life.'

'I know it does, dear. But then, the decision is Barbara's after all. James is a good fellow – you know that for yourself. He will certainly care for her. He will be still be able to work. His mind is active enough, even without his earnings he can offer our Barbara security, a lovely home and above all else, Patricia, they love each other. Come on now, no tears today, powder your nose and be happy for them.' Dropping his head he softly added, 'Things could have been worse you know, much worse.'

In the pretty bedroom that had been hers as a child, Barbara pulled her wedding dress over her head, carefully so as not to disarrange her hair. The dress was a simple one: a delicate shade of yellow, cut straight across the bodice with two thin shoulder-straps, over which she wore a loose bolero that fell to be gathered into a band at the waist. Heavy Belgian lace formed cuffs for the sleeves.

Her dark hair had been teased into an up-swept hairdo. A few wisps escaped at the nape of her neck and in front of her ears to show below the soft cream-coloured, straw, wide-brimmed hat that she wore. A narrow band of the same Belgian lace was the only adornment on the hat.

Her flowers were a small posy of pale yellow roses, interwoven with maidenhair fern.

'Ready, darling?' her father's voice crackled with emotion. 'Turn around and let me look at you,' he ordered. Barbara did as he asked. 'You look beautiful,' her father said softly. Coming forward he bent to kiss her. A gentle kiss that said it all.

No motorcars for Barbara today, or for the main wedding guests. Colin Peterson, who still had charge of her father's small stables, and Clem Tompson were driving open carriages each drawn by a pair of well-matched horses.

Folk had gathered to line the long narrow High Street of Alfriston. Perched insecurely on the cramped high pavements they were a jolly lot. Some waving balloons, others calling their good wishes. The quaint shops with bottle-glass bow windows that overhung the pavement carried placards: 'Good luck to Barbara and James!' The story of this wedding and all that had gone before had touched the hearts of local people and they had turned out to show their goodwill.

There was no shortage of ushers. Neil Chapman, Peter Bradley, who had made them so welcome on his boat at

Henley, Anthony Holt, now engaged to James's sister Chloe, and Mark Bradley, son of one of the senior partners of the law firm that employed James. All were dressed for the occasion.

Barbara and her father descended from the carriage at the end of the lane and walked the path through the well-mown grass to the entrance of St Andrew's Church.

Barbara had no bridesmaids, only Penny to stand behind her to take her flowers when the time came.

It was not until Barbara entered the church, saw the sun shining through the high stained glass windows that rose high above the altar and heard the organ notes that she faltered.

Her arm was through the crook of her father's elbow and he used his free hand to tighten his grip on her. 'Brave girl,' he whispered.

She was vaguely aware of seeing people she knew: Mrs Clarkson, who had been a gem this last few weeks, and – wonder of wonders – sitting beside her was Mrs Winters! Oh, that was nice of her mother to have invited her.

'God bless you,' Mrs Winters whispered softly.

Barbara smiled her thanks.

Without the help and kindness of Mrs Winters she would never have survived all that time she had lived in Battersea. But she wasn't going to dwell on the past. Not today.

Her heart lurched as her eyes met those of James. There was nothing pathetic about James, so elegantly attired in his morning suit as he sat bolt upright in his wheelchair. His brother Rodney, acting as his best man, looked tall and stately standing on the right-hand side of James.

As Barbara and her father neared the front pews she was aware that these seats were occupied by those for whom she cared and who cared for her. Tim and Elizabeth with their three children. James's parents, his sister Ann and her husband Jack Tully with their twins, Lucy and Harry. Rodney's wife Elaine sat on the other side of little Lucy and was obviously amused at some remark the child had made, for she was dipping her head to hide her smiles.

Barbara felt the tension ease. This was such a happy day. She would have two families now. Brothers and sisters, nieces and nephews, she and James wouldn't have to face the uncertainty on their own in the years that lay ahead.

The vicar, splendid in his robes, gave a smile of encouragement to Barbara as she took her place besides James.

The ceremony began.

When it came to Barbara's responses she turned her head, gazed directly into James's eyes and with all the love that was in her heart she vowed, 'I will.'

James made his responses in a strong voice, smiled up at her, took her left hand in his and, gently but firmly, slipped onto her outstretched finger the gold band that signified they were man and wife.

Behind her, both their mothers were weeping, others too perhaps, but Barbara was filled with joy. No more misgivings, she and James would face the future together.

Chapter Twenty

ON THE SURFACE of things life in the new Ferguson household had settled into an even pace.

Modernised now, to a great extent the charm of the house remained unchanged. Beautiful wood had been restored and polished, the staircase with its carved banister rails set to rights by craftmen who loved their work. Some of the most beautiful pieces of furniture had been left to James by his grandparents. A tall rosewood bureau, mahogany desk, two high-backed hall chairs with ivory inlaid decoration and two beautiful lounge chairs carved with graceful lines.

She was happy for James, when soon after their marriage, with Paul driving the car, he took off for London four days a week to resume business with his law firm. The silent emptiness they left behind them in the house was terrible and, for Barbara, depressing. She needed to divert herself by doing something useful.

Barbara sat alone in the kitchen, lingering over a third cup of tea. James and Paul had left for London more than an hour ago. She looked out the window at the persistent rain that had been falling since early yesterday evening. A right old dreary day this was going to be!

'Right – make a move,' she ordered herself. 'Don't sit here moping.'

Darting upstairs she made sure all the windows were

closed. With speed she changed her dress for a suit, found shoes and a handbag that matched, and went to phone her mother-in-law.

'Could you do with a visitor?' she grinned when Muriel Ferguson answered her call.

'Anything wrong?'

'No. No, everything is fine; I'm just feeling bored. James is in town for the day.'

A sigh of relief came down the line. 'You're more than welcome, love to see you. Chloe is home for the day. Bring a pair of stout shoes, if this rain lets up we can go tramping over the Downs – or along the beach, come to that.'

Twenty minutes later, Barbara sprinted through the rain to the garage, settled herself comfortably in the driving seat of her car and within minutes was on her way to Eastbourne, pleased at the prospect of having Chloe's company.

It stopped raining, the sky became brighter and Barbara's mood lifted as she drove through the fresh countryside.

Her mother-in-law opened the front door, her face shining with pleasure as she hugged Barbara.

Appetising smells were rising up from the kitchen.

'Coffee an' home-made gingerbread is all ready and I've put a casserole in the oven which won't spoil, no matter what time we decide to eat.'

'You're an angel,' Barbara said and meant it. 'If I'd have stayed on my own today I would have wallowed in self-pity.'

'Well, you're here now and Chloe is so pleased.'

Cake and coffee were consumed quickly.

Two Thermos flasks were filled with boiling water, packed into a wicker basket that already held jars of tea, coffee and sugar. Another flask was filled with cold milk, spoons were held secure by a box of the still-warm ginger-bread and a packet of biscuits.

'Make sure there are three walking sticks in the boot, and wellingtons, just in case,' Muriel called up the stairs to Chloe, who had been given the job of taking the hamper to the car.

The wet May morning had given way to a sunny, warm afternoon. Twenty minutes later, Muriel Ferguson turned the car left and drove beneath the wide canopy that displayed the name: 'BUTCHER'S WHOLE BOTTOM, OWNED AND PROTECTED BY THE FORESTRY COMMISSION'.

Along a tree-lined path and she brought the car to a halt beside several other cars, all parked in order on the shingle-covered ground. Dogs of every shape, colour and form romped across the grass and set off for the woods, their owners in tow.

'Difficult to know who takes who for a walk up here,' Chloe laughed.

'When I was at school we had two dogs and my father used to bring us all up here at weekends,' Barbara reflected aloud. 'No matter what the weather, snow, ice, torrential rain, we never ever arrived here and found no other cars. Such a popular place isn't it?'

Chloe laughed, 'Beats me why the locals always refer to this place as Butcher's Bottom Hole.'

'Me too,' said her mother. 'Suppose it's easier to say quickly than Butcher's Whole Bottom. Whatever, it has always been a very popular place and one has to admit a truly marvellous place. Your father always states that one could come here every day for a month and take a different route.'

She twisted her body around to look at the two girls seated still in the back of the car and asked, 'Well, are we going for a walk or not?'

Shoes off and wellington boots now on, each armed with a stout crook-handled walking stick, they set off. The beginning of the woods had a well-trodden track running through thinly-spaced, tall trees along which people walked in both directions. Not one person passed another without a greeting. 'Afternoon. Lovely now isn't it?'

'Yes, cleared up nicely.'

'Oh, look at that dog! Isn't he lovely?'

'Spoilt rotten, that what he is, all this petting, he laps it up.'

How could one have a black mood in a place like this? Barbara mused to herself, as she stood by while Muriel bent and patted an Old English sheepdog. Half a mile further on, tracks branched off to the right and to the left of where they were walking.

'Let's take the right side,' Chloe insisted. 'The roads on this side wind up higher and the views are magnificent.'

Making good use of their sticks, they began to climb. It was very quiet now. Warm like a summer's afternoon. The trees were taller, the bracken dense, the breeze soft against their cheeks. It took some time to reach the top. Thankfully they sank down among the rough grass and bracken fronds. There was no need for conversation. The view was magnificent!

Old farmhouses with their great barns and outbuildings were strung out at intervals in the distance. Fields of gold, green and brown covered the earth like a patchwork quilt, so that there was no way of knowing where one farm started or another finished. The only sound was the distant hum of farm machinery.

'Up you get,' Chloe broke into their thoughts. 'We've a long way to go yet.'

Another mile along a pathway bordered by bushes of yellow gorse and wild flowers and they came to a path that led downwards.

'I'm going to make my way slowly back to the car,' Muriel decided. 'I'll set the chairs out, have a snooze and I'll make you a drink when you get back.'

'Are you sure you'll be all right?' Chloe questioned her mother.

'Quite sure. You two young ones go are far as you like. I'll see you later.'

They watched as Muriel followed the road which led right down to where they had set off from, then they turned off the track and took a narrow, high-hedged lane that wound up and over even higher.

'I wish I'd never worn these wellingtons, my feet are burning,' Chloe complained as they came to a white-barred gate and a rough path that had been hewn out of the hillside.

'I remember this path, it's a short cut; rough going but eventually one does come out near to where the car is parked,' Barbara said, having first taken several minutes to get her breath back.

'Not yet,' pleaded Chloe, walking beneath a great, leafy tree and thinking how nice it was to be in the shade. 'Park your bottom down here for a while. I've got some chewy fruit-sweets in my pocket, they'll refresh your mouth, do till we get back an' can have a drink.'

'Oh smashing! Barbara ripped at the paper of the sweet with her teeth, the sweets were a bit sticky from having been in Chloe's pocket for so long.

With her back resting against the tree, and her bottom wriggled comfortably into the dry growth of ferns, she tossed a handful of pine cones into the air and sighed contentedly.

'Gosh, I'm glad I came over today and even more glad that you were home, Chloe. I feel a different person for having walked up here. It feels as if we're sitting on top of the world.'

'Mother said you were down in the dumps when she came off the phone this morning. Anything you want to talk about? I can be quite a good listener you know.'

Chloe truly liked her sister-in-law. Now she was worried that Barbara might be regretting her decision to marry her brother. More so when Barbara made no answer.

'Bit of a strain, is it, coping with James?' Chloe sighed, sympathy had been in her voice.

'Not at all!' Barbara rushed quickly to dispel any thoughts that things weren't going right between herself and James. 'James is every inch his own man. One hundred per cent. More so now that he is back in the city, practising law, doing work that he trained for years to be able to do. No, Chloe, it's me. I just don't know what to do to fill my time.'

'I'm sorry,' Chloe softly told her. 'I didn't mean to pry. As long as you and James are happy, that's all the whole family prays for.'

Barbara reached over and took Chloe's hand in hers. 'I know, dear.' Then on impulse she sat up straight and said, 'Chloe, James and I love each other. Probably it isn't natural that either of us can live without full sex. I can't pretend that it doesn't matter all the time. Mostly it doesn't. We get by. We do really love each other and we make love. In our own way. I had such a bad time in my first marriage I sometimes think I am grateful not to have to cope with that side of things.'

Chloe hung her head and murmured. 'Poor Barbara.'

'Chloe, you won't tell anybody about this?'

'Barbara, you know I won't,' Chloe scolded.

Colour had flushed up into Barbara's cheeks. It embarrassed her to talk to anybody of what went on between her and James. It was personal and wonderful for them both. Not enough at times. But then it had to be.

Not every night did she take the stairs to her own bedroom to lie alone in the double bed. She would lie in James's bed, in his arms, and relish in the fact that he adored her and she him. He was tender, attentive, ever conscientious of her needs. Sometimes they would talk into the early hours of the morning. James making sure that she knew of what work he was doing, of cases in which he was involved and relating to her any interesting gossip that often came from the Old Bailey.

The fact that Barbara had blushed had brought an awkward silence between them, a silence that Chloe sought to break but didn't know how.

Barbara was still struggling to hide the intensity of her feelings, but determination showed in her dark eyes.

'What I'd really like to do, Chloe, is get a job. Voluntary work of some kind. I'd like to help others. Especially children,' Barbara added wistfully.

'Well I'll be blowed!' Chloe exclaimed, pushing boister-

ously at Barbara's shoulder. 'The person you want to talk
to is my Anthony,' she said proudly.

'Why Anthony?'

'Just listen and I'll explain. For ages a group of doctors
that Anthony works with have wanted to set up a clinic in
London to help children. Children that are not classed as
hospital cases but need help never the less. Young mothers
that can't cope, babies that have disabilities, unwanted
babies that are found to have been neglected, that sort of
child.'

Barbara's eyes glowed with enthusiasm.

'Go on,' she urged Chloe.

'Well, three months ago a clinic was set up in Vauxhall.'

'How wonderful,' Barbara showed her approval. 'Has it
turned out to be a success?'

'It certainly has. The clinic had only been in operation
a month when money began to pour in. From sources one
would never expect, Anthony said.'

'I want to help,' Barbara declared. 'And don't say James
won't let me.'

'As I said, the best person to talk to about this is Anthony.
He's been involved with this project long before the clinic
was opened.'

'Will you ask him? Tell him I'd like to offer my services.
Once or twice a week at least, I don't mind what job he
finds for me to do.'

'I'll ask him,' Chloe agreed. 'But make sure you discuss
it with James.'

'Oh I will. I promise.'

'Good. You sound a whole lot brighter now. Ready for
the traipse back? You do realise that on this path we have

to climb even higher before we start to descend down to where the car is parked?'

'Let's get started then. That cup of tea your mother promised would be ready will go down a treat, eh?'

The dark panelling of the walls gleamed in the light from two standard lamps and the log fire that burned in the huge fireplace. Soon they wouldn't need a fire in the evenings; with summer well and truly on the way they would be able to spend more time outdoors in the garden.

James smiled at Barbara as she looked around the room. The hearth held a basket piled high with logs, the vases on the side-tables held masses of spring flowers. There was age and tradition here in this house, yet it did not lack a sense of comfort nor yet the homely touches of books, magazines and board-games scattered around the room.

'Would you like a drink, darling?' James asked as he propelled his wheelchair to the cabinet.

'Yes please,' Barbara answered enthusiastically.

James mixed the drinks, whisky and dry-ginger for each of them, while Barbara moved towards the windows.

'Going to be a nice day tomorrow, look at that red sky.'

James came up behind her, handed her the drink, then sat back and studied her. She was thirty-one, small-boned and slender, quite beautiful with her dark colouring and dark-brown eyes. He still couldn't fathom why she had agreed to marry him. He knew everything now of her life with Michael, she had held nothing back in the telling except perhaps the most intimate details. God – what she must have been through. It was no wonder at first he had thought her bubbly personality to be somehow tensed, even forced.

Tonight she seemed relaxed, different somehow, very happy. Oh, he hoped so. They had both known the limitations they faced when they had taken the vow, until death us do part. He silently prayed that he would always be able to make her happy.

As if she had caught his thoughts Barbara raised her glass and said, 'To us, James.'

It wasn't until after they had eaten their evening dinner that Barbara broached the subject.

'James, have you heard about this clinic that doctors in London have set up to help children?'

'Yes, actually it was your father who was telling me. A voluntary group, I understand. Working under very limited conditions. Three portable buildings set up on a disused bomb-site. Must be very dedicated men.'

'Chloe was telling me today that Anthony is very much involved in the project. James, I'd like to offer my services, as an unpaid volunteer. Would you mind?'

She saw his eyes widen in amazement. 'The children they are trying to help will be poor desperate mites.'

'All the more reason why I should do this. Or don't you think I could be of any help?' she challenged.

'If I agree, will you promise not to do too many hours?'

'I promise, James. It's just that the days are so long when you are away in town and my life has no meaning. This is something useful I really would like to do. Please.'

'It won't be nice work, not all the time,' he warned.

Barbara gazed intently at him. 'Are you saying I may offer my services?'

'Could I stop you?' he smiled broadly.

'You intended to agree all along,' she accused.

'Whatever makes you happy. All right,' James capitulated. 'But remember, two days a week at most.'

Barbara's face radiated pleasure. 'Oh, James, thank you!'

He held out his arms. Barbara knelt on the carpet and he brought her to his chest as though she were a tiny child, herself in need of comfort and help.

Would working with children be good for her? Or would the sights she was bound to see break her heart?

It was four weeks now since Barbara had worked her first day at the London clinic. This Tuesday she had arrived earlier than usual. Anthony, too, came in ahead of his schedule. They sat together in the partitioned-off reception room, before the staff came on duty and the mothers with their babies began to arrive.

'I feel so guilty,' Barbara confessed. 'So many of these small children are suffering badly and their wretched mothers don't seem able to cope, those that could haven't enough money to get by on.'

'Barbara, you're doing a great job here,' Anthony said. 'You mustn't try to take everyone's troubles so seriously. But somehow I feel there is more to this conversation than you have so far told me. Something in particular is worrying you. I am right, aren't I?'

'Maybe, I could be wrong.'

'Wrong about what?'

'Well, I suppose it's best someone else is aware that we have a thief working here. I've fretted about it long enough.'

'Barbara, tell me, make me understand what has been going on,' Anthony commanded.

'The first week I was here, half-a-crown disappeared from my purse. I put it down to the fact that I must have

314

been mistaken, though I was almost sure that I wasn't. The second week it was a ten-shilling note. The week after, nothing; so I let the matter drop, but last week I brought with me chocolate buttons, dolly-mixtures and some jelly babies. I thought it would calm the kiddies, make them less frightened if we gave them a few sweeties.'

'That was a nice idea,' Anthony smiled.

'It would have been,' said Barbara. 'When I went to my bag there wasn't a sign of any sweets. I thought I must have been imagining things, perhaps have left them at home. I hadn't. They had been taken, all right. Silly isn't it? Such paltry little things.'

'You've no real evidence, I suppose?'

'Only that the two cleaning women were going at it hammer and tongs when I went in to the cloakroom last week. Mary, the quiet one, was saying it wasn't right, while Joan, the loud-mouthed one, was telling her she should mind her own business.'

'Morning,' several voices chorused and the sound of the metal doors clanging shut could be heard. The nurses were arriving.

'We'll talk about this later on,' said Anthony, his eyes serious as they watched Barbara leave the room.

During the whole of the shift Barbara felt troubled. Should she just have left the matter alone, be more careful where she left her bag in future? But then again, she couldn't walk around clutching it all the time, and the area given over to the staff was very small. To tell the truth she felt sorry for Joan. Convinced that it was her that had taken the items, she could bring herself to imagine why. Also, that loud domineering attitude that the woman adopted could be a brazen front she presented to the world to cover up her own short-comings. Working in this clinic had certainly opened Barbara's eyes to just how privileged a life she herself led. It also summoned up memories of the time when she had lived in Battersea. Memories she would far rather forget.

She had once thought that the area where she and Michael had lived together could have been described as reaching the bottom of the barrel.

How little she had known.

The tenant buildings around this area where the clinic had been set up were ten times worse. Dirt-encrusted, old blocks of flats where no sunlight seemed able to penetrate, surrounded by bomb-sites now cleared of most the debris, they had become unsightly rubbish tips. A place where the fight against dirt must be a losing battle and disease an ever-frightening threat.

The clinic closed at two. The cleaning women came for only two hours, twelve until two. From the narrow corridor Barbara watched as Mary donned her coat and Joan lingered checking items in her straw shopping bag.

'Goodbye, Mary, I will see you next Tuesday,' Barbara said quietly.

'Cheerio, Mrs Ferguson,' Mary answered.

'Can you hang on a minute, Joan, please,' asked Barbara, her heart beating very fast.

'No, I can't, I've got me kids to pick up,' came the sullen reply, from this skinny woman with thin, mousy-coloured hair.

Barbara blocked her way. 'May I have a look in your shopping bag, Joan?'

'What yer gonna look for? These packets of sweets an' bloody chocolate biscuits? Is this what you're after?' Joan asked, pulling several items from her shopping bag and holding them high almost in triumph.

Barbara was taken back by the woman's matter-of-fact acceptance that she had stolen the articles.

'They don't belong to you,' Barbara warned. 'Would you like to tell me why you took them and all the other things, including money.'

''Old on there, missus 'igh an' bloody mighty. You ain't got no proof that I took anything other than what I've got 'ere in me bag, an' seeing as 'ow I ain't left the premises yet, 'ow d'yer know that I'm gonna pinch 'em, eh? Go on answer me that.'

Barbara stared at her, but she held her ground. 'All I'm asking is that you come back into the room and tell me why you thought you were more entitled to a few sweets than some of the poor little mites that come here for treatment.'

Joan pointed a finger at Barbara, 'You fink these are fer me? Well let me tell yer one fing: while you're 'ere playing the bloody lady bountiful, 'anding out sweets an' making out yer some kind of Florence Nightingale, I've got four kids at 'ome who ain't 'ardly ever seen sweets, let alone chocolate biscuits. My kids deserve a treat now an' again just as much as anybody else's kids do, only I ain't the type what goes round pleading in yer so-called clinics. I've always bin taught, God 'elps those what 'elp themselves.' Her rage had to dry up, at least for the moment, she was out of breath.

Barbara seized her chance. 'If you don't come and sit down and talk this through rationally I shall call the police.'

'Fer a few bloody sweets!' A worried look had appeared

on Joan's face. 'What d'yer want me ter do?' she asked in a rush of anxiety.

'Just sit down and talk.'

'What about?'

'Oh, come on, Joan, you're not that stupid, and it wasn't only sweets, you have had twelve and six out of my purse.'

Joan sagged in shock. 'I never fought yer would miss it.' But she had the grace to turn on her heel and go back into the staff room.

Joan's mouth was working but no words came, she crumpled down onto a chair, pulling her threadbare cardigan tightly across her flat chest.

Barbara wanted to weep for the woman. She'd known the time when she had had to go begging to Mrs Winters for a loan in order to buy food.

'Is your husband out of work?' Barbara asked.

'Ain't got no 'usband.'

'I'm so sorry, but you don't have to cope on your own. If only you had spoken to one of the doctors when you applied for the job, I'm sure some help would have been offered you. How long have you been a widow?'

'I never said I was a bloody widow.'

'Sorry, I assumed – '

'Well, I was married at the beginning of the War, got meself pregnant on 'is first leave. After the second time, when I was swollen up like a balloon, he never came 'ome no more.'

'What about the father of the other children?'

'Mind yer own damn business. I don't ask yer about what you do, do I?' She had a point, Barbara conceded to herself.

'All right, Joan. We'll forget the whole thing. I expect

your kiddies look forward to you bringing them home something, but will you promise me one thing?' Barbara was being gentle now.

Joan looked pathetically relieved. 'What is it I'm supposed to promise?'

Barbara swallowed. 'Will you let me arrange for a social worker to visit you?'

'No! No interfering bloody busy-bodies. I've 'ad some of them ter put up wiv in the past. None of 'em ain't coming over my doorstep. I mean it.'

'All right. If I leave it until I'm here again next Tuesday, would you agree to talk to someone if I offered to be there to help? I promise it would only be for your good and for the good of your children. There are many allowances that I am sure you would be entitled to, and many people only too pleased to help.'

'Yeah,' Joan sneered. 'And the rest! What about the things?'

'If you mean the things you've already taken, as you so rightly pointed out I have no proof. As to what you have in your bag, I am more than happy for you to take them home as a little gift for your kiddies.'

'Ruddy good of yer, I must say. Bet it makes yer feel bleedin' good, don't it?'

Oh dear, Joan wasn't going to give in gracefully. Compared to all the robbing and killings that went on, what Joan had done had been nothing. In a crazy sort of way Barbara even admired her. She was fighting for her children in what was possibly the only way she knew how. A little laugh escaped her. 'I'll see you next week then.' Barbara bent and picked up the straw shopping bag and handed it to Joan with a smile.

Joan took it from her without voicing any more objections.

Barbara woke up next day with a sore throat and what promised to be a heavy cold. Numerous hot drinks and large amounts of aspirin did nothing to help. By the weekend she was worse and James insisted on calling the doctor.

'You've picked up a virus, my dear,' he announced, having taken Barbara's temperature and listened to her chest with his stethoscope.

'Stay in bed, keep warm, drink plenty and see that you take the tablets I've prescribed for you.'

It got worse, not better. A dry hacking cough, every bone in her body ached, a hammer continually beating in her head, Barbara was only too glad to stay in bed.

Her mother came over daily and one morning she made a declaration that had both James and Barbara sighing with relief.

'I've found a daily treasure for you, and I do mean a treasure.' Patricia gave a self-satisfied grin before saying, 'Her name is Mrs Margaret Harvey, youngest sister of our Mrs Clarkson. Extremely fortunate to get her,' she said proudly. 'She lives at Wannock. For years she's been a daily up at Ratton Manor, but the old gentleman died three months ago. We've Mrs Clarkson to thank: she put the word in for you, been on for ages that you two needed someone to take care of you. There was a time your father and I thought Mrs Clarkson was considering deserting us to come to you herself.'

'Oh bless her,' Barbara grinned. 'She always has had a soft spot for me and I know she adores James.'

'Well, you will be set up now.'

'I'm sure we shall,' Barbara readily agreed. 'Please thank her for me, Mummy. I have felt so guilty, all the extra work has fallen on Paul's shoulders, he's been bringing me up trays and goodness knows what else he has been having to do downstairs.'

'Well lie back now and concentrate on getting better. Maggie, as she insists on being called, is well and truly installed. Ironing sheets when I got here this morning.'

'Such a relief,' sighed Barbara. 'Mother, will you ring Anthony for me, please? And if you can't get hold of him, ring Chloe.'

'Darling, you aren't still worried about not being able to go to that clinic, are you?'

'Not really . . . well yes, Anthony will understanad. There is a matter that I must get sorted. The sooner the better.'

'All right, dear, I'll go downstairs now and make us all some coffee and while the kettle is boiling I'll phone Anthony.'

Barbara was downstairs, a travelling-rug wrapped around her knees. She sat in the lounge with the bottom half of the sash-window open to the garden. It was a lovely June evening, the weather had turned warmer, she felt very much better but as weak as a kitten.

Today she and James were giving their first dinner-party. There would be ten people sitting down to the meal: both hers and James's parents, Penny and Neil, Chloe and Anthony, James and herself.

James had insisted that a local couple who specialised in outside catering be allowed to do the cooking.

Maggie Harvey was to be here also – at her own insistence. Plump, rosy-faced, friendly Maggie had already endeared herself to both Barbara and James, and even Paul wasn't adverse to a bit of spoiling when it came to Maggie's cooking.

Barbara watched the first car turn into the drive, and smiled with pleasure when she saw it was Anthony. It wasn't hard to guess why he had deliberately showed up early.

He walked across the lawn. 'How's the invalid?' he called.

'Anything but!' she called back.

He put a leg over the windowsill and climbed into the room.

'Total fraud then, are you?' he asked, bending his head to plant a kiss on her cheek.

'I'm fine now, raring to go, though I must admit whatever that damned virus was it certainly knocked the stuffing out of me. But Anthony, please, before the others get here, tell me about Joan. Did she turn up for work the day after our little rumpus? I've been so worried as to what kind of hornet's nest I might have stirred up there.'

'Hey, hang on. Not so fast. That's the reason I'm here so early, to put your mind at rest. It's amazing really, Barbara, as things have turned out you did Joan Crosbie an enormous favour and, more to the point, she is grateful.'

Seeing the look of astonishment on Barbara's face, Anthony laughed, 'True! Honestly. She even made a point of asking me to thank you. Quite a climb down, eh?'

'I'm still not with you,' Barbara exclaimed in exasperation.

'We've managed to straighten her affairs out; not as well as we would have wished, but at least we have got some help for her. God alone knows she needed it! Too proud, that's half her trouble. Do you know, one of the children that she is struggling to bring up isn't her own?'

Barbara raised her eyebrows and Anthony answered her unspoken question, 'The little lad had been abandoned. Seems his mother ran off with another man, father managed for a while then he left the boy with a neighbour – the neighbour being Joan. She's never seen hair nor hide of the father since. That was eighteen months ago. Poorly fed and clothed but clean, oh yes, very clean was our social worker's report. Children happy. All of them quite bright. Joan was scraping by, doing three part-time cleaning jobs. Fifty shillings a week at most to pay the rent and feed and clothe all of them.'

'In what way are matters better for her now?' Barbara was anxious to know.

'Every way. I promise you. She's accepted the fact that she does need help and I'm told she is on quite a friendly footing with her social worker. Hard to believe isn't it?'

'Oh, Anthony, I'm *so* pleased, I really have worried about that woman and her children. I can't wait to come back to the clinic.'

'Ah! . . . That's another thing I wanted to talk to you about.'

'What? You aren't softening the blow? Saying you don't want me to return?'

'Not exactly.'

'That means yes, doesn't it? I know what you're going to say, I've given it a lot of thought. Me being different, well-dressed, having money, has annoyed those woman. I don't fit in, do I?'

'It's not that, well, to be honest, more or less that's true, but please, Barbara, hear me out; I have a proposition I want to put to you, a very worthwhile project.'

He spoke with such sincerity that Barbara decided to reserve her judgement. At that moment James propelled himself into the room, followed by Paul carrying a tray of drinks.

Quickly Anthony said, 'Barbara, it's not a private matter, we can all discuss it after dinner. I promise you will be interested.' With that she had to be content.

'Anthony, good to see you, how are you?'

'Fine, James, and you? Plenty of work in your line of business, I hear.'

'Criminals never take holidays,' was James's quick retort. They all laughed.

'I'll put the tray down here,' Paul said. 'Mr Ferguson's car is just turning in the gate, I'll let them in.'

'Is Chloe with her parents?' James asked.

'Yes, she rang to tell me not to pick her up. She'd decided to come with her mother and father,' Anthony told them as he moved towards the door to greet his fiancée.

The caterers had done them proud. Seafood platter as a starter, followed by buttered asparagus tips, roast leg of English lamb, baby onions in creamy sauce with several dishes of fresh young vegetables, tiny new potatoes and crispy roast ones, almond-topped open apple tart with thick clotted cream. Petits fours and coffee now being served, Barbara's father and Robert Ferguson asked permission to smoke. With the grand smell of rich Havana cigars now pervading the room, they settled down to serious conversation.

'So,' Barbara said, turning her head towards Anthony,

'are you going to keep me in suspense all the evening or are you going to tell me about this new scheme of yours?'

'Anthony been having a go at you, has he?' Muriel Ferguson had butted in before Anthony had a chance to answer.

Barbara laughed at her mother-in-law, saying, 'I'm a glutton for punishment.'

'Well you're certainly asking for it this time. If this is about what I think it is, then there'll be no stopping him. It's Anthony's pet subject.'

'Mother!' cried Chloe. 'Give Anthony a chance to plead his own case.'

James, seated at the other end of the table, caught Barbara's eye and they both grinned.

'Isn't it just?' Penny murmured. 'I've heard him go on about this before now.'

'Isn't it just *what*?' Neil asked. 'You've lost me.'

Everyone laughed.

'Isn't it just Anthony's pet subject,' Chloe's father explained. 'We'd do better if we all kept quiet and gave the poor fellow a chance to say what he is obviously dying to tell us.'

Anthony drained his coffee cup, his eyes glittered with assurance as he turned to face them all.

'I suppose I do go on about this subject, I make no apology; that's because it is very serious. I don't have to convince Chloe. She's seen it first hand.

'It all began for me when I came up against the atrocious way mentally-retarded children and those who are handicapped were written off. There always has been, and probably always will be, much speculation amongst the medical profession as to the rights and wrongs of various treatments.'

Anthony paused and when everyone remained silent he continued, 'My own opinion in respect of specific children, is that their condition is often made worse by cruelty and neglect. More attention and a lot more love would benefit so many of our small patients.'

Anthony now had the attention of them all – especially Barbara, who found herself following his every word with interest. She had known he was totally dedicated to his work, but just how deeply he cared came as a surprise. She wanted him to continue, to hear everything he had to say on this subject.

'I became acquainted with Ivy Pearson through the out-patients department at the hospital. She is Matron of Coombe Haven, which is a residential home in Surrey, quite near South Croydon station, well known for the remarkable work it does for under-privileged children. It is a home for any child up to the age of twelve who is in need of specialist care for several reasons. Some of the children have been abused, beaten, you wouldn't believe the cruelty. Others are deformed and therefore unwanted and a few are mentally impaired. The home depends largely for funds on voluntary contributions. I felt very privileged when, some time ago, I was asked to become a member of the committee.'

Anthony stopped speaking and smiled his thanks to Barbara as she refilled his coffee cup.

James was the first to break the silence, 'Organisations, such as you are describing, Anthony, already exist for children of the Church of England faith, Roman Catholics and those from Jewish families. What makes this home different?'

'Because it is of no special religious denomination and

the children are not what one would term "ill". They are classed as backward or deformed and for that reason society as a whole doesn't want to know them. Left to the system they would be written off. Hidden from the world.'

'Is this what you had in mind for me to be part of?' Barbara asked timidly.

'Well, yes. There are never enough money or helpers,' Anthony was saying now. 'We have to give a lot of thought to just how best to help each child.'

He raised his head, gazed at everyone seated further down the table, making sure he wasn't boring anyone.

'Some think our methods are unconventional, we have to take things slowly. We set up meetings, argue until everyone is agreeable, prepare our notes and hopefully we have enough volunteers to press ahead. Perhaps Chloe would like to tell you more about how they work one-to-one with a patient.'

Barbara looked at Chloe in surprise. 'Do you work there?' she asked.

'Unfortunately no. I would have told you before this if I did; I just don't have the time. I do visit sometimes – so does Mother, more often than I do.'

'What I do mostly is rattle the begging bowl,' Chloe's mother answered. 'I organise fetes, coffee mornings, bring-and-buy sales, things like that. Barbara, your mother held a coffee morning for us not so long ago and we have in mind to rope the men in soon: we're setting up a mock auction when Penny has persuaded Neil to be our auctioneer.'

Neil Chapman groaned. Penny tapped the back of his hand with her teaspoon: 'You know very well you're anticipating the event with glee. You'll wring loads of money out of your friends without turning a hair. Won't you, darling?'

Neil smiled his answer, laying it on thick, 'For you my angel, *anything.*'

'Come for a day, Barbara,' Anthony suddenly urged. 'See one of the volunteers working with a child who has never walked, yet whose legs are not withered. She or he will massage for an hour at a time. Others may read a story to a child who just will not speak, there being no apparent reason why he or she can't. The helpers will ask questions, show the pictures in the book, pressing and probing for answers. Sometimes it can turn out to be a very rewarding experience.'

Barbara glanced across the table to where her father sat. He had kept quiet all this time.

She raised her eyebrows in question.

He smiled his encouragement and, turning her head to face James, she was heartened to see that he too was silently applauding what he knew was to be her decision.

'Anthony, I'd very much like to be involved,' Barbara quietly said. 'You've more than convinced all of us that it is indeed a worthy cause.'

Chapter Twenty-one

MAY HAD GIVEN way to June and June into July before Barbara was really fit enough to make her first visit to Coombe Haven. She had travelled by train from Eastbourne to South Croydon station, where Anthony had promised to meet her. He had stressed that he would only have time to make the necessary introductions as this was not the day that he did his stint of voluntary work at the home.

Barbara felt a little apprehensive as she stepped down from the carriage. This soon vanished as she spotted Anthony waving and smiling at her from the end of the platform; the sunlight sparkling off his gold-rimmed glasses, he looked quite boyish, even eager – as if he were considering this outing to be a great adventure.

His arm around her shoulders, he said, 'The car is parked almost outside the station, we'll be there in ten minutes. Am sorry, Barbara, I can't stay, pressure of work an' all that. Still, I'm sure you'll enjoy your visit and Paul rang me to say James will be finished in court about four, so he said they will pick you up and you can all travel home together.'

Barbara gave an audible sigh of relief. 'Oh, that's nice, better than travelling back on the train in the rush hour.'

Everybody expects the Matron of a home to be stiff and starchy. Ivy Pearson didn't fit that description in the least.

Barbara liked her instantly. Ivy exuded competence, humour and kindness to such a degree that she instantly put Barbara at her ease. A large woman, gaunt and long-necked, though her eyes were kindly and lit up her whole face, as she explained to Barbara the progress some of the children had made since having been admitted to Coombe Haven. Continuing on their tour of the building, Barbara noticed that in spite of her size Ivy's every gesture was graceful and when handling the children she was always so gentle.

In the kitchen four women were gathered.

'These young ladies attend to the morning cleaning, breakfast and lunch,' Ivy Pearson explained. 'Working until two o'clock. Two other married women take over for the afternoon until the night-workers come on duty. We also employ three full-time workers in our own laundry which is housed in a separate building in the grounds.'

'Maisie, Shirley, Ethel and Rose,' Matron introduced the women to Barbara. 'They are indispensable when it comes to the running of this place and the children trust them. This, ladies, is Mrs Barbara Ferguson, hopefully we shall be seeing her on a regular basis after today.'

Four pairs of eyes were sizing Barbara up, making her wait while they formed their opinion of her.

Three had the appearance of the working classes, sallow complexion, drawn-in cheeks and hair dragged back from their faces. The fourth woman, Rose, tended to be plump, yet she was pretty and round-faced like a country bred girl. She seemed to have decided that Barbara was a friend, for she held out her hand, saying, 'Hallo, Miss, you'll find it's a nice place 'ere.'

The others gave in. 'Ow d'yer do, Miss,' they chorused. Barbara nodded, smiled, and said, 'Nice to meet you all.' Down a long corridor and Ivy opened a door into what appeared to be a large play room. 'Listen everyone, I want you to meet Barbara Ferguson,' she called loudly. 'She's our new volunteer.'

Three young women simultaneously called a cheery, 'Hallo Barbara,' while a dozen or so pairs of children's eyes surveyed her cautiously.

Against the wall were chintz-covered chairs, and an old upright piano, its lid being raised showed its keys had turned yellow. The room was bathed in sunlight and heavy with the smell of fresh flowers.

A very much lived-in room, books and toys were strewn over the floor, a furry teddy bear, muddled wooden blocks, a gaily painted pedal-motorcar. Liveliness was the word that sprang to Barbara's mind.

'Right, apart from upstairs, and the treatment room, which we will leave for the moment, that's the end of the grand tour. We'll go back to my office and have a cup of tea.'

Following Matron without question, Barbara decided that she was a fast talker who looked one squarely in the eye and made an instant judgement. She had already formed the opinion, from listening to her non-stop account of the work that was carried out at Coombe Haven, that it was her energetic enthusiasm for the home and its patients that in turn gave her the wholehearted devotion of the staff.

With the tea brewed and a cup now set in front of Barbara, they were entirely at ease with each other.

'I don't mean to make us sound like angels of mercy,' Matron began, 'all the same, we can't operate on a nine-to-five basis. Once the kids here touch your heart, and some will, there is nothing more rewarding than having one of them respond to you. Now if we are to have you

331

with us, shall I call you Barbara? And you call me Ivy. We all tend to use Christian names here.'

Barbara opened her mouth to reply, but Ivy was already racing on, 'I know you don't have any experience, but all you need for now is common sense and a caring attitude. Now when can you start and how many days will you be available?'

Barbara hesitated. She badly wanted to become involved with this well worthwhile project, but at the same time was frightened of being seen to be a failure. It hadn't occurred to her that she would be asked to plunge right in without some period of training.

'Would you like me to stay now? Well, until about four o'clock?' she fearfully asked.

'Good girl,' Ivy smiled approvingly. 'Hang your jacket through there and I'll take you to meet some of the children. There's one little boy in particular that I want you to see.'

Striding purposefully through corridors, Ivy turned her head and called, 'Not going too fast for you, am I? I want you to see what is known as the treatment room.'

There was no need for Barbara to form a reply. Ivy came to a halt in front of an open doorway, proudly she said, 'You've no idea of the amount of effort and time that some of our ladies put in here.'

Barbara's heart warmed towards her, she so obviously loved her work and believed in it.

'I can imagine. What a lovely well laid-out room this is.'

The room was large, bright and sunny, its tall windows looking out across lawns and flower beds. Around the wall there were three medical couches on which small children lay, each with a lady assistant in charge for safekeeping. On the floor two little girls were playing a game, using coloured counters and plastic cups.

Ivy approached the nearest couch and smiling at Barbara, she said, 'This is Hilda Whitely: she handles the physical exercises of the youngest children.'

Hilda was a short, attractive fair-haired girl about Barbara's own age.

She smiled, warmly acknowledging the introduction, but all she said was, ''Allo.'

Ivy grinned. 'Hilda is a true Londoner, as you will soon find out.' They moved on and Ivy, lowering her head, whispered, 'Heart of gold, that one.'

At the next group, Ivy said, 'This is Barbara Ferguson, from today she will be joining us. Brenda Smith I think you already know, you worked with her for a short while in the clinic at Vauxhall.'

'Yes, hallo Barbara. Welcome, it will be nice having you helping out here.'

'Thank you, Brenda, I'm looking forward to it.'

'Next to Brenda, is Catherine Bateman, she is everyone's dogsbody.' Catherine was a stout dark-haired girl of thirty-five or so.

'Hallo, Barbara, yeah I get every thankless task,' she said humorously.

'And last but by no means least our youngest member of staff, Julie Stevenson, she is always willing and able.'

A pretty youngster, no more than nineteen, smiled brightly at Barbara.

'Hallo,' they greeted each other.

At the far end of the room a white-coated man sat at a leather-topped desk, his back to the windows.

'Come and meet a dedicated man,' Ivy said softly to

Barbara. 'One of two full-time doctors that are employed here.'

As they walked towards him, the doctor rose to his feet, his hand outstretched in welcome.

'Our new recruit, eh? I'm Richard Turner.'

'Barbara Ferguson.' They both smiled, and shook hands.

Barbara guessed he was about forty, but somehow he appeared much older. A thin, worried face and grey, serious eyes that seemed to change as he smiled.

He seems nice, Barbara thought, with some satisfaction; it won't be hard to work with him.

Ivy said, 'We haven't fed Barbara yet. How about you, Richard, have you eaten?'

'It doesn't matter. About lunch, I mean. Please don't worry.' Barbara felt awkward.

Doctor Turner had sat down, leaning forward with his elbows on the edge of the desk. 'Aren't you hungry?' he asked Barbara.

Barbara didn't answer.

'I'm starving,' Ivy declared. 'So come along, let's all go and eat.'

To tell the truth Barbara had had a very long morning. Leaving home so early, having only had a bowl of cereal for her breakfast, she was feeling hungry, so she gratefully took her cue from both of them.

Having a meal together would break the ice, help Barbara to settle in, was what Matron was thinking and she made sure that it was in an entirely natural and easy fashion that the three of them went to the kitchen.

There was a smell of steak-and-kidney pies, mouth-watering.

'Are you eating here, or in the dining room?' Rose cheerfully asked.

'As it's so late we'll have it here, at the big table. Don't you worry, Rose; we'll see to ourselves,' Ivy Pearson assured her.

Leaving Barbara and the doctor to sit themselves down, Ivy went to the huge stove, took a pair of oven-gloves from a hook on the wall, and crouching down she opened the oven and took out a tray of individual meat-pies.

'They aren't dried up, are they?' Rose asked anxiously.

'No, just right,' Ivy said, setting the tray down onto the table.

Rose placed a tureen beside it. 'I put all the veg that was over in the one dish to keep it warm,' she said, taking the lid off of the dish and allowing steamy smells to rise. 'There's plenty of lovely gravy in the copper pan on the stove. If you're all right then I'm gonna go an' finish clearing up in the dining room.'

Some time later, Ivy asked, 'Have you two had enough to eat?'

Richard nodded.

Barbara said, 'Oh, yes thank you, it was a lovely meal. Did Rose make the pies?'

'Rose? No. We have a cook. She's here by six every morning, goes home at lunchtime. Marvellous, you'll see, she's been with us some years now. Would you like tea or coffee?'

'You know I don't like tea,' Richard shot in.

'I wasn't asking you,' Ivy laughed.

'Coffee is fine for me,' Barbara quickly told them, watching Ivy open a huge fridge to take a bottle of milk from the shelf on the door.

When the coffee had been made and a cup set in front of each of them, Richard leant towards Ivy and asked, 'Have you considered Barbara to work with the Rowlings boy?'

Barbara turned and stared, wondering who the Rowlings boy could be.

'Yes, I have. It was my intention to introduce young Sammy to Barbara when we set out on our tour. Somehow we got sidetracked. Perhaps you would like to fill her in on some of the boy's background?'

Richard had insisted that he too wished for Barbara to address him by his Christian name and now, smiling at him, she queried, 'Richard?'

He straightened up, folded his arms across his chest.

'Begin at the beginning,' Ivy prompted gently.

'I get a bit embarrassed when speaking of this boy. His name is Samuel Rowlings, he's two-years-old, and I'm sorry to have to tell you, one of our failures – not that we've given up hope, not by any means. Both myself and David Bennett, that's my colleague, have racked our brains for a solution for this child.'

Barbara was impressed by the sincerity that showed in Richard's whole manner.

Abruptly now, he took up the story, 'Samuel Rowlings was born with a harelip. Other than that we have found no physical deformities whatsoever. The mother was pregnant when she got married . . . far too young, hard on the father as well as herself. A trying time. Six months after the baby was born the father upped and left the pair of them. Disappeared. To give the young girl her due, after the initial shock had worn off, she did her best for nearly a year. Not in the happiest of circumstances. She had no family and the father's family openly showed their disapproval of his choice.

'The girl committed suicide. Baby was found in an upstairs bedroom. The mother had not turned up at the welfare clinic for two weeks and staff became worried.

'The welfare officer almost fell over Samuel – the body of Samuel she had thought at the time. As it was, he was filthy but alive. His mother's body was in the next room. Empty drink bottles were strewn everywhere. Dark-brown coloured, empty tablet bottles lay beside her.

'Samuel's legs and bottom were raw with sores from his stinking napkin. He was in a shocking state.

'He was given a series of injections against the germs. Even his eyes were almost closed, filled with yellow pus.

'His mother had been dead four days. She hadn't ill-treated him. We are quite sure about that, she had reached the end of her tether. Couldn't cope any longer. Not on her own.

'If only she had sought more help, or had a family she could turn to.' Richard reached in his pocket and brought out a packet of cigarettes, 'D'you mind?'

Both women shook their heads.

He took one from the packet and struck a match. When it was alight, Barbara asked, 'Had she no one?'

'No. She grew up in a home. Later was farmed out to several different foster families. Married at eighteen, had Samuel six months later. Too young!'

'*Yes*! Far too young,' Ivy Pearson muttered almost to herself. 'It would be nice if – ' she broke off mid-sentence.

'If what?' Barbara asked.

'If that child could relate to someone, if someone could show him some love.'

'The boy has to learn to trust a person first,' Richard said quietly and then added, 'and learn to speak.'

'*What?*'

'That's right,' Ivy told a shocked Barbara. 'Sammy has never uttered a word to anyone from the day he was found. He has had an operation to repair the roof of his mouth and later perhaps he will have surgery to his top lip. There is no reason why he doesn't talk, he just doesn't.'

In the shiny, sunny kitchen, you could have heard a pin drop. Each person was deep in thought, until Richard spoke, 'Are you going to take Barbara along to meet Sammy?'

It was a sort of dismissal, but a kindly one. Ivy sighed, 'I think I'd better. Let her see him for herself.'

There seemed to be so little of him. His skin was creamy-smooth, his face unblemished except for the red, sore-looking patch on his top lip. His tousled hair was a mass . of tight, fair curls which clung to his head. He sat in the centre of a playpen, surrounded by soft toys. As they approached, he lifted his head and stared at Barbara, only to drop it almost immediately.

Ivy smiled at Barbara over Samuel's head, 'He's shy. He's pretending you aren't here, he doesn't want to look at you.' She bent her head to say to the little boy, 'Come on you silly-billy, this is a nice lady who has come to see you.'

The poor little mite grunted angrily under his breath and crouched down slightly as if to hide.

Barbara quietly said, 'Hallo.'

'Say hallo, Sammy,' Ivy prompted. Then said, 'Don't be lazy, Sammy. You could say hallo Barbara, if you wanted to, Bar-bar-a, that's this lady's name. It's easy, listen, Bar-bar-a, you try.'

Ivy rose to her feet. Softly, sadly, she said, 'As usual he isn't going to utter a word.'

'What does he do all day?'

'Barbara, he does all the normal things the other children do. He eats well, though he won't feed himself. We still aren't sure if there is any permanent damage to his right arm, he doesn't use it much; his right leg is very weak too, though there again, doctors can find no reason why it should be. He plays, he sleeps, and in the afternoon he goes out in the grounds. When we have outings, we have our own special bus, he comes along, always seems to enjoy the ride.'

'I see he has plenty of toys, does he like picture books?'

'Mostly he tries to tear the pages out. He does seem to pay attention if someone is reading to him, or explaining a picture.'

'You're fond of him, Ivy, aren't you?'

'Yes, I just wish he would respond.'

'Does he make friends with the other children?'

'Some. He gets very annoyed if they touch him. Probably he'll be better when he's older. If he has a preference for anyone it's Hilda, and she seems able to cope with him better than most.'

Sadness swept through Barbara. Tears welled up in her eyes.

Ivy said quietly, 'Are . . . you all right?'

'Yes,' Barbara, answered. But she wasn't.

Her first thoughts had been, how could a young mother take her own life, abandon a tiny mite, not giving a thought as to how or where he might be brought up. Then suddenly she was reproaching herself.

Who am I to level such an accusation! If I'm such a kind and caring person, how come I signed my own baby away without even having set eyes on him? Did I know to whom he was going? I still only have Sister Francis's word that he would be adopted by a very good family.

A guilty conscience was something she thought she had put behind her. But it had caught up with her. God pays his debts, she tortured herself.

Barbara looked so sad that Ivy asked, 'Would you like to help get some of the children ready for their walk?'

Barbara didn't trust herself to answer. She was so near to tears, she just nodded.

Ivy felt she had to say something. This new volunteer was so obviously upset. 'Don't be disapproving or try to pass judgement will you, Barbara? It's not nice that these kiddies get rejected, cast aside; we all know that, but people have a thing about handicapped or disfigured children. They look away most times. It's hard enough if there are two parents. One on their own . . . Well.'

Barbara asked herself, what could she possibly say to that?

Sounds of adults talking and laughing drifted in from the corridor.

'Ah! That will be the Red Cross ladies. You'll like them, Barbara. Their headquarters are only a short distance away and they have a rota of helpers who come in and feed the children, and others who come in the afternoon and help our own staff to take the kiddies out. For walks or outings we only put one child into the care of one volunteer. Safer that way.'

'Come on, cocker!'

The loud voice made Barbara jump. She turned to see Hilda Whitely bending over the side of the playpen.

'Time t'get yer outdoor clothes on, Sammy. We're gonna go out in the gardens, might even see the dogs. Yer like the doggies don't you, luv, they bark at yer. One of these fine days yer might even 'ave something t'say t'them, eh?'

Hilda lifted him over the side and set him down. Sammy, eyes downcast, began to totter unsteadily towards the corner of the room. There he stood, face to the wall, his little head slumped forward onto his chest.

'No, no, yer fat-'ead,' Hilda ran to him. ''Ere, put yer arm in this sleeve. All the others will be gone if we don't 'urry up and then yer won't like that, now will yer?'

Within seconds, Hilda had Sammy dressed in a bright-red linen coat and a small peaked cap with a badge on it. She hesitated, looking at Ivy, and if Barbara had turned around she would have seen the direct look each gave the other and the little wink that was exchanged between them.

Then Hilda said, 'I 'ave t'go an' get one of the pushchairs out of the cloakroom. Will you 'old Samuel for a minute?'

Barbara dithered, 'Will he come to me?'

'Course 'ee will.'

Hilda lifted the boy up, hoisting him towards Barbara.

'I shan't be a tick, Sammy,' Hilda assured him, and she turned and went out of the room.

Sammy looked right into Barbara's eyes as she put her arms around him and drew him close. Near to, his harelip looked very red, and sore. He smelt of talcum powder and fresh soap. Lovely. Suddenly she felt his fingers grip her shoulders and then she felt pain, such pain that it made her eyes water and her nose hurt.

Sammy had brought his head back and butted Barbara straight in the face. Now he wriggled and twisted, using his knees to give himself leverage against her chest, yet he never uttered a sound. Barbara almost dropped him, probably would have if Ivy had not intervened.

'Ready then, my old son,' Hilda was back with the pushchair.

She took one look at Barbara, dabbing her nose with a white handkerchief and mouthed the word, 'Sorry.' When she had Samuel safely strapped in the chair, she raised her eyebrows at Barbara and said, 'Bit determined, ain't he? Wriggles like an eel, but 'ee'll get used t'yer, yer'll see.'

Ivy was worried. Had she pushed things too fast?

'Had enough?' she asked. 'Or shall we go out into the grounds and watch what goes on?'

Barbara found herself chuckling, imagining what she was going to say to James when he saw her battered face.

'Was a bit unexpected, wasn't it?' Ivy couldn't help herself – she burst out laughing.

'I'll live,' a smiling Barbara assured her. 'Lead on.'

Barbara was amazed at both the size and the beauty of the gardens. Huge rhododendron bushes flanked the high stone walls, and azaleas in such colours as Barbara had never seen before. Across wide, green lawns a play area had been set up. Small, low swings, gaily painted roundabouts, helter-skelter slides and a sandpit. There were a dozen or so children there, each with an adult to keep a watchful eye on them. Cries of delight and chuckles of pleasure could clearly be heard.

It wasn't hard for Barbara to pick out Sammy, her eye soon focused on his bright-red blazer.

Hilda had him chained in a swing that had a box-like seat with safety rails at each side. She was gently pushing him back and forth, not from behind, but from in front, so that he could see her at all times. 'One a penny, two a penny, three four five,' she crooned as she bent almost double in order to be able to see Sammy's face.

Ivy and Barbara watched in silence for a few minutes until Hilda slowed the swing down and lifted Sammy to the ground. They couldn't hear what she was saying to him, but there was no mistaking that she planted a kiss on his cheek before patting his bottom and pushing him in the direction of the sandpit.

He wobbled off, reeling to the right, followed closely by Hilda.

Barbara turned to face Ivy. 'He drags that right leg, doesn't he?'

'Afraid so.'

'Do you do anything about it?'

'Yes. He gets daily massage and exercise. Not for as long as we would like, but we only have so many volunteers that can spare that amount of time.'

'Is that what you would like me to do?'

'Is it what you would want to do?'

'Very much so, if you think it comes within my capabilities.'

'I certainly do, and naturally we wouldn't leave you on your own, not to begin with. Could you manage a whole day every week?'

'I could manage two days if you're sure that I would be of some help.'

Ivy Pearson smiled broadly, 'I'm positive, Barbara. A

willing volunteer is almost always worth two of every paid employee.'

'Would I be working with Samuel?'

'You've no idea of how much I was hoping you would want to. It wouldn't be solely with Sammy,' she laughed aloud. 'He has to sleep sometime. The doctors will do something about repairing his lip when he is a little older but there is no guarantee that he will ever walk really well.'

Barbara glanced at her watch. 'It's just on four,' Ivy confirmed. 'You'd better see about getting yourself ready, your husband will be here soon.'

Several thoughts were racing through Barbara's mind as they walked back to the house.

Never ever walk properly! *Oh yes he will!* Barbara vowed to herself. If I have to help him exercise for the rest of my life I swear to God, he'll walk properly one day.

Chapter Twenty-two

BARBARA GAVE AN unconscious sigh as she drew a writing-pad and pen from her desk. Her thoughts were so tangled that she had decided she would put her feelings down on paper in a letter to Elizabeth.

Her visits to Coombe Haven had become very import-ant, or so Ivy Pearson assured her. Barbara was not so confident. Of one thing she was certain – each visit had come to mean a great deal to her. Not that she had made a lot of progress with young Sammy, he still hadn't uttered a single word in all the weeks she had been going there. Signs of recognition, yes, even going so far as to climb onto her lap.

Occasionally even that could go wrong. Seated with his back to her chest, Sammy would bounce up and down, demanding silently that Barbara gave him a ride on her knees. Fearing that he might fall she would tighten her arms around his waist, holding him close. Twice he had resisted this action. His little head had gone forward, only to be thrust up and backwards, quickly slamming hard into Bar-bara's face. One such tantrum had resulted in Barbara having a black eye.

Both Paul and James had been highly amused, a fact that neither of them tried to hide, as they travelled home to Jevington.

'Quite the little boxer!' Paul had exclaimed.

'I'd put our Samuel down as a heavy-weight, don't you

agree?' James had replied, tears of laughter showing in his eyes.

The fact that the two men had met Sammy, on more than one occasion, had to be accredited to Brenda Smith. Having met each other at the clinic in Vauxhall, Brenda knew that their interest in what Barbara was doing was vital. And so it had come about.

Seeing Paul turn the car into the drive early one afternoon, she had approached Matron, 'Would you mind if I offered Barbara's husband and his male nurse a cup of tea?'

'By all means, Brenda. By the way, where is Barbara?'

'Still over at the sandpit.'

The two women looked knowingly at each other.

The result had been that Paul and James arrived at the sandpit, in the nick of time.

'I want another chocolate biscuit!' a little girl named Jill was screaming, but Julie Stevenson, her carer, said, 'No, you've already eaten yours. There was only enough for one each.'

Sammy hadn't started on his biscuit; he was watching Steven, a bigger boy, pat the end of an upturned bucket which he had helped to fill with sand, plop it over, and then carefully lift the bucket away, to produce a perfect shaped turret for the edge of the sand castle they were making.

The little girl saw her chance. She reached out and snatched the biscuit from Sammy's hand.

Sammy's face turned red and he hit Jill with his shovel.

'No, no!' Barbara cried.

Steven, the big boy, pushed Sammy. He fell and hit his head on the bucket. Paul jumped into the pit, looked at

Sammy's head, 'He's not hurt,' he told Barbara, amazed that the small boy hadn't screamed.

'He hit me with his shovel!'

'That's true,' Julie told her little charge, 'But, Jill, you have got to learn that you can't have everything you want and you certainly mustn't take things away from other children.'

James groaned in mock despair, 'Good God! How often do you have to settle clashes like this?'

'Just lively kids,' Barbara explained. 'More often than not a pain in the neck, but all perfectly normal.'

'Come on,' Paul said to the still screaming little girl, swinging her up in the air. 'How would you like a ride in my friend's carriage?'

The child eyed the wheelchair with mistrust.

With a broad grin Paul dumped her onto James's knees and turned back to the group of by now wide-eyed children.

'Shall I help you to make sand-pies?' Paul smiled the question at Sammy and was rewarded with a nod of his head.

When it was time for the children to return to the house they made comical procession. Jill still sat on James's lap, queening it over the other little girls, showing she was enjoying the ride. Sammy, legs wide apart, was being carried on the shoulders of Paul and to compensate the other children, Hilda Whitely walked backwards, facing the group, beating time and singing loudly, ''Umpty Dumpty sat on a wall, 'Umpty Dumpty 'ad a big fall . . .'

Ivy Pearson had rushed to the window on hearing the noise.

'Well, I'll be sugared!' she exclaimed, hardly able to believe her eyes.

A city gentlemen, wearing a dark pinstriped suit, in a wheelchair, with Jill, their most cantankerous little girl, riding on his knees. And to top that a huge fellow had Sammy astride his shoulders. Sammy, who normally shied away from men! As for Hilda, she had thought that nothing that one could do would surprise her, but she'd come up tops today. Talk about leading the band!

'You think Sammy is a nice little boy?' Barbara had asked anxiously, as Paul had driven them home.

Being quite used to the conversation being solely about Samuel Rowlings on these journeys, James wasn't put out; indeed he was thrilled to know that his wife had taken up such a worthwhile occupation. Now he smiled as he answered her truthfully.

'Yes, yes, he's a really likeable little lad and very brave into the bargain.'

Barbara nodded happily, 'I know. I'm so glad you've seen him for yourself. I've wanted to hear your opinion for ages.'

'I had a word with Ivy Pearson while you were getting yourself ready.'

'Oh! What did she say?'

'She said that although Samuel still doesn't speak, he has come a long way since you have been helping at Coombe Haven. She also said for Paul and myself to drop in whenever we were able.'

'Ivy's so patient with the children,' Barbara remarked. 'She really loves them, you know.'

James observed, 'Because in one way or another they are all orphans of the storm.'

'Probably. I feel grateful to Anthony, and to your sister

Chloe, for having introduced me to Coombe Haven in the first place.'

So a pattern was formed and James had never found cause to complain, or to regret his decision to become personally involved.

'Barbara?'

Her husband's voice behind her in the doorway broke into Barbara's thoughts.

'Barbara . . . what are you doing in here on such a lovely autumn afternoon? We won't get many more opportunities like this. It will soon be winter. You said you were coming out into the garden and were going to write a letter to Elizabeth.'

'I am, darling. Here – you can take my pad and pen and I'll carry this tray; I've squeezed some lemons and made a jug of squash.'

It was Sunday. Paul Soames had taken his lady-friend, Maureen O'Connor, to Brighton for the day. With time, James had become a little more independent. He had learnt to do some things himself but it did worry Barbara: what would happen if Paul decided to marry his lady-friend and leave James? Time enough to meet trouble when it comes knocking on the door, she told herself.

With two chairs set out on the lawn, a table between them and a glass of lemonade within easy reach, James became absorbed in the Sunday papers and Barbara settled to writing her letter.

October 29th

My dear Elizabeth,

Well here I am, having stayed the course at Coombe Haven for four months. Am writing, because I feel I can say so much more, express my feelings better, than I'm able to when we have our weekly natter on the telephone.

My feelings have been mixed, thrilled with Samuel's progress one day, down in the dumps the next because he sometimes reacts so violently towards me. Such a sad little boy. And lonely. Though he is never alone, children and adults around him all the time. It's as if he has a shell around him and no one seems to be able to make the break through.

Elizabeth, with three kiddies of your own you must be wise as to how they act and think. Tell me, please, do you think that Sammy realises that he has no one? No family of his own? It would make your heart bleed to see his little face when I say goodbye to him. I always make a point of assuring him that I am coming back.

As you know, I go to Coombe Haven Tuesdays and Thursdays. It's a long break between Thursday and the following Tuesday. Samuel is quite hostile when I do return. How I wish to God that boy would speak. If it were only to rant and rave at me.

Penny has visited Coombe Haven a couple of times, she was quite taken up with Sammy. 'Nice enough to eat!' she declared.

Funny enough, he didn't object to Penny picking him up. Maybe because she isn't hesitant, goes for it, laughs a lot and is always in command. Do you think that is possible?

The biggest thrill I get is when, perhaps, I put my hand out and brush the hair away from Sammy's eyes, he'll make a grab for my forefinger, rolling his own chubby little fingers around it like a sausage. He'll hold on to it for ages. It's the nearest I ever get to a cuddle from him.

Elizabeth, I meant this to be a cheerful letter and here I am writing of all my misgivings when I should be asking after you and Tim. What of William and John? Growing fast I expect. Are they doing well at school? And baby Hannah? We don't see enough of each other, do we? I must get James to agree to come to Windsor for a weekend.

Which brings me to another point. I'm a coward or I would have started off with this.

James wants to attend a do being given by the Law Society. Thing is, it is being held in Scotland, over three days. James wants for us both to go and then for us to stay on at the hotel for a further ten days or so. I know he's right to insist – we haven't had a holiday and this would be the ideal break. Paul has offered to accompany us, bring his lady-friend as well, so it would be great for them.

But oh Elizabeth, the thought of leaving Sammy without a visit for maybe more than two weeks fills me with dread. Be like deserting a sinking ship. Worse! He would be entitled to believe I had abandoned him. Another rejection.

I have made some headway with him. I'm sure I have. There are times when I could shout out loud with pleasure because of a fleeting moment when I catch an expression on his little face, and for the briefest instant a smile will transform his solemn features.

I know I must put James first, yet I feel the next few weeks with Samuel will probably be more important than all the rest put together.

Why can't we all be as wise as King Solomon?

Ah Elizabeth, I suppose I shall go to Scotland, or rather I should say WE shall go to Scotland. Will ring you before we leave.

Our love to you all,

Barbara.

She sat back, thinking of Tim and Elizabeth, their children growing up in that uncomplicated family, with security and so much love.

She looked across at James. He was still young, only thirty-eight. Life wasn't fair. Still, he hadn't let the accident ruin his life. He wasn't bitter, never regarded himself as a cripple. He worked hard at keeping himself fit. His pale-blue, short-sleeved shirt hung loosely over lightweight cream linen trousers. He felt her gaze and looked up directly at her, and she felt a glow spread over her. His arms were brown, his face tanned from the good summer weather they had had, and his belly was as flat as a pancake.

He leaned over and reached for his glass, his forearm brushing across her lower thigh. She watched the muscles in his forearm flex when he pulled the table nearer.

She touched his hand, felt the warmth and the springy hairs which covered the back of it. Oh James! she breathed to herself. I love you so.

They didn't have everything in life, but then who does? Life could be a whole lot worse. They had their moments when some nights she lay in his arms and he proved beyond doubt that she was the only woman for him and she certainly needed no convincing that marrying James had been the absolutely right thing for her to have done.

As if knowing something of what Barbara was thinking, James leaned across, his lips seeking hers.

Oliver, their big Labrador retriever, wriggled to his feet, cross at being disturbed, then moved to the shade of a tree and flopped down again.

James laughed, 'That dog has a wonderful life.'

Barbara smiled warmly. 'And so my darling, do we, and please God, the best is yet to come.'

Barbara couldn't help herself. The tears were spilling over, falling warmly on to the back of her hand before she had time to brush them away.

'*Please*, Sammy,' she begged. On her knees beside him on the carpet, she tried to swing his body round to face her. He would have none of it.

'Leave 'im be, Barbara,' Hilda advised. 'Most likely 'ee will pine, but that might just do 'im a bit of good. Yer never can tell. Good Lord, you're entitled t'have a break, same as the rest of us. I'll see ter 'im. That's a promise, cross me 'eart. I won't let 'im forget that you're gonna come back. Now do us both a favour an' sling yer 'ook, go on, while the going's good, else you'll 'ave us all in bloody tears before you're finished.'

Apparently the seminar had been a great success. Certainly James was in a good mood as he asked Paul and Maureen to join them for a drink before they set out for their evening walk.

There weren't many guests left in the hotel now, the four of them had enjoyed a lovely dinner, taking their time over it, and were now sitting in the comfortable lounge with coffee set out in front of them.

'Brandy, Paul?' James asked and when Paul nodded, he added, 'And liqueurs, is it? For you two lovely ladies?'

The waiter brought their drinks and just as Barbara was about to raise her glass, Paul said, 'Maureen and I have something to tell you both.'

Barbara's heart sank down into her boots.

Taking hold of Maureen's hand, Paul smiled as he said, 'We've decided to get married.'

Barbara tried her best to smile and Paul, watching her, knew exactly what she was thinking. He spoke quickly.

'I have a proposition to put to you both, if you don't think I am being too presumptuous.'

'Paul!' James cut him off quickly. 'I thought you regarded Barbara and myself as friends?'

'Oh, I do,' Paul hastened to assure him. 'The last thing I want to do is to leave you. Working for you, James, suits me very well.'

'So, spit out what you were about to say.'

'The cottage in your grounds – with some renovations it would be a grand place for Maureen and myself to set up house. Don't think you're aware of it, but Maureen is a barmaid-cum-waitress at The Smugglers in Alfriston. She has a room there. Lives in. All her family are still in Ireland. We have been having lengthy discussions about this for ages. She'll be over the moon if you agree.'

Barbara looked first at Maureen, who by now was blushing. Then she turned to James, their eyes met and they both smiled.

'Congratulations!' James and Barbara said simultaneously. James was shaking hands with Paul, Barbara was kissing Maureen, then found she was being hugged by Paul while Maureen rose and bent to plant a kiss on James's cheek.

His eyes wide with happiness, Paul sat back. 'What a relief,' he murmured. Maureen, who had always appeared self-conscious when around Barbara, now smiled happily. 'Oh thank you both. 'Tis such a lovely cottage, we'll be able to fix it up fine. I'll keep on with me job for a while, but the joy of it, to come home to me own place instead of just having me own room.'

James became serious, turned to Paul first and then to Maureen, 'I would like to pay all expenses for your wedding – Barbara's and my wedding gift to you both.'

'We'll not be having a grand wedding, Mister James,' Maureen hastened to say.

'We'll go into all of that when we get home. I dare say Barbara and some of her friends will relish the idea of going shopping with you and doing all the things you girls do in preparation for a wedding. Meanwhile, will you please drop the Mister. Maureen and Paul, you are to us, and Barbara and James we are to you. All right?'

It was a happy pair of lovers that set off for their walk, and a relieved married pair that remained behind in the hotel to toast them once again with fresh drinks that James had quickly asked the barman to bring to their table.

This hotel, in Dunoon, had been selected by the Law Society. First off, both Barbara and James had been disappointed that it wasn't on the edge of a loch or set amongst Scotland's mountains. Now it suited them to stay in Dunoon for their extra days, one of the main reasons being

Elizabeth Waite

that the resort had a long level promenade, not far from
the hotel, which enabled Barbara and James to take a
leisurely walk of an evening. Besides which, the hotel was
of the older type, not plush, giving excellent food and
service. Barbara especially liked the fact that log-fires were
lit in all the public rooms early in the afternoon.

They hired a car, dressed casually, and the four of them
toured the spectacular Western Highlands, making sure they
spent one day on the shore of the lovely Loch Lomond.
The only fly in the ointment being Barbara's remorse at
having left young Sammy.

James, well aware of how his wife felt, did his best to
reassure her.

Early one afternoon, they arrived at a particularly lovely
spot.

Having made sure that Barbara and James were quite
comfortably settled in a cottage that served cream teas,
Maureen and Paul set off to stride away across heather-
covered hills.

The cottage had tremendous views, made all the better
by the glowing autumn foliage.

Barbara was looking out of the windows, quite happily
watching several squirrels scampering up and down the
trees, when James put a hand on her knee, making her
jump, intruding on her thoughts.

'Tell you what, Barbara,' he said. 'When we get back to
London, we don't need to go straight home, we could
book ourselves into Brown's Hotel in Dover Street for the
night and go pay a visit to Coombe Haven.'

'Oh James, I *do* love you,' she squeezed his arm. 'You're
sure you don't mind? You won't be too tired?'

'Well,' he paused, as if he were giving thought to the

question. 'We aren't exactly slumming it on the train, are we? Gourmet food, excellent sleeping berths, we'll arrive fresh as daisies.'

'Oh, you!' She pushed his arm this time, a scone that was halfway to his mouth got there faster, cream, squashed from the filling, now spread along his top and bottom lip.

Barbara roared out laughing.

James bought Scotch whisky for his colleagues, and a bottle for each of their fathers. Barbara bought lots of tins of butter-shortbread for the children at Coombe Haven, a teddy bear dressed in a kilt for Sammy, and a warm tartan shawl for Mrs Clarkson and Maggie Harvey. For her mother and also for James's mother, she couldn't resist silver brooches, fashioned in the shape of a twig of heather.

They had been back in London for less than two hours. Washed and refreshed, they stood beneath the canopy on the top step of the entrance to Brown's Hotel, watching as the doorman raised his hat and whistled up a taxi for them. There was no shortage of offers of help from the staff when it came to manoeuvring James's wheelchair down the steps and into the cab. Paul saw that everything went smoothly, waiting until Barbara was seated up front with the driver before getting into the back seat to sit beside James. Maureen had travelled straight on to Eastbourne: she was due to start work the next morning.

There was no mistaking the warmth in the welcome Ivy Pearson gave them. In the doorway to the playroom, Barbara stood still for a moment, uncertain, the thumping of her heart loud in her ears, nervousness making her legs tremble.

Hilda Whitely sensed her presence, looked up, put a finger to her lips and mouthed the word, 'Shush.' Hilda than quietly got up from the chair on which she had been sitting and backed herself out of the room.

Smiling broadly at Barbara, she gave her a gentle push, sending her forwards.

The sight that met her eyes brought her almost to tears. Sammy was snugly dressed in a pale-blue jersey, sitting on the floor actually looking at the pages of a picture book. Oh, he is a handsome child, was her first thought: his tight, fair curls still clung to his head, falling down over his forehead as he bent forward. With his chubby face and rosy cheeks, the scar on his lip didn't matter. Strong dimpled little hands held the book. 'I can't help it,' she muttered beneath her breath, 'I adore him.'

Further down the room children were rattling tins, piles of bricks were being knocked over and carers were helping others to do their exercises. Sammy was oblivious to everything that was going on around him.

'Sammy,' Barbara's voice was scarcely more than a whisper.

He turned, he stared. His lips didn't move but he made a noise. Not words but sounds, just sounds. He stood up, tottered towards her, then stopped a few feet away.

'Ba . . . ba . . . bar . . . bar . . . a,' his voice was low and hoarse.

Barbara was unaware that James had wheeled himself up close, that Hilda and Ivy were halfway into the room, silently applauding.

Her heart was filled with so much love for this little mite she didn't know what to do first.

'You said it! Yes you did, my lovely, you said it. My name. Barbara, you said it!'

The little boy stared at her a few seconds longer and then he began to cry. The first tears Barbara had ever seen him shed.

'Slowly,' James urged. 'Don't frighten him.'

There was no stopping her.

Arms out wide she ran, swooping him up, holding him close, wrapping him in safety, smothering him with love.

She didn't dare let herself believe it. He didn't resist, instead he nestled his head into her neck: he was crying softly, rubbing his wet face against her bare skin.

Heavenly! She was finally cuddling him.

'Don't cry, my pet, please, don't cry,' she crooned to him. 'See, I *did* come back.'

Keeping Sammy in her arms she turned towards James, there were tears in his eyes.

'Did you hear him? Did you? He said my name. After all this time he said my name!'

'Yes darling, I heard,' James smiled. He was more moved than he would have cared to admit. Watching Barbara, and Sammy, who was still clinging to her, he had this protective feeling towards the little lad, that as the weeks had gone by had got ever stronger and was by now becoming so familiar.

Behind her, Barbara heard footsteps coming down the room. She turned her head and saw Hilda, who, when she reached her side, stood looking at the pair of them.

'Fank the good Lord f 'that!' Hilda let out a great sigh of relief. 'I've bin saying Bar-bar-a over an' over again, till I'm blue in the face. Even bin saying it in me sleep, so me 'ole man tells me. 'Ee finks I've gone a bit funny like, found meself a woman friend, if yer know what I mean.

Yer got t'laugh at my Bill, he's bin going all round our council estate asking 'oo the 'ell is Barbara?'

Even James couldn't control his mirth!

Barbara, still rocking Sammy back and forth, was laughing fit to bust.

'I think you'd all better come along to the dining room,' Ivy instructed them, putting on her stern matron's voice.

Barbara lowered Sammy to the floor. He wouldn't let go his hold, grasping a handful of her dress, his eyes never leaving her face.

'Come on, a little bird told me it's shepherd's pie today. Your favourite. If you give me a smile, just one, I'll come and sit beside you.'

He managed a smile all right. It lit up his whole face.

Ivy Pearson, severely dressed, still very much the matron, waited until they were round the bend in the corridor, out of sight, and then she leant against the wall and fumbled in the pocket of her dress for a handkerchief. Her sight kept blurring with tears.

Chapter Twenty-three

JAMES HAD BROKEN with his routine and taken a day off from the City to attend an open-day at Coombe Haven. Invitations to the press and local dignitaries had also been sent out. The weather had been kind: for November it was a grand day, clear and dry even if it was a little cold. They had managed to set up several stalls in the grounds besides the various activities that were going on in the house.

The day had not originally been organised as a fund-raising event but the results, judging by the number of people that had turned up, must be good.

'Ladies and Gentlemen!'

Doctor Richard Turner and his colleague Doctor David Bennett were both standing on chairs, near to the sale-of-work table, looking out at the crowds that had gathered on the lawn.

Voices were hushed and heads turned expectantly in their direction.

'Thank you.' Having got everyone's attention, Richard held up a sheet of paper.

'Just before we all go into the house for a hot cup of tea, the committee of this children's home have asked us to thank you all for your generosity. The results of today's gathering will, I'm sure, gladden the hearts of all who are involved with Coombe Haven. As most of you are aware, many of our workers are volunteers and the few that are paid a wage are dedicated to the children far beyond the call of their duties. Serving and giving as they all do, they are inspired by and grateful for the money which has been donated today. Such has been the success of this operation, so we have already been told, that it has resulted not only in donations of cash, many of which are from unexpected quarters, but offers have been made of equipment from various firms in the district. Equipment that the home so badly needs and which will be very much appreciated. I speak for us all and on behalf of the children, when I say, we are truly grateful. If you would like to know more of the workings of Coombe Haven, my friend, David, here, will be only too happy to give you one of our brochures.'

Sounds of gladness and goodwill rippled around the grounds.

Sammy, whose little legs wouldn't carry him any further, was riding piggyback on Barbara as they made their way back to the house.

'James and Paul were looking for you two.'

At the sound of Richard's voice behind her, Barbara stood still, turned around and waited for him to catch up with her.

'They said to tell you they would see you inside.'

'Oh, right. We were just making tracks, getting chilly now.'

Barbara bent down and let Sammy slip to the ground.

'Had a good time, haven't we?' she said to the little boy. 'Tell Doctor Richard you had a ride on a pony.'

Sammy looked up at the doctor, smiled, nodded, but never answered.

'Still hasn't much to say for himself,' Richard's tone reflected concern.

'Oh, he's still very wary of folk. Chatters away to me sometimes now, nineteen to the dozen.'

Sammy must have felt he was being ignored.

With a lot of force he flung his arms around Richard's knees and butted the doctor's legs with his head.

Neither Richard nor Barbara took any notice. They stood there, still carrying on their conversation.

Sammy slammed his whole body against Richard's legs again, this time causing him to take a step backwards.

'He doesn't relish sharing you, Barbara, does he? He wants the whole of your attention. Not that anyone can blame him for that,' he added with a grin. 'He's an amusing little character on the days you're here, withdraws back into his shell other times. Pity. He will eventually have to learn to trust others.'

Barbara was still pondering on Richard's words when she entered the dining room and saw Paul waving her to a table where he and James were already seated.

'Here, take my cup,' Paul offered. 'I've only just fetched it, it is still hot.'

'No, I'll go, you stay where you are. I'll get Sammy some squash at the same time.'

'Hallo Sammy, old chap, have you had a great time?' Paul, doing as he was told, had bent down to take charge of the small boy, lifting him up onto a chair.

James stretched his arm across the table, took a chocolate cake from the plate of assorted fancy cakes and offered it to Sammy.

The boy's lips twitched into half a smile but he made no sound.

With the cake half-eaten, Sammy slipped down from his

chair, put one foot on to the platform of James's wheelchair and climbed up into his lap.

'Ride,' he demanded.

'Say please,' James told him without thinking.

'Please,' Sammy obediently said.

Paul laughed to himself.

James let off the brake and let the chair roll back and forth.

Barbara, arriving back with a tea-tray, couldn't believe her eyes. It was such a happy scene. Paul Soames nodded his head, let his eyelid drop in a saucy wink, as if to say: see, even James is taken up with the little toddler.

Her thoughts were still troubling her. What if Richard had been trying to warn her that soon Sammy might have to leave Coombe Haven? Foster-parents would be found for him.

It didn't bear thinking about!

Yet that very idea had been there all the time. She mustn't brood on it. Lose Sammy! She was so strongly opposed to the idea that it made her feel sick.

Sammy banged her with his fist and said, 'Look!'

Barbara looked, and saw his sticky fingers, his beaming, chocolate-smeared face, and she pulled him from James's lap into her arms and hugged him.

James watched and heard her say, 'You little monkey. I love you. D'you know that?'

Sammy didn't answer.

She tickled him, he wriggled, laughing loudly.

His laughter eased her tension.

Visitors were leaving, only the part-time volunteers and a few employees such as Hilda had remained to help with the clearing-up.

'Isn't it time you were going home, Hilda?' Barbara asked, as she helped Hilda to stack dirty cups and saucers onto a tray.

'It's all right, Barbara; me 'ole man is on two till ten t'day, he won't be there now anyway.'

'Have you got any children? I've never thought to ask you before now.'

'Bless yer 'eart, course I 'ave. Two boys, ten an' twelve. Me mum will see t'them, give 'em their tea. 'Sides, they take more notice of 'er than they ever do of me or their father. Do anything fer their Gran they will.'

'Oh, you're lucky, having your mother nearby. That's how you manage to be able to work. Peace of mind, eh, knowing someone is there when they come home from school?'

Hilda laughed as she passed an empty tray to Barbara, and lifted the loaded one to take to the kitchen.

'Me mum lives wiv us. Me dad died eight years ago, couldn't leave me poor 'ole mum t'get by on 'er own, could I?'

Barbara was thoughtful as she regarded Hilda setting off, most likely to give a hand with the washing-up. Happy soul was Hilda, ever ready to give help where it was needed. So, there was a family of five living in the Whitelys' council house. She knew about this estate, where Hilda lived: very unusual type of houses they were. Built years ago, more as country cottages, when Croydon was still very much part of Surrey. The front doors opened straight onto the pavement. They were very small dwellings, without bathrooms and yet to hear Hilda, she was quite sure that the Whitelys were a very happy, contented family.

Life was a puzzle at times.

There was James and herself living in the country, plenty of room in a beautiful house, horses to ride whenever the fancy took her, lovely walks and not very far from the sea. What more could a woman want from life than this? She had comfort, security, love and tenderness. The one vital thing that was missing was children. Whatever else she might possess that was what she didn't have. And never could have.

'Ladies.'

Ivy Pearson waved her arms in the air to silence the talking that was going on in the dining room.

'May I have your attention for a moment, please?'

There was a sudden hush amongst the adults, but not the children, who merely glanced up at Matron and then went on with their chattering.

'Just before you all go home, may I raise the question of Christmas? We have been most generously offered toys and even entertainment, spread over the holiday. We shall as usual be having agency nurses to come in to supplement our live-in staff. The children will want for nothing. If, however, some of you volunteers could manage some form of involvement, no matter how small, it would be greatly appreciated. Thank you all for the effort you have put into making a success of today.'

Matron gave a friendly wave, signifying the end of her little talk, and turned to descend from the platform.

The swell of voices broke out afresh.

Barbara was stunned. Christmas!

Couldn't she just imagine it, without being able to see Sammy?

Yes! was her own answer. Vividly!

Her gaze took in the fact that Paul was busy stacking

chairs against the wall, but James was lounging back in his chair studying her intently.

It was on the tip of her tongue to demand to know what they were going to do about Samuel during the Christmas holiday, but knowing such a question at this moment would only hurt James's feelings, she gave a little shrug of her shoulders and went back to stacking dirty crockery onto trays.

''Ave a look at Sammy, e's more than 'alf asleep,' Hilda nudged Barbara with her elbow.

'Oh bless him.' He was curled up on the carpet, one leg tucked underneath his bottom, his head resting on his arm.

Barbara bent to pick up a wooden brick that was jammed beneath his elbow, and speaking softly she said, 'Come on, my darling, you mustn't go to sleep on the floor, someone will tread on you if I leave you lying here.'

Without a word Sammy held out his arms to her and when she had him curled up in her arms he stuck his thumb in his mouth and, sucking contentedly, closed his eyes again and drifted off to sleep.

'There's a good boy,' she murmured, not really knowing what to do with him now, but not wishing to part from him. Very soon Paul would be telling them it was time to set off for home.

'I'll take him, Barbara,' Hilda said. 'The nurses are taking most of the little ones up to their cots.'

Barbara stroked his silky, soft, curly hair and whispered, 'Bye-bye, Sammy. I'll see you on Tuesday.'

She was relieved that as she passed him over to Hilda's outstretched arms, he didn't stir, nor did he open his eyes.

She paused before going to join James.

All children need parents. A child shouldn't be shifted

from pillar to post. It would be a poor, lonely life if that was all that Sammy would have to look forward to.

'Let's go,' Barbara said to Paul as she buttoned up her coat.

James sensed the effort this was costing her, and he felt extraordinarily moved. He recalled the time at Henley, when Barbara had first told him of the rough treatment she had received at the hands of Michael and his mate, and how subsequently she had refused to even look at her own baby. He had clung to the hope that his love for her would eventually wipe out all the nightmares of her past. It might have, had not fate intervened. His accident had banished all hope that they would ever have children of their own.

'I'm ready,' Barbara looked into his face, saw his blue eyes, full of love and understanding, and the sweetness of a soft smile came to her lips.

She said faintly, 'We can't leave him here. Not for Christmas.'

'No. I'll see what can be done. We'll sort something out.'

She breathed out. Thank God for James. She closed her eyes and tried to say a prayer, but somehow the right words wouldn't come.

She wasn't asking to have Sammy for good. Just for Christmas. Was that too much to ask?

Apparently it was. The answer was No.

Barbara could see the reasoning of the doctors and the members of the committee, but that didn't make it any easier to bear.

James had dreaded having to tell her of their decision.

'They are right, you know, Barbara; we just didn't take

he time to consider what we were asking. As Anthony
pointed out, normally home visits are encouraged, at least
for the older children, but under strict supervision and in
calm, quiet circumstances.'

'Christmas time being the wrong time,' Barbara said
thoughtfully.

'Well, yes. Lots of people in and out. Festivities and
presents, could be bewildering for a small child in strange
surroundings, don't you agree?'

Barbara found herself saying, 'Yes', when all she wanted
to do was scream in frustration.

James manoeuvred his wheelchair nearer to where Barbara stood looking through the lounge windows. He felt
self-conscious about what he was going to say to her.
Would he be touching a raw nerve?

'Barbara, would you . . . well, could you . . . bring yourself to think about adoption?'

It hadn't been easy to say. Would she reproach him
because that was exactly what she had done to her own
son?

'I've spoken to my partners,' he plunged on, as she
remained silent. 'The firm would handle all the legal aspects
for us, and I only ventured to ask because the panel of
doctors at Coombe Haven said that was one of the possibilities they were considering in Samuel's case. They would,
of course, have to trace his father. No one envisaged trouble
from that quarter.'

Barbara was agitated. She found it was much easier not
to cry if she screwed her eyes up tight and refused to open
them.

'I don't mind if you want to cry,' James told her, endeavouring to show her just how much he did understand.

'I'm doing my best not to.'

'Sammy will be fine. Matron will see to him and she won't be the only one.'

Barbara knew he spoke the truth, yet none the more for that Christmas would seem a never-ending holiday this year.

Chapter Twenty-four

WITH THE COMING of the New Year, endless discussions were under way as to the suitability of James and Barbara Ferguson to become adoptive parents of two-year-old Samuel Rowlings.

On two weekends, a fortnight apart, they had been allowed to have Sammy home for two days. The first time had been a strain. He had clung to Barbara, wouldn't let her out of his sight, and had withdrawn back into his shell, scarcely uttering more than one word at a time during the whole of his stay. The second time had seen an improvement. Paul and Maureen O'Connor had spent the Saturday with them, helping to amuse Sammy and making him laugh.

Sunday, Penny and Neil had arrived, and as James had been quick to remark, 'Who on this earth could resist the charms of the beautiful Penny?' She not only had Sammy talking, she had him yelling with joy at the tricks she got up to for his benefit.

James was a hundred per cent certain that this was what he wanted. Given the chance he had vowed to himself that he would love and care for Samuel, never treating him any less than if he had been his son by birth.

For Barbara it was different.

God alone knew just how much she longed to bring Sammy home to their house and never have to take him back to Coombe Haven.

To wash and undress him and put him to bed. To read him stories. To wake up in the morning and go into his bedroom, find him all warm and still smelling of sleep. To bathe his knees when he fell over, to try and understand when he had a fit of bad temper, to be there for him. Always!

She was, however, faced with one of the most painful decisions she had ever had to make. She had to give herself definite answers to certain questions and on no account must she lie to herself. Could she agree with James, that they take Sammy and make him their son for the right reasons – or was she striving to atone for having given up her own child for adoption?

Whichever way she looked at it, Barbara decided she would be firm in her mind by the time it came to making the ultimate resolution. It was in a much happier frame of mind that she took Sammy back to Coombe Haven on the Monday after his second visit and stayed the day with him.

Paul and James picked her up from Croydon soon after three and they were back at the house by five o'clock.

Getting out of the car, Barbara noticed Maggie Harvey was watching her from the lounge window. Why was Maggie still here? She usually set their evening meal ready and went home about half past three.

Maggie had the door open before Barbara could set her key in the lock. 'Mr Holsworthy rang you, twice,' she reported, trying to hide her anxiety. 'He said to tell you Elizabeth has been taken into hospital and would you or James ring him at this number as soon as you got home.'

'Did he say what was wrong with Elizabeth?' Barbara took the slip of paper.

'No, only that she had been involved in an accident, but

Mr Warren phoned from the nursing home, he sounded very upset.'

Barbara turned to Paul and James in anguish. 'Something has happened to Elizabeth.'

James held his hand out to her, 'Paul will get the number for us. Thank you for staying, Maggie.'

'I'll see you all in the morning.' Maggie wanted to get away home, before she started crying.

They gathered around the phone in the hall.

'You're through to the General Hospital,' Paul said, handing the telephone to James.

Barbara couldn't bear the suspense. Neither could she interrupt the only side of the conversation that she could hear.

'Tim, don't worry yourself about Mr Warren, Paul will go straight over to the home and fetch him here. Yes, I know we have to face that possibility,' James was speaking so gently. 'We'll be here all night if you feel like ringing again later. It won't do any good if we go to pieces, Tim. We'll be with you first thing in the morning, but we'll speak again as soon as I've told Barbara what has happened.'

'Three days ago Elizabeth had a nasty fall. She was riding her bicycle, on her way to a meeting of the Women's Institute at the local village hall. Gashed her face and arm rather badly.' James's matter-of-fact tone heartened Barbara for an instant.

'The bad news is, during the examination the doctor discovered a lump in her left breast. They have admitted Elizabeth to hospital and today she has undergone a series of tests. We shall know the results in the morning.'

Barbara looked at him in dismay, her face white with shock.

'Come on now,' he said gently, 'let's not panic. It might not even be a tumour.'

'Have they taken X-rays?'

'Apparently an X-ray doesn't tell the doctors what they need to know.'

This wasn't real – it was a nightmare. Suppose it was breast cancer? The thought of sweet, gentle, Elizabeth being exposed to that kind of surgery!

'Did Tim say if there was any way of knowing yet?'

'If there was the doctors weren't saying,' James told them both. 'Tim said they had done their best to reassure him.'

'I wish we could go to Windsor right now.' Barbara was struggling to keep her voice calm.

'We'll go in the morning, get a real early start. Most important thing now is to comfort her father. Poor old chap. Tim felt he had to ring the home and the warden kindly offered to notify Mr Warren. He must be worried sick.'

Elizabeth sighed, 'I'll go up and make the bed in one of the spare rooms, he'll stay here with us, of course. Do you think, James, that he will be up to making the journey to Windsor?'

'I really don't know. Let's cross that bridge when we come to it. At worst we could leave him here with Maggie. For tonight the old man will feel much better knowing that he is with friends who really care about him and his daughter. Now go upstairs and see to his bed. Paul will be back shortly and we'll all have dinner together.'

It was a struggle for Barbara to swallow her food. She was grateful that Paul was there and that he and James kept the

conversation going, making sure that Mr Warren didn't
dwell too much on what had happened to Elizabeth.

In bed with James – she couldn't bear to be alone –
Barbara lay awake, going over and over in her mind what
might happen if things turned out badly. Why, oh why
should this happen to Elizabeth, of all people?

There was no justice!

Staring into the darkness, she prayed as she had never
done before.

'Barbara,' James reached for her, taking her into his arms.
'Elizabeth will be all right. Don't torment yourself, it won't
help.'

'I keep thinking of the children. Did Tim say who was
looking after them?'

'No, but we'll find all that out in the morning. Now go
to sleep, my darling,' his voice was soothing.

'I'll try,' she whispered.

It was close to dawn before she fell into a troubled sleep.
Maggie opening the bedroom door woke her and James.

Glancing at their alarm clock James saw it was only six
thirty. 'I came early to make you all some breakfast. I
presume you are going to Windsor.'

Barbara lay still, trying to prepare herself to face whatever
this day was going to bring. Her eyes followed Maggie as
she poured out the tea and took a cup round to James's
side of the bed.

'I've taken a tray into Mr Warren and Paul was up and
about when I got here,' Maggie said.

James made several phone calls but when Paul drove the
car up to the front door, he, Barbara and Elizabeth's father
were in the porchway, dressed and waiting. Barbara held

the door open as James propelled his chair out in to the
cold, sunlit morning. She turned and looked back, Maggie
came at her with a rush, her strong arms going round
Barbara's waist.

'I'll be praying you find things all right. Now don't take
on so, ring me if you get a chance and if you're not back
by the time I go home I'll take Oliver with me. I'll give
him a bit of a run anyway, seeing as how Paul hasn't
taken him out this morning.'

'You're a treasure. You know that, don't you?' Barbara
said, brushing angrily at her eyes to wipe away the tears.

'Hope the traffic's light this morning,' Paul muttered, a
hand at her elbow as he helped her into the car. 'We should
be at the hospital in about two and a half hours.'

Barbara went into Elizabeth's room on her own. Tim was
sitting beside the bed. Elizabeth looked as if she had been
in a fight!

Dressed in a stiff, white, hospital gown rather than one
of her own pretty nightdresses, her silky brown hair looked
in need of a good brush. There was an angry looking bruise
on her left cheek and a gash that ran the length of her
chin, this wound had been stitched with black thread which
served to make it look raw and ugly.

'Barbara!' Elizabeth pulled herself up on her elbows.
'Oh, it is lovely to see you but you shouldn't have come
all this way. There isn't any need.'

'No need! Don't talk daft. Since when didn't we come
running when one or the other of us was in trouble?'

'Well, now you are here, don't look so worried, darling,
I'm going to be fine. You'll see.'

'Fine! You can't even ride a bike now, so I hear, without

falling off,' Barbara was doing her best to keep her tone light. Inside her heart was pounding.

'Thank you for coming, Barbara,' Tim rose to his feet and kissed her on both cheeks. He looked ghastly.

Before she could tell him that his father-in-law was outside with James and Paul, a nurse came into the room.

With a cheerfulness obviously meant to reassure them, she explained, 'I shall have to ask you to leave for a little while. Doctor Wimbourne will be here shortly with Mr Shard, and you, Mr Holsworthy, really should get some rest. We don't want to end up with you as a patient, now do we?'

Turning to Barbara, she urged, 'Take him along to the cafeteria, see that he drinks a good hot cup of tea and has something to eat.'

Paul queued up at the self-service counter, coming back to the table where they were sitting with a loaded tray.

'You've got to eat,' James told Tim, brushing aside his protests.

Tim did his best, only to please them, but all he could think about was Elizabeth. 'We had no hint of it,' he told them. '*Nothing.*'

'It'll probably turn out to be nothing,' James said.

No one answered him.

Two men in white coats approached. Tim obviously knew one of them, he rose to his feet. 'Hallo, Doctor Wimbourne. These are family friends.' He made the introductions. 'I'd like them to hear what you have to say.'

The doctor smiled and nodded, 'This is Mr Shard, he will

be the surgeon looking after your wife. We've scheduled for her surgery at nine o'clock tomorrow morning.'

'Then it is a tumour?' Barbara interrupted, the colour draining from her face.

'We have to face that possibility,' Mr Shard said gently. 'We have just discussed this with Mrs Holsworthy. If the biopsy shows that the growth is malignant, we'll go ahead and do a mastectomy immediately.'

Barbara flinched.

'But,' Mr Shard quickly added, 'we don't even know that it's malignant yet, so let's not fear the worse. Most tumours prove to be benign.'

'Does my wife really understand what might happen?'

'She understands, Tim,' Doctor Wimbourne said softly.

'Will I be able to go back in and see her before we leave?' Barbara struggled to keep the fear out of her voice.

'You'll all be able to see her as soon as the nurses have tidied her up. Please only two at a time, and don't stay too long.'

'Thank you, Doctor Wimbourne.'

James went in to the side ward with Barbara, he did his best to keep the conversation cheerful.

Barbara was choked right up when she came out of the room, having said an emotional goodbye to Elizabeth.

'She'll be all right,' James held out his hand to her, though to tell the truth he was feeling utterly helpless. 'Tim will phone us as soon as there is any news. We will all pray and you'll see, Elizabeth will come through with flying colours.'

In bed, Barbara lay awake. Staring into the darkness, wishing morning would come.

It was the longest day of their lives. Penny came and the two friends hugged each other. Lost for words.

Maggie made endless pots of tea and coffee.

It was three o'clock before the phone rang. On the second ring James picked up the receiver.

'It was malignant! Elizabeth hasn't come round yet, but the doctors are optimistic.'

Tim sounded whacked out but he insisted to James that he was spending the night in the hospital, 'I'll ring you again first thing in the morning. Goodnight James.'

Two days and there wasn't much change. On the third day Paul drove them back to Windsor.

They took it in turns to sit with Elizabeth. When the sun had set and dusk was settling outside the windows, they all feared the worse.

'I wish to God she'd wake up,' Barbara couldn't keep the tears from falling.

Paul patted Barbara's shoulder. 'I'm going with James to the bathroom and I'll get some tea for us on the way back. I won't be long.'

Barbara got to her feet, stretched and crossed to the open doorway. Nurses and doctors were going about their duties. Patients in wheelchairs and on crutches, others walking dressed in slippers and dressing-gowns, were talking to each other in the corridor. Visitors were arriving, clutching bunches of flowers. It was hard to believe.

She tried to focus on the fact that miracles did happen. She closed her eyes: Dear God, she has three little children, they need her.

'Barbara . . .' James's voice came to her from a room across the hall. She looked, his face was serious. Doctor

Wimbourne was talking to Elizabeth's father, Paul and James.

Barbara hesitated, took a deep breath and covered the distance between them.

'I am so sorry,' Doctor Wimbourne placed his hand on her arm. 'We did everything possible.'

'Thank you,' she had to force herself to say it.

Doctor Wimbourne turned to face the men, 'Your son-in-law is in Mr Shard's office, Mr Warren. If you and your friends would like to go and join him . . . he will be able to explain matters far better than I.'

Barbara felt she was sleep walking as Mr Warren took her arm, guiding her along behind Paul and James.

Mr Shard's voice droned on, 'In any surgical operation there is always an element of risk.'

'Mr Shard,' Barbara interrupted, 'we were told earlier that Elizabeth came through the operation well.'

'And so she did, my dear,' his voice held not only a note of sympathy but sincerity also.

'What happened after the operation is in medical terms, a pulmonary embolus. Unfortunately it is a complication that can occur after major surgery.'

Barbara shuddered.

Elizabeth's father must have asked a question. Mr Shard had swivelled his chair around to face the old gentleman.

'You are quite right, Mr Warren. A blood clot detached from the wall of a deep vein is swept into the bloodstream through the heart and along the pulmonary artery to the lung.'

Mr Warren tried hard to choke off a sob. Although his voice was only a whisper, they all heard him say, 'You never expect your children to die before you do yourself.' There was nothing more anyone could say.

Mr Shard rose to his feet, 'Please.' Tim had made to rise. 'Stay where you are. My office is at your disposal.' He hesitated, 'I am so sorry, words fail me.' With that he left the room, closing the door quietly behind him.

Oh Elizabeth! Elizabeth, kind, generous friend. Why? Why? She never did an unkind thing to anyone in her life.

Oh God, her poor children. How sad these little ones would grow up without a mother.

Scalding tears were running unchecked down Barbara's face. She was choking. Her nose was running and she felt so mad she wanted to smash anything that she could lay her hands on.

They left the office and waited in the reception room while Tim and his father-in-law went in to stay a while longer with Elizabeth, only now it wasn't Elizabeth. Only her body.

Tim and Mr Warren came out from the side ward. They both looked as if they had aged ten years.

Now it was the turn of Barbara and James to say their goodbyes to their dear friend and when they came back to join the men Barbara managed to a weak smile. 'Come on, you're coming home with us,' she said to Tim.

Elizabeth's body was being brought home to Alfriston to lie beside her mother in the small churchyard of St Andrew's, the parish church. Tim had gone to pieces, not caring whether he lived or died. James had made all the arrangements, urging Tim to sign all the necessary documents. William, John and Hannah were still in Yorkshire with Tim's parents, who weren't going to be able to attend the funeral. Both of them were elderly and Mr Holsworthy had confided to James, on the telephone, that he feared his wife was suffering the early states of senility. When Barbara had learnt of this she wondered briefly if she should insist that Tim bring the children home for the funeral and then decided against it.

The church was packed. Folk who had seen Elizabeth grow up in this peaceful village questioned the ways of a God of love that would take the life of a young wife and mother and leave her father – an old man and widower – to grieve and her husband to be driven half out of his mind.

Even before the flowers had died on the freshly-dug pile earth on Elizabeth's grave, Tim had left them.

Without hint or warning he had gone. Not back to work, Neil Chapman had been on the telephone daily to report that no one at the office had seen hide nor hair of him.

Letters and telephone calls from Tim's father in Yorkshire had then worried everyone as to how the old gentleman was coping with three children.

'What about the boys' schooling, James? Someone has to start considering things like that.' The children being so far away in Yorkshire was worrying Barbara more than she would admit.

James swung his chair away from the table and drew up close to her. 'You're right of course. In the long term there are loads of problems that need to be sorted; meanwhile, as soon as I get to the office tomorrow I will get my secretary to telephone the welfare people, they'll contact Yorkshire and make sure that help is at hand.'

Barbara wiped her mouth with her serviette, they'd finished dinner and sweet and coffee could wait a while.

'James, there's another matter I want to talk to you about: Sammy! I'm longing to see him and yet I dread to think what his reaction will be. It's been ten days since I've been near Coombe Haven.'

'That's hardly been your fault, my darling. Matron will have done her best to explain your absence to Samuel.'

'That's all very well,' she moaned. 'How do you go about telling a two-year-old little boy that you hadn't been near nor by him because one of your best friends had died.'

'Now stop blaming yourself,' James said sternly. 'It has been a trying time for all of us. Unfortunately, as in many things, innocent people get caught up in the repercussions; in this case, sadly it is a little boy. All you can do is have patience, show him that you *do* love him and hope for the best.'

Hope for the best was right, but she feared the worst!

Barbara had arrived at Coombe Haven so early that the children hadn't quite finished their breakfast. She stood in the doorway of the dining room watching, unable to control the trembling of her legs.

Hilda put the last spoonful of boiled egg into Sammy's mouth, wiped his lips clean and lifted him down from his chair. Today he was dressed in blue dungarees and a canary-yellow shirt. He looked gorgeous! His hair was still unruly, a mass of tight curls. She wanted to rush in, to swing him up in her arms, hug him tight, but decided not to.

'Sammy,' she called, opening her arms wide, praying he would come to her. He didn't move.

'Yer daft 'apeth,' said Hilda briskly and gave him a push

with her hand. 'Go and give Barbara a kiss, I kept telling yer, didn't I, that she would be back? Well, she's come back – so go on, be quick.'

Sammy walked slowly. 'No, no, no,' he muttered to himself. Suddenly his pace quickened, he flew across the room, his right leg dragging badly in such motion.

Barbara let go of her handbag and bent her knees to receive the little arms that she hoped would lock around her neck. That wasn't what happened. Fists flying, feet kicking, his cheeks turning a flaming red with sheer temper, Sammy laid into Barbara, so unexpectedly that she lost her balance and reeled over backwards to lie on the floor.

Hilda ran to her assistance. Barbara waved her away. She sat up but remained on the floor. Sammy was crying now, not softly as he used to, but great yells and screams, letting out all his resentment until the yells turned to hiccups, his breathing became tight and his face was a bleary mess. Still Barbara sat on the floor and waited.

Reluctantly, at last, he leaned against her. Lifted his head and examined her face long and hard. 'You didn't come.'

The words broke her heart.

'Oh Sammy. I couldn't come. I wasn't well.' It was a bad lie, but the best she could think of.

Slowly the red-rimmed blue eyes melted in forgiveness and his arms crept up to cling around her neck.

Barbara let out a long sigh of relief. Calmly, gently, she put her arms around his wriggling, warm, sweet-smelling little body; he shuddered and the movement frightened her. Carefully she got to her feet, still clasping him in her arms.

If only she could shield this small boy from all the knocks

of this world. Surely he had had more than his fair share already in his young life?

She made a promise to herself: in future she would do everything that she possibly could to see that he never had reason to cry like that ever again.

In a very short space of time, Samuel Rowlings became very much part of Barbara's and James's life. They had him home for two days on alternate weekends, gaining so much pleasure from his visits that life without him now was unthinkable.

'Let's take him to the seaside, next time he's here,' Maureen O'Connor sounded as excited as a child herself.

'Well,' she said, seeing that not only Paul but Barbara and James were also laughing at her. 'That wee mite would creep his way into the hearts of the saints, so he would. Tell me now, be honest, which one of you could refuse him the moon, if that's what he was yearning for? Sure an' away that angelic look he turns on would melt the heart of our Blessed Lady, never mind us poor mortals.'

It was true, Barbara thought to herself. That lively, lovely boy had everyone he came into contact with eating out of his hand. Her own parents adored him. James's entire family had taken him to their hearts. Even Colin Peterson and Clem Tompson were talking about teaching the lad to ride.

It was still only the first week in May, not yet exactly summer, but that didn't deter Maureen, she was determined to have her way. Cold as the weather was, Sammy's next visit was enlivened by a visit to Norman's Bay. A mile further on than Eastbourne, Norman's Bay boasted a silver, sandy beach at low tide. Wrapped up well in jerseys, woolly hats and scarves, they made a colourful picture as they set off down the almost deserted beach. Leaving Paul and James to watch from the open doors of the car, Maureen and Barbara held tightly to Sammy's hands, swinging him back and forth as they ran. Sometimes his little feet left the shingle to swish through the air, much to Sammy's delight as he yelled, 'Again, again!'

The little boy had never seen the sea before and was, at first, terrified of the noise it made and of its bouncing waves. Barbara stood one side of him and Maureen on the other, right at the edge of the water, pulling him backwards as the waves rolled in to lap at their wellington boots. Sammy tore off his gloves, and once or twice bent to trail his hand in the foam that was left behind as the waves receded with the tide.

'Come back,' he called out, his eyes wide with wonder, his cheeks rosy with the excitement of it all.

'Brrr, it's too cold to stay here,' Barbara declared loudly. 'We'll look amongst the stones on the way back up to the car, see if we can find some pretty shells, shall we?'

Maureen dried Samuel's hands on the towel she had brought with her, Barbara brushed the sand from the seat of his damp dungarees because twice he had decided to sit himself down.

'Come along – ' she stooped and hoisted Sammy up into her arms, and led the way back up the beach.

'I see the sea!' Sammy yelled, throwing himself at Paul's legs.

'We know – we've been watching you.'

Sammy wriggled free and Paul helped him to clamber up onto the back seat of the car, landing with a thump into James's lap.

'I see the sea,' he repeated. 'Look.' He unclenched his

little fists and held out a collection of shiny shells. 'Mine,' he declared as James went to touch them.

'May I see them? *Please*,' James pretended to plead.

Sammy considered for a moment, opened one fist and said, 'Yes.'

'Was the sea nice?' James asked.

'Wet,' he shouted, then chuckled as he took back the two shells that James had been inspecting.

Slowly, one at a time, Sammy laid the shells out in a circle on the seat of the car. He was totally absorbed in this occupation. His dimpled fingers were red with the cold. He persevered in laying them right side up.

Watching him, filled with fondness, James wondered about Sammy's vulnerability. He felt so protective of this child that seemed to have found his way into his heart, not to mention that of Barbara and the rest of their friends and family. Let's hope the matter would be resolved to the satisfaction of all concerned, it was certainly taking a long time, he thought.

The whole situation was tricky, to say the least of it. When he had first suggested to Barbara that they might consider adopting Samuel, she had, at first, appeared to be frightened, then overcome with joy. He was well aware that for the two of them to take this extraordinary step was somehow a marvellous opportunity. But not one to be taken lightly.

Once his firm had agreed to set the wheels in motion the subject had been avoided. With no questions from Barbara, no answers had to be found by him. Which was just as well, for he had none to give.

Everything hinged on gaining the consent of Samuel's

father and as to yet, despite great efforts, he had not been traced.

Barbara climbed into the car and lifted Sammy from James's lap to sit on the seat between them. She looked across and saw the expression on her husband's face. He was not looking at her, he was looking at Sammy. He was looking really proud, as proud as if the little boy was their own flesh and blood.

Chapter Twenty-five

THE WEEKEND THEY would long remember with regret began with the arrival of Penny and Neil Chapman. Conversation was light and friendly until dinner was over.

Barbara passed the mints round. Penny put a restraining hand on her arm, 'How long is it since you or James have seen Tim?'

'I can't put my finger on the exact date,' Barbara answered. 'Tim has only stayed here with us once since Elizabeth's funeral. I've written to him, he doesn't answer and his telephone appears to have been disconnected.'

Neil sighed, sat down close to James. 'Sorry,' he said. 'There's no way of wrapping this up.'

'You're going to tell us that Tim has gone to pieces, hasn't been to work?' James muttered. 'He was in a pretty bad way when we last saw him. We tried, so did Paul, weren't able to get through to him. Letting himself go, if you want the truth. Barbara tried to persuade him to go up to Yorkshire, see something of the twins and Hannah. It can't have been easy on those children, can it?'

'He's fast becoming an alcoholic,' Neil's voice was low as he made the statement.

'What?'

'That's right, James, no other word for it. He hasn't been home to Windsor in weeks, he's taken a flat in London. I think the drinking started as a little something to help him

389

get over Elizabeth's death. Who could blame him for that? Poor sod.'

Neil stood up and began to pace the carpet.

'How did you find out?' Barbara wanted to know.

Neil shook his head. 'You don't want to hear all the details. Believe me – you don't. In fact I would much rather you girls took yourselves upstairs, or wherever, and left me to tell James the facts.'

'Wait a minute, Neil. This is a rotten shame and if there is anything we can do – ' Barbara's voice trembled.

'It's not a shame, Barbara, it's a illness.'

'Well if Tim is so ill, shouldn't we be taking him to see a doctor?'

'You think we haven't tried?' Penny cut in. 'He won't go.'

'Perhaps we ought to make sure that a doctor pays a visit to this flat of his, don't you think so Neil?' By now James was the only one who was speaking softly.

'My father has already done that. He values Tim, not only as a friend but as a good employee. Tim handled some of our largest accounts. He's missed in the firm.'

'What happened?' James asked.

With a half-smile on his lips, Neil reluctantly told them, 'Tim laid one on the doctor. He was stoned out of his mind. Punched the doctor straight in the face.'

Both the girls sighed.

Barbara spoke first, 'Such a pity! We'll have to find a way to help him.'

Penny cleared her throat, 'There's more. Worse in a way.'

'Worse?' James frowned. 'How?'

'Neil and I went up to Yorkshire. We thought his parents

might be able to help. Poor souls, they need help themselves.'

Neil took up the story. 'We couldn't bring ourselves to tell his father about Tim's alcoholism. They certainly have enough troubles of their own without us adding to them.'

'Yes,' Penny chipped in. 'That visit was a ghastly nightmare. I've never felt so helpless in the whole of my life.'

'I won't wrap it up. I'll give it to you straight.' Even to himself Neil's voice sounded angry. 'Tim's father was not strong enough to cope with the situation. His loyalties were torn between the grandchildren and his wife. He has sent the twins to a boarding school, and the social workers have found a place for Hannah with foster-parents. It would have been madness for him to have done otherwise. There are so many complications with Mrs Holsworthy now. Her husband clings to the hope that she will recover, but of course she never will. It isn't safe to leave her alone for a minute. Poor woman has lost so much weight and her mind, well, eventually I suppose she will have to be admitted to a home.'

'But why did the children have to stay in Yorkshire?' Barbara asked. 'Why couldn't Tim have made arrangements for them to be looked after in their own home?'

'I've asked myself that same question time without number, and I haven't been able to come up with any sensible answer,' Penny sounded resentful.

'I know how you must be feeling,' Barbara reassured her. 'Bad enough that the children lost their mother, surely the one person they need to be with is their father, not an elderly grandfather and a grandmother who is desperately ill.'

'Stop getting so hot under the collar, you two, it won't

help to solve anything,' James brought himself back into the discussion. 'I think we are all agreed that something will have to be done. With the long summer holidays coming up it would be wrong to leave those children up there in school, and the baby with strangers. They are used to us and with the nice weather they can play in the fields and run wild down by the sea. There are enough of us, with our families to help, to surely see to three children. We owe it to Elizabeth.'

'That's exactly what Penny and I agreed,' Paul smiled now. 'And this seems the right time to tell you: we have rented a cottage down here for three months, we intend to look for a place to buy, we've had enough of London, besides – ' he paused, turning to Penny. 'You want to tell them?'

'I'm going to have a baby.'

The words weren't out of Penny's mouth before Barbara was by her side. 'Oh, congratulations! That's wonderful, how long?'

'Three months, a Christmas baby if all goes well.'

'It will, of course it will. James, isn't it marvellous! We'll have them as neighbours again and a new baby into the bargain.'

'Hold your horses,' Neil laughed. 'We haven't found anything to buy yet. Besides, to get back to the serious question, what are we going to do about Tim?'

It was James who answered for them all, 'Enjoy the weekend, the weather is set to be fine and warm, and first thing Monday morning we'll all travel up to town together and pay a visit to Tim in this new flat of his. Between us we should be able to talk some sense into him.'

'Or get some help for him. It's very possible that he is

going to resent our interfering in what he will regard as his own business.'

James stared at Neil as he finished speaking. He realised with some astonishment that he was angry about the way Tim had palmed his children off onto his parents.

'Well,' he said aloud. 'All of us turning up out of the blue should take the wind out of his sails.'

The flat that Tim had rented was part of a Victorian mansion in Gloucester Road, Kensington. By good chance they found two parking places in the carpark quite close to Gloucester Road station. As a group they arrived at the foot of the wide marble steps that led up to the front door.

'Stay there,' Neil said to the girls and turned to Paul who was standing beside James's wheelchair. 'I'll go up and ring the bell. Looks as if there is a list of occupants' names on that wall there.' He ran up the steps, before he had reached the top step the massive door was flung open wide, and a slim tall man in a well-fitting suit, wearing a trilby hat, made to push past Neil.

'Who the hell are you?' the man rudely asked.

Neil was silenced by astonishment; he stared, opened-mouthed.

'Well? I asked you a question.'

Recovering quickly Neil said, 'I'm looking for a Timothy Holsworthy.'

Before he could say another word the man began to pull at his arm. 'I say, I do apologise, it's been a heck of a night for me, and now this. I'm Detective Sergeant Whicker, Kensington Police.'

Neil turned and glanced at Penny and the others still waiting anxiously on the pavement.

'I think you had all better come in,' the detective indicated with a nod of his head.

Minutes later, they were assembled in a very large, well-furnished room, which lay on the right hand side of the wide hallway, overlooking the busy Gloucester Road. Detective Whicker kicked the door shut, flung a bunch of keys and two white envelopes onto a table, looked at each of them in turn, then in a very quiet voice said, 'Before I ask you to identify yourselves, I'm very sorry but I have to tell you that Mr Holsworthy is dead.'

Penny said, 'Oh no, I'm sorry, but I think you're making a terrible mistake.'

Neil reached for her hand and held it between both of his.

Barbara moved to stand between James and Paul.

The silence in the room now was disturbing. The awareness of the truth of what the man said, hit them all. To Barbara it was really frightening. She flinched from the stare of this stranger. She had a feeling she had been along this road before, when Michael died.

James spoke first. 'I'm a partner in a law firm, Bradley and Summerford. If you will outline to us what has happened, I will take it from there.'

The detective recognised the voice of authority.

'Tenant in the flat opposite spoke to an officer early this morning. The lady was worried, no sign of Mr Holsworthy. The constable knocked, got no reply, contacted the station for permission to enter. The gentleman was dead. Two letters beside him, one addressed to the coroner, the second –' he broke off, went to the table and picked up the two letters, peering closely at the writing, 'is addressed to James Ferguson.'

Second Chance

Somewhere in the house a telephone rang, a motorhorn sounded out in the street and a dog could be heard barking. No one in the room moved or spoke. Suddenly everything came together. Shock, pity for Tim, regret that they hadn't acted more quickly, impatience and anger that Tim should take the easy way out, dumping the whole mess on his elderly father. Everything.

But mainly, what Barbara was feeling was panic, and at the same time she was so afraid.

Detective Whicker cleared his throat. 'I'm sorry. Always a nasty business. I must be on my way.'

'I take it we can get all the information, identification, date of inquest, and such like, from the station; is that right, Detective Whicker?' James asked.

Reluctant to confirm too much, the policeman took a card from his wallet, handed it to James, before he formed an answer. 'Telephone number is on there, sir. My superior will give you all the assistance you need. If you don't mind though, sir, I shall have to see you all off the premises. I have to lock up, keep the place tight until our boys have finished all the paper work.'

They came out of the house into brilliant sunshine and a clear blue sky. James reached for Barbara's hand and together they looked upwards, the sun felt warm and bright on their faces.

'James, tell me,' Barbara whispered, 'tell me, between us haven't we had enough trouble to last a lifetime? I don't think I can take much more.'

'Listen to me! We weren't to know that things had got to such a pitch with Tim. Blaming ourselves isn't going to help anyone, least of all his three children. You think because Tim couldn't face the thought of living without

Elizabeth, he didn't give one iota for the twins and Hannah? Do you?'

'Yes,' Barbara said cruelly.

'My feelings exactly,' said Penny, as she covered her face with her hands. 'We might feel differently later, but at the moment I can't help it. I don't think he gave a thought as to what would happen to his kids. He hasn't been near them in months.'

'Hey, steady on, old girl,' Neil put his arms around his wife's shoulders. 'We none of us know how we would react in the same circumstances. God forbid we ever have to find out.'

'I think perhaps we had better make a move,' Paul said. 'You girls stay there with James. Neil and I will fetch the cars.'

Barbara's and Penny's mood had shifted, the anger had subsided, absolute shock had taken over.

'If only,' Barbara muttered to no one in particular.

Penny knew exactly what she meant.

If only they had come up to town on Saturday morning, straight after their discussion on Friday evening. The weather had been lovely, the sunshine hot, they had spent a relaxed happy weekend together.

Tim had been on his own.

Everything had been left in order. A valid will. Everything he owned, was left in trust, equally shared, between his three children.

The letter to the coroner stated that Tim had decided that William, John and Hannah should go to live with James and Barbara Ferguson, if they were willing, and that he wished for the Court to appoint James Ferguson as their legal guardian.

The letter, written to James, had been very brief: 'Try to forgive me. There is no life without Elizabeth.'

'A sad business,' James said, his eyes shining with tears as he passed the note to Barbara.

She read it, looked away. Too choked to answer.

James waited. 'Do you want us to take the children?'

Barbara nodded her head, 'Why is it we never realise how much we love a person, until that person dies? Those children are orphans. Why? Why?'

There was no answer.

'Only the children matter now,' James remarked. 'The kindest thing we can do is bring them home, care for them, show them we really love them, want them, let them know that this is their home.'

'I'll do my best,' Barbara declared.

'I know. I know you will. Once they, and we, get over the blinding pain of loss and the terrible shock of it all, together we'll both do our best to make sure that they feel secure and that they have a happy life.'

It was agreed that the three children should stay in Yorkshire until the end of July when the boys' term at the boarding school would end.

A nagging thought was hammering away in Barbara's head. She could cope. She was determined to cope. Finding a school for the twins would be no problem. Hannah was a different matter, she was not yet two-and-a-half-years-old.

Maureen had offered to give up her job at The Smuggler's in order to help Barbara. James had immediately offered her full-time employment, which she had gladly accepted.

What a blessing in disguise Maureen O'Connor had turned out to be. Now Maureen Soames. She and Paul had slipped away quietly to Eastbourne one weekend and had been married in Eastbourne Town Hall.

Deprived of the opportunity to pay for a reception, James had bought them several beautiful pieces of furniture to go into the cottage which had been renovated so well.

With Maggie Harvey coming in daily Monday to Friday and now Maureen on hand to do whatever needed doing, which would include driving the boys to school and meeting them in the afternoons, Barbara counted herself very lucky indeed. The main problem now being, how would she fit in her visits to Coombe Haven? So far she hadn't missed any, and she had no intention of doing so.

For once fate intervened in a kindly way.

It was the second Thursday in July. Barbara was at Coombe Haven, out in the garden with most of the other helpers and almost all of the children. With Sammy contented enough in the sandpit, Barbara leant back on her elbows and turned her face to the sun.

'You're looking much better, in fact you look bright-eyed and bushy-tailed. Something good must have happened to you for a change. About time, I'd say.' Brenda Smith was smiling across at Barbara from the swing-chairs.

'Not really, Brenda,' Barbara called. 'It's just that it's such a lovely morning, everything's all bright and colourful. To tell you the truth I could use some good news.'

'Oh, about young Sam, you mean? Officialdom never was noted for their speedy results, we all know that. Besides in Samuel's case, he still has a father somewhere, must be taking time to get a trace of him. Out of the blue, you'll see, the conclusion will be a happy ending.'

Her enthusiasm was endearing. 'You really think so?'

'Yes I do.' She looked at her watch. 'It's lunchtime.'

Barbara sat up and called to Sammy, stretching out her arms to lift him up onto the grass.

Brenda said again, only loudly this time, 'It's time for lunch.'

In a group, ladies and children, they moved towards the house.

'I'll take 'im,' Hilda said as Barbara reached the dining room. 'Matron wants a word wiv you.'

Ivy's expression, as she waved Barbara to a chair, had Barbara's spirits soaring.

'You've had some news?'

'Yes. They've traced the father.'

'And?'

'He's living in New Zealand, he's married again. Apparently he had no objection to his son being put up for adoption.'

'Why didn't someone tell me? Why didn't they discuss it with me.'

'I don't know. It's just their way I suppose.'

'And when will it all go through? Become legal?'

Seeing Ivy frown and the straight set of her mouth was suddenly frightening to Barbara, and she was pleased when Ivy spoke again.

'It isn't that I want to dampen your hopes but I can't stand by and watch you be disappointed.'

'How can I be disappointed when you've just said that Samuel's father has agreed for him to be adopted?'

'It's not as simple as that, Barbara, and you know it.

Adoption is a lengthy business, the courts have to be thoroughly satisfied before their final consent is given.'

Lengthy business! Barbara felt sick at the thought of it.

'There is one ray of hope. With the approval of the committee of this home there is always a chance that the Court would allow you and James to have custodianship of Samuel. As the child has already been made a ward of court that would not be an unusual step for them to take.'

Barbara stared at her. Then suddenly, she shook her head and laughed, 'I should pay more attention to what my husband tells me. He spoke of this some weeks ago. It appears that you are now telling me exactly what James said his partners were aiming for. Custody, under supervision, while an adoption order is considered.'

Ivy Pearson bent and picked up a piece of paper from the floor, folded it neatly and stared out of the window and prayed, 'Don't let this nice couple be turned down. They can give a good home to a little boy that nobody else wanted because he was disfigured. And most of all they will give him love and he will love them in return. When a child from this home is offered a fresh start it makes this job so worthwhile.'

The house rang with laughter. There had never been a better summer and James was convinced that he had never before seen Barbara looking so happy. It had taken a while for William and John to settle in, but with James taking a month off from the office and Paul around at all times, not to mention Clem down in the stables, the boys had never once been left to their own devices. Hannah had taken to living in Jevington like a duck takes to water. The little girl had attached herself to Sammy straight off; he still being scared of strangers, and a little bit jealous if the truth be known, refused to speak to her at first.

'Perseverance must be little Hannah's middle name,' James remarked as he sat beside Barbara beneath the tree, listening to her repeat nursery rhymes.

'Jack an' Jill went up the . . .' Hannah paused, and waited. Sammy jerked his head forward, took a deep breath and yelled: 'Hill!' Hannah put her two dimpled little hands together and clapped.

Sam chuckled at his own cleverness.

James swallowed hard. He still found it unbelievable that they had four children living under their roof.

Barbara smiled. She had established a great rapport with Helen Brown, the social worker who dropped in unannounced from time to time to see how Samuel was faring. None the more for that, she would feel a whole lot more at peace with the world once the court had made the order permitting James and herself to become the legal parents of Samuel Rowlings.

She chided herself to have more patience. The day would come, she had to believe that much, when Sammy's name would be entered in the Adopted Children's Register. All the new information could be recorded and then Samuel would be issued a new full birth certificate.

From that day forth she would sleep more soundly. When that day dawned he would become, legally, Samuel Ferguson. Son of James and Barbara Ferguson.

Chapter Twenty-six

WEEKENDS WERE ALWAYS special and this one was going to be marvellous. Tomorrow would be Easter Sunday 1965. Barbara and James were about to celebrate their tenth wedding anniversary. Everyone would be here. The house would come alive, resounding with boisterous laughter.

Barbara looked out into the garden to where James and Paul were preparing everything for tomorrow.

'The marquee has gone up a treat,' James told her as he wheeled himself into the kitchen.

'That's great, a safeguard in case it rains, though the forecast is good. Would you like a cup of tea?'

'That's what I've come in for,' he smiled.

'And there's me thinking it was because you love to look at me!'

'Pour the tea out, woman, and don't be getting ideas like that into your head!'

Barbara, feeling a glow as she always did when James was around, took the cosy from the pot and filled a cup for him.

'Boys arriving home tonight?' he asked idly.

'I'm not sure. Expect they will ring later. If not tonight, you can bet your boots they'll be home by the crack of dawn.'

'Fill one of those big mugs with tea and I'll take it out to Paul when I've drunk mine.'

With the kitchen to herself again, Barbara poured herself

a second cup of tea and sat slowly sipping it, letting her mind wander back over these past ten years. She couldn't believe how quickly they had flown, nor how happy they had been.

Before she had wed James, she had been through hell. Having told the details of her first marriage to James, details she had never told another living person, it had made no difference to him; he had insisted that his love for her was so great that he would settle for nothing short of marriage. How could she not love him with all of her heart?

Even then disaster had struck. James had almost lost his life in that car crash. When finally they had started their married life she had felt herself to be worthless. James, with sheer guts and determination, had gone back to practising law, while all she had to do was keep the house clean and tidy. James's sister, Chloe, and her husband Anthony, had come to her rescue – only Anthony wasn't her husband then, she reminded herself.

The clinic in Vauxhall had been her first try at voluntary work. At this memory, Barbara felt herself shudder: the poverty and the shameful way some little children were made to suffer. Then had come Coombe Haven and Sammy. It was as if a lifeline had been thrown to her. A chance to redress some of the wrongs of her earlier life.

Next there had been the death of Elizabeth. To this day she had never been able to come to terms with that, and James and she had been devastated when Tim had taken his own life.

'The lights are not working properly.'

Paul had thrust his head through the open kitchen window and the sound of his voice brought her back to the present with a start.

'What?'

Paul laughed. 'You were miles away, weren't you? I said I can't get the lights to work; the first lot we've put up amongst the trees are fine, the ones we are trying to string nearer to the house need some new bulbs. I'm taking the car down to the village, just thought I'd let you know.'

'Fine. I'm glad the marquee is up, ready for the caterers. I couldn't face organising all the food that we shall need.'

The telephone rang, Paul waved a hand, calling, 'I won't be long,' and Barbara went to take the call.

'Mum!'

Her heart leapt with joy.

'It's me, John. Wills has gone to take some of his books back to the research lab, but we'll both be getting a lift; should be home by seven.'

'All right my darling, we'll keep dinner for you.'

'Good-oh, hope it's a roast. See you later.'

She heard the click of the phone as it went dead. She held the receiver against her cheek for a second before she replaced it.

Mum! It always thrilled her to hear the twins call her and James 'Mum and Dad'. James had never officially adopted Elizabeth and Tim's three children, he hadn't thought it right to take away their surname. Legal Guardian had served well. Neither had they asked to be called anything other than Barbara and James. It had come about when the boys had been attending Eastbourne College; always encouraged to bring their friends home, the twins had soon fallen into the habit of saying 'This is our Mother and Father,' when making the introductions. The habit had never altered. Incredible. They were both in their first term at Sussex University now. Her mind went wandering off again. How well she remembered the Christmas that they had been born.

She had come home to her parents, battered and bruised in both mind and body. She had also given birth to a son. And without giving a thought to the consequences or to the heartbreak she would have to endure, she had agreed to have him adopted.

Only weeks later she and Penny had been Christmas shopping in London, touring stores like Hamleys where they had bought soft toys as presents for Elizabeth's newborn babies. Without knowing the tragic truth, Penny had dragged her off to visit Elizabeth in the nursing home where she had had to hide her own feelings as she watched Penny drool over those two tiny boys.

Envious, that's how she had felt. Guilty too. Oh yes, very guilty. With her mind so much in the past today, Barbara found herself hoping and praying that, whoever the couple were, and wherever they lived, that had adopted her child, they might love him and care for him as much as she and James cared for the four children that had come to be the light of their lives. She felt that must be so, they wouldn't have adopted a child if they weren't intending to be loving parents. They would be repaid ten-fold if her experience was anything to go by.

Toot-toot. That was the mini. Maureen was back from the school run. Barbara quicken her steps and she had the front door open as Maureen pulled the car to a halt.

Oh, just look at Sam! How *did* he manage to look so grubby when he came out of school, whereas Hannah, with books held under her arm and a satchel slung over one shoulder, still looked as if she had stepped out of a bandbox.

Amazing the bond that still existed between these two. Oh, they had their squabbles like any other normal brother and sister, but harm one and you had the other one to deal with. Barbara felt her heart swell with love as she watched them come flying towards her.

Hannah reached her first. Everything was dropped onto the porch step, arms were flung around her mother's waist and her cheek was being given a warm wet kiss.

'Hallo Mum, may I go down to the stables as soon as I've changed?'

'Give yourself time to get into the house,' Barbara laughed as she hugged Hannah.

Wham! not much altered with Sam. He got his mother's attention one way or another, Barbara thought to herself as he too planted a kiss on her cheek.

'Mum, I'm starving.' He could still look so pitiful when he chose.

'You always are,' she teased.

There was just a year between these two. Hannah being eleven was the spitting image of her mother; she also had the same kind, gentle nature that Elizabeth had had. She was truly a lovely child and being the only girl around the place, men and boys alike were very protective of her.

With Sammy it was uncanny. At the age of twelve he hadn't lost his fair complexion, not yet his head of tight fair curls – much to his annoyance. He hated being teased about his curls and would spend a great deal of time in the bathroom trying to flatten them straight with a wet comb. His colouring being so very much the same as James's made him a natural Ferguson, and no one needed telling twice how proud both she and James were to have him as their legal son.

Twice Sam had been into hospital, each time to have an operation on his top lip and to the roof of his mouth. The ugly red gash, which had been so prominent on his top lip, had long since disappeared. All that remained of his harelip now was a thin white scar. William and John were forever telling him that nobody noticed it, but if it worried him they reassured him he could always grow a moustache when he grew older.

Once he had come to the dinner-table with a black pencil line drawn over the scar and extended to form a moustache. Barbara had been terrified as to what his reaction would be if anyone laughed.

It had been Sammy himself who had broken the silence, laughing out loud as he had said. 'Now you know what I shall look like when I am old!'

His words had had them all in hysterics, more so when his father had said he needn't wash it off until after dinner.

Buttering tea-cakes and filling glasses with milk to keep these two going until dinnertime, Barbara laughed to herself. There had been no shortage of joy and laughter since the four children had come into this house.

Barbara woke early, she had spent the night downstairs in James's bed, as she did so much more often as time had gone by. The sun was already shining through an opening in the curtains: it was going to be a lovely day. She turned in his arms, and buried her face in his chest.

'Happy anniversary, my darling,' he whispered against her hair.

Barbara thought for one awful moment that she was going to start the day by crying. Don't be so ridiculous, she told herself, what in heaven's name have you got to cry about? 'I love you, James, very very much.'

'I love you too,' he answered, 'I don't think you can possibly know just how much.'

Now she did cry.

James laughed and held her close.

They lay there, making plans for the day. 'So many people are going to be here.'

'Yes,' James agreed. 'And if we don't get a move on they will start arriving before we are even dressed.'

It was not only a lovely day. It was wonderful.

Barbara sat at a table just inside the marquee. James was seated in his chair across from her. 'Just look at them all,' she murmured.

Most of the adults had come inside for their lunch which was being served superbly by the caterers.

There were grandparents, parents, god-parents and friends. Outside a great mass of children were enjoying themselves.

James's brother Rodney and his wife Elaine waved. Over to the right stood Jack Tully who was married to James's sister Ann.

'Good God!' Barbara suddenly said to James. 'Just goes to show that we don't see enough of our families. Look at the size of Ann's children: Harry and Lucy must be turned eighteen by now.'

'Here's to many more happy years.' A head came over Barbara's shoulder and she twisted round to kiss Chloe. Anthony was shaking hands with James.

'I've just rescued Oliver from the clutches of a gang of youngsters: they were trying to have rides on his back, but that dog wasn't standing for that,' Anthony told them, fighting to keep the laughter out of his voice. 'It's a job to know to whom all these children belong to on a day like this.'

'Well I expect your two were in the fray somewhere,' Barbara replied.

'Our two weren't.' Penny came round the back of James's wheelchair and flopped down onto a seat beside Barbara.

'Hannah has taken our Jane off to the stables. I begged them to keep themselves clean but I've a feeling I was talking to myself. Clive is all right, he and Sam have got the grandfathers to organise a three-legged race when we've all finished eating.'

Barbara covered Penny's hand with one of her own, feeling enormous pleasure that her dear friend was here today. Not that she didn't see a great deal of Penny. Neil had bought 'Walled in House', a mile or so up the road: a rambling old farm house that, in the last eight years, had come alive, restored by skilful workmen to its former glory and enhanced by the birth of their son, Clive, and two years later their daughter Jane.

The daylight was almost gone.

Paul and Neil, like two pied-pipers, led the way through the garden to the field beyond; children followed, a straggling laden procession.

Between the wall and the orchard, far away from the stables, wooden frames had been set up to hold the fireworks and here everyone set down their boxes and formed a circle.

Whoosh, the first rocket made for the sky, sending a

shower of coloured sparks shooting outwards. Young voices were raised in glee as the firework display got underway.

Only the youngest members of the families had accompanied the children, the older ones preferring the warmth of the house and a well-earned drink.

Barbara and James were out on the porch alone.

'Have you enjoyed today, Barbara?' James's voice was unusually soft.

'More than I can put into words,' she answered.

'So you don't mind spending another ten years with me then?'

'Oh James! More than that! Another *fifty*, please God.'

'We'll both be very old by then, maybe we'll be grand-parents, or even great-grandparents, who knows?'

'Who knows indeed!' They both laughed and James took hold of her hand, and together they waited for their children to come back up to the house. A house that had become a family home for all of them.

WHEELING AND DEALING

Elizabeth Waite

Ella has lived in the East End of London all her life and when her husband is determined to move to Epsom to be near the racecourse he frequents and loves, Ella's refusal to move with him breaks up their marriage. It's been a tempestuous marriage – sometimes they had money, often not and when he was doing well, he liked the ladies…

Once the marriage breaks up, Ella loses the will to keep smart, trim and fit. Until her mother steps in, determined to pick up the pieces. And it works – Ella gets a job as a barmaid in the British Legion club which gives her an income and a social life. She begins to take pride in her appearance again and, when Dennis turns up for a drink one night, he is taken by surprise – and remembers what attracted him to her in the first place. But can Dennis win back his wife? Ella has to decide if Dennis has changed – or indeed can change – his wheeler-dealer ways…

978 0 7515 3611 9

Other bestselling titles available by mail